THE LOST GOSPELS OF MARIAM AND JUDAS

authorHOUSE®

AuthorHouse™
1663 Liberty Drive
Bloomington, IN 47403
www.authorhouse.com
Phone: 833-262-8899

Published by AuthorHouse   09/09/2021

ISBN: 978-1-6655-3231-0 (sc)
ISBN: 978-1-6655-3232-7 (hc)
ISBN: 978-1-6655-3233-4 (e)

Library of Congress Control Number: 2021914680

Print information available on the last page.

This book is printed on acid-free paper.

Για,
Ντιάνα -
Προστατευτής άγριων πτηνών,
Κυνηγός για την τέλεια συντακτική δομή

THE GALILEE

I followed my father's footsteps in the sandy soil as we climbed the hill, another hill of the many we had crossed in our long journey from Bethany. My father had slung over his back his bag of tools and a bundle of our possessions. I carried another bundle on my back and the donkey I led carried as his burden clay water jugs, a stack of firewood and other supplies. Behind me walked my mother who carried a smaller bundle of clothing balanced with poise on her head, a white cloth spread below it, blocking the hot sun's rays from her face, neck and shoulders. The donkey was tired from the long journey. The donkey was plodding his hoofs in a shuffle. I laid my hand on the donkey's head and spoke quiet words of encouragement to the beast. He snuffled at me.

At the top of the hill my father stopped, looked ahead then turned to look at us coming up behind him. I squinted my eyes against the bright sun and watched a hawk soaring high in sky, its keen eyes searching for prey. I wish I had the bird's freedom of flight to make the traveling easier. A few more steps and I stood next to my father at the top of the hill. My mother walked up and stood beside us. My father pointed. He told us, "Nazareth."

My eyes followed his pointing hand and I saw in the shimmering distance a village perched on a plateau below the height of the hill where we stood. There were the people's homes, with patches of green that would be their gardens. We would go down this rocky hill then cross a dry ravine that would run fast with water in the rainy season, then climb one more hill to our destination. The rough terrain was especially difficult for my mother. Looking at this hill to descend and the next to climb, I knew it would be late in the day before we arrived at Nazareth.

My mother said, "Bless us, ADONAI, and let us find peace and work and lodging in Nazareth." She bowed her head and placed her fingertips to her forehead.

Looking down I saw at the bottom of the hill a group of four boys. These were the first people we had seen since leaving the River Jordan to cross west through the Jezreel Valley at the south base of the Tabor Mount. My father started down the hill and we followed him. At the bottom of the hill I could now see that three of the boys were provoking the other. The fourth boy was younger than the others. He looked to be the same age as myself, which was thirteen years. The fourth boy had a hunting sling in his hand that was being pulled away from him by the oldest and biggest of the other three.

The older boy pushed the younger boy, and said to him, "You can't hunt. Give me the sling. Run home to stada." Then the boy being insulted threw a hard punch to the others face, yelling, "Shut your mouth or I will kill you." The other two boys jumped on the young boy and now all three were attacking him.

No matter how hard the young boy fought, he did not have a chance against three. He was being punched and pulled from three directions and now the young boy was on the ground being kicked by all three of the attackers. We were still a stone's throw distance from the group of boys. My father had stopped walking and we came beside him. I said, "It is not fair. There are three of them to his one."

My father replied, "It is not our concern."

"But father, you are always telling me that we should help those in need. I want to help him."

"We do not know the rights and wrongs of this affair. Perhaps he deserves the beating."

"Then let them beat him one at a time, not all at once." I turned to my mother. "Mother should we let three beat one?"

My mother answered my question with a question, "What would you do?"

"I will fight one so he only has two to fight."

My mother looked at my father and said in a weary voice, "He is the son of his father."

My father laughed, nodded his head towards the fight, and said to me, "Go then."

I stepped to the donkey and selected a hard stick of firewood. The stick was the length of me to my chin, a slender but good stout weapon. Pulling it from the stack I turned and ran to the fight.

Two of the boys were holding the younger boy down while the older of them kicked the younger boy. Running up from behind them, they being unaware of my approach, I swung the stick in a vicious arc, hitting the kicking one across his shoulders and the back of his head. I knocked that boy down, he fell hard to the ground. The other two boys looked up in shock. That gave the boy being held down a chance to jerk an arm free and he grabbed a fist sized rock from the ground next to him. He smashed the rock into the face of one of the attackers, that boy yelling in pain and falling back.

Now there was only one attacker left and the young boy tore into him with a vengeance, pummeling his face with his hard fists. In moments the fight was over. The three attackers were lying on the ground moaning. The young boy who was being attacked stood and turned to look at me. I was leaning on my stick of firewood, the other boy was breathing hard, spitting out blood.

The boy who had been outnumbered and being beaten raised his arm. He showed me his open right hand in the sign of peaceful greeting, and said to me, "Many thanks for your help. My name is Yeshua. I am called Yeshua the Nazarene."

I raised my hand and replied, "I am Judas. The son of Simon Iscariot."

My name is Judas Iscariot. I am going to tell you what happened, what really happened, to me, and to my friend, Yeshua.

NAZARETH. MY NAME IS JUDAS ISCARIOT

We entered the village of Nazareth. I was leading the donkey, walking beside Yeshua, my mother and father alongside us. I saw this was a village of about a half a hundred homes most with garden patches and many with mangers for the livestock. In the center of the village there was a well, fed by a spring at the base of a rocky outcrop. The well's sides were stacked stones covered in a troweled plaster that held the water from draining off into the ground around it. We stopped at the well and used a stoneware jug to draw water. We gratefully drank the cool fresh water. I poured water into a chiseled notch on a stone for the donkey.

Looking about I saw the houses of the inhabitants were made of stacked stone and sundried clay bricks. The roofs were covered with reed mats. These were sticks of wood branches weaved together and covered with a rough coat of plaster to block the rain.

Yeshua took us to his home. It was a simple home like the others in the village, but very clean. I could see the work of a craftsman in its design and construction. We entered through a gate to the courtyard of the home and I saw an old man working on a piece of wood with a mallet and chisel under an overhang to block the sun. On the other side of the courtyard was the family's food preparation area and two women, one young and the other older, were cooking something in a large pot hanging from a chain over the fire. Another young woman was grinding grains of wheat between two round flat rocks. She was preparing the dough for bread, mixing it with salt, yeast and water, adding dried grapes for sweetening, then shaping the dough into thin round loaves to be cooked in a dome of stacked stones, a fire burning hotly within it. Another young woman was tending the cooking loaves.

The old man turned at the noise of us entering. He called out, "Mary, we have visitors." From inside the house another young woman came out with some weaving cloth in her hands.

Yeshua said to them, "Yosef, Mother, this is my friend, Judas, and his mother and father."

My father stepped forward and said to the old man, "I am Simon, the son of Jacob Iscariot of Kerioth," and pointing to us, said "This is my wife Cyborea and our son, Judas."

The old man greeted us, "Welcome to our home. I am Yosef, the son of Jacob Heli. This is my wife, Mary Salome and her mother Anne. These are my daughters Mary Jacob, Salome, and Joanna, and this is my stepson, Yeshua."

The older woman turned, looked at my father, and said in a voice of joy, "My brother!" And she and my father stepped quickly to each other to embrace. "My sister! I am so happy to see you!"

Of all the houses in Nazareth we had come to the one where my father would find his sister. My mother touched her forehead and exclaimed, "This is a sign of good tidings from ADONAI."

Yosef looked at Yeshua's bruised face and said to him, "I see you have already become acquainted with Yeshua. Fighting again, eh? What are you fighting about this time?"

One of the young women who had been tending the cooking, Mary Salome, walked over and took Yeshua's face in her hands, asking him, "Are you alright my son?"

Yosef asked Yeshua again, "What are you fighting about?"

Yeshua, who seemed embarrassed by his mother's maternal attentions, pulled his face away and replied, "Nothing. It was nothing."

Yosef reached out and took Yeshua's hands, turned them over, saw his skinned bloody knuckles, and asked, "Can you work tomorrow?"

Yeshua replies, "Yes. I tell you it was nothing."

My father told Yosef, "Your stepson is a fighter. He fights three at once. And beat them." He turned to Mary Salome, the mother of Yeshua, and said, "Mary, the last time I saw you was many years ago and you were but a babe. I am your uncle. I am pleased to meet you and your family."

Mary Salome smiled, "It was providence that you came upon Yeshua in your journey."

Yosef asked Yeshua, "Why are you fighting three? Is one at a time not good enough for you?"

Yeshua turned to me and said, grinning through a split lip, "It was only two after Judas took down one of them."

Mary turned to me, "Bless you for helping Yeshua."

I clapped Yeshua on the back, and told his mother, "Yeshua would have beaten them without my help."

Yosef shook his bearded head, telling Yeshua, "I have told you many times, your energies would be better spent learning to use the tools of a tekton. The Law says a father must teach his son a trade so that he doesn't have to take up a despised occupation, such as tax collector, usurer, moneychanger, dung collector, gambler with dice, or a brothel-keeper. All of them will burn in Hades for eternity."

Yeshua, exasperated, told him, "I am learning to be a tekton. I will soon be ready to run my own crew."

Yosef said, "Not if you break your hands or your head fighting all the time you will not."

My father said to Yosef, "I am a tekton and I am training my son to be a tekton. We are going to Zippori for work. I understand there is much building activity in Zippori."

Yosef replied, "Yes. Herod Antipas, the rabid fox, has decreed that Zippori will be a trade center. Many Romans and wealthy Haribum are building homes there. Most everyone here in Nazareth walks to Zippori for work. You are welcome to eat with us, spend the night, and then accompany us to town in the morning. The job I work on is hiring. Perhaps you can find work there."

My mother said, "Bless you for your hospitality". She turned to Mary Salome, "Mary, may I help you prepare the meal? We have four quail Judas caught today and some wild onions and dandelion greens I found that we can add to the pot."

I had gutted the birds when I caught them. I took them from my bag and handed them to Mary Salome. She and my mother plucked the birds, rubbed the meat in salt then seared the meat over the flames of the fire. They cut the meat into pieces and added it to the boiling stew. They put the onions and greens in the pot, adding garlic, mustard seed and dill. The smell made my stomach growl.

I watched my mother and Mary Salome tend to the cooking. Mary Salome, Yeshua's mother, was very young. I was surprised at her youth, she must have been just a girl when Yeshua was born. Amongst the pagans, the Philistines and the Habirum of the Sadducee sect, a daughter under twelve was entirely in the power and possession of her father. He could arrange her betrothal and collect the value of the wedding contract in advance, or even sell her into slavery. A girl twelve years and one day could be married. Only when a girl reached the age of twelve years and a half could she choose her own husband. I saw that Yosef's daughters had been given the freedom of choice as they were older than twelve and a half and seemed to be not betrothed.

Yosef and my father went to the piece of wood and tools Yosef had been working on when we arrived. Yosef, with his long grey hair and beard, was very old compared to Mary Salome. In this land where girls are married young, and usually to older men, these two were unnaturally years apart in difference. If Yosef was Yeshua's stepfather, I wondered, who was his real father?

While I was standing looking around and anticipating the food, the gate opened and two young men came in. I was introduced to them as Yosef's sons, Jude and Joses. I was to learn Yosef had two other sons, James and Simon. Yosef had been married before. His previous wife had perished from sickness. Yosef had then taken Mary Salome for his wife.

The food was ready. The women carried the pot and bread in. We entered Yeshua's home. We gathered at the large table, and Yosef said the prayer. We dipped the bread in olive oil and honey to accompany the stew made of barley and vegetables. The meat from the quail added to the flavor. I listened as Yosef and my father talked during supper. My family, and Yosef and his wife Mary Salome, and all our spread out relations, were of the Pharisee's, tracing our ancestral lines back to the House of King David. King David took seven women to wife and begat of them nineteen sons. My father's line was of the son

Shephatiah, by the wife Abital. Yosef, Yeshua's stepfather, was from the line of the son Daniel, by Abigail. And Mary Salome's line traced back to Nathan, by Bathsheba.

While we ate the evening meal, my father told Yosef we had started our journey from Bethany, where I was born and lived until now. Bethany was on the Mount Olivet, near to Jerusalem. We walked the Roman road, the King's Highway, through the Valley of Achor to Jericho. There we had crossed the River Jordan to the east bank, into the Plains of Moab, and traveled north through the lands of Perea and Gilead so as to bypass the land of the Cuthites on the west side of the river. We followed the east bank of the River Jordan north to where it met the dry riverbed of the River Yarmuk that ran south and west out of the wilderness of the Golan. There we crossed to the west bank of the River Jordan at the ruins of the abandoned town of Bet Yerah. We continued west into the Jezreel Valley lying between Carmel Mount to the south and Tabor Mount on the north, arriving finally to Nazareth. It was a journey of five suns.

Yosef asked my father why we had left Bethany. My father replied, "I was building homes in Bethany and some stone setting in Jerusalem. It was steady work. Then Herod Antipas started work on his palace in Herodium. Herod Antipas decreed that all tektons must work for him and, dog that he is, was paying only half wages. I thought to move to En Gedi, the oasis and waterfall at the Salt Sea, to live among the Essenes. There are many Habirum there who are farming. Then our cousin, Yokhanan HaMatbi, came to visit and told me that Zippori was being rebuilt. So I thought to try our luck here instead."

Yosef shook his head, "Herod Antipas. The Imudean grandson of a slave. He will steal the bread from your plate."

My father said, "He is not a lawful ruler of the people. The Law tells us. – *You shall not set over yourself a foreign man who is not your brother* –. The slave, the Imudean grandfather, he was not Habirum and now his grandson rules over our land."

They were speaking of the tetrarch of Galilee, Herod Antipas. He was the son of Herod I, who the Romans called Herod Great.

The Roman senators had appointed Herod I governor of the lands of Galilee about fifty eight years before. Ten years after that, the Romans made Herod I their client king of Judah. Herod I had died two years before my birth. Upon his death, fifteen years ago, his lands had been divided among his sons. The son Herod Antipas had been given the lands of Galilee and Perea. South of Galilee and west of the River Jordan was the land of Judah, home of the Temple in Jerusalem and now governed by the Romans directly.

It was common knowledge that Herod I was not Habirum. His father, named Herod Antipater, was from the pagan land of the Arabah Imudeans, to the far south and west of the Salt Sea. Herod Antipater had been born to slaves serving at the temple for the Roman god Apollo. The temple of Apollo was in the town of Ashkelon, a port city north of Gaza on the shore of the Great Sea. The town was on the Roman road Via Maris that ran north from Aegyptus to Phoenicia. Herod Antipater, being born to slaves, he himself was slave, owned by the temple overseer.

At a young age, just a boy, he was bought from the temple by a wealthy Greek merchant who admired him and lusted to make Herod Antipater his concubinus. The man would dress the young Herod Antipater in the robes of a woman, paint color on his lips, anoint him with perfumes and use him as a lover. Later, when the man died, of poisoning by the hand of Herod Antipater himself some say, he freed the now young man by manumission in his will and left him his home and a large sum of coins. Now being a freedman of wealth, the grandfather inserted himself into the circle of the powerful Roman ruling class, currying favor and gaining influence. Herod Antipater rose from humble beginnings as a temple slave, to slave concubinus of a pederast, to a privileged man of wealth. Herod Antipater filled his home with slaves of his own, for his household chores and for his bed, both young girls and young boys. The former slave, Herod Antipater set himself the task of building a family dynasty. As with most families of great wealth, the original secret source of their fortune was a shameful dark history they seek to bury.

Then the son of Herod Antipater, Herod I, with Roman backing, had seized Jerusalem and Judah from Antigonus the Parthian. Herod I had all members of the ruling council Sanhedrin executed, including his father-in-law. All forty five men were killed by strangulation and sword because Herod I suspected their Hasmonean family connections could threaten his rule. Herod I had plundered the Temple treasury and all the documents secured there for safekeeping by Habirum families. In those documents were the birth records those families used to trace their lineages to confirm their rights and social standings. Herod I burned those records with the intention of clouding the truth of his own background. Herod I claimed to be of a Habirum family who had returned to Judah long before from the exile in Babylonia. Luckily many families had copies of their documents so Herod's treachery was ultimately not useful to him, and no one believed his false story of him being of Habirum.

This was the beginning of the Herodians who ruled the land of the Habirum. They appointed men as illegitimate high priests of the Temple Mount. Herod I had consolidated his power by making a pagan from Babylonia, called Simon, the high priest of the Temple Mount. Simon had a half-sister, the one called Mariamne the Great Beauty, and Herod I lusted for her. Simon was not of the priestly lineage from the time of Moses brother, Aaron, and thus could not officiate at the Temple rites. The sister Mariamne was of the Hasmoneans, related to Judah Maccabeus, so Herod I used that lineage to defy the Law and appointed him anyway. Thus Simon became the high priest and leader of the Sanhedrin council of elders, subservient to Herod I and furthering the unlawful rule of Herod's kingdom.

For the last fifteen years, his son, Herod Antipas, the grandson of the slave, was ruler by proxy from Rome of the land of the Habirum. The Herodian line of priests at the Temple continued, with sons and nephews and other male family placed in office and on the altar. Herod Antipas was a cruel man. Where his father had taxed the people for his building projects, Herod Antipas taxed them mercilessly to send tribute to the emperor in Rome and to increase the wealth of his own treasury.

Herod Antipas dealt swiftly with criminals and any person he considered to be a threat to his throne. The most common punishment was the cruci fixus which he used throughout his kingdom. In Jerusalem, just outside the northwest walls of the city on the hill of Golgatha was the killing ground known as the place of the skulls. Herod Antipas had different ways to crucify a person. Normally their arms would be spread on a cross beam and spikes driven through their forearms just below the wrists. Their feet would be spiked on the post. Sometimes Herod Antipas would have them nailed to the cross upside down, so their legs would not carry their weight, thus increasing their torment. Sometimes he would not have their legs broken, which made their hanging longer, because with broken legs death came sooner due to suffocation. The place of the skulls was near to the city so everyone could witness the cruci fixus and know the fate that awaited them if they came to the attention of Herod Antipas.

Another way Herod Antipas enjoyed executing his victims was to tie their wrists to their ankles and then they were placed into a large sturdy bag of raw, bloody untanned animal skins. Into the bag with the victim would be put wild dogs and feral cats and snakes, and then, after the screaming victim was tortured for a period of time for Herod's amusement, the bag was thrown into a hole in the ground and all within buried alive. Herod Antipas was a barbaric savage man who even had his wives, his wives mothers, his sons, and other members of his family murdered if he suspected them of treachery. Indeed, it was said the Roman emperor, Augustus had remarked that he would rather be Herod Antipas' dog than a member of his family.

Herod Antipas lived at his palace in the rebuilt Zippori or his capital at Caesarea Maritama and was building a new palace at the port of Tiberius on the sea of Chinnereth. He would travel about his kingdom with a military bodyguard, showing the strength of his rule, exacting tribute from all he would visit. Herod Antipas only came to the holy city of Jerusalem for the festivals such as Passover. He didn't live at Jerusalem because of the rank smell of the Valley of

Hinnom at the southern end of the city. This place was usually called the Valley of Dung.

The Valley of Dung was the dumping ground for the city. The dung collectors would go through the streets, an oxen pulling their wagonload of barrels, pouring the citizens buckets of dung into the barrels. When the barrels were full the collector would pass through the Dung Gate, at the southeast of the city wall, to the dumping ground. All manner of dung and trash and filth the city produced was taken to the Valley of Dung. The bodies of dead animals and the bodies of those crucified on the cross were destined for the Valley of Dung, to the fires. It was the despised occupation of certain individuals, the lowest of slaves and criminals who had been spared from cruci fixus, to keep the fires burning and placing the cadavers, dung and trash into the fires. Before the accumulated filth could be set fire and burned to ashes the piles would be infested with waves of burrowing maggots, plagued by countless swarms of greasy well fed rats, and festered by thick clouds of buzzing flies. The overseer of this work was a hulking brute of a man who drove his charges with the whip and used his spear on any who could work no longer or who tried to escape, adding their cadavers to the burning piles. At night the wild dogs would roam and feed and fight and rut and howl. The noise they made was like the torment of lost souls. The fires burned constantly, making black stinking smoke that in the hot dry months when the winds blew from the south out of the Arabahian desert, would cover the city like a low hanging fog. It was a humid, sticky, stinking fog that brought misery and sickness to the people.

The constant burning fires, the black smoke and the stench of the Valley of Dung was said by the prophet Isaiah to be akin to Sheol, the place of eternal damnation. The Valley of Dung was also known as the Valley of Slaughter. This is the place where in earlier times the Canaanites had made sacrifices to the pagan god Ba'al and the fire god Molech. Parents would sacrifice their children by passing them through the fire, burning them to death, to appease their pagan gods, while the multitude banged drums and wailed to block the screams of those being burnt. This abomination was abolished by King Josiah who was sent by ADONAI to rid the Temple of pagans.

Our home in Bethany was north and west of the city, on the north slope of Mount Olivet. We were far enough from the Valley of Dung so it was a rare day when we would even get a breath of the corrupt air from the fires. Only when we went into Jerusalem for the Passover, and if my father had work there, would we have to breathe the stench of the Valley of Dung. I had taken my schooling by tutor at home or at a wise man's place of study in our hometown of Bethany and so was not in the city very often.

While eating I looked about with curiosity and saw their home was a large rectangle arranged with curtained separate areas for sleeping. There was a paved stone floor with plastered joints and the plaster ran up the walls to seal the stones of the wall. I saw a corner of the large open room was arranged as their home's praying and worship place. There was a low table of wood, crafted by this family of skilled tektons, and on it I saw many scrolls. After supper, curious, I asked Yosef for permission to look at the scrolls. Yosef nodded his head at Yeshua and told him to show me. The scrolls were written in Aramaic and Hebrew and Greek. I have studied the Book and the Laws and the letters in Hebrew, Aramaic and Greek. I thought I was well taught but I had not seen the words of these philosophers, who the Greeks called, filósofoi. Yeshua read from the scrolls in a learned manner. I wanted to ask Yeshua questions about these philosophers but the hour was late. It was the end of the day. The water clock was filled, the candles were blown out, and it was time for sleep.

ZIPPORI. MY NAME IS JUDAS ISCARIOT

My father woke me in the dark before the dawn, before the first hour which started at sunrise. Sitting up I saw that my mother and Mary Salome and Yosef were also awake, preparing for the walk to Zippori. Mary Salome was by Yeshua's pallet, waking him.

After a bite of the food left over from supper the night before, we all gathered in the courtyard. The men had their tool bags over their shoulders. Mary had some vegetables she had grown in her garden that she would sell in the market. My mother was helping her to carry them. The daughters carried some cloth they had weaved. The market in Zippori was an important source of coins for this family and the others in Nazareth.

Yosef had told us the night before that Zippori was about three milia passum distant, a walk about one movement of the sun dial. A milia passum was the Roman measurement of one thousand paces, each being marked by a stone milliarium on the roadside. We would walk there, work, then walk back, getting home to Nazareth in the evening. The days now were long but later the days would grow shorter. On those short days we would leave at dark and return at dark. This was done every day, except for the Shabbat of course.

Before yesterday's supper Yeshua's mother had given Yeshua a bit of oil mixed with herbs. I went with him to the well where he washed and placed the salve on his face. By the fountain I asked him why those boys had attacked him. Yeshua just shook his head, saying it was nothing and continued to wash. When the sun came up I could see that his face had purple bruises from the beating. But this morning he was cheerful, the beating forgotten. Yeshua's eyes were as blue as the summer sky and his hair was more light than dark, a light brown. Yosef, his stepfather, and his mother, Mary Salome, had dark hair and dark eyes and Yeshua's skin was lighter than theirs. Except for his mother's quick smile, he looked nothing like either of them.

As time passed and I came to know Yeshua better, I would see that sometimes Yeshua was lighthearted and joking but at other times he seemed to be worrying over some personal grievance. At those times he was quick to use his fists on any of the boys and younger men who offended him. For his youth, he had a reputation as a ruthless fighter when in a scrape. The other boys of the village gave him respect and a wide berth. I was always ready to back him up if he was outnumbered. We were both hard fighters, our reputations preceded us. Except for our friendship he was a loner. The other people in Nazareth shunned him for some reason and that had made Yeshua a stranger to them. He had no friends, except me, he told me. I was proud to be Yeshua's friend. Perhaps we became close because I too was an oddity. I had reddish colored hair. Red hair was considered bad luck among the Habirum. But my mother always told me that I looked like the archangel Uriel who had red hair. She said Uriel was the flame of God. My mother said that of all the seven archangels it was Uriel who warned Noah of the coming flood, and by doing so saved humanity.

During the walk to Zippori, my father asked Yosef about the time he had taken his family to Aegyptus, and what he had done while there. Yosef told my father they left in the year of the bright star when Yeshua had been born, thirteen years before. That was the same year I had been born, but not same month. Herod I had pulled the same trick that had caused my father to leave Bethany. Herod I used the Roman law, ad opus publicum, or works to the public, to force tektons to work solely for him. Yosef said he would rather glean the harvested fields for scraps and be hungry, than work for the Roman lackey son of slaves. So he had packed up his family and left Galilee. They had gone to the land of the Aegyptus. Yosef said he had been born and raised in Alexandria where he had learned to be a tekton working with his father. Yosef had traveled to many places in the land of the pharaohs while a young man, so it was a natural place to escape the servitude of Herod I. They had first gone to the town of Heliopolis where many Habirum lived. The Aegyptus people called Heliopolis the place of the sun. The place of the sun had a temple to the Aegyptus sun god, AmunRa. At that temple was a tekhenu, what the Greeks called an obelisk that was older than the time of Moses, if the stories could be believed. The four sided obelisk was made of carved red granite. The base of each side was wide as a man stretching both arms could reach and the obelisk was as tall as three men. The obelisk had mysterious carvings on it, the meanings of which were unknown.

I interrupted to ask Yosef, "Who built this tekehun?"

He told me, "No one knows what manner of people were builders of the monument, or what gods they prayed to. Yeshua can tell you more about the land of the Aegyptus later. Here is the town. We will arrange the women in the market place then go to our work."

We passed by the sentries through the gate at the outer wall, across an open area to the inner wall and gate, then into Zippori. The two walls and gates meant invaders could be attacked from the ramparts on both walls, to be shot by archers and burned with pitch thrown from overhead. Past the gates was the main road leading into the town. It was a roadway of paved stones with thick round columns on each side rising in the air marking the way to the temple and the palace of Herod Antipas. The columns were not carved stone but were stacked segments of the Roman opus caementicium, a manmade assembly. Using pulvis puteolanus, ash from a burning mountain, and mixing it with water and sand, the assembly was formed to shape by tektons using wooden falsework. Once the mixture hardened and the falsework removed, the opus caementicium was like stones.

Entering Zippori that first early morning I was surprised at the crowds and industry I saw. There was a great bustle as the people moved about setting up to display their wares in the market. The sights and sounds of construction indicated workers making progress.

We followed the columns to the large open market square. Propped against the walls of the buildings and out in the middle were orderly rows of all manner of things for sale and barter. Merchants and villagers displayed fruits and vegetables, grains for bread, dried fishes and the pungent fish sauce called garum, poultry and eggs, pottery, cloth and weavings. Tailors sewed material for robes and clothing. There were bakers and millers, sellers of spices and salt, a currier who worked the cured leather forming sandals, belts and other useful items, candle makers and a seller of pitch for torches. The pitch came from the southern area of the Salt Sea the Romans called Lake Asphaltites. There were also makers of jewelry and amulets, a tent maker, those who collected and sold camel dung and wood for fire making. A smith who was busy stoking his forge hot to make nails and tools. There were wine sellers and water sellers. A man dressed in a colorful robe and turban from Arabah bought, sold and traded horses. A barber cut hair and shaved beards. The barber would also pull a rotten tooth, open a vein or supply a purgative to discharge the evil humors of bile and phlegm. There was a scrivener who charged to write contracts and letters, and a notary to witness the contracts. Some who sold cooked foods were taking morsels off their fires in exchange for coin, my mouth watering at the aromas. It was a carnival of sights and sounds and smells that happened every day, except on the Shabbat.

Along roads leading off the square were located less savory establishments such as taverns where publicans would serve the drunkards. Outside the taverns were the pimps who promoted the talents of their slaves, female and male, young mostly but some older whores for customers with fewer coins to spend. The whores stood or squat awaiting the next paying customer. There were money lenders and gamblers, and collecting Roman tribute from all, the tax collector. The tax collector would collect from each merchant and seller a bargained cost to conduct business, depending on the value of their goods sold. At the end of one road, downwind from the city, was the tanner. This was a despised occupation as the tanner soaked the animal hides in vats of liquefied dung, which created a sickening odor, to treat and render the animal hides to leather. Just like in Jerusalem, the tanner was kept far from the town center. I thought it amusing that the tax collector was neighbor to the tanner.

My family and Yeshua's did not need much from the market. We grew most of our own foods, we made most of our own tools, and the women weaved cloth and made the clothes we wore. We had no need of the colorful things prized by the Romans and the Sadducees and pagans. We purchased candles and salt mostly, the rest was of no use.

At the Passover in Jerusalem there were Habirum who had come from all parts of the world. I had seen strange people there, but here in Zippori I saw many new things. There was a dark skinned woolly headed tribe Yeshua told me were Nubians from Aithiopes, far south on the River Nile, in the land the Romans call Afrikkus. Yeshua said the Nubians brought from their country ivory, precious stones, slaves and wild beasts for the Roman games in the new amphitheater Herod Antipas had built. Gladiators would fight the beasts, or the beasts would be let loose on criminals who would be bloodthirstily devoured for the mobs entertainment.

There were Roman men wearing red togas over their white tunics being carried about in their lecticas by slaves. The Roman women wore ankle length Aegyptus cotton or silk stolas with a cloak thrown over the shoulders. Some of the Romans had blonde hair and I even saw one Roman with red hair that was as bright as a corn poppy in bloom. This town was truly a mixing pot of different peoples.

Having worked with my father on projects within the walls of Jerusalem I was used to groups of people crowded together in a large town atmosphere. However the town of Zippori was different in that it was newer and cleaner than Jerusalem. Jerusalem had people living there since before the days of King David, generations upon generations ago. Jerusalem had once been home to Canaanites and Jebusites, and the town was called Jebus. King David, to take the town for the Habirum, had chosen a dark night without the light of the moon. He and his warriors had crawled through a tunneled water shaft into the city from the spring called Gihon that was outside the city walls. King David took the city guards by surprise, slitting their throats, and quietly opened the gates for his army, thus conquering Jebus.

King David renamed the settlement Jerusalem and made it his capital. Jerusalem was on a hill surrounded by deep rocky valleys. King David fortified it by surrounding the town with new walls. He also secured the water spring shaft so no one could repeat his tricky attack. He then enclosed the valley with a new wall, enlarging the town and the population had increased. King Hezekiah, generations later, further secured the water source by digging a tunnel through solid rock that brought water from the Gihon spring under the city walls to the Pool of Siloam in the Valley of Tyropoeon.

Just as in Jerusalem, and all places where large numbers of people lived in close proximity, Zippori had a town dump. They used a valley, a ravine, for dumping. Where the dump in Jerusalem was olden back to King David, the dump in the newer town here was not as filled or smelly as the older one in Jerusalem. As the number of people living in Zippori increased, the dung and filth would one day fill the ravine. The dump burned the town's offal, as is done throughout the land.

My father said to Yosef, "It is bigger and busier than I expected. I understand that Herod Antipas has renamed Zippori, calling it the Roman word, Autocratoris."

Yosef replied, "The town is named Zippori after the wife of Moses, the daughter of Jethro. It will always be known as Zippori by the Habirum, no matter what Herod Antipas calls it. Herod, that fox, taxes the Habirum for his many building projects including this, what he says will be the ornament of the Galilee. On the coast of the Great Sea is the port city he built. He calls it Caesarea Maritama to honor his Roman emperor."

My father said, "On the eastern shore of the Salt Sea, Herod Antipas has rebuilt the fortress he calls Machaerus. It sits on a high hill. They store water in cisterns to supply the people if they are besieged. It is easy to protect and would take an army to conquer. Have you seen it?"

"No, I have not been to the land of the Nabateaan's in Petra, but I have been told of their temple carved into the face of a cliff. I understand it is impressive stone work."

"The Nabateaan's are no more. They were great fighters for many generations and allies of our great general Judah Maccabeus, but the Romans under the command of Marcus Aemilius Scaurus has defeated the Nabateaan's. Now Herod Antipas rules their kingdom."

Yosef, shook his bearded head, muttering, "That fox. He will not rest until the whole world is his kingdom."

Yosef told my father, "Be careful of who you speak to here in Zippori. There is a group of Habirum who are bound to making troubles. They despise the Sadducees. We all despise the Sadducees, the dogs for the Romans, but this group are zealots and will bring Roman retribution on us all with their troubles."

"I will bear that in mind."

My father looked at me. "You hear that? Take care of who you speak to in this foreign land."

Then Yeshua said, "The Book of Isaiah tells us. – *He donned righteousness like armor and a helmet of salvation on His head. He donned garments of vengeance as His attire and clothed Himself in zealousness like a coat* –. Perhaps these troublesome Habirum have something to say we should hear."

I would soon realize that Yeshua was in the habit of questioning all that seemed normal to others. Yeshua was different from other people in his thinking and attitudes.

We arrived at our place of work which was a palatial villa in the Roman style being built for a rich Sadducee. Yosef introduced my father to the foreman who, after a short conversation, immediately hired him. Skilled tektons, those who are talented with working in wood, stone and metal are valued hands. Yosef and Yeshua were building wooden timber falsework to support the opus caementicium columns and arches that surrounded an outside open area, called the atrium. This atrium had a rectangular implurium, a pool, for swimming and collecting rain water. I looked over the edge of the unfinished pool and saw several craftsmen laying bright chips of colored stone at the bottom and sides for an artistic mosaic. At one end of the atrium would be a garden for herbs and flowers. This villa was obviously for a very wealthy man as it had many rooms. The largest most finely detailed rooms would be for the master and his family, with more rooms for the many slaves who would live there and care for the family. The slaves would include cooks and household staff including the house steward to supervise them, a schoolmaster to tutor the children, and guardsmen to protect the family and property. There was a room for exercise, what the Greeks called the gymnós. Piping was laid from the aqueduct to bring water directly into the home for cooking and washing and bathing. There would be no need of the public bath houses with their stink and sweat of the mob for this privileged family. I saw this villa would have the Roman three stages of bathing, the frigidarium for the first soapy cold bath, then the warm tepidarium for relaxing, then the caldarium for the final hot soak.

The surrounding walls and supporting pillars of the villa were finished. Now we would use cedar timbers for the ceiling beams and cedar planking for the flat roof. The cedar wood was imported from the forests of Lebanon at great expense. The flat roof was an outside gathering area where the family would get the evening breezes and take supper. From the outside the home would have solid, plain impenetrable walls, with gated entries to provide security. The plainness of the outside hid the luxury inside.

My father was set to chiseling stones for the arched doorways and I was his helper, as was Yeshua the helper to his father cutting and hammering the wooden falsework. We kept busy until the sixth hour, when the sun was directly overhead, then all work stopped for a short break to have food and water. Afterwards we continued the labor until the eleventh hour according to the sun dial when the foreman called the end of work for the day.

We went to the market to fetch the women and then we all started the walk back to Nazareth. Outside the town we came upon an old man who was seated on the ground inside a circle he had drawn in the sand. The old man had long white hair and a long white beard. His long hair and beard made him appear to be covered by a white cloth, like his face and arms was poking through holes in the white covering. The man had a carved wooden wand in each hand that he was holding over his head while he muttered some incantation. I asked Yeshua what the old man was doing.

Yeshua said he was, "Pulling truth from AmunRa, the sun god."

At that Yeshua's step-father, Yosef, said, "He is a necromancer. The Book of Micah, the prophet, tells us. – *I will eliminate witchcraft from your domain, and there will be no diviners among you* –."

Then he and Yeshua cheerfully argued the sayings in the Book about magicians. Yeshua told him, "Not all words of the Book speak ill of magicians. The words in the Book of Exodus tell us. – *ADONAI said to Moses and Aaron, When Pharaoh speaks to you, saying, 'Provide a wonder for yourselves,' you shall say to Aaron, 'Take your staff and cast it down before Pharaoh. It will become a snake!' Pharaoh summoned his wise men and sorcerers and necromancers of Aegyptus. They too did their incantations. Each one cast down his staff and they became snakes. But the staff of Aaron swallowed their staffs* –. Also in Exodus are the words. – *And they took soot of the furnace, and stood before Pharaoh, and Moses threw it up heavenward, and it became a boil breaking forth with blains upon man and upon beast. And the pharaoh's magicians could not stand before Moses because of the boils, for the boils were upon the magicians and upon all the people of Aegyptus* –."

And then Yosef told Yeshua, "But the Book of Deuteronomy tells us. – *There shall not be found among you one who practices divinations, an astrologer, one who reads omens, a sorcerer, or an animal charmer, or one who consults the dead* –. Psalms tells us. – *Hearkeneth not to the voice of charmers, Or of the most cunning binder of spells* –."

And for the rest of the walk back to Nazareth Yeshua and Yosef talked of The Book as knowledgeable men. I had before only heard such thoughts from the priests in the synagogues. I wondered how Yeshua, in his youth, could discuss The Word so knowingly. I, like other boys of the Pharisees, had studied the Torah and the Laws with a learned man until the age of thirteen when I left the schooling to work at learning my father's trade. In our sect, the Pharisees, some boys continued their studies past the age of thirteen. Those boys would grow to become the scribes, the guardians of the tradition. But after I turned thirteen, when I became accountable for my actions, I had chosen to work with my father and learn to carve stone into lasting things of beauty and usefulness.

The hour was late when we arrived back in Nazareth. There was time for supper fixed by the women while the men tended to the animals and other chores. Then it was dark, the water clock was filled, the candles were blown out, and all laid down for a well-deserved rest.

The next day was like the first, an early rise, a bite of food, the walk to Zippori and a day of hard labor. In the second half of the day, after the high sun break, Yeshua and I were sent to fetch stones from a pile brought fresh from the quarry. We had some time to talk while we worked. I asked Yeshua how it was he could read Greek so well. He told me that as a child living in Aegyptus he had studied with a wise man who taught him Greek and other subjects. Yeshua said he was carried there as a babe in his mother's arms and they had only returned the year before. He told me that his mother and Yosef and all Yosef's children had walked to Bethlehem, where he was born, then they continued on to Gaza. They sailed in a boat to a town called Pelusium at the mouth of the Tamiathis branch of the great River Nile. Yeshua told me the river current travels north downstream to the Great Sea but the winds blow south from the Great Sea. The wind blew them upriver to the city of Heliopolis. They had lived there and other places in Aegyptus. Of course, Yeshua said, he was only a babe and did not remember the journey there, it was just as his mother had told him. But he did remember growing up there, the wonders he had seen in that land of old and what he had learned, and of the trip when they came back the same way to the land of the Habirum.

The next day was a repeat of the first two, except at sundown would be the beginning of the Shabbat. At the end of the work day we returned to Nazareth. We had moved into a house near to Yeshua's that was vacant, it needed work and my father contracted with the owner to repair it in exchange for a reduced property payment. My family would contribute and share victuals with Yeshua's family for the evening meals.

We gathered for the sixth day supper. A traditional place was set for and to honor the prophet Elijah and another for Mariam, who watched over her brother, the baby Moses, in his crib of river reeds.

We would eat before sundown and the next day, the Shabbat, have only the mid-day and evening meal. Shabbat was a holy day when the Laws of purity and cleanliness were observed as laid out in The Book. For the Essenes, some of whom are our cousins, and who had taken the Vows of Discipline to join that sect, the cleanliness was even more observed as they refrained even from defecation during the Shabbat.

Before the supper Yosef read holy words from a scroll then after supper we all sat and talked until it was late and time for rest after that day's hard work. The next day was one of rest and study of The Word. In the morning we went to a small synagogue in Nazareth where we worshipped. The women were included in the Pharisee synagogue, being equal in all things with the men. The seven prophetesses, Huldah, Sarah, Miriam, Deborah, Hannah, Abigail and Esther were shown to be wise and strong and the Pharisees showed women the respect they deserved.

The Sadducees did not allow their women to join the men during holy services. This was just one disagreement that we Pharisees had with the Sadducees. We believed the synagogue was a house of assembly, worship and prayer. The Pharisees believed any Habirum could speak to ADONAI in the synagogue. The Sadducees insisted that the Temple, with Herodian appointed priests officiating, was the only linkage to ADONAI. This was to the Sadducees benefit as they controlled the Temple treasury, and controlled the monopoly on the selling of the sacrificial doves and sheep as the offerings. The Herodians, not of true Habirum lineage, had control of all Judah for their Roman overlords. They worshipped the coin of Caesar. Some day we prayed, the Romans and Herodians would be driven from the land of the Habirum.

During the day of rest Yeshua and I found time to sit in the shade of a grove of trees. I told Yeshua I was very interested in what Aegyptus had been like. Yeshua told me, "My father and older stepbrothers worked as tektons, I was too young for work so was sent to study. One of my teachers had been born and raised in the Habirum community of Alexandria, Aegyptus. He knew about the Aegyptus from their earlier times. He told me about the Aegyptus gods and goddesses."

Yeshua told me about the many places Yosef had taken them for his work. There was a place called Giza, where there were great monuments so old they were mostly buried in the sands, covered by the countless years of winds and storms. The monuments had been standing so long no one knew how or when they had been built. Carved into those stone monuments were symbols that told mysterious stories. Yeshua said that the wise man told him some secrets about the monuments, secrets about who built them. He said he would tell me that later. It was something he was not to speak of during the day of Shabbat.

Yeshua had a leather pouch sewed to a loop of braided Kaneh Bosem, the stalks from the Kannabaeus plant. The loop was for hanging the pouch over the shoulder. This Kaneh Bosem was very useful for making rope and for ship's sails and clothing. Inside the pouch was a short wooden stick with strange carvings on it. Also in the pouch was a length of leather to be worn about the neck with an amulet carved from red jasper hanging from it. He also had a black rock and a white stone. Yeshua said he found these treasures exploring the Aegyptus monuments.

Yeshua said the healers of Aegyptus used the Kannabaeus plant to cure all manner of ailments. Yeshua told me the Aegyptus used Kannabaeus also for ritual praying to their gods. They would burn the leaves, then breathe the smoke. The inhaled smoke caused one to relax and have awakened dreams and visions.

"Have you experienced these awakened dreams?" I asked him.

"No. Not yet," he replied, "But one day I think I will try the Kannabaeus for the awakened dreams. I remember that Yosef once used it for a problem he had with a stoppage in his defecation. An Aegyptus man practiced in their healing arts placed a plug of the Kannabaeus coated with olive oil in his back passage. The next day Yosef returned from the field smiling as if a great weight had been lifted from him."

The days became weeks and the seasons changed from planting to harvest to the time of the rains. During this time Yeshua and I worked as apprentice tektons learning to be craftsmen and eventually run our own crews. We found time for adventures. We hunted in the forested woods on the slopes of Tabor Mount. We used our bows and arrows and set traps, to catch meat our mothers added to the stew pot for the evening meals. Running in the hills hunting, and working the hard labor in Zippori, made us swift and strong, our bodies strengthening to muscular young men.

We kept hidden in a small cave on the Mount Tabor wooden arms of war we sparred with. We pretended we were warriors of the Judah Maccabeus clan. He was the Habirum leader who led the revolt against the Seleucid Empire, freeing the land of the Habirum and cleansing the Temple. Our wooden weapons were the double edged dagger, the short stabbing sword, the long sword and the javelin. We practiced with these weapons so that we would be worthy opponents if called to war.

We helped with the daily chores. We gathered deadfall and brush and cut firewood. We tended to the animals. We helped to patch the woven reed and brush roofs, covering that with layers of plaster made of clay, sand and water, sealing the roofs for the rains. Yeshua told me stories of the land of the Aegyptus, of the lost civilization and its mysteries. We talked of one day traveling beyond the hills of Galilee, to see the wonders of the farther world. For the first time in both of our lives we had a true friend and companion. The suns and moons passed, the seasons changed. We grew and changed. But the Galilee remained more or less the same, day in and day out.

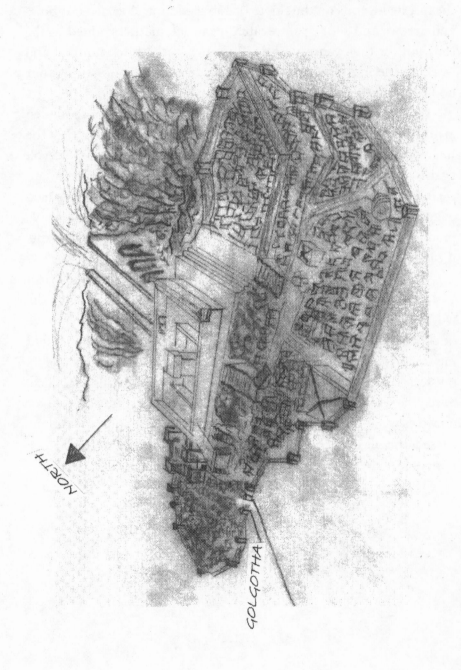

NORTH

GOLGOTHA

JERUSALEM. MY NAME IS JUDAS ISCARIOT

In the month Nisan, all the families in Nazareth made the journey to Jerusalem, as did all the Habirum in Galilee for the Pesach, the Passover festival. We would go the same route as our journey from Bethany to Nazareth, a journey of five suns. I counted it as an adventure, but Yeshua in the days preceding the trip grew moody. He was irritable with all except me and even with me he did not josh and joke as before. For some reason Yeshua did not look forward to going to Jerusalem. Whatever the reason, he kept it to himself.

The day before the journey we went to synagogue for prayer. After the service and the breaking of fast Yeshua seemed to be in a foul temper and insisted on being alone most of the day. His mother, Mary, and Yosef and the other children seemed to be used to his mood and left him to his own. I was worried that I had somehow insulted him but outside, before he walked away toward the Mount, he told me, "Do not trouble yourself, my friend. It is a private matter. A question in my own mind that troubles me. One day I will have the answer. Now I ask only that you do not take this to be a reflection on you." Yeshua walked away, brooding.

We left at the dawn for the journey to Jerusalem and the Passover festival. My father and mother and I would travel with Yosef's family including his two married sons with their wives and children. Donkeys were loaded with the supplies we would need while at the festival including the cooking things and the portable homes we used for traveling. These portable homes were made of goat skins sewn together and laid over a structure of tree branches. The goat hair would swell when wet keeping out the rain. Over time a family's home would became a large covering as the family grew. As Isaiah tells us. – *Broaden the place of your tent and let the curtains of your dwellings stretch out, stint not; lengthen your cords and strengthen your pegs* –. A family's tent was divided into two parts, the first part was for the men. Behind that was a curtain, making a separate part for the women.

The road was filled with travelers going to the festival. Many of them had been traveling for days and some for weeks, as Habirum came from all parts of the land, some of them even crossing the Great Sea. On the fifth day we arrived as the sun was beginning to lean to the west and made our camp at the Mount Olivet. Our camp was near to where the Essenes gathered. Many Essenes were in our clan as we were related by birth and marriage. The city of Jerusalem had more people living in it than many villages combined, and during the festival the population increased several times over. The Mount Olivet, the Garden of Gethsemane and Bethany, were considered within the Temple precincts so here we made our camp, away from the crowded city.

While we were taking supper that first eve of our arrival, Yeshua's stepbrother, Joses, told us an amusing story. When they had returned from Aegyptus, two years before, they had come straight to Jerusalem as it was the Passover Festival., Yeshua argued with some of the Temple priests the meaning of certain words in Exodus. The conversation had become feisty, ended with harsh words and threats from the priests.

Yeshua, said Joses, told the priests that ADONAI passing over the houses that were marked with blood on the lintel and door posts, was like a story from the Aegyptus goddess Taweret. Yeshua told the agitated priests the story in Exodus was a demonstration of conjuring and magic.

I asked, "Who is this Taweret?"

Yeshua said Taweret is the Aegyptus goddess of childbirth and fertility. "The River Nile is reborn each year by the magic of Taweret. She has the body of the hippopotamus, the tail of a crocodilia, and the legs of a lion. In Exodus the evil eye was averted using the blood of the Pesach offering, just like the magic of Taweret protects one from the evil eye. All peoples of Aegyptus make offerings to Taweret for protection against the evil eye."

Joses told us the priests were angry that Yeshua, this boy of young years, would dare to question the words of ADONAI.

"Yes," said Yosef, to Yeshua, "I had to talk fast to get you out of that difficulty. Let us not debate the priests this year."

Yeshua opened his eyes wide, spread his arms and addressed us all, sitting before the campfire, "I was not arguing with them. I was only pointing out that words can have different meanings. The wise men tell us, 'Drink not froth, for it gives cold in the head. Nor blow it away, for that gives headache.'" Yeshua asked us, "These are words with a hidden meaning, are they not? Are not those words meant to blind the evil eye?"

My father told Yeshua, "Words can cut like a knife. It is best to not take the knife from the sheath, unless you mean to draw blood. The Law tells us, in another hidden meaning. – *One must be certain to drain all the blood from the meat –.*"

Yeshua nodded his head thoughtfully. "Well said. I shall take your advice,"

The next morning Yeshua and I took a walk about the city. Jerusalem was divided into two parts by a city wall that ran from east to west. The area of the Upper City was where the Temple stood. The palaces of Herod Antipas and his high priest, Caliphas, were located there. Also in the Upper City, next to the Temple, was the Antonia Fortress, the home of the Roman troops assigned to keep order in the city. One entered the city through the gates that were closed and guarded at night by the Roman soldiers. From the gates, stone paved roadways led to all points in the city. In the Upper City and the Lower City were thousands of resident's homes and a multitude of market stalls.

The markets in Jerusalem were as colorful as the one in Zippori. The market here at Jerusalem had even more variety of goods for sale or barter. Products came to Jerusalem from everywhere such as herbs and spices, peppers and garlic, and figs and fruits from Aegyptus and other lands. Papyrus for scrolls came from the town of Byblos, a seaport in Phoenicia. The scribes would gather their scrolls together into one single document, calling it ta biblia, the book.

There were alabaster jars of ointments and perfumers selling scents. Skilled tailors displayed lengths of the brilliant blue and purplish red cloths for the robes prized by the wealthy. There were goldsmiths and silversmiths who sold bowls, plates and cups for lavish suppers, also they displayed rings and bracelets accented with precious stones. There was the stone on which slaves stood, to be bought by those who practiced such pagan atrocities as owning their fellow human beings. There were the sellers of wood for the wood offerings to the Temple. In the markets and at the Temple itself were the moneychangers who would exchange the peoples foreign coins for the Tyrian silver shekel, the only form of currency the Temple priests would accept for the taxes and offerings. A flood of the silver denarius, drachmas and staters, and gold aureus, and copper assarions and leptons, poured into the city, then into the Temple, during the festivals. The Sadducee priests of the Temple collected taxes for all that was imported into and sold in Jerusalem, enriching the treasury.

This year I was to visit and see the Temple from another perspective, Yeshua's, as he saw things different from other people. Yeshua questioned the things most people took as normal. As I walked with him about the Temple, Yeshua talked about the priests and their practices in a quizzical and sometimes derisive manner.

Yeshua pointed out that the people were obligated to make the offerings to the Temple. They would buy the unblemished sheep and white doves which the seller had to pay taxes on, then people would make sacrifices to the altar, which was another form of tax. The Sadducee priests of the Herodian dynasty performed the sacrifices. The priests cut the animal's throats, threw the blood on the fire, gave a part of the meat to the man making the sacrifice, but kept the hides and a share of the meat for the priests themselves to eat. The priests sold the hides for an additional profit. Yeshua pointed out that the priests got the sheepskins, free meat, and also charged coins for this service. Yeshua wondered how rich the treasury was, and how much Herod Antipas took from it.

"Nehemiah tells us. – *The people instituted upon themselves the commandment to give one third of a shekel yearly toward the service of the Temple of our God –*. Of course that is every Haribum in the world, so it must be a large amount," I pointed out.

Yeshua said, "That may be as it is written, but in truth, the tax has increased to half a shekel. The temple collects many more shekels than that. Look, the people are lined up to purchase the white doves and sheep for sacrifice. They pay for the offerings and each are required to pay the second tithe also, one tenth of the produce of their land. The second tithe must be used to purchase food and wine for their meals and all they require while they are at the festival. The treasury of this temple, call it the treasury of Herod Antipas, must be rich beyond imagining."

I stood looking around at the thousands crowded into Jerusalem to go to the Temple, all intent on their need to make the offerings, for that is what the Sadducee priests told them ADONAI demanded of them. I saw that what Yeshua said was the truth. The people were being used as burnt offerings themselves by the Sadducee priests of Herod Antipas. The people were like the doves and sheep they offered for sacrifice. The people were the sacrifices. Looking about at these thousands of people, I felt the tears of pity for my people burning my eyes.

I turned to look at Yeshua, and I saw the hard look on his face. There were no tears in his eyes, no pity on his expression. I saw only a burning rage. I understood now why he disliked coming to Jerusalem for the festival. It was the hypocrisy of the Temple priests he found maddening, and it was the fervor and ecstasy of the people allowing themselves to be used by the Sadducee priests that baffled him.

Yeshua was right. The amount of coins the Temple collected during this festival alone must be a staggering weight, enough to crush Samson himself. The daily pay for a laborer was one Greek drachma or one Roman silver denarius, they being equal, and depending on who was paying. Skilled tektons made more than laborers and crew leaders even more than that. Two drachma was equal to one half shekel so a man worked two days a year just to pay the Temple tax. Every Habirum in the world had to pay that, then they had to buy the offerings, and pay the second tithe when they attended the festivals.

I stood and watched the mass of people, buying the offerings and paying for the sacrifices. They were wailing and beseeching to ADONAI for His blessing. Yeshua pointed at a very old woman, struggling to make her way to the altar. The woman had no offering but her fist was clenched tightly. As we watched she dropped two small copper leptons onto the altar. A lepton was the smallest unit of coin. The lepton coin was known as mites.

Yeshua said, "She, out of her poverty, put in all that she had, her whole livelihood. The widow feeds the priests, but she herself will have no supper tonight." Yeshua stepped to the woman, pushing the crowd aside, and assisted her from the altar steps. He walked her to a clear space, then leaned to whisper in her ear. I saw him place some coins in her hand. She embraced him, I could see her crying on his chest while Yeshua patted her on the back. Then he stood watching as she left the Temple through the Eastern Gate.

The Book tell us that Jerusalem, on this Mount, is the special place of ADONAI. This is the center of the world, the place where ADONAI resides. In The Beginning, ADONAI stood upon the Foundation Stone, and from there He created the world. It was dust from the Mount that ADONAI formed to make the first human, Adam.

I, of course, believed this was true. But Yeshua scoffed at the notion, telling me, "The Aegyptus have their own story of the creation of the world. Their story is older than that, so perhaps they are right in their thinking."

"What is it they believe?" I asked.

"They believe the god AmunRa changed the void of darkness into light. They believe AmunRa has a force beyond anything we can comprehend. They believe AmunRa created other gods to work for him. The other gods made the sky and land and water and all the creatures. That his gods included Osiris and his sister and consort, Isis. They believe Isis bore a miracle child, fathered by Osiris, without copulation. The Aegyptus believe that AmunRa changed disorder and chaos into structure and harmony. Perhaps the Aegyptus are right. Perhaps ADONAI is just another name for AmunRa. Perhaps when

Moses led the people out of Aegyptus the people brought AmunRa with them. We end a prayer with the word, Amen. The Aegyptus end their prayers to AmunRa by saying, Amun. Is it the same god, just called by a different name?"

Yeshua was a talker, a philosopher, a spinner of stories. Listening to Yeshua talk could sometimes make the brain ache. I could see why Yosef told him there were things he must not speak of in the land of the Habirum. "So do you not believe the Word is true?"

Yeshua pondered on my question for a moment. "I believe I must seek the truth." He pointed at the milling thousands of worshipers. "It is difficult to see how that can be the truth. Could it be possible that all of those people, in their hysteria, can be right? Their subservience to the Sadducee priests of Herod Antipas shows me their reasoning may be muddled."

I had no ready answer to Yeshua's thought. I told him I would think on it.

Yeshua and I explored the area around the Temple and the holy city. While I looked at everything with interest, Yeshua seemed to have eyes only for the Roman soldiers who guarded the city. It was if Yeshua was looking for some soldier in particular. He even approached some of them, and talked to them. I, of course, thought he was mad. "Why do you speak to these Romans?" I asked him. Yeshua responded by shaking his head, saying nothing. I warned him the soldiers might draw out their sword and cut him down. He looked at me with a grim smile and said, "The sword cuts both ways. To, and from."

I asked Yeshua, "Do you seek a Roman soldier in particular? Is that why you talk to these Romans?"

Yeshua looked at me, a grim countenance on his face. "Yes. The Roman soldier's name is Abdes Panthera."

I asked him, "Why is this Roman so important to you that you would risk bringing yourself to the attention of the Romans?"

Yeshua looked away. Long moments passed while he seemed to be deep in thought. Finally he said, "I owe him a debt of honor. I will repay that debt one day."

I hesitated to inquire further, it seemed to be a private affair. I only said to Yeshua, "Then I will help you to find this Roman."

Yeshua looked at me. I could see a slow burning rage in his eyes. He said to me, "You are my friend, truly, but this can only bring trouble and I do not want the trouble to be on you."

I told him, "You are my friend, truly, and whatever trouble you encounter, I will gladly share."

Yeshua said, "And if I told you that when I find Panthera there will death. What then would you say?"

"Whatever is the ending of this, I will be at your side."

Yeshua clapped me on the back and said, "Very well. I welcome your strong arm and your eyes to watch my back. One day I will catch this Panthera. I will catch him, and I will kill him, and you shall witness my revenge."

"May I ask what the revenge will be for?"

Yeshua looked at the group of Roman soldiers, looking for the one. His hard face and his determination for the blood feud sent a chill down my back. He said, "Panthera is a sinner and a criminal. For his sin, and for his crime, he will die."

Yeshua and I hunted, adding meat to the stew pot. One day while we were hunting, to the north and west of the city, words from Genesis presented themselves to us. Isaac said to his son, Esau. – *Now therefore take, I pray thee, thy weapons, thy quiver and thy bow, and go out to the field, and take me venison –.*

We had surprised a buck who fled away through the ravines. We ran far and soon were in the Ayalon Valley. The deer led us further north into the woods of Mount Ephraim, and we were now in the southern part of the land of the Samaria, home of the Cuthites. Our arrows found their mark and the buck fell. While we were cleaning it and preparing to pack it out back to camp, two men and two teenage boys of the Cuthites came from the woods and surrounded us. The older and bigger of the men told us the deer belonged to them as it was in their land, where we were not welcome. Yeshua and I stood, back to back.

Yeshua told them, "Leave now while you can walk away."

That man laughed and went to push past Yeshua to the deer. Faster than can be told the fight was on. For our youth we were matched in strength but not size to the men. They had the advantage also in that the two boys were like ticks clinging on us as we fought the men. They fought for simple stupid greed. We fought for the honor of our tribe. There were hard hits from both sides then they tired. Our stamina prevailed, and the advantage became ours. Yeshua head butted the boy's face, breaking his nose, then threw several punches to his man's head. The man staggered back, then reached under his cloak and drew out a dagger. The man came at Yeshua viciously, swishing the dagger at Yeshua. The man leaped and swung the dagger at Yeshua's face, going for his eyes, nicking his cheek. The fight that could and should have been settled by the strength of fist had suddenly turned deadly, with blindness, and even death, as the outcome.

Yeshua almost fell to the ground but he came up with a handful of sand and threw it in the man's eyes. While the man backed, cursing, with one hand to his face, Yeshua kicked him between the legs then stepped quickly in, grabbed the arm with the dagger, and pulled the man off balance. Yeshua tripped him then slammed him to the ground hard on his face, the wind erupting from the man's lungs with a loud exhalation. Yeshua grabbed the man's leg at the foot, bent the man's leg over his back, and then fell on it with his full weight, snapping the man's knee like a brittle stick. The man screamed and fainted from the pain.

I fought some room to maneuver and drew my staff from its sling on my back. Swinging it like a whirling magician weaving a wild spell I hit my man upside his head, dropping him. The two boys turned and ran. We knew they were going to their camp for reinforcements. My opponent was trying to rise, cursing us. I clubbed him about the head with the staff rendering him insensible. I gave him a couple of extra knocks to his foolish head for his use of profanity.

Yeshua grabbed up the buck onto his shoulders and I gathered our bows and quivers. Then we ran like the wind for our camp. Our clan feasted on the venison. Blessings to Isaac and Esau, the venison was delicious.

When we arrived in camp with the dressed game, Yeshua and I were bloody and dirty indicating some sort of trouble. We told my father and Yosef what had happened so our clan could be prepared in case the Cuthites came looking for revenge. I knew the Cuthites and the Habirum were enemies, but not the whole reason why. We sat at the campfire and my father and Yosef told of the history of the Cuthites in the land of Samaria.

Yosef said, "The blood feud we have with the Cuthites from the land of Samaria is the reason we cross the River Jordan to the side of the rising sun. We do not travel through their land as many of them take joy in preying on those who are not of their tribe. The Cuthites claim to be of the tribes of Ephraim, but everyone knows they are descendants of the Assyrians."

"That is so," said my father. "And they worship the pagan god Nergal, their god of war and destruction. They have a temple on Mount Gerizim where they claim Moses received the commandments from ADONAI, instead of at the Temple Mount, as we believe. They pay tribute to and parley with the Romans."

Yosef told us, "The Cuthites are favored by Rome, being given the fertile lands of the Plain of Sharon. The Plain of Sharon has rich soil they use for grazing herds of cattle and sheep, and to grow abundant crops. They do not share their bounty with the Habirum, but instead place the harvests on ships bound for Roman Italia."

My father said, "In the time of Judah of Gamala, Judah started a revolt over paying taxes to Publius Sulpicius Quirinius, the Roman legate governor of Judah. Yeshua, you and Judas would be the age of eight harvests. The Cuthites swore allegiance to Rome and fought Judah. The Cuthites began calling their temple, Zeus Hellionios, and were given special consideration. The Cuthites are treacherous. Beware the Cuthites and venture not into the land of Samaria. In future do not chase game into their lands. You were lucky today that it was two men and two boys. Had it been four men, you would be food for the vultures. They would be eating the venison, the vultures would be eating you."

I could see Yeshua sitting near the fire, chewing then swallowing. He shook his head with a puzzled look on his face. He asked, "But why do we fight over whether their Mount Gerizim is the place of Moses? Exodus only tells us Mount Sinai was between Aegyptus and Arabah in the Wilderness of Zin, and that there were twelve wells of water and seventy date palms. No one truly knows where the Mount Sinai is located. Some say that is far from here, south, down to the Sea of Reeds. But even if it is that far, it is certainly not a forty year walk from here to there. Besides, Mount Gerizim has the pulvis puteolanus from the burning mountain the Romans use for their opus caementicium in their aqueducts and building. Has anyone seen the burning mountain ash come from the Wilderness of Zin? Not I. Have you?"

Yosef shook his bearded head and told my father, "Yeshua will debate with the donkey."

The Passover festival ended. We left to return to Nazareth and a return to our everyday lives.

NAZARETH. MY NAME IS JUDAS ISCARIOT

The Galilee, along the Jezreel Valley, was a land of bounty. The Jezreel Valley was fertile, lying in the Plain of Esdraelon between Mount Tabor and Mount Gilboa. The Valley received more rain than Judah further to the south. Most of the land of the Habirum in Galilee was fertile. Crops were grown such as the grains, wheat and barley. The many vineyards grew grapes for wine. Olives were pulled from the trees by the handful. Bees were kept for honey. Different types of nuts fell from the trees and made a carpet on the ground. There was grazing for cattle and sheep and goats roamed the hills tended by their shepherds. This was a land of fertility, blessed by ADONAI. This was truly the land of milk and honey my people had been given by ADONAI after our exodus from Aegyptus. It should have been a paradise. Why then was it not, and why was there conflict? Why, especially, was there conflict in the Jezreel Valley?

As I grew older and learned more about the history of my people and the land we lived in, I came to understand that the Jezreel Valley had always been a fiercely contested place. It fell in the center of all the world's civilizations. It was the main trade route for the movement of people and the goods they traded. Armies fought for that land and its bounty. The Jezreel Valley was the crossing point for armies from north to south and from east to west. The soil was soaked in blood since the beginning of time. Towns, villages and cities were built, fought over, destroyed and plundered. The warriors slaughtered their foes, taking the women and children as slaves. Then new towns, new villages and cities were rebuilt atop those ruins. Then there was more fighting, from generation through generation.

The Book said that the world began in the Garden of Eden and the land of the Habirum, with its bounty, was that garden. It seemed that everyone wanted to fight for Eden, and to possess it. To the west of Nazareth was the old city of Megiddo, once a citadel of King Josiah. Megiddo was captured and razed to dust by Pharaoh Necho II, resulting in Josiah's death. It was now just a great mound, a hill that was grazed on by sheep. Many said that Megiddo would one day be the place of the last fight of the world, bringing an end to the world.

The conflict for the land of the Habirum continued under the Roman occupiers. But there was always hope that freedom would one day come. There was even fighting amongst the Habirum themselves. That is why Israel and Judah was split into two separate kingdoms after the death of King Solomon. Probably the whole world was a rough and vicious place. As it says in Genesis. – *And the earth was corrupt before God, and the earth was filled with violence and robbery –*.

There were only two laws that the people knew, the Laws of the Book, and the law of the Roman emperor. The Roman laws were administered by Herod Antipas in the Galilee. In Jerusalem the governor, Pontius Pilate ruled. These men exercised the power of life and death over the Habirum. The Roman law benefitted only the Romans and their collaborators, the Sadducee. When your neighbor could take the injustices no more, they sometimes chose to rebel against the laws of the emperor. There was only one punishment for inciting rebellion and for thievery, and that was to be nailed to a cross. The Romans were expert at rendering this punishment, which they called, the cruci fixus.

As the seasons passed Yeshua and I became skilled tektons. I became a master stone carver and mason, and Yeshua became a master working with wood. We learned metal working and forged our own tools. We heated and blended the ores, forming iron, bronze and copper to make instruments of such quality that other workers paid us to make tools for them. The foreman made us team leaders and placed men under our supervision. We replaced our wooden weapons, the dagger, the short sword, the long sword and the javelin, with razor sharp iron weapons. We kept these stashed in our secret cave on Mount Tabor where we continued to spar to perfect our skills. Yeshua was better in close fighting with the dagger and swords but I was better with the bow. I practiced until I could draw, shoot and place six deadly iron tipped arrows in a space no bigger than a man's hand from a distance of six horse lengths. Yeshua and I were master tektons and becoming skilled with the arms of warfare.

ZIPPORI. MY NAME IS JUDAS ISCARIOT

One day Yeshua and I were walking through Zippori. Yeshua saw some Roman soldiers lounging and lazing, drinking wine, and flirting with the women. A Roman standard was leaning against a wall. The crest caught Yeshua's interest.

Yeshua approached the soldiers and asked if they knew a man called Abdes Panthera.

The oldest of the soldiers said, "Yes, I know Panthera. He is a good fighter. Why do you ask of him?"

Yeshua said his family owes Abdes Panthera a debt and wishes to repay him. "Can you tell me where he can be found?"

The soldier replied, "Panthera served here in Roman Judah. His legion was sent to the province of Gaul, to Colonia Narbo Martius."

I saw that Yeshua was very interested. This is the first time someone has known of Panthera. "Where, pray tell, is Gaul?" he asked the soldier.

The soldier pointed north and west. "Gaul is across the Great Sea."

Yeshua asked, "How does one get to Gaul? How many suns journey is it? Can one walk to it from here"

The soldier laughed at the young man's ignorance. He is loose with the wine and finds this amusing. To impress his friends and show his knowledge, he drew a crude map on the wooden table with the point of his dagger.

The map he drew was an oval shape with an opening at the far left end. "This is the Great Sea. It is fed from the Greater Sea beyond this gap in the land between Hispania and Afrikkus." He scratched with his dagger on the table, "This is where we are at, the Roman province of Judah." Then he scratched another mark far to the other side of the oval at its top. "This is Gaul."

Yeshua asked him, "How far is this Gaul? How does one get there? How many days of horseback ride is it?"

The centurion laughed. "Are you a sailor or a farmer? You cannot get there on horse. You must sail the Great Sea in a boat."

Yeshua told him, "I am a carpenter. Perhaps I will build a boat and sail to this land of Gaul, to this Narbo Martius."

While Yeshua had been talking, I was standing to the side, watching these Romans. They had welcomed this distraction to go along with their wine. They looked at Yeshua as if he were a stupid farmer to be joked at. To get the information Yeshua had allowed them their laugh. If they only knew Yeshua's intent they would not find this so funny.

Yeshua thanked the soldier and bid him a good day. The man laughed, "Be sure to build a boat that does not leak. It is a long journey."

From there Yeshua went into the city in search of a certain wise man. This Habirum was said to have traveled to many lands. I walked with him. He was quiet and determined. He had finally found where this Abdes Panthera could be.

We found the wise man in a synagogue. He was a very old man with a long white beard. Yeshua told him he sought information about the Great Sea and a land called Gaul and a town called Colonia Narbo Martius. The wise man was studying scrolls by the light of candles. He asked Yeshua for what purpose he sought this information. Yeshua told him he had been to Aegyptus and his travels had made him curious about other lands. The wise man asked Yeshua some questions about Aegyptus and when Yeshua spoke knowingly of that land, the wise man invited us to sit with him.

The wise man told us in his younger days he had sailed the Great Sea with his father and brothers to Italia. He told us the Romans call the Great Sea, Mare Nostrum. "Mare Nostrum, Our Sea. They not only claim the whole world is their property, but they also claim the Great Sea."

He said the furthest he had sailed had been to the island of Corsica. The land of Gaul was just north of Corsica. The wise man opened a scroll showing a map and Yeshua and I watched as he traced his fingers over it.

He showed us the land of ADONAI, where we are. His finger pointed to the sea of Chinnereth to the east of us and the Salt Sea to the south. Going west he pointed to the city called Alexandria of Aegyptus in the land of Afrikkus where the Nile River met the Great Sea. North and west of that, sticking down into the Great Sea like a long leg with a boot at its end, was the land of the Romans, called Italia. More west of that was the land of Gaul.

Yeshua asked the wise man how many days sailing it would be to Gaul. He said, "It is a great journey. One must cross the Great Sea in a worthy craft. It is a journey of at least one moon to Gaul if you are lucky, two moons if the wind is against you and you get in the wrong currents. You must take careful notice of the currents or your craft will be caught in a circle and you will drift endlessly."

"One must choose a place on the coast to begin the journey. There are two places. Joppa is a harbor about sixty of the Roman milia passum south of us. Half that distance is Caesarea Maritama but it is thick with Romans who would tax you to death before you even got in your boat. The best is Joppa. Many Habirum fisherman call Joppa home."

The Romans set in the ground a marking stone, a milliarium, at each milia passum. These stones are how they mark their territory, like a dog raises his leg to mark his spot. I asked the wise man, "I have heard it said that the Romans, on all their roads, place a stone marker at each milia passum. These stones have a carved number on it, the number showing how many milia passum it is back to Rome from that marker. Is that true?"

"Yes. The Romans consider their city of Rome in Italia to be the center of the world. Each of those milia passum mark the distance to the center of that city, to their Foro Romano. I have seen this place. There are many buildings and plazas. It is where they have their celebrations to their pagan gods and their Senate meet to decide their laws. Also there is the coliseum where the gladiators fight each other to the death and where criminals are slaughtered by wild beasts for the enjoyment of the mob. I have seen their center of the world, and it was not, as they say, something to write home about."

The wise man studied the candle flames for a moment, his brow wrinkled in thought. He shook his head and said quietly, almost as if he were talking to the candles themselves, "The center of the world? Such arrogance! – *Pride goeth before destruction, and a haughty spirit before a fall* –." He asked, "Where is it written?"

Yeshua and I at the same time answered him, "Proverbs." And he smiled at us as though we were good students.

Yeshua asked him about the dangerous currents he spoke of. The wise man showed us how the current in the north part of the Great Sea goes west and the current in the south of the Great Sea goes east. He showed us on the scroll how one must sail north then west around the island of Kyprus, "Do not go ashore on the island of Kyprus. That is where the copper mines are. You might find yourselves taken prisoner by the Roman soldiers and sold into slavery to work the mines. The only escape from that is death."

"Then follow the coast to stay north of the island of Rhodes. From there you enter into the Sea of Creta where there are many smaller islands, that is the land of the Achaians. Continue west keeping the land in sight to your right hand side. Stay north of the island of Creta. Steer west to the Ionian Sea to the Strait of Messana that lies between the island of Sicilia and the land of Italia. Here you must take care for the currents and tides in the Strait of Messana can be very rough and dangerous. You must pick a calm day before you pass through the Strait of Messana. Once you are through the Strait of Messana steer north and follow the coast of Italia to the north of the island of Corse. Steer west to the port town of Massilia in Gaul. There is a community of Habirum in Massilia. West along the shore is Colonia Narbo Martius. I recommend you do not go there as it is a Roman military port. If you make it to Massilia you are in the land of Gaul."

Yeshua asked him, "How will I know the shore I land on is the one of which you speak?"

The wise man smiled and said with a twinkle in his eye, "Going into unfamiliar lands is an adventure. – *Those who go down to the sea in ships, who do their work in great waters. They have seen the deeds of*

ADONAI, and His wonders in the watery deep –. It sounds like you are planning a grand journey. If I were not so old I would go with you."

Using the charred end of a stick of wood from the fire, Yeshua drew on another piece of wood the map the wise man had shown us. Yeshua thanked the wise man and we left. Walking away I had not seen Yeshua so excited before. Now he knew where this Roman soldier, Abdes Panthera, was to be found. "Now," said, Yeshua, "I must learn to build a boat."

The work continued in Zippori. The rapid growth was fueled by the work of the tetrarch, Herod Antipas, and his favor with Rome. The projects included his palaces and fortresses. There was public work such as building and maintaining the aqueducts and roadways. There was work on the coliseums and theaters for the amusement of the mob. Herod had thousands of masons and wood workers on these projects. Any work in a holy place could only be done by priests. The priests were trained to be tektons but they were not very good at it, and this took work from the Habirum. All Herod's projects required great sums of monies, monies he got from taxing the Habirum. Everyone was required to pay these taxes, creating hardships on all. There was much grumbling amongst the Habirum who had to pay

these taxes. The projects Yeshua and our clan worked on were not for Herod but for the rich Sadducee who collaborated with Herod and the Romans. We were thankful for the work and coins it paid but held the rich Sadducee in contempt for their subservience to the Romans.

One day a man came to the luxurious villa we were building. He was a short but muscularly built man. He was a few years older than I. His smiling face was surrounded by a mass of black curly hair and a thick beard. He gave the impression of a man who enjoyed life and laughed at its ironies. He greeted Yosef with a slap on the back and Yosef seemed delighted to see him. Yeshua also greeted him enthusiastically, laughing in pleasure. Yosef introduced us and I realized I had a distant cousin I had not met. His name was Thaddaeus Barabbas. He was the son of a learned man and from the town of Cana. Thaddaeus Barabbas was a stone chiseler who was looking for work. I took him on and was glad to have him on my crew. He not only could lift and wrestle the largest stones into place, he could also use his mallet and chisels and large hands to make the most delicate and intricate of cuts into the stones.

One day we were told a new shipment of stones and timbers had arrived from the quarry and forest. Yeshua and I were instructed by the foreman to go and select the best materials for the project. We took Thaddaeus Barabbas with us to assist with the loading. While there I disputed with another man over a selection of stones and we set to fight over the choice. The man had two others with him and Yeshua stood ready in case they joined with their man against me. Thaddaeus Barabbas laughed and walked over to the man, talking reasonably in a seeming attempt to ward off the coming fight. As he passed me he said in a quiet voice, "Allow me." He said to their leader, pointing with his right arm to the huge pile of stones from the quarry, "See now, there is plenty for all." Then his left arm shot out, his huge left fist delivering a crushing blow to the side of the man's head knocking him down unconscious. Thaddaeus Barabbas then grabbed the other two by their tunics and with a great jerk pulled them together banging their heads against one another and they too fell to the ground, knocked senseless. Turning to us with a booming laugh Thaddaeus Barabbas said, "I think they have changed their minds."

Thaddaeus Barabbas moved to Nazareth with his pretty pregnant wife. All the clan pitched in to assist him in building a home near to Yosef's. With all working the home was raised in a day and there was a supper afterwards to celebrate. Thaddaeus Barabbas was a welcome addition to our clan. Thaddaeus Barabbas was not only a skilled stonemason and formidable fighter but he also had a great sense of fun. He always had a laugh and a smile for everyone he met.

At the end of one work day when we had come home to Nazareth, Thaddaeus Barabbas and Yeshua and I were sitting under the shade of some trees having a rest and a talk. We saw a cloud of dust down the road, signaling a group of horsemen were approaching. Soon there came into view a group of Roman cavalry. We sat quietly and watched them approach. Everyone in the village had gone into their homes, only we three continued to sit under the trees. They rode into the village to the well and watered their horses. The cavalrymen wore armor breastplates of metal. Each had buckled to their waists the spatha, the long sword, with a shield on their left arm and a long spear, the javelin, in their right hands. A turmae, thirty cavalrymen, like this were trained to charge and slaughter their enemy like foxes slaughtering hens in the coop.

Their leader watered his horse, said something to his men, then turned, spurred his horse and rode toward us. Riding right up to us in an insolent manner, his dust caking us, he halted his horse and said to us, "We seek a bandit who has stolen coins from a merchant in Zippori. The bandit stuck a dagger into the merchant during the robbery. The bandit was injured in the leg by the merchants slave. The merchant says this bandit is a short fat man. Have you seen a stranger, a short fat man who may be limping, pass through your village?" He sat on his horse, looking down at us from under the shade of his bronze helmet. The helmet had on the top a colorful ridge of feathers, the identifying crest of this unit of cavalry.

Thaddaeus Barabbas answered for us, "You are the only strangers who have come to our village."

The man sat on his horse, studying our faces as if he were looking for signs of a lie in our eyes. Then without another word he pulled the horse's head to the side and rode away waving his arm at his men to follow. We sat silently, watching them go until they were in the distance. Thaddaeus Barabbas said, his normally smiling face twisted with hatred, "The Roman pigs ride over our land. Their horses slobber in our water and leave their dung on our soil. They act as if they are the masters and we are their slaves. One day we will be rid of them."

I said, "Not today we won't. Three against thirty armed men on horseback. That would be a short fight."

Thaddaeus Barabbas replied, "Yes it would. I will take the first twenty, you two can split the rest."

I said, "Samson slew one thousand Philistines using the jawbone of a donkey. I suppose those thirty donkeys would fall easily."

Yeshua said, "No. They will not fall easily. There are more of them than lice on the dogs, and they breed like rats, their numbers growing more by the year. We will only be rid of them if all the people rise and mark the ground with their blood, leaving no living thing of them alive. All of the Habirum, in all the land, must draw together to fight."

I knew Yeshua meant the divided land must unite. After the death of King Solomon his son, Rehoboam, assembled all the warriors of the house of Judah. They would attack the northern tribes and force them to accept his rule. The Word of ADONAI came to the prophet Shemaiah. – *Ye shall not go up, nor fight against your brethren the children of Israel* – and the Land had not been united since the days of Solomon. When King Nebuchadnezzar of Babylon conquered Judah, destroying the Temple and taking the people of Judah as slave, Jerusalem was laid waste. The northern Pharisee tribe of our people stayed in the hills of Galilee and kept faith with ADONAI. Yeshua was saying that all the Habirum must put aside their tribal differences if the fight against the Romans was to triumph.

Yeshua stood and looked at the turmae as if to make sure they had left. "We can defend our homes and families from them if need be. To make troubles would only have you nailed to the cross. In the time of Pompey, the escaped slave, gladiator and warrior, Spartacus, led his army against Rome. His army was defeated. The Romans crucified six thousand of the captured fighters of Spartacus, one every twenty paces, for all to witness the power of Rome. The Roman general Varus, crucified Judah of Gamala and two thousand of his followers for protesting taxes. Pontius Pilate sends more Habirum to Golgatha, the place of the skull, even now. No, we must be prepared to defend our homes but to attack them would only bring sorrow to the women. Before there could ever be another revolt all the Habirum must rise in anger."

I told him, "The people would need more than anger. They would need weapons. One cannot fight a cavalryman with a mason's mallet."

Thaddaeus Barabbas said, "Yes, I would prefer a sharper weapon than a donkey's jawbone. All men to the fight would need something better. As Samuel tells us. – *Sharpen every man his plowshare, and his coulter, and his axe, and his mattock –*."

King David had slain Goliath. The Philistines had the knowledge of making iron, and by slaying Goliath and defeating the Philistines the Habirum gained that knowledge and skill. The Habirum could then make their own iron swords, spears and arrow points. Yeshua looked at me and we both turned to Thaddaeus Barabbas. Yeshua asked him, "Would you like to see something better than a jawbone?"

We took Thaddaeus Barabbas to the Mount to our secret cave. Thaddaeus Barabbas marveled at our weapons. He complimented the quality and sharpness of their edges, telling us, "The emperor's armorer could not make them better."

We talked about the necessity of defending our homes if the Romans attacked. We each took a blood oath swearing allegiance to the others. In time past, there had been King David's Three Mighty Warriors. They were Ishbaal, Eleazar, and Shammah. They defended the home of ADONAI and the Habirum. We would defend our home too. Swearing this oath on Mount Tabor was fitting, as this was where the men of Naphtali and Zebulun had joined with Deborah and Barak's forces to defeat the Canaanite army of King Jabin.

THE GALILEE. MY NAME IS JUDAS ISCARIOT

This year, like the year before, the rains did not come. The year before we had lived off the grains we had stored from the previous harvest. The skies stayed dry and now the hot sun burned the seeds in the fields and gardens. The wells dried, there was rationing, and the cisterns the rains usually filled, only had dust in them.

There was starvation among the people but Herod's taxes continued for his building projects and to send tribute to the Roman emperor. To feed the ambition of Herod, he sent gifts to rulers of foreign lands including the ruler of the island of Kyprus where Herod was allowed to mine for copper. Herod also sent gifts to the rulers of Byblos in the land of the Phoenicians, and to Damascus, Nicopolis, and Laodicea, Tripolis, Athens and others. All these gifts were paid for by the taxes Herod imposed on the Habirum. Many people had to borrow from the hated tax collectors in order to feed their families. If the family could not repay the loans, the tax collector would seize the family's land. The family would stay living there, but working now for the tax collector who took the greatest portion of all the land produced.

In the city of Jerusalem and the immediate surrounding area, the Temple normally had a program of caring for the widows, the poor, and the cripples and beggars. That care included a daily ration of food called the poor bowl. The poor bowl was a portion of bread and beans and a bite of fruit. During the famine even the poor bowl was hit by the shortages and the poor and crippled suffered. Our clan was fortunate in that, as skilled tektons, we were able to earn coins for our work in Zippori, but even the rich Sadducees began to scale back on the work they commissioned. The drought and famine hit the whole land and all suffered.

The Valley of Jezreel was in normal times abundant with green growing crops but now was brown and dry. The game Yeshua and I hunted and provided for the suppers was welcome to the table but the deer and birds suffered in the drought. The dry forests on the Tabor Mount grew scarce with wildlife. When the grain stored from the previous harvest had been used even the daily bread was gone from the supper table. All prayed for the drought to end. – *Who waterest the mountains from Thine upper chambers? Who causeth the grass to spring up for the cattle? Who brings forth bread out of the earth?* – Who indeed?

In times past, when drought and famine laid waste to the land, the stress of circumstances would cause entire tribes to migrate to the land of the Aegyptus where the regularity of the River Nile nourished life. The Canaanites, Jebusites, Moabites, Ammonites, Arameans, Hittite, Ugarite, and the ancestors of our people, the Habirum who made the exodus out of Aegyptus, all would return to the River Nile seeking water. – *ADONAI said unto Moses, 'Gather the people together, and I will give them water'* –. Even the Cuthites along the coast of the Great Sea suffered, for the salt in the water of the Great Sea made it unfit for watering of any crop.

It was during this time that the wife of Thaddaeus Barabbas, Zeruiah, named after the sister of King David, went into labor with their first child. The women gathered in the home of Thaddaeus Barabbas to assist Zeruiah as she labored.

Something went wrong with the birth, the babe was breeched and Zeruiah's screams filled the village for hours and hours. We men were gathered, praying for Zeruiah and the babe's safe delivery. Finally her screams stopped but there were no sounds of joy from the women. Instead Thaddaeus Barabbas was told his wife had died from loss of blood and the babe was stillborn.

I had never seen a man suffer like did Thaddaeus Barabbas. He cried and screamed and raged and could not be consoled. He left us to be alone, walking away across the dry fields. He would never be the same person again as he became morose and angry. This would change him in other ways, as time went on.

The drought continued and there was suffering across the land. Many people said that ADONAI had forsaken the Habirum and was punishing us because of our turning away from Him, blaming it mostly on the Sadducees who worshipped the coin of Caesar.

THE RIVER JORDAN. MY NAME IS JUDAS ISCARIOT

There was talk of a man named Yokhanan, who was called, the Baptizer. Yokhanan the Baptizer lived in the desert. They said this man wore clothing of camel's hair with a leathern girdle about his loins, and his meat was locusts and wild honey. They said that he was of the Essenes. My father wondered if this could be our cousin, Yokhanan HaMatbil. Curious, we decided to see for ourselves. We traveled south past the town of Jericho then struck east where we crossed the River Jordan. Lake Merom, in the far north, drained to the River Jordan which replenished the sea of Chinnereth, then the River Jordan continued south finally ending at the Salt Sea. Our destination would be north and east of the Salt Sea.

As we got close to our destination we saw multitudes of Habirum also journeying to see and hear this man. The river was low due to the drought. People from the east, the land of Perea and the tetrarchy of Herod Philip were also gathered listening to this man. Herod Philip was the brother of Herod Antipas by a different mother, the fifth wife of Herod Great. As we got closer we were finally able to see him and my father said, "It is he, our cousin, Yokhanan HaMatbil."

Yokhanan was telling the throng, "Repent ye, for the kingdom of heaven is at hand. A coming judgment is upon the land. It will be a baptism with fire. The axe will be laid unto the root of the trees, therefore every tree which bringeth not forth good fruit is hewn down, and cast into the fire. ADONAI said to

Malachi. – *Behold, the day is coming, burning like an oven, when all the wicked people and all the evildoers will be like straw, and that coming day will burn them up, says ADONAI. And you will trample the wicked, for they will be ashes under the soles of your feet –."*

Yokhanan the Baptizer looked into the crowd and said to a group of better dressed people who were standing apart from the rest, "You, you pagans and Sadducees, O' you generation of vipers, who hath warned you to flee from the wrath to come?"

Those people now wailed, beat their breasts and begged Yokhanan the Baptizer to show them the way. Yokhanan the Baptizer led them to the water and one by one dipped them, saying, "I indeed baptize you with water unto repentance."

The words of Yokhanan the Baptizer spoke to the frustrations we all felt under the domination of the Romans and their parasites that bled us dry. Even in the time of drought, Herod showed the Habirum no mercy, taxing the very food and water we needed for life.

Yokhanan the Baptizer began speaking again. He compared the Roman rule now to the bloody days of Antiochus IV Epiphanes of the Seleucid, and his conquest of Jerusalem. Of how Antiochus had pillaged and destroyed the temple, murdered the Habirum men, and carried ten thousand women and children away as slaves. How the men not killed in battle had been enslaved and set to building his new fortress and citadel, his overseers whipping the workers with rods, the disobedient nailed to the cross or their bodies torn to pieces and thrown to the dogs. How he had fouled the temple grounds with the sacrifice of swine and forbid the worship of ADONAI and destroyed any of The Book that was found.

Yokhanan the Baptizer told that this Antiochus, not content with his first conquest, had again waged war on the Habirum. In the second war Antiochus ordered his soldiers to cut down without mercy all of those whom they met and to slay those who took refuge in their homes. There was a massacre of the young and the old. There was a killing of women and children, and a slaughter of virgins and infants. In the space of three days, eighty thousand were lost, forty thousand meeting a violent death, and the same number being sold into slavery.

Yokhanan the Baptizer told how Judah Maccabaeus started a revolt. How Judah raised an army of Habirum and led his army against the Seleucid Empire and defeated them. Yokhanan the Baptizer told how this had brought freedom to the Habirum for one hundred and thirty years.

"Hark the words ADONAI said to Malachi. – *Behold, I send you Elijah the prophet before the coming of the great and awesome day of ADONAI –*."

Someone in the crowd called out, "Are you the prophet?"

Yokhanan the Baptizer asked the man, "Why then did you go out? To see a prophet? I am the voice of one crying out in the desert. The word of ADONAI you already know. And ADONAI said to Moses. – *Bring out the children of Israel from the land of Aegyptus according to their armies –*."

Yokhanan the Baptizer continued, "The prophet you seek is in your own heart. The army you seek stands before you, and that army is you! You, and those standing next to you are the army. ADONAI tells us in Exodus. – *I shall make all your enemies turn the back of the neck to you. I shall deliver the inhabitants of the Land into your hands, and you shall drive them away from before you –*."

"The accursed Romans, and their dogs, the Sadducee, are murderers, thieves and robbers. They are money changers, harlots, sinners and adulterers. All they touch becomes tainted. Tainted coin must not be used for alms to the poor nor must it defile the Temple."

Yokhanan the Baptizer was, I could see, calling for revolt against the Romans. While we stood there Thaddaeus Barabbas joined us. We had not seen Thaddaeus Barabbas for many suns. He looked as if he had been living rough, his clothing dirty, his hair and beard twisted into knots. The last time I had seen him he had been lifeless, as if he cared no more for living. Now he had a bright light burning in his eye. Thaddaeus Barabbas told us, "Yokhanan speaks the truth."

Yeshua said, "Truly, I say to you, among those born of women there has risen no one greater than Yokhanan the Baptizer. He is Elijah, the one the prophets said would come."

All in our clan joined the line to be dipped by Yokhanan in the water of the River Jordan. Yokhanan worked tirelessly until the darkness was upon us. He sat in our camp that night, talking with us by the light of the campfire until the hour was late. In the morning we left to return to Nazareth, our spirits lifted and our resolve hardened.

Life and work continued and in the meantime the words of Yokhanan began to spread throughout Galilee. It wasn't long before Yokhanan the Baptizer came to the attention of Herod Antipas. Herod was worried that trouble could be caused by Yokhanan the Baptizer, but Herod hesitated in dealing with this problem because he feared that arresting Yokhanan the Baptizer could incite the very riots he hoped to avoid.

NAZARETH. MY NAME IS JUDAS ISCARIOT

Herod Antipas had recently divorced his first wife, Phasaelis, so he could marry a woman named Herodias. Herodias had been married to his half-brother, Herod II, but left him for Herod Antipas. Herodias was the full sister to Herod Antipas' half-brother, Herod of Chalcis. She was said to be a great beauty, and Herod Antipas decided she would be his, even if she was a close relation in his clan. Yokhanan the Baptizer denounced this union as wicked saying, ""It is not lawful for thee to have her to wife."

Then one day word came that speaking against Herodias was what caused Herod Antipas to finally have Yokhanan the Baptizer arrested and charged with the crime of treason. Yokhanan the Baptizer was imprisoned in the fortress of Machaerus. This was a setback to the winds of revolt that Yokhanan the Baptizer had started brewing and all waited to hear what would become of Yokhanan the Baptizer.

Yokhanan the Baptizer was locked away for two long years. During that time, life in Nazareth and the work in Zippori continued. The drought ended, the crops grew bountiful, and the springs and wells filled again. This appeased the population and most people grew content with their lot in life and returned to their comforts, forgetting the words of Yokhanan the Baptizer. Some people, though, could not forget.

Thaddaeus Barabbas left Nazareth for good and became a bandit. He lived in the hills and came out only to rob the Roman collaborators. He drew men to his group that had lost their homes and land to the tax collectors during the drought. He would occasionally come through Nazareth and I could see that purpose had returned to his life, if not joy. That purpose he had found was to wreak havoc upon the Romans and their collaborators in any way he could find, including leaving the Romans dead in the field. – *Thy carcasses shall be food unto all fowls of the air, and unto the beasts of the earth* –. This of course, made him a wanted man. The Romans hunted him and if they caught him, there was only one punishment, he would be nailed to the cross. One day on the Mount, in the shade of the forest trees, Thaddaeus Barabbas talked to Yeshua and me. He was attempting to get us to join his band of bandits.

Yeshua told him, "The drought has ended. The people have forgotten their sufferings. When the people are hungry they are angry. When there is meat on the table they rejoice. You and your three men are not enough to fight the Romans. All you will get for your troubles will be nailed to the cross."

Thaddaeus Barabbas said to Yeshua, "I remind you of the prophecy, my cousin.

Yeshua replied, "I have no need to be reminded of that child's bed story. I heard it from my mother all my life. It is nonsense."

"I remind you anyway, whether you heed the word or not is your choice today, but one day you will have to choose. On the day of your birth, just as it is written in the Book of Numbers, the bright star shone in the sky, heralding the messiah's return to free the Habirum. That light in the sky was. – A *pillar of fire by night –.*"

Yeshua shook his head, saying, "There are problems with that old story, my cousin."

Yeshua began counting the fingers on his hand. "First, I was not the only man child born on that day. Second, the bright star shone for a week, not just that one day. Third, for one to believe that light was a sign is ridiculous because anyone who studies the sky knows the planets and stars move in accordance with a regularity like the sands falling in the hourglass. As it says in Genesis. – *Let there be luminaries in the firmament of the heaven to separate between the day and the night; and they shall serve as signs, and for festivals, and for days and years –.*"

"The sands falling in the glass are just numbers, one full moon to the next. Some people fool themselves into believing that numbers are signs. Indeed, the sum of the numbers adding to twelve are considered magic by some. They study the twelve constellations and believe they mark more than just the time of planting and harvest. They believe the twelve prophets and the twelve tribes are more than just numbers. Whether you believe all that nonsense or not is beside the point. The reality is we have all witnessed darkness during the day that is caused by the moon blocking the sun. That is no miracle and is no daemon haunting the earth. It has been proven by the wise men the bright star you speak of was really just two planets hanging in the sky in such a way as to seem to be one bright light. Every boy is taught those planets are called Venus and Jupiter by the pagan Romans. Our people say Venus is the Queen of Heaven and Jupiter is called Righteousness. That light in the sky means nothing. The sign of a messiah? Nonsense. Besides, everyone who has claimed to be the messiah, and there have been many, all end up nailed to the Roman cross. Their cadavers are thrown to the wild dogs in the Valley of Dung. That is what claiming to be the messiah will get you."

"You fear the Romans?"

Yeshua narrowed his eyes and his face turned hard. He spoke slowly and carefully, "I warn you, my cousin, Thaddaeus Barabbas. Do not question my willingness to protect our women and our homes. I will fight and I will kill any Romans who trespass intending violence. But I will not stupidly sacrifice myself for the entertainment of the pagans at their place of the skull."

Thaddaeus Barabbas was insistent, "But, Yeshua, among all those born under that star, be it a sign of the prophecy or not, only you are of the house of David. And only you from the house of David was born in Bethlehem under the light of that star."

"My mother is of the line of David, yes, but that proves nothing. The Greek arts of viewing the heavens, their astronomy and astrology, show us the truth of the matter. The prophecy is just the interpretation of dreams and divination, which prove nothing."

"It proves the prophecy is true. As Micah, the prophet tells us. – *Bethlehem, from you someone will emerge to be a ruler over Israel. He will stand up and lead with the strength of ADONAI. Your hand will be raised over your enemies, and all your adversaries will be eliminated –*."

Yeshua snorted, "Bed time stories. To frighten children in their dreams."

"David was born in Bethlehem, and the prophecy says the one who follows him will be born there too. Jeremiah tells us. – *In those days, and at that time, Will I cause a shoot of righteousness to grow up unto David, and he shall execute justice and righteousness in the land. In those days shall Judah be saved, and Jerusalem shall dwell safely* –. David was the messiah who brought the Habirum together. The Habirum were all scattered tribes. It was David who made them into an army."

Yeshua shook his head at Thaddaeus Barabbas. "You, of all people. I thought you had a level thinking head. Your head is as thick as the stones you carve."

Stung by Yeshua's words, Thaddaeus Barabbas jerked himself to his feet. "Yeshua, my cousin. One day you will see your destiny. You were born to fight. You were tutored in the scholarly arts to know why you must fight. You have taught yourself to be an armorer to make the weapons of war and you have trained yourself in the use of those weapons of war. Yeshua, we have only the one enemy to fight, the Romans. They are the enemy that desecrates our Temple and spreads their filth across our land like maggots on the corpse. They are the enemy that taxes our lifeblood, and the enemy that treats us as slave. ADONAI will not bless the land and bless the people until the people themselves defend the land of ADONAI."

"Thaddaeus Barabbas, my cousin. I have told you before, the people will not rise and fight the Romans. Let me remind you of a story, except this one is undoubtedly true. The last time the people rose to fight, when we were all three but children, the one they call Judah the Gamalan, calling himself messiah, started the revolt against the taxes. He raised an army who attempted to overthrow the Romans. Judah and his army fought for two years, then they were vanquished in battle by the Romans. Judah was killed along with thousands of his men. Then the Romans nailed to the cross thousands more Habirum men, and women who had supported Judah."

Yeshua stood, walked to Thaddaeus Barabbas. "My cousin. I respect the fire burning in your heart and soul. But tell me, if you would please, how would any further revolt be successful? How could we win against Herod Antipas and Rome, when history shows the futility of the trying?"

Thaddaeus Barabbas stood quietly, with tears streaming down his cheeks to wet his beard, tears for the memory of his wife. "I only know that I must fight. I must not stop fighting. To stop fighting is to die."

Then Thaddaeus Barabbas embraced Yeshua. He turned to me, embraced me. Turning to go he stopped and looked long and hard at Yeshua. "Think on these words how King David gathered his army. – *His brethren and all his father's house went down thither to him. And every one that was in distress, and every one that was in debt, and every one that was discontented, gathered themselves unto him, and he became captain over them, and there were with him about four hundred men –."*

"Yeshua, if you gather four hundred men, then four thousand will follow you, then forty thousand more. Warriors will follow you and the land will be free of the Romans. I only know that the Habirum must have a leader. The people will fight for and follow a leader. They will follow the leader that it is spoken of in the prophecy. One day you will believe the words of the prophecy. It is your fate." Then our cousin, Thaddaeus Barabbas, left us to return to his fight, the fight that kept him alive, in his grief.

ZIPPORI. MY NAME IS JUDAS ISCARIOT

One day we were working in Zippori and a great cry went up among the citizenry. Men and women were out in the streets. The men were yelling and the women were wailing. We went out to discover the cause of the commotion, and that is when we were told that Yokhanan the Baptizer had been executed by Herod Antipas.

We were told that Herod Antipas had been having a banquet at his palace in the fortress of Machaerus. During the drunken feast, the daughter of Herod's new wife, named Salome, had danced a spectacle for Herod and his guests. The alluring erotic dance of Salome had bewitched Herod Antipas. When the dance was over the drunken Herod was so taken with her he promised to give her anything, half of his kingdom if she desired, and he would not deny her.

Salome asked her mother, Herodias, what she should ask for. Herodias told her to ask for the head of Yokhanan the Baptizer on a platter. When Salome presented Herod with her request Herod had consented and sent word to the prison to have Yokhanan beheaded. The platter with Yokhanan's bloodied head on it, was brought to Salome. Herodias rejoiced as she hated Yokhanan the Baptizer for his criticism of her marriage to Herod Antipas.

Salome asked her mother what she should do with the head of Yokhanan the Baptizer. Herodias had it thrown over the wall into the dung heap. We were told that some of Yokhanan's followers had stolen the headless body of Yokhanan from the dung heap and buried it in the desert. This news sent Yeshua howling with grief. He cried, "Herodias planned this evil thing in her evil heart. The drunken Herod did this sin for a dance? A dance from the batzonna daughter? Why?"

The crowds were protesting this brutal treatment of the Baptizer who they thought would bring freedom from the Romans. The Habirum rioted and the Sadducee were routed from their shops and homes. The Roman soldiers and cavalry came and beat and arrested and killed many Pharisees. Yeshua and I, and our fathers, quickly loaded our tools in the bags. Then we ran for the market to gather the women to protect them and get everyone home to Nazareth. We came around a corner to the market and suddenly were in the middle of a pitched battle between some rioting young Pharisee Habirum men and a group of soldiers and cavalrymen from the garrison. The Romans were outnumbered but had the benefit of having weapons to use against the Habirum who were armed only with sticks, stones and torches.

We found the women hiding in an alcove behind where they displayed their wares. More cavalrymen galloped in and joined the melee. The Romans discriminated against no one, all of us were the enemy to be put down. My father and Yosef were hurrying the women along and Yeshua and I were protecting the rear as we made our escape. A horseman chose me as a target and charged with his javelin. I dodged his attack but he reined his horse around and came at me again. The ground was wet from a water sellers broken pots. I slipped and fell. Trying to rise I could see the foot long razor sharp point of the javelin was going to spear me like a fish.

Suddenly Yeshua jumped in front of the horse and pushed a burning torch in its face. The horse screamed and reared like a wild animal. The horse's hooves slipped on the water soaked paved stones. The horse went over backwards landing on the cavalryman pinning him to the ground. Yeshua grabbed up the javelin the man dropped and thrust it up into the man's throat. The sharp point of the javelin penetrated the man's throat, spearing his brain. Yeshua pulled the man's sword from its sheath. I was on my feet now and looked about for our fathers and the women.

Just then I heard a woman screaming. I turned to see that it was a teenage girl. Two soldiers had murdered her mother and father, and now had the girl on the ground ripping off her clothes. The Romans would rape the girl, lying in her own mother and father's blood, then take her for slave, or just murder her also.

Yeshua gave a yell and charged the soldiers, running one through the back with the sword. That soldier was pushed into the other soldier, knocking into him, and they both went down. The young girl scrambled to her feet, covered herself with her torn clothing and ran away screaming. Yeshua pulled the bloody sword from the man's back and swung it down onto the other soldier's sword arm hacking it off at the elbow. The iron sword hit the stone pavement so hard it broke off in half. Yeshua, screaming like a berserker, used the stub of the sword to hack at the soldier's neck until he chopped the man's head from his body. Yeshua was consumed by a blinding rage.

My father ran up to me and yelled, "We must go!"

I ran to Yeshua and grabbed him by the arm, yelling his name and shaking him roughly, jerking him out of his madness. He dropped the broken sword and we all ran for the gate before the Romans could close it trapping us inside the city to be hunted down and killed like dogs. At the gate many Habirum were fighting the Roman soldiers, stopping the soldiers from closing the gate so that other Habirum could escape. Through the gate we ran, and outside the city walls caught up with the others. As we hustled toward Nazareth, my father described to Yosef what had happened. Yosef said to Yeshua, "You killed three Romans. There were witnesses. You could be identified. The Romans will come for you. You must stay away from Nazareth for a time, until this darkness passes. You must go and hide."

Yeshua asked, "Where shall I go?"

Yosef told him, "Escape for thy life. Go east to the River Jordan where it meets the River Yarmuk, then go further east, far into the wilderness of the Golan. Speak to no one. Take care not to be seen."

"How long must I stay in the Golan?"

"A moon, stay away a moon. Then return at night, in secret. We will know by then if the Romans hunt you."

Yeshua had lost his bag of tools. He had nothing but his tunic that was dark with the Roman's blood, and his leather bag with his Aegyptus treasures slung over his shoulder. I put my tools in my father's bag then we threw into my bag what we had to give Yeshua some provisions. There was some food, a flask of water, a flint and an iron knife. Yeshua's mother, Mary Salome, was crying and holding Yeshua in her arms.

Yeshua gave her one last hug, embraced us all, then he turned and ran.

We watched as Yeshua ran east toward the wilderness. Behind us the sky was smoky black from the fires in the city

We turned to the south and hurried for Nazareth.

TEMPLE OF ISIS. MY NAME IS
MARIAM OF MAGDALA

I was born in the town of Magdala on the west shore of the sea of Chinnereth. I am the high priestess of the Temple of the Goddess Isis. The temple is located ten of the Roman milia passum east of the town of Gergesa, which is a fishing town on the east shore of the sea. The Temple stands in an oasis fed from a watercourse that bubbles up from deep in the earth. We are at the edge of the Nahal Samakh ravine that runs fast during the rainy season, filling our water storages, but in the hot months is a dry rocky path. One can follow this path west to Gergesa, or one can follow it east where it withdraws into the wilderness. Few go into the wilderness, and of those, even fewer return. The wilderness is an arid, wild and dangerous place of savage inhabitants and wild beasts, such as lions, scorpions and vipers. Some say the wilderness is haunted by daemons.

The Temple is many generations older than I. The women of my family are the keepers of the beliefs and practices of the Goddess Isis and her Temple. All girl children in our tribe are trained and study the Beliefs from their first days. Then one female from each generation is chosen to maintain the Temple and continue the Belief. That girl, chosen before her first menses stays virgin and pure until her death. The younger girl assists the high priestess, learning more of the Belief and then becomes high priestess herself when the older dies or steps aside.

I am a Pharisee Habirum. I worship both ADONAI and the Goddess Isis, and see no contradiction in my beliefs. My ancestry on my mother's side is traced back to Ruth, the great grandmother of King David. Ruth married Boaz, of the tribe of Judah, who called Bethlehem his home. My people have worshipped Isis since the days, many generations ago, when they were in bondage to the Pharaoh in Aegyptus. I speak, read and write the languages

Habirum, Aramaic, Greek and Latīna, and am thoroughly schooled in the healing arts.

One morning there was much excitement for a stranger had been found dead lying on the ground in front of the temple. I went out to see. It was a man in his middle twenties of age, perhaps a few years younger than I. There were many injuries to his body I could see through the rags of his clothing. One of his legs was swollen and discolored. The leg was red, yellow and black, as if from the bite of a poisonous creature. When I bent to touch him he reached out his arm and his hand covered mine. I could see he was not dead, just at the limit of his strength. His body was hard and sinewy, his muscles well formed, though he was gaunt from his travels.

The man opened his eyes and looked at me. I saw his eyes were as blue as a precious stone. I could see he had suffered in his journeys. He was cut and scratched and he was caked with dirt and dust over his sunburnt skin. I asked him his name. He tried but couldn't speak as he was parched, his lips cracked by the heat and sun. A servant bent and poured some water in his mouth. He drank thirstily. Then he spoke and told me his name was Yeshua. I asked him where he was from. He said he was Yeshua of Nazareth.

We have had strangers show up at the Temple and village before as it is the only oasis for many days walk. These travelers were sometimes injured and normally I would have them taken to the village where the women would tend to them. I was about to have this man taken there when I saw around his neck a leather thong and on the thong was a carved stone of red jasper that was his amulet. Many people carried amulets for luck and good health and to ward off evil spirits. His amulet was beautifully carved and looked to be very old. I took it in my hand. I was astonished to see the amulet was the tyet, the Knot of Isis. Something struck me about this stranger with blue eyes with the Isis tyet. I wandered where he had gotten it. He was looking up at me as I leaned over him, he whispered, "You are an angel. An angel with red hair and green eyes. Am I in heaven?"

I asked him, "Where did you get this stone?"

Whispering, he replied, "At the Isle of Philae."

I was shocked. "Have you been to Philae?"

He managed to whisper, "Yes," but then his strength was gone and he passed out.

Now I will tell you what happened, what really happened to Yeshua, and what really happened to me, and to us.

I instructed my assistant, the one who would follow me as High Priestess and who was the daughter of my second sister, to have this man taken inside. I gave him over to the servants to be taken to the baths and washed. Then I anointed him with herbs and oils for his skin was cut and bruised in many places. His swollen leg was treated with the acetic acid of lemons and covered with the juice from squashed leaves of the aloe plant. I blew smoke from the aromatic Kannabaeus plant in his nostrils, relaxing him so he would rest. He slept the rest of that day and to sunrise the next.

When he awoke the next morning I was beside his pallet. He looked at me and said, "For I was thirsty and you gave me drink, I was injured and you healed me, I was hungry and you gave me food, I am a stranger and you welcome me. You are the angel that brought me from the wilderness. I owe you my life. I hope one day to repay your kindness."

Yeshua and I spoke in Aramaic and Greek and the Habirum language of our ancestors as there might be no word in Aramaic or Greek for the thought. Aramaic, spoken and written, was the language of negotiation, contracts and trade amongst the Habirum. It was the common tongue in Israel and Judah, except for the Romans whose language was the guttural, harsh sounding Latīna.

For the next few days his leg was soaked in a mineral bath and treated with juices of the plants. Soon he was able to stand. His leg was still stiff and he could not walk far but he improved daily. He was weak from starvation and thirst, but with food and care his youth and strength overcame his injuries and he was soon glowing with health.

Yeshua told me he had been in the wilderness for forty days and forty nights. He described the wilderness as a barren place of hilly terrain lost in a maze of valleys and ravines, where rock piled upon rock and the blinding sun heated the earth like a blazing fire. He said he had seen green plants growing at the top of a steep craggy hill. He began climbing, searching for the water that fed the plants, when a viper hiding in the rocks had struck him on the leg. He had fallen down the hill loosening the rocks, and then he was covered by the rock slide at the bottom.

Listening to Yeshua's story reminded me of the travails of David, as told by Samuel. How David had survived in the wilderness of Ziph, where only the wild goats climbed the rocks. – *And his soul thirsteth in a dry and weary land, where no water is* –.

Yeshua told me he had lain there in the rock pile for a sun and moon, in the sweat of a fever. He began crawling at the dawn of the next day and crawled for three suns until he saw in the distance the green palms of our oasis, arriving when the moon was directly overhead. He said he had awoken to see my red hair blazing like embers in the morning sun. He said my green eyes dazzled him. He told me I was, "The angel who brought me deliverance."

I asked him why he had been in the wilderness. He looked worried, and wondered if the Romans ever came to the Temple? I told Yeshua the Romans did not bother us, that we were far off the road and hardly anyone ever came here except those wishing to worship Isis.

Yeshua asked me if I knew of Yokhanan the Baptizer and his execution by Herod Antipas. I told Yeshua that the news of this had come to us but the Romans had not been to the Temple with any concerns about it. "Why," I asked Yeshua, "How does this concern him?"

Yeshua then told me Yokhanan the Baptizer was a cousin in his tribe, and how Yokhanan had talked of revolt against the Romans and how he had been beheaded by the drunken Herod who lusted for his wife's daughter. Then Yeshua told me about the riot in Zippori. He told me about the Roman soldiers who had murdered the mother and father and were attempting to rape the girl. He told me how he had killed three Roman soldiers and how he might be a hunted man.

The Romans were known for their brutality and harsh rule. That is why the Temple, I told Yeshua, was far from their normal travels. If it was the Romans he was hiding from in the wilderness, then he could take sanctuary here, at the Temple. Yeshua thanked me for my hospitality. He said he would welcome the shelter until his leg was well and he could travel again. He said he wanted to bring me no problems and would go as soon as he was able.

Yeshua got stronger each day. During those days he told me of his travels and life in Aegyptus. I was spell bound by his stories. Yeshua told me of his time at the Isle of Philae, and he asked me to tell him of the Goddess Isis.

I told him the worship of Isis was many thousands of years old and had come out of Aegyptus. Isis was a goddess of AmunRa's realm but she had limited power. The Aegyptus god AmunRa was the supreme god who created everything and had power over everything. The goddess Isis had gotten her greater magic and power from AmunRa. Isis had tricked AmunRa into telling her his real name which was the source of his power. Isis created a snake that bit AmunRa, making him ill with the creature's venom. Isis told AmunRa she would cure him if he would tell her his real name. AmunRa acceded to her demand, telling Isis his real name. Now Isis had the same powers as AmunRa. Isis used her powers and magic for good, whereas AmunRa had used his power and magic to torment men and women for his own amusement.

I told Yeshua how the brother of Isis, the god Osiris, had been murdered by his brother, Set, because Set was jealous of his brother. Also, Osiris had married their sister, Isis, whom Set lusted for. Set had murdered Osiris then dismembered the body of Osiris and scattered the pieces throughout the world. Isis, his sister and now his widow, hunted the parts and pieces of Osiris and restored his body. Isis made Osiris whole again, except for the penis, which had been eaten by a crocodile. Isis restored his body, and then brought him to life by transforming herself into a bird, flapping her wings over his face to force air into his lungs, and raised him from the dead. Then, using her magic, they copulated, without physical union. Isis was still a virgin and she bore him their son which was a miracle. Their child, Horus, was the god of the sky, the sun being his right eye and the moon his left eye. Horus, as a falcon, flew across the sky each day and night, bringing the sun and the moon to the world.

"Isis has been revered for thousands of years, by the Aegyptus, then the Greeks, and now the Romans. Not the Roman aristocracy, but many Romans of the common people worship Isis. At first she was spread from Aegyptus by those who came with Alexander the Macedonian, now she is spread in all the lands the Romans rule. There are temples to Isis from Londinium to Damascus, from Afrikkus to the Dark Sea in Asiana."

Yeshua sat, nodding his head in agreement. "In Aegyptus there was the temple to Isis at the isle of Philae and another at Heliopolis, and in my travels I saw her likeness carved into the stone of many of the great monuments. All over Aegyptus there are people who worship the goddess Isis." He lifted his amulet to look at it more closely. "I see her power is great. Perhaps Isis gave me this amulet all those years ago, knowing it would bring me to you." Yeshua kissed his amulet, while looking into my eyes.

We sat quietly for a moment, smiling at each other in a companionable silence. I was very glad Isis had brought Yeshua to the temple.

Yeshua said he had been just a babe when they arrived in Aegyptus. Over the next years his stepfather's work had taken them to many places in Aegyptus. He told me they traveled to strangely named towns such as Oxyrhyuchus and Crocodilopolis. On an island in the swift waters of the River Nile was a place called Elephantine. Yeshua said at Elephantine was a ruined temple, where in the days of Cyrus the Great's kingdom and rule over Aegyptus, there was a border outpost and garrison manned by Habirum mercenaries, loyal to Cyrus. When Cyrus had conquered the Babylonians and allowed the Habirum their freedom, some of those freed had stayed and made a home on the island.

I told Yeshua I had always dreamed of journeying to the land of Isis, and listened to him attentively as he told me of his adventures there. Yeshua told me his stepfather was a skilled tekton able to find work anywhere, and that he had a lively curiosity that drew him to far lands to study their mysteries. Yeshua told me his stepfather was commissioned to do some work on the Isle of Philae. Yeshua and his family sailed the Nile upriver in a boat made from bundles of papyrus reeds lashed together tightly. The reeds swelled when wet, allowing the boat to float. A sail caught the winds from the north, from the Great Sea, pushing the boat against the current. When the wind wasn't blowing all hands rowed oars pulling the boat upriver. Yeshua told me the Isle of Philae was in that part of the river called the First Cataract, where the water ran rapidly in waves over the rocks that were above the surface, making travel by boat difficult and even dangerous. The journey upriver had lasted a full moon.

Yeshua said that as their boat came round a bend in the river and approached the island he could see sheer cliffs with an Aegyptus temple complex high on the top, the sculptured towers rising high against the sky. As they came nearer, the boat captain expertly weaving between dangerous rocks in the river, they landed at steps carved out of the rocky face of the cliff. Climbing the steps to the top, Yeshua said the view of the land in all directions was magnificent. The Temple itself was beautifully constructed by skilled tektons. The Temple was of elegant proportions. The entrance was guarded by two enormous lions sculpted from the rock face of the cliffs. Also at the entrance were two tall stone obelisks, with Aegyptus symbols carved on them. Yeshua said other monuments he had seen in Aegyptus had been damaged by vandals and the ravages of time, but the Temple of Isis was maintained in respectful condition, still in use by those who worshipped the Goddess. At the Temple were women priests in white robes, and Yeshua had watched their sunset and sunrise ceremonies to honor the Goddess Isis.

In my mind's eye I could see the beauty of the Temple as Yeshua described it. "Oh, Yeshua, to have been there with you would be a dream come true. All my life I have studied the teachings of Isis, but listening to you I can finally see her home."

From his leather bag he took out and showed me his Aegyptus treasures. Yeshua told me he had been digging for the foundation of a building his stepfather was constructing on the Isle of Philae and found the Isis tyet amulet and the wand that may have belonged to some long dead magician. The wand had strange symbols carved into the wood. Yeshua rubbed the wand with beeswax, keeping the wood and symbols in perfect condition.

I asked Yeshua of his family. He told me his mother was of the House of David and the tribe of Judah. We expressed surprise when I told him I also was of the House of David. He exclaimed, "So! We are distant cousins! Since we are related, I might just give you a kiss on the cheek. One cousin, to another. What do you say to that?"

I had to smile at his brazen cheekiness. "Perhaps, another day. And your fathers line. Who are they?"

Yeshua's smile left him. He sat silent for a long moment. He looked at the ground, shaking his head, "I do not speak of him."

I wondered how his father had wronged him, for Yeshua to deny him thus. "Then tell me more of your adventures in Aegyptus."

From his bag Yeshu pulled out and showed me more of his Aegyptus treasures. One was a smooth bead the size of a walnut. It was gleaming and of a whitish transparent color. Yeshua said I should hold it close to my eye. When I did I could see through it and beyond. All the things I could see through it were of a dreamy texture. "It's beautiful," I told Yeshua, "What is it?"

Yeshua told me it was rough unformed glass. He had found it during his explorations of a cave on the Isle of Philae. We had a few items of glass here at the Temple, drinking cups and platters that had been donated by worshippers of Isis, but I had not seen something like this bead before.

Yeshua said the Aegyptus had learned to make glass by accident. Some men transporting goods on the River Nile made camp on the shore in a desolate spot. When they could find no rocks to set their cooking pots on at the campfire, they used some chunks of mineral from their load, the mineral called niter. The fire melted the niter and it dripped down onto the sand of the river bank. The melted niter and sand joined making a streaming liquid. The liquid cooled and hardened, and thus was born this new glass. The Aegyptus had perfected the art of making the rough glass into things of beauty and usefulness.

Another treasure from his bag was a shimmering black rock. It was the size of his fist and very heavy. The stone shined purplish in the candle light. Yeshua showed me how his iron knife stuck to the rock and held it, even upside down. Yeshua had found this rock also in Aegyptus, in the desert, while exploring beyond the great monuments of Giza. He said the wise man told him it came from the stars, in the vastness of the unknown, where the Watchers came from.

"I have read of the Watchers in Daniel." I asked Yeshua, "What do you know of these Watchers?"

"The story in Daniel has the king of Babylon, Nebuchadnezzar, receiving a vision from a Watcher. But it is in the Book of Enoch where the Watchers are truly told of."

"I have heard of the Book of Enoch but I have not seen it. Who are these Watchers?"

"The Watchers are the sons of ADONAI. They are holy angels, sent from ADONAI's home in the sky. The Watchers are named, Shâmḥâzâî, who was the leader of the other Watchers, Arâkîbâ, Râmêêl, Kôkâbîêl, Tâmîêl, Dânêl, Êzêqêêl, Bârâqîjâl, Asâêl, Armârôs, Bâtârêl, Anânêl, Zâqîêl, and Sâmsâpêêl and more, for a total of two hundred."

I asked Yeshua, "For what purpose did ADONAI send these Watchers to earth?"

"The Book of Enoch says the Watchers were sent by ADONAI to watch over humans and instruct them in useful knowledge. The Watchers taught men agercultura, the secret of seeds and plantings and harvests, and the use of herbs for healing. Men were taught the art of mathematics, those things which are certain. Men learned building skills so that men could assist the Watchers in the construction of the great monuments on the River Nile. But the Watchers lost their way. The Watchers became corrupt. The Watchers began to lust for the daughters of men. The Watchers saw the daughters of men were fair, and the Watchers decided they would have the daughters of men. They took them wives of whomsoever they chose. The sons of ADONAI came in unto the daughters of men, and they bore children to them. Enoch writes these children were great giants. These children were called the Nephilim. The Book of Genesis tells us the Nephilim were the mighty men of old, men of renown. These children, the Nephilim, were begat by the Watchers and the daughters of men in unholy union. Then the children of the Watchers and the daughters of men, the Nephilim, instructed humans in forbidden knowledge, making humans corrupt."

"What knowledge is forbidden?"

"Some of the arts of magic. How to use the power of wicked daemons to cast spells and strikes against other humans. The Nephilim taught humans the meaning of signs and numbers and their uses in sorcery and necromancy. Humans learned the secret of metals and the skills of forging arms of war. These things caused humans to become impure in the sight of ADONAI. ADONAI saw the Nephilim were defiling mankind and leading them astray into sacrificing and worshipping daemons and pagan gods. That is why ADONAI sent down the seven archangels. The seven archangels are Michael, Raphael, Gabriel, Uriel, Saraqael, Raguel, and Remiel, The seven archangels were sent to clean the earth of the Nephilim. The Watchers, who revolted from ADONAIA, fell from grace when they lay with the daughters of men. Their children, the Nephilim spread evil and impurity throughout the earth. It was for this uncleanliness that ADONAI washed away all the impurities in the great flood."

"Yeshua, do you believe this story of the Watchers and the Nephilim?"

"Many places in the holy book tell us that angels are the messengers of ADONAI. ADONAI sent angels to Moses, to Joshua, Hagar, and Balaam, to Lot and to Abraham. When the Habirum were taken to Babylon, the Habirum forgot ADONAI and worshipped Anu, the Babylon god of the heavens. When the Habirum were released and free to return to Jerusalem, Ezra, the scribe and priest, taught the laws of ADONAI to those who did not know them. But even before that there were tales of gods and angels. There have always been other gods, and they had their own angels. The Aegyptus god was AmunRa, the supreme, who made the world. And your goddess, Isis, came from Aegyptus. Perhaps before them came the Watchers and the Nephilim, from the stars in the night sky"

The sun had set. Yeshua and I were seated on carpets before the altar of Isis. The candlelight made Yeshua's face fall into light and shade as he turned his head when he spoke. His tale was transporting, taking me to a place I had not contemplated before. I shivered, from the evening chill, or from his words, I did not know.

"What became of these Nephilim?"

"Enoch says there was a war between the sons of darkness, the Nephilim, and the sons of light, the archangels. Using the might and fury of ADONAI, the archangels destroyed the Nephilim, but this war caused the collapse of all that man had constructed in a great flood that covered the whole world. The useful knowledge the Watchers had taught humans was mostly lost after the great cataclysm and flood. Perhaps that is why the great monuments of Aegyptus were abandoned and left to the desert storms. Humans did not know how they were to be used, and they lost the skills needed to maintain them."

"And you believe these Watchers and Nephilim are real?"

"Why are the Watchers and the Nephilim told of in the holy book? They are told of in Genesis, and Numbers, and Ezekiel, and Enoch, and Daniel. Daniel tells that Nebuchadnezzar had a troubling vision that affrighted him. None of the king's magicians, the enchanters and the Chaldeans who were trained in astronomy and astrology, could interpret the vision. Only Daniel could interpret the vision. Daniel told Nebuchadnezzar. – *My lord, the dream be to them that hate thee, and the interpretation thereof to thine adversaries. This is the interpretation, O king, and it is the decree of the Most High, which is come upon my lord the king, that thou shalt be driven from men, and thy dwelling shall be with the beasts of the field* –. Mariam, if we believe some of the holy book, why not believe all of it? And if we doubt some of the holy book, why not doubt all of it?"

I asked, "Do you believe these Watchers were from the stars in the night sky? Do you believe they were the angel messengers of ADONAI?"

Yeshua said, "I only believe I must seek the truth. Genesis tells us ADONAI created man and woman in his own image. I take that to mean humans have a mind like ADONAI, not that we know everything as ADONAI does, but that we must seek to know. Is it not possible that ADONAI meant for man and woman to question all things, and to seek knowledge?"

Yeshua asked me, "If the gods of the time of Isis from Aegyptus are older than the ADONAI of the Habirum, and if the Watchers are the ones who built the great monuments in Aegyptus, could the Watchers, with their powers, have been like gods to the Aegyptus people? Could Isis be the daughter of a woman who lay with a Watcher? Could this AmunRa of Aegyptus be the leader of the Watchers, the one named Shâmḥâzâî? Could he be the one who Isis tricked into telling her his real name, which is the source of her power? Could Asherah, the sacred consort of ADONAI, be Isis, or the mother of Isis?"

I had never before considered such a thing and told Yeshua I would have to think on what he said. I told him these were new and somewhat unsettling thoughts. Yeshua made me see things differently. I had never before met someone who made me think of such thoughts.

The days passed and became weeks. Yeshua was able to move comfortably, indeed, he found some tools and began making some needed repairs to the Temple. The only other man at the Temple was my mother's brother, Aaron. Aaron's wife was named Elisheba, she was chief cook at the Temple. My uncle was an older man but strong and capable. He welcomed Yeshua's knowledge and skills as a tekton. Working with wood they made needed repairs and built some furniture. Using a mallet, chisel and mortar on the stonework Yeshua made the walls weathertight. Mixing and spreading plaster on the reed mat roofing he sealed the roof for the rainy season.

Yeshua showed me tricks of hand magic and conjuring he had learned in Aegyptus and I showed Yeshua the healing magic of Isis that was in the plants, ferns and minerals of the earth. I showed him the Temple scrolls of pharmacopoeia. The scrolls were very old, having been handed down from the other priestesses in my family for hundreds of years. I told Yeshua that there had once been more of the scrolls of Isis but they had been burned in the fire set by the Caesar Julius that destroyed the Library Alexandria in Aegyptus. Now the only copies where here, in the Temple.

I studied with Yeshua the scrolls of Isis. I told him the aromatic smoke and boiled tincture of the Kannabaeus plant was used to relax the body, to cure seizures and stomach ailments, and bring happiness to the saddened. I showed him the writings that described how the oils of the aloe and linseed plants, the castor berries, the palm trees, the beans from the gengent and poppy seeds, and a hundred others, were used for their curative powers. As it says in Ezekiel. – *And by the river upon the bank thereof, on this side and on that side, shall grow every tree for food, and the fruit thereof shall be for food, and the leaf thereof for healing* –. Yeshua devoured the knowledge. He spent hours studying the scrolls.

The soils in the area of the Temple grew wattle trees. Birds feed on the nectar from the green and rose colored leaf pods. Yeshua gathered the pods from the trees, crushed them in a mortar and pestle, then added charcoal dust and spit to make ink. He made a quill from bird feathers and used the ink on linen, copying the words from the scrolls to make his own pharmacopoeia. I saw that Yeshua could became a true healer and magician.

One day Yeshua was studying the scrolls and he asked me, "Is there a cure for what torments the soul?"

I asked him, "What sort of torment troubles the soul?"

Yeshua then told me of the conversations he had with his cousins, Yokhanan the Baptizer, and Judas Iscariot and Thaddaeus Barabbas, and how they had spoken of revolt and ridding the land of the Romans. Yeshua said he had prayed to ADONAI for guidance about what he himself should do in this struggle. Yeshua told me his prayers had not been answered, and then he told me of his secret and the question that tormented his soul.

Yeshua himself was a learned man, having been taught all manner of things in Aegyptus and his studies in the synagogues here in the land of the Habirum. Yeshua told me that his studies had made him question whether there was a god, or any gods, at all. Yeshua questioned the Habirum god, the gods of Aegyptus, the gods of Rome, the gods of Greece, the Watchers from the stars, and wondered why, if there were a god or gods, then why did the gods allow such suffering of the people? Why did the gods not answer people's prayers for plentiful harvests? Why did the gods allow droughts and allow the people to suffer starvation? Why, it seemed, did the gods favor the rich and mighty while the poor and oppressed struggled? Did the gods themselves hold back the rains and make the droughts? Did the gods themselves willingly cause the people to suffer starvations and deprivations and sickness and poverty? Were the gods blind or indifferent to people's sufferings or were the gods themselves evil? Did the gods cause the suffering? Why, Yeshua wondered, did the gods make the Romans the more powerful over the Habirum and keep them in bondage like the pharaoh made them suffer. And Yeshua wondered, if he took up arms against the Romans, would the gods favor him with the strength to be victorious?

These were the questions that tormented Yeshua's soul.

We were in the Temple, sitting on soft cloths and furs before the altar of Isis. Yeshua lifted his bag, stood, walked to me, and said, "I wish to make you a gift of my treasures from Aegyptus for saving my life."

"No," I told him, "These are your treasures. They have brought you good fortune. To part with them could bring you bad luck. I cannot let you do that."

Yeshua knelt before me, and said, "The best luck of my life was meeting you. If you will not take them all, please choose one. You must let me repay my debt to you."

I told Yeshua, "You do me great honor. You must keep your wand for the carvings on it are your talisman. Your tyet of Isis brought you here, showed you the way to the Temple and may show you safe paths in the future. The black rock from the stars I believe you may need someday. I will gladly accept the glass bead, and when I look into it, I will always see you."

Yeshua pulled the glass bead from the bag, held it in his fist and put his fist to his chest. He told me, "From my heart I give you this. And know this, I will always hold you in my heart, for your kindness, for your beauty and for that you have saved my life."

Yeshua took my hand and placed the glass bead into it. I held this small treasure in my palm, then placed my hand and the bead to my heart. The glass bead was warm from his body heat, where it touched my breasts.

Kneeling before me, our faces were inches apart, our eyes locked. His blue eyes and my green eyes looked into each other. We looked through to the hearts of each of us. My breathing grew fast. I felt sensations I had never known before. A long moment passed, then in an unspoken understanding we slowly pulled away from the other. We both knew this was not to be. Yeshua was of the Pharisees, and their men stayed celibate until marriage. I, of course, was virgin, dedicated to the Goddess Isis.

Yeshua stood and walked to a window, he stood quietly, looking out, the sunshine illuminating him. I sat and looked at him. He was tall and sturdy, his muscled legs rooted solidly to the earth. His arms and his chest strong, his chest holding the blood that beat through his good heart. His long hair was bleached fair by the sun. Such a good man, I thought. I was thankful he had survived his ordeal in the wilderness. Yeshua had been with us for three full moons. Perhaps it would be best, for both of us, if he did leave soon.

Yeshua was awake and dressed with his bag over his shoulder the next morning when I came from my chambers. "I am well," he said. "I should go in case the Romans were to come and cause you problems."

We broke our night fast, I insisted he must have food before he began his journey. During the meal I told him I had considered what he told me, about the torment in his soul.

"Yeshua, there is a plant that opens one's mind to receive a vision, a vision that is for them only. This plant is a powerful substance and must be used with care. I will administer this plant to you. I believe that if you used this plant now, before you go, it may provide the balm to your torment. Would you try it?"

Yeshua asked, "Have you used this plant yourself?"

"Yes. All who study and train to be the priestess of the Temple do this to prepare for their duties and to know how it may affect others."

"When you used this plant, did you have a vision?"

"Yes."

"Can you tell me your vision?"

"My vision was of a land of peace and harmony. Where the sun was softer and not hot and blinding as here. The soil was fertile and not dry sand like here. Where rivers and streams flowed and the water was clean and clear. The ground was covered by a carpet of green grasses and colored flowers and the trees grew as far as the eye could see. The soil produced all manner of foods and the vines were full of grapes. My vision must have been a foretelling of a heaven that awaits me. My vision showed me that one day I would be in this beautiful place."

"Your vision is of a heaven. I hope to one day go to and see such a place. Yes, I will try this plant you speak of."

I told him, "There are certain preparations one must take before the substance is ingested. You must do exactly as it is written in the pharmacopoeia." I told him he would take no food the rest of the day to the time of the end of his vision, and that I would fast with him. He must fast to prepare his body and mind, and I would fast to prepare for the vigil. I told him I would watch over him while he went on his vision quest.

For the rest of that day we both fasted and took no food. He drank only boiled water. The water was boiled in a copper jug then the jug placed in the stream to cool. A pinch of salt and the juice of lemons was added to the cooled water for him to drink. I dosed him with swallows of colocynthis and the oil of castor for their purgative effects. By the next dawn Yeshua was cleansed of all impurities in his body.

At the dawn the servants took Yeshua to the baths. The fires had warmed the room. I supervised as he stood and was scrubbed with cleansing agents, and pitchers of hot then cool waters were poured over him as his body was washed and rinsed. Then he climbed into the heated waters of the bathing pool and soaked while his face was shaven clean of beard. When the soaking was complete he stood and was rubbed dry. His long brownish sun bleached hair was combed and tied in a loose bundle to hang down his back. His body was oiled, and then he was dressed in an ankle length robe of soft linen.

Yeshua was placed on cushions on the floor before the altar of Isis. The fires were built up to warm the room, the candles gave the room a soft glow, and incense sweetened the air. I was seated on cushions next to him to be able to watch over him when he left his physical body to journey in his vision. My assistant was seated next to me as this would be training for her. Two servants were seated the other side of him.

I told Yeshua, "You must promise to lie on the cushions. You are not to stand and move about. If you stand and move about you could injure yourself. In your vision you will be able to walk where you please, and to run, fleet of foot. You will be able to fly across the skies as a falcon. You will be able to swim as a fish if you want. You will leave your physical body here, but in your journey, in your vision, you may go where it pleases you. If you begin to rise I will place my hand on your brow and you will feel a pleasing weight that holds your physical body in place. Yeshua, I will watch over your physical body. You will be safe in my care. Do you promise me you will lie on the cushions and travel only in your vision?"

Yeshua lay there, trusting me, looking at me with his beautiful blue eyes. "Yes," he said. "I promise to lie still. And I will promise also that I will honor anything you ever ask of me."

I smiled. "You promise to honor anything I ask?"

"Yes."

"Yeshua, are you of sound mind and good judgment right now?"

"Of course."

"And you promise anything I request of you?"

"Yes. I will do anything you ask of me. That is my promise and my word to you."

I found Yeshua's words pleasing. This was a sincere promise he was making to me. It was the first time in my life to be made such a promise by a man. All the same, I had to smile at him. "Yeshua, do you not know it is dangerous to promise to a woman anything she asks?"

Yeshua smiled with his lips and his eyes and his honest face. "I am of sound mind and good judgment and I know what I say."

"Very well. Let us begin."

I would use the dried caps of a certain type of mushroom that is rare and grows in the wet grass beside the Nahal Samakh ravine in the warm months when the morning dew is heavy. The mushroom blooms only from the full moon to the first light of the morning sun. It must be searched for early in the grey dawn, found, picked and then stored carefully. It is extremely important to get the dosage just right. Too much can cause madness, too little only inflames the stomach causing spasms. For a man of Yeshua's size, weight and strong health, I made the dosage equal to what filled my cupped palm.

I raised the relaxed head of Yeshua off the pillow and told him he must chew, make saliva, and swallow, make more saliva and swallow more. I fed the substance to his mouth and his eyes crossed and his face puckered from the bitter taste. I encouraged him to continue until it was done. Yeshua continued to chew and make saliva and swallow until my hand was empty. When he had swallowed it all, I gave him clean boiled cool water flavored with juice of lemons. I told him to rinse his mouth but not drink it down. He rinsed, he spat into a bowl, then rinsed and spat until the water was gone and the bitter taste had been relieved. I laid his head back on the pillow and told him to close his eyes and rest.

He lay quietly. I sat on cushions next to him and watched the lights and shadows from the candles play across his face. He had a strong face that could be chiseled in stone that showed character and strength of purpose. His high forehead indicated a great intelligence, and the gentleness of his eyes and mouth showed his empathy.

In less than a half movement of the sun dial, Yeshua's eyes suddenly opened wide, he grabbed at his stomach and sat straight up. The servant had the large bowl ready, shoved it under Yeshua's face and he vomited into it. The servant took the bowl away. The other servant washed his face, then dried his face with clean scented cloths. I gave Yeshua more of the clean water to rinse his mouth. He swished and spat until he felt cleaned again. He lay back on the pillow with a groan.

"Am I poisoned?" he asked.

"No, that is normal. The body did not need the plant any longer, all the juice from the plant is now in your blood. Now the vision will begin."

"Did you know that would happen? That I would be sickened?"

"Yes. It is the way of the plant. If I had told you, would you have consented to do this?"

"No. Definitely not."

"Of course. That is why I did not tell you. Now lie there, relax and close your eyes. Welcome the vision. You will find the answer you seek."

For three movements of the sun dial I sat quietly and watched Yeshua as he lay there in the embrace of his vision. He spoke, he listened, he questioned, he laughed, he cried, he reached out his arms opening and closing his hands, he thrust with weapons, he pulled to him some things he saw and pushed away other things he saw. Several times I had to lay my hand on his brow to keep him from rising. Each time I did so, his body relaxed, but his vision continued. He called softly names of those he loved and yelled names of those he fought. He tossed and sweated in his exertions. He sometimes spoke in a language I did not understand, as if he was speaking to someone who had gifted him with their tongue. He finally lay easy, spent. Another movement of the sun dial passed while he lay quietly, completing his vision, and then Yeshua opened his eyes. His face and body were still and relaxed, the vision had come to him, and now the vision was revealed to him. Yeshua turned his head and looked at me. I looked into his eyes, and I could see he was at peace with himself. Whatever he had sought in his vision, he had found it.

Yeshua was taken to the bathing pool again, washed then dressed in a clean robe. He rested for a while, lying still as a babe in a dreamless sleep. I too cleaned and washed, then I put on a fresh gown. Before the sun set we met at the table and broke fast. There was served only light foods, for, as I told Yeshua, his body and mind needed nourishment but the foods must digest easily after his experience. We took supper together. Yeshua was quiet, his mood contemplative. He was remembering and thinking on his vision. I respected his quiet and waited for him to speak.

We had eaten what the body required and were replete. The sun finished its journey to the west, leaving the room in darkness, the only light the candles burning on the table. Yeshua sat for a long time staring into the candle's flames. Then he looked at me and said, "Thank you for allowing me to have this vision. My soul is at rest and my mind is at ease. I know now the answer to my question. I know now what I must do."

I asked, "Can you share with me your vision?"

"Yes, I will share with you gladly. – *I saw in the visions of my head, and, behold, a watcher and a holy one came down from heaven. He cried aloud, and said thus. Hew down the tree, and cut off its branches. Shake off its leaves, and scatter its fruit –*."

"Mariam. In my vision I found the voice of ADONAI, who is called different names by different peoples and takes different forms to those people. But ADONAI is really the same, no matter the name or form given to ADONAI. ADONAI is your Isis. ADONAI is the seven archangels. ADONAI is AmunRa, the Aegyptus sun god. ADONAI is in the air we breathe, the water we drink, the food we eat. ADONAI is in the soil and the rocks and in the sky. ADONAI is in the trees and the birds that rest in them, in the streams and in the fish. ADONAI is in the human soul and that is what gives humans the ability to be more than the beasts who act only out of instinct. ADONAI in the human soul is how humans can think and reason. It is what allows humans to show charity and compassion and generosity and, if necessary, to decide to take up arms to fight for what is right and true and good. But when a human cannot find ADONAI within themselves, then they are like the beasts who act from instinct and not reason. Some humans may have lost ADONAI within themselves, some may deny ADONAI within themselves. And those are the beasts. Those beasts are the Roman emperor and his lackeys. Those are the ones who must answer to ADONAI. In my vision ADONAI spoke to me. ADONAI showed me what I must do. ADONAI said unto me. – *You are a tool of war. Through you I smash the horse and the rider. Through you I smash the chariot and the rider. ADONAI goes with you, to fight for you with your enemies. You shall smite all your enemies' warriors by the blade of the sword. ADONAI shall make you mighty in battle –.*"

"Mariam. The words of ADONAI tell me to lead our people from the bondage of the Romans. ADONAI tells me I am His battle axe and weapon of war. I am to break in pieces the Romans. I am to drive them from our land, and if they will not go willingly, I am to cut them down and leave no living thing among them alive. ADONAI has spoken, telling me. – *Fear them not, for I have delivered them into thy hand, there shall not a man of them stand against thee –.*"

"I am to prepare for war, I am to rouse the warriors, and I am to rally all the fighting men and attack!"

I said to Yeshua, "This quest you propose is a dangerous one."

"It is not a quest I propose but one I accept. It is a quest that has been commanded of me. It is more dangerous to be subservient, for to live in bondage and fear is to lose one's soul, and if one loses their soul they are doomed to damnation. I will fight the Romans and ADONAI shall be my shield. ADONAI made the earth with his might. He established the world with His wisdom, and with His understanding spread out the heavens. And with His strength I shall destroy the Romans."

The beat of my heart quickened. My skin tingled with goose bumps and my hands curled to become fists. I knew Yeshua was right. To live free of the Romans! "Take me with you on your quest. I will fight with you."

"No. You know that cannot be. The danger will be great. I cannot allow you to be in such danger. I respect and treasure your bravery, and it will inspire me in battle."

Yeshua stood and walked to me. He laid his hand on my shoulder, and told me, "I leave at the dawn. And know this. I leave my heart here with you. My heart is yours. I give it to you gladly." His warm strong hand squeezed my arm, the touch lasting a long moment.

I stood and took Yeshua's hand in mine. I led him to the altar of Isis. I knelt before the altar and pulled him down to kneel with me. I prayed to Isis and to ADONAI. "– *I will say of ADONAI, who is my refuge and my fortress, ADONAI, in whom I trust, He will cover thee with His pinions, and under His wings shalt thou take refuge. His truth is a shield and a buckler. Thou shalt not be afraid of the terror by night, nor of the arrow that flieth by day. A thousand may fall at Thy side, and ten thousand at Thy right hand. It shall not come nigh thee* –. Amen."

Yeshua looked at me. He stood and pulled me to my feet. He took my face in his hands and held me tenderly. He leaned forward and gave me a chaste kiss on the cheek. "Your prayer for my safety and for my victory I will cherish forever." Then he turned and walked to his chambers to rest.

The next morning very early, before the grey skies of dawn, I came from my chambers to find that Yeshua had already gone. I understood that he had said his goodbye the night before, and did not wish to prolong our parting. Yeshua had been with us a short time. He had been gone only a very short time. I could almost feel his presence still in the room, but he was gone. I missed him. There was an emptiness in my heart that I knew would be impossible to fill.

I went to the altar to make my morning prayer. Lying on the altar was the leather thong with Yeshua's knot of Isis. A long braided lock of Yeshua's hair was intertwined with the tyet that he had left for me. I lifted the leather over my head and placed the tyet to my heart.

I knelt to pray. I asked ADONAI to place His power in Yeshua's hand, for him to break the Romans with a rod of iron. That he may dash them in pieces like a potter's vessel and that he may smite through the loins of them that rise up against him and that they rise not again. And the blessing of ADONAI be with him in strength, and his arm be mighty. I prayed to Isis for her to shine the protection of her light all around Yeshua like a shield of the strongest iron, and to keep him safe.

"Amen."

ZIPPORI. MY NAME IS JUDAS ISCARIOT

One day working in Zippori, during the midday break, I walked to the fountain to fill my water flask. The city had many fountains, fed directly from the aqueducts. The rich Romans and Sadducees paid for the aqueducts water to be diverted into their villas for their own bathing pools and private fountains. The villa was not complete so the water was not flowing in the villa's fountain yet. This fountain was closest to the workplace.

A few men and women were filling water jugs at the fountain, some were freed, some were slaves who wore the leathern yoke about their necks with the owners name burnt onto it. The Romans and Sadducees held slaves, but not the Pharisees or Essenes. We considered slavery to be against God's will, as ADONAI said to Moses. – *I am the Lord, and I will bring you out from under the burdens of the Egyptians, and I will deliver you from their bondage* –. We interpreted that to mean all peoples were to be free, to not be slave. There were laws for the treatment of slaves but most Romans and the Sadducees treated their animals better than they treated their slaves. Slavery was an abomination before ADONAI.

I drank then stood for a moment enjoying the cool of the water spilling over my hands as I filled my flask again. The other people had finished and left, I was alone at the fountain. Then a man in a cloak with the hood over his head came and stood by me. The man said in a quick quiet voice, "Judas, it is I, Yeshua. Quiet. Don't say anything. Don't look at me. Just listen."

I was astounded. Yeshua had been gone for one hundred suns. An entire season had passed. We all thought he must have perished in the wilderness. There had been much sorrow for him. Now I wanted to throw my arms around him and yell, but I stood still and listened.

"It is good to see you my friend, we have much to talk about. But first I need to know if I am hunted by the Romans?"

In a quiet voice I told him, "No. There were many killed that day, Both Habirum and Romans were killed. There were fires and much damage. The city was closed and work was stopped for a few days but then all resumed as normal. No one ever identified you. The Romans came neither to Nazareth nor here to the workplace. Tell me, where have you been?"

"Tomorrow is the Shabbat. Is our secret cave on the Mount still safe?"

"Yes."

"I will meet you on the Mount after morning prayers. Say nothing of me to no one. I will tell you why tomorrow."

Then as silently as he had arrived, he disappeared into the crowd and was gone.

Yeshua! Praise ADONAI!

The next morning I arrived at our secret place. Yeshua was not there. I wondered if I had imagined him talking to me the day before. Then I heard the song of a bird behind me. I turned to see Yeshua standing there in the shade of a tree. He was covered by his cloak, with the hood thrown back, showing his smiling face. We pounded each other on the back, laughing and talking at the same time at the pleasure of our reunion.

"You look healthy, my friend," I told him. "The wilderness must be like a relaxation at the Roman spa."

"And you, my friend, you look healthy too. Hard work must agree with you."

All the day we talked. Yeshua told me of his time in the wilderness. He told me of the beauty of the stars at night, the quiet of the land, the emptiness and solitude that prompted thinking and searching for the answers we all seek. He told me of the difficulties and dangers of the wilderness, about the lack of water and food, and the snakebite, and the rock slide, and his crawling out of there for three days dragging his rotting leg behind him. He told me of the oasis, and he said he had been cured of the poison venom by an angel with red hair.

I was entranced, an angel! I asked him to tell me more of this angel.

Yeshua said, "She is not an angel of the heavens. She is an angel of this earth. I did not have to wait for death to take me to her, she came to me in my hour of need."

Yeshua told me that the angel had saved his life, and that the angel had shown him the door to a secret passage in his own mind. In that secret passageway he had a vision, and that was what he wanted to talk to me about. The vision allowed him to journey to far off places and to witness things that have no explanation. Most important, Yeshua told me, in his vision ADONAI spoke to him, and ADONAI showed him his soul, and what was in his soul, and how he must direct the energy of his soul.

Yeshua said he heard the words of ADONAI, "And ADONAI spoke to me thus. – *The Lord will cause thine enemies that rise up against thee to be smitten before thee. They shall come out against thee one way, and shall flee before thee seven ways –*. ADONAI has commanded me to rid the land of the Romans. I am to gather warriors and drive the Romans away."

In his vision ADONAI commanded Yeshua to cut down the Romans where they stood if they would not leave, to deny them sanctuary, to take their weapons to use against them, to take their water and food, to thirst them and to starve them. He was to cut them from the soil and leave their root and seed to dry to dust in the sun. Yeshua said this is what ADONAI commanded of him, to be ADONAI's ax and chop them down.

"I am to gather an army and make a war on the Romans. I have spoken to no other man of this. Only you and I know of this. Judas, will you join me in this quest?"

We were sitting on the ground. I stood and reached out for Yeshua's hand. He offered me his hand and I pulled him to his feet. We stood facing each other. "Then I am your first warrior. I will join your quest. Your quest shall be my quest. I will stand by your side. My weapons will strike with yours to drive out the Romans. I am honored that you thought of me first. How shall we begin?"

"Tell me, Judas. How is our cousin, Thaddaeus Barabbas? Have you seen him lately?"

It so happened that Thaddaeus Barabbas was camped not far away on the Mount and I knew exactly how to find him. Yeshua and I left for his camp.

Just before sunset Yeshua and I came down from the Mount. We entered into Nazareth the back way. He wanted to keep his arrival a secret for now. When we entered his home everyone was shocked, surprised, gladdened. His mother Mary Salome held him tight, sobbing, "My son. My son. My prayers are answered."

We sat at the table. Yosef said the prayers, thanking ADONAI for Yeshua's deliverance. We took supper and there was joy in every bite. Yeshua told us all to keep his arrival a secret. "I will tell you why this must be so later. Right now let me look upon you and rejoice. My prayers to come back to you and find you all healthy have been answered."

The next morning before the dawn, Yeshua and I went to the Mount Tabor and our cave. We loaded our weapons onto a donkey and disguised the weapons amongst bundled sheaves of cut grasses and straw that we tied to the crosstree on the donkey's back. We dressed in poor clothing as if we were farmers taking the feed to market for sale. We carried bags containing supplies and provisions.

Our destination was the town of Capernaum on the northern shore of the sea of Chinnereth. It would be a fast walk of one sun. We would not take the Roman road called Via Maris which was a direct route, but would go across the Plain of Zebulon going through the remote countryside. We did this to avoid the tax collectors and Roman military patrols on the Roman road.

We arrived in the hills above Capernaum when the sun was setting. We made camp to await the dawn. After a nights rest, before the sun had risen, we were at the seashore waiting for the fishermen to arrive. The sea of Chinnereth supported hundreds of fishermen in towns all along its shore. The port town of Capernaum at the north end of the Sea was known for its bounty of fishing. Their catch was the red belly musht, and sardines, and biny. These delicacies were cleaned, then preserved by being salted and drizzled with olive oil, or just arranged on racks to dry in the sun then packed in barrels and sold throughout the land. Another delicacy Capernaum was known for was their manufacture of a pungent fish sauce, the garum, used for seasoning foods. When the fish were cleaned, the scraps and heads and innards were placed in shallow trays and allowed to ferment in the sun until the unsightly and odorous pile dissolved to a thick paste. Some people slathered the sauce on their foods at every meal. I used it sparingly. It tended to swell my stomach with the uncomfortable gasses and caused the unsociable foul winds from the back passage.

Capernaum was a busy town lying on the trade route between Damascus and Jerusalem. It had good roads, toll booths, and a small Roman military garrison. We would need to tread carefully as our load of weapons, and our mission, was sure to draw unwanted Roman attention.

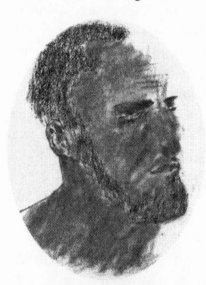

We were looking for two brothers we had met when we went to see Yokhanan the Baptizer at the River Jordan. These brothers were the sons of the fisherman Jonah. The names of the sons were Andrew barJonah and Simon Peter barJonah. They, like us, were of the Pharisees tribe. They had come to our camp with Yokhanan at the end of that day and sat with us at the fire while we talked of ridding the land of the Romans.

Walking the shoreline, leading the donkey, we soon came upon the two brothers preparing their boat for the days fishing. They looked up as we approached. It had been over two years since we had been introduced but they recognized us.

Yeshua said to them, "Andrew and Simon Peter. Have you found a way to continue the struggle against the Romans since the death of Yokhanan?"

Simon Peter replied, "No. Have you?"

Yeshua said to them, "Yes. I have seen our triumph in a vision. I know what must be done. Follow me, and I will make you fishers of men."

We sat at their boat on the shore and Yeshua told them of the troubles in Zippori after the news of Yokhanan the Baptizer's murder by the Roman lackey, Herod Antipas. Yeshua told them how he killed the Roman soldiers and his escape to the wilderness. Yeshua told them of the beauty of the emptiness of the wilderness and his tribulations there. He told them of the angel who cured him and who had given him the vision. In that vision was the plan how to free the land of the Romans.

Andrew asked Yeshua what the plan was. Then Yeshua spoke to them of twelve men who would be military captains of the new army of the Habirum. They would be twelve men who would represent the new Twelve Tribes. In times past, there were the twelve tribes, Reuben, Simeon, Levi, Judah, Issachar, Zebulun, Dan, Naphtali, Gad, Asher, Yosef, and Benjamin. Yeshua said we would begin the new Twelve Tribes. The twelve captains of the new twelve tribes would organize their warriors for a coordinated strike at the enemy in stealth and darkness, from one end of the land to the other.

Andrew and Simon Peter were excited. Both saying, "Yes, I will join the fight."

Yeshua told Andrew and Simon Peter that we would travel and recruit more warriors. Yeshua told them that I, Judas, was the right hand of Yeshua. Their kinsman who had been at the camp, Thaddaeus Barabbas, was his left hand. Thaddaeus Barabbas was spying out the enemy and he would meet us at the place of the first attack. Yeshua told them that I, Judas, was the first of the twelve, Thaddaeus Barabbas was the second, and with the two of them joining, we would now need eight more trustworthy strong warriors to make the twelve chosen ones.

Yeshua said, "Among all the captains, Judas is first. Like King David's chief of the captains, Jashobeam, you will take the order of Judas as my orders. Thaddaeus Barabbas also speaks for me. When Judas and Thaddaeus Barabbas speak, take their words as mine. Judas will also be treasurer, handling our finances. We need more men. Do you know of any warriors we can trust to approach?"

At that, Andrew and Simon Peter left their boat on the shore and led us to James and John, the sons of Zebedee. The brothers and their father were repairing their nets as we approached. Simon Peter greeted them and introduced us, telling James and John and their father Zebedee that these were kinsmen who had been at the camp with Yokhanan the Baptizer. Zebedee and his sons had also been followers of Yokhanan the Baptizer. When Yeshua told them about the army he was raising to free the land of Roman rule the sons immediately joined us. The father was very old and could not join us but he told us he wished he could go with us, to fight for freedom. Now there were six of the twelve.

Yeshua said we would need six more captains and Simon

Peter told us in Bethsaida was a man who was a boat builder. The best way to travel was to use a boat to get from town to town on the shores of the sea of Chinnereth.

Andrew and Simon Peter said we would pass their houses on the way to Bethsaida and they would get a bag of supplies for themselves. When we entered Simon Peter's home his wife was kneeling beside a pallet on the floor, tending to another woman. Simon Peter told us this was his wife's mother, and she suffered from a fever that would not break no matter what they tried.

Yeshua went to her and sat on the floor at her side. He asked the wife of Simon Peter to tell him how long the fever had lasted and what treatments she had used to help her mother. She described giving her mother purgatives. The woman lay there conscious but weak. Yeshua said to her daughter, "I believe I may be able to help your mother. May I treat her?"

Simon Peter's wife was desperate and ready to try anything to save her mother. She agreed, and then Yeshua bent over the woman and told her, "You have the strength within yourself to cure yourself. I will act as your guide to help you find that strength." Yeshua asked the woman if she was willing to search for that strength and if she consented to allow Yeshua to be her guide. The woman whispered, "Yes."

Yeshua asked the daughter to fetch clean cloths and lemons. Yeshua asked Simon Peter to bring in two buckets of fresh water. Yeshua took some of the fresh water and put it into a pan he placed at the fire to boil. We all sat quietly and watched as Yeshua dampened the cloths in the bucket of cool water and wrapped the cloths about the woman's head, neck, shoulders and on her lower legs and feet. He took one cloth and asked Simon Peter's wife to place it on her mother's breasts while the men turned their heads away. This was done, then Yeshua took out his pharmacopeia and mixed some powders, oils and potions together that he placed into a clean drinking cup.

When the water boiled, Yeshua poured it into the cup over the mixture he had concocted and squeezed the juice of a lemon into that. He raised the woman's head and helped her to drink. Yeshua took another pinch of a green herb from his pharmacopeia and placed the herb in the bowl of a small pipe. Yeshua told the woman this was the herb Kannabaeus and that it would relax her healing spirit. Yeshua lit the herb in the pipe, sucked the smoke into his mouth and then blew it gently into the woman's nostrils, instructing her to breathe the smoke. After the herb in the pipe was smoked to ash, the woman seemed to go into a very relaxed state and she lay resting. Yeshua took the cloths from the woman's feet and rubbed her feet with the cut lemons, spreading the juice thoroughly. Then he began to massage the woman's feet. He asked the woman to tell him when he found the tender spots on her feet. When she did he concentrated his efforts at those places. While he massaged her feet he sang soothing words to a song in a language I did not understand.

I could see with my own eyes as the woman relaxed under Yeshua's ministrations. Instead of tossing in her fever, she fell into a deep sleep. It was the middle of the day when all this began and Yeshua sat with Simon Peter's wife's mother until the next dawn. All the while he kept the cloths cooled with fresh water and fed her more of the tea he had concocted, while continuing to massage her feet and legs, arms, neck and shoulders.

At the sunrise the woman's fever had broken. She was sitting upright leaning against the wall, tired and weak, but healed. Yeshua was sitting beside her, listening attentively as she spoke softly to him. Yeshua, I had observed over time, had the art of listening. He could make the other person feel as if they were his only consideration and all they said was important and interesting. After a time Yeshua told her, "Rise and go. Your faith in yourself has made you whole." He helped the woman to stand. Her daughter took her through the curtain for her to wash and be refreshed.

Shortly the two women returned to the main room of their house. We all gathered and broke our night fast together. We ate bread and fresh fish cooked on a spit over the fire. Simon Peter's wife's mother took food with us. After the meal we began to take our leave when Simon Peter's mother in law said she would go with us. She said she wanted to help in the fight against the Romans.

Yeshua shook his head and told her kindly, "There will be danger. It is no place for you."

The woman replied, "A fighting man needs nourishment. You cannot gather and cook food and fight at the same time. A fighting man needs his strength and strength comes from food. I will come with you on your quest and I will gather and cook foods for you to eat and be strong."

I could see Yeshua was trying to talk her out of this notion when he said, "But you are still weak from the fever. How can you travel?"

The woman stood straight and told him, "I am not so weak that I cannot steer a donkey."

Then Simon Peter's wife said, "I too will come on your quest and help my mother with the cooking."

Yeshua asked her, "What of your home and children?"

Andrew's wife told us, "I will care for the children. It is for the children that you fight the Romans, so the children do not live in servitude." She hugged Simon Peter's wife, "Have no fear for the little ones. I will care for them and protect them."

At that Yeshua told us all, "Very well. Our army grows by the day! Our weapons against the Romans shall be the sword and the cooking pot."

We left Capernaum for Bethsaida to find the man named Philip. Bethsaida was a walk of one movement of the sundial along the shoreline. As we left the house, I was surprised to see a crowd gathered in the roadway. Apparently word of Yeshua's healing of Simon Peter's wife's mother had spread among the people of this town. Among the crowd was a Roman centurion. The centurion was dressed in  his red uniform showing he was an officer of the guard. He had his sword in its scabbard at his belt. He was holding his helmet in his right hand. The centurion was a medium built blonde haired man of regular features, shaved clean of beard in the Roman style.

I said in a low voice to Yeshua, "This man is not a welcome sight."

Yeshua answered, "He holds his helmet in his sword hand. I do not believe him to be a threat. All of you wait here. I will talk to him," and Yeshua walked directly to the centurion, stopping a pace away. "Greetings, centurion. What is it you seek?"

The centurion said, "My name is Cornelius. I seek the healer, the one called Yeshua. Is that you?" The centurion looked at the sword hanging from Yeshua's belt, but he made no comment, instead fixing his gaze on Yeshua in an open honest manner.

"Yes. I am Yeshua. I am blessed to know some of the healing arts. Are you feeling unwell?"

"It is not for me I come to you but for my servant. She is very sickened in her body. I must travel to Caesarea Maritama, she cannot be moved and I dare not leave her. I fear for her life. I ask that you attend to her. I will pay you."

Everyone knew of Caesarea Maritama. It was built by the father of Herod Antipas and named Caesarea in honor of the emperor Augustus. It was a major trading port with a deep harbor. The town received fresh water fed by an aqueduct from a spring in the hills of Mount Carmel. It had a Roman amphitheater for staging the Roman spectacles. The town had one of the palaces of the tetrarch Herod Antipas. The governor, Pontius Pilate, also had a home there.

Yeshua stood looking at the centurion, his head tilted to the side and a quizzical expression on his face. "Have the Roman doctors been sent for?"

"Yes. A doctor bled her and fed her purgatives, but she has gotten worse. The doctor's treatment made her worse. The doctor told me to make a sacrifice to the gods for her to be well, then he left her to her fate. They say you are a healer. I ask, please, that you come with me."

Yeshua nodded his head, "I will come with you to see your servant. Just a moment while I speak to my friends."

I told Yeshua, "This could be a trap. There might be Romans waiting, to set an ambush for you."

"I do not think so. The centurion called the sick woman a servant, but it is obvious she must be his woman. I do not think even the Romans would play such a trick. If it is a trick the Romans will pay in blood. Let us go with this man on our way out of town."

The centurion led his horse and we walked with him to his place of lodging. Yeshua conversed with the man as we walked. Cornelius told Yeshua he was with the Cohors II Italica Civium Romanorum from the land of Italia. He had been sent to Capernaum for temporary duty but was now returning to the garrison at Caesarea Maritama. Yeshua asked Cornelius questions about Italia and I could see Yeshua was using this opportunity to learn more about our enemy, the Romans. I knew that soldiers, legionaries, and centurion officers served twenty five years in the Roman army to their retirement and pension and, if they were not already Roman born, received Roman citizenship. They were forbidden to marry while serving. Many, such as this man, bent the rule by taking a concubine, calling the woman a servant. I had to agree that the man looked distressed so the woman must be important to him. The Romans, it seemed, could also be subject to pains of the heart.

Walking fast we were soon there. The neighborhood was one of working citizens and the homes modest. I did not see any soldiers lurking about. The centurion opened the door and bid Yeshua to enter. I looked over Yeshua's shoulder into the room and only saw a woman lying on a bed in the corner. I went back to the shade of a tree. Simon Peter, Andrew, James and John and I sat to wait the outcome of Yeshua's healing.

We sat outside the centurion's home until the end of the day. At times we heard Yeshua singing songs in that strange language, but other than that, the house might as well be deserted for the lack of movement. At the setting of the sun, marking the beginning of a new day, the door opened and Yeshua and the centurion came out. We walked toward them. The man had his money purse in his hand and was attempting to pay, but Yeshua refused any compensation. Yeshua told the centurion, "Do violence to no man. Accuse no one falsely. Show mercy to others in need and your debt is paid."

"But you have saved her life, and in doing so, saved mine, for I love this woman with all my heart. All I have I will give to you for your healing."

In the gathering twilight Yeshua stepped to the man. He extended his right arm and he and the Roman grasped each other by the forearm, in the handshake of peace. Yeshua telling him, "In the holy book of our people, King Solomon tells us in Ecclesiastes. – *To every thing there is a season, and a time to every purpose under the heaven. A time to kill, and a time to heal. A time to love, and a time to hate. A time for war, and a time for peace –*. Cornelius, today has been a time to heal and a time for peace. Take your lady and go in peace, Roman. Perhaps we may meet again someday."

I stood there shocked to the core of my being, for I saw there were tears rolling down the centurion's cheeks. He said no more. He gave Yeshua's arm a firm shake then bowed his head and turned, going into the room to his woman.

By the time we left, the hour was late. We returned to Simon Peter's home to shelter for the night. Sitting at the fire in Simon Peter's home, I asked Yeshua a question that had puzzled me all the day. "If you say the Romans are our enemy, and if they ask for an egg we are to give them a viper, why did you heal the Roman's woman?"

Yeshua sat staring at the fire. "Proverbs tell us. – *The merciful man doeth good to his own soul. But he that is cruel troubleth his own flesh –*. What had that poor woman done to us that we should treat her unkindly? That centurion, Cornelius, yesterday and tomorrow he is the face of the enemy. But today he is a man troubled in his heart for the woman he loves. Today he was not a good man nor was he a bad man. He was just a man."

'What ailment did the woman suffer from?"

"She had a palsy that affected her swallowing of food. When she did not eat she weakened. When she weakened her muscles would cramp and tremble. I treated her with the Kannabaeus. The magic of the plant eased her to take nourishment. I left some of the Kannabaeus with them so Cornelius will give her a little when she is in pain. She will be well to receive the love of the centurion. The centurion will in turn be warmed by her love and companionship. To find someone to love without reservation is difficult, but once found is a treasure to cherish. To lose someone you love means losing a part of one's heart and soul."

I sat staring at Yeshua. What under the sun was the matter with him? I had never heard him express such sentimental nonsense before. Was he going soft in the head?

Early the next morning we departed Capernaum to travel to Bethsaida. As we walked along the shoreline of the sea of Chinnereth, I looked about with curiosity. I had not been this far north in the Galilee before. At this junction where the northern River Jordan feeds the sea of Chinnereth, I saw this was not only an area of fishermen but also farming. The fields were rich with crops. There were ditches

dug and lined with plastered stones that brought the river's water to the fields. I saw the ditches were ingeniously constructed to run north to south, so the river's water constantly ran fresh to the fields. These ditches fed smaller cross ditches that ran east to west to irrigate the entire planting area. A land of milk and honey! Truly, this was a land worth fighting for.

We went to the boatyard of Philip where we found him working. Andrew and Simon Peter introduced us, but before Yeshua spoke of his vision, Yeshua noticed a man sitting to the side in the shade with a cloth covering his eyes. Yeshua went to him and asked what ailed him. The man said his eyes hurt him and he feared he was going blind. Philip told Yeshua the man is his uncle and a craftsman with many skills and his talents were sorely missed. Yeshua gently removed the cloth. Standing to the side I could see the man's eyes were covered in a dried matter.

Yeshua told the man he had a substance from his pharmacopoeia that could clear his eyes for him to see again. "Will you allow me to treat you?" The man readily agreed. First Yeshua heated some water in a pan on the fire. When the water was warm Yeshua dipped a cloth in it and used the wet cloth to clean the man's eyes of the matter. Then Yeshua took from his bag several items including a small clay vial plugged with a cork stopper. Yeshua shook some powder from the vial onto his palm then he spat in his palm to moisten the powder. He rubbed it into and around the man's eyes. Within minutes the man was sitting up and smiling, looking at everything as if it was his first time seeing. Everyone thought it miraculous! Their friend and coworker was cured of his malady.

Yeshua told us this powder was a mixture of crushed fennel seed and the ash called pulvis puteolanus from the burning mountain of Etna in Sicilia in the land of Roman Italia. Yeshua gave the man a small amount of the powder and told him to wash his eyes with it each morning for the next five suns.

I asked Yeshua where he had gotten this powder and he told me, "From the angel with red hair that saved my life." That brought Yeshua to tell Philip the reason we had come to see him. Yeshua told Philip of his vision and of the quest commanded of him to break the rule of the Romans and bring freedom to the Habirum.

Yeshua said, "ADONAI spoke to Moses. – *I whet my glittering sword. I will render vengeance to my adversaries. I will make my arrows drunk with blood. My sword shall devour flesh. And doth make expiation for the land of the people* –. The Habirum must be governed only by the Habirum. The Law tells us we must fight to free the land from the Romans."

Philip said to Yeshua, "If your ability to fight is equal to your healing powers, then the Romans will fall before you. Now that my uncle has vision again he can take care of the business. I will join your quest." Philip became the seventh of the twelve.

Philip encouraged his cousin, Nathanael Bartholomew, another boat maker and skilled with the art of sailing to join the quest. Nathanael Bartholomew seemed reluctant, saying to Philip, "Can anything good come out of Nazareth?"

Yeshua put out his hand to Nathanael Bartholomew and told him, "You are an Israelite in whom is no deceit. Join our quest and you shall see if anything good can come out of Nazareth."

Nathanael Bartholomew looked at his kinsman, who was cured,

and then turned to Yeshua, "I see you are plain spoken as well as a healer. I will fight with you for freedom," and clasped Yeshua's hand in his. Nathanael Bartholomew joined as a welcome addition, the eighth captain.

Yeshua told us, "You are the first eight of what will be twelve captains. The twelve captains will command the twelve new tribes of the united kingdom of Israel and Judah. The twelve captains of the army will each choose two good men to serve as your right and left hands. We will go now to search out the next four captains, then we begin."

Yeshua and I went to the donkey that was loaded with our arms of war. Away from the others I asked him, "When you were treating Simon's wife and the centurion's woman, you sang songs in a strange tongue. What was the language you were speaking?"

Yeshua said, "When I was a child growing up in Aegyptus I learned to speak their language. But I have not used it in the years since we returned to Nazareth. I thought I had forgotten it, but in my vision I saw the words and remembered how to speak them. I also remember the songs of Aegyptus and the letters of their language. The secret passageway that took me to my vision also revealed to me forgotten chambers in my mind."

We unloaded the bundles of straw with their hidden weapons and loaded them into Philip's boat. Then we climbed aboard and sailed southwest to a town called Har HaOsher, what some called the Mount of Beatitudes. Philip told us he knew many men there who had followed Yokhanan the Baptizer and who hungered for another leader. I observed with interest how Philip handled the sail and steering rudder.

Yeshua asked Philip many questions about sailing the boat and how it was built. Philip told us the hulls of the boats were made of sawn boards of the fir tree that come from the land of Senir, and the hull was made watertight with pitch from Lake Asphaltitus at the south end of the Salt Sea. The mast was cedar from Lebanon, the oars were of oak from Basham. The sails were woven Kaneh Bosem from the Kannabaeus plant, made in the town of Tyre. While they talked I lay back with the sun on my face, thinking this was much better than walking or riding a donkey. It was a very comfortable means of travel. It was so pleasant I drifted off to a deep sleep.

I woke when the boat was beached at the shore. We walked a short distance and came to a village at the base of the hills. Philip spoke to several men who became excited and ran off to bring more. Men and women began gathering until the village was full. Yeshua walked to the top of the hill so that he could see all that had gathered.

Yeshua spoke to the multitude thus.

"ADONAI sent an angel to me. The angel showed me a vision. In that vision ADONAI commanded of me to prepare for war! To rouse the warriors! To let all the fighting men draw near and attack!"

"Behold, a sower went forth to sow his seed. And it came to pass, as he sowed, some fell by the way side, and it was trodden down, and the fowls of the air came and devoured it up. Some seed fell on stony ground where it had not much earth. Because it had no depth of earth, it was scorched, and because it had no root, it withered away. And some fell upon a rock, it withered away, because it lacked moisture. And some fell among thorns, and the thorns grew up with it, and choked it, and it yielded no fruit. But other fell into good ground, and did yield fruit that sprang up, and increased, and bear fruit, some a hundredfold, some sixtyfold, and some thirtyfold."

"He that hath ears to hear, let him hear. Our army is of good seed and good ground. Each day we grow and each week we will get more men and grow even stronger. Soon all the land of the Habirum will join our quest. Soon the land of the Habirum will be free of the Romans."

"You must choose. Your choice is freedom, or the slavery of Caesar."

"No one can serve two masters, for either he will hate the one and love the other, or he will be devoted to the one and despise the other. If a kingdom be divided against itself, that kingdom cannot stand. And if a house be divided against itself, that house cannot stand. The Romans divide our house. The Romans must fall. The Romans are the rich and the full and the laughing ones. But woe unto them that are rich! Woe unto they that are full! Woe unto they that laugh now! For they shall mourn and weep. Do not give dogs what is holy, and do not throw your pearls before pigs, lest they trample them underfoot and turn to attack you."

"You are the salt of the earth. Blessed are you who hunger and thirst for righteousness, for you shall be satisfied. Ask, and it will be given to you. Seek, and you will find. Knock, and it will be opened to you. You have heard that it was said, you shall love your neighbor and hate your enemy, and you have heard that it was said, an eye for an eye and a tooth for a tooth. The message from ADONAI is the Habirum are the neighbors and Rome is the enemy. O Jerusalem, Jerusalem. Your hour is at hand. You are the light of the world. A city set on a hill cannot be hidden."

"Everyone then who hears these words of mine and does them will be like a wise man who built his house on the rock. If a Roman seeks your counsel say nothing. If a Roman seeks your comfort and asks for bread, you will give him a stone. If a Roman asks for a fish, you will give him a serpent. If a Roman asks you for an egg, you will give him a scorpion."

"Think not that I am come to send peace on earth. I come not to send peace, but a sword. If you have no sword, sell your cloak and buy one. Do not think that I have come to abolish the Law or the Prophets. I have not come to abolish them but to fulfill them."

And then I saw when Yeshua finished these sayings, the crowds were astonished at his teaching for he was teaching them as one who had authority and not as their scribes. Yeshua came down from his perch on the hill and moved among the throng. I saw they were all full of hope and ready for the quest to bring freedom.

It was then later in the day and the time to take supper was approaching. When the day began to wear away, a man of that town said to Yeshua, "This is a desert place. Send the multitude away that they may go into the towns and villages round about, and lodge, and buy themselves victuals. For they have nothing to eat."

Yeshua answered, "They need not depart. Give ye them to eat. How many loaves have ye? Go and see."

Andrew said, "A lad here hath five barley loaves and two small fishes, but what are they among so many?"

Yeshua said, "Bring them hither to me. Make the men sit down by fifties in a company." Now there was much green grass in the place. So the men sat down, in ranks, by fifties. When the men and the women were assembled thus Yeshua said to them, "Think upon my words, and await my return, then you will supper."

Then Yeshua gathered the seven of us together, and we were myself, Andrew, Simon Peter, James and John, Philip and Bartholomew. Yeshua told us we were going for victuals to feed the many. "Let us return to the port." Yeshua turned to the seated throng and said in a carrying voice, "The first twenty men to stand come with me."

At his words twenty of the most eager came to him. With Yeshua in the lead we all walked to the sea and saw a boat tied to the wharf being loaded with goods. Yeshua asked Philip, "This boat has foods to transport. Is this captain a dog for the Romans?"

Philip replied, "I know of this captain. He is Habirum but his livelihood is from the Romans. He is not a bad man. But not a good man. He is just a man." Yeshua looked at us and said, "Here and now it begins." Yeshua told the twenty men who accompanied us to wait on the shore.

Yeshua went up the gangplank onto the boat and we seven followed him. The men who labored, working for day wages to load the boat, stopped to see what the interruption was about. Yeshua inquired as to who was the captain of this vessel. A portly man who was checking off items on a scroll replied, "I am captain. Who are you?"

At that Yeshua threw back his robe to reveal the sword on a belt at his waist. "Who I am is not the question you should ask. You should ask yourself, what is the meaning of these words? – *A generous person will prosper, and whoever refreshes others will be refreshed –.*"

The portly captain looked confused by Yeshua's words. He looked alarmed at the sight of the sword and wary at the sight of us seven standing with Yeshua plus the twenty men on the shore. "You talk in riddles. What is your business?"

Yeshua pointed behind him, up the hill. "There are five hundred hungry people back there and I am here to get them victuals for supper. I see that you are loading barrels of salted fish and loaves of bread. I tell you that you will prosper and be refreshed if you share these victuals with those who hunger. – *He that hath a bountiful eye shall be blessed. For he giveth of his bread to the poor –.*"

I saw that the captain was a very worried man. He said to Yeshua, "These fish and loaves are the property of the Romans to be sold at market in Jerusalem. Perhaps I can share some. If you have coins to pay?"

"I have no need of coin from Caesar. I say to you, render therefore unto Caesar the things which be Caesar's and unto ADONAI the things which be ADONAI's. Does the Book of ADONAI not tell us. – *Behold, I have given you every herb yielding seed which is upon the face of all the earth, and every tree in which is the fruit of a tree yielding seed. To you it shall be for food –.* I ask you only one time. Will you share and refresh those that hunger and thus prosper in the light of ADONAI. Or will you choose to bleed for the Romans?"

At those words Yeshua put his hand on his sword and told the captain, "Choose now and choose sensibly." The captain chose to share. Yeshua had the twenty men that accompanied us come aboard and each lifted a load of the foods to their shoulders.

While the men were loading, Yeshua questioned the captain on his route to Jerusalem. "How do you sail to Jerusalem from here?"

The captain explained to Yeshua that it was the season for the River Jordan to run high and they would sail south to the shore east of the town of Jericho. There the foods would be loaded on camels for the walk to Jerusalem on the Roman road. Yeshua looked thoughtful, "How many days sail on the river is this journey?"

The captain told Yeshua, "North to south the sea of Chinnereth is about forty five milia passum, then another one hundred down the River Jordan as it twists and turns on itself. It is a sail of about ten days to the landing on the river where we meet the camels. We must anchor at night on the River Jordan because of dangerous rapids and rocks that cannot be run during the dark hours. The river runs full now after the rain season, but it cannot be sailed during the dry months."

I could see Yeshua was gathering this information to be used, somehow, in our quest against the Romans. The captain asked Yeshua what multitude he fed that required such an amount of foodstuffs. "And what am I to say to the Romans when I arrive with part of their load missing?"

Yeshua grinned wolfishly. "Go ye, and tell that fox, O Jerusalem, Jerusalem." Yeshua thanked the captain for his hospitality and generosity and we left to return to the meeting place.

With Yeshua in the lead and we seven as guards plus the twenty men all carrying a load we left the port. We walked along the path and were approached by a man who identified himself as Levi Matthew, the local tax collector. Levi Matthew inquired as to the value of the foodstuffs being carted and who was to pay the tax due the emperor.

Yeshua said to him, "Come with me and I will show you the value of these foods. Then you shall be the judge of the tax to be paid."

I could see that Levi Matthew was surprised. I knew that normally the person who was taxed would argue and bargain to minimize the tax to be paid. But here was a man who would allow him, the tax collector, to place the value on the goods. He seemed curious and agreed to accompany us.

When we arrived at the meeting place the people rejoiced at the sight of the food as their hunger was great. Yeshua said to Levi Matthew, "You are Habirum. Yet you tax Habirum? What say ye to this? What value do you place on providing for the hungry? What value do you place on life? What tax would you charge for someone's life? Blessed are they who hunger now, for they will be satisfied. Blessed are they who weep now, for they will laugh. Tell me, Levi Matthew, what tax do you say must be paid on these people's lives?"

When the tax collector, Levi Matthew, saw that Yeshua had brought the fish and loaves to feed these people who hungered, and not to profit himself, he knelt before Yeshua and said to him, "I see that you are a wise man. I know that I am but a sinner. I sin for the Romans. I sin to tax my fellow Habirum for the Romans. I ask for forgiveness."

Yeshua lifted the man to his feet. "I did not come to call the righteous, but sinners to repentance. Tell me Levi Matthew, what would you say if I told you there was no need for taxing the people? What would you say if I told you that the Romans and their taxes could be ridden from our land?"

We ate while Yeshua questioned Levi Matthew. We seven captains sat with them and listened. Levi Matthew said, in answer to Yeshua's question, "The kingdom of Herod I was divided among his three sons. Herod Antipas received the Galilee and Perea. Herod Philip was given Auranitis, Batanea and Gaulanitis. Herod Archelaus was given Idumea, Samaria and Judah, but his lands were taken from him. Judah then become a Roman province. All these lands are claimed by Rome, so the brothers Herod rule only by the blessing of the Romans. The Herod's tax the Habirum to pay the Romans. It is the way of things."

Yeshua questioned Levi Matthew of his knowledge of the Romans and how much taxes they collected. What Levi Matthew told Yeshua was an astonishment to us all. I wrote this on a scroll I had so that I would be sure to remember it correctly.

Levi Matthew told us, "In the lands of Judah and Israel, ruled by the brothers Herod for the Romans, the taxes collected each year are more than eighteen million drachmas."

We all stopped chewing and sat there with our mouths open like the village simpleminded person. Philip tried to speak and began coughing, having swallowed the wrong way, and we had to beat on his back to clear his lungs to breathe. Yeshua said to Levi Matthew, "You speak of a sum of coins that is truly a golden mountain. What do they do with all this coin?"

"Most goes to Rome to pay tribute. A large part is used by the Herods for their building of fortresses and palaces. Some is sent to foreign leaders as gifts. The costs of maintaining the Temple are substantial. The coins the priests collect from the offerings and sale of hides is supposed to contribute to that expense but most goes into the priest's own pockets. The coin in the Temple, the sacred treasure, is supposed to belong to the Habirum for use only at the Temple. Pontius Pilate took for himself a vast sum of the sacred treasure to build the aqueduct from the water spring at Masada to the Temple in Jerusalem."

Yeshua shook his head, "Pontius Pilate. Rome's thief and murderer. Each day he sends our people to the place of the skulls."

Levi Matthew said, "Yes. When the people gathered to protest the spending of the sacred treasure on the aqueduct, Pilate had his Cuthite mercenaries hiding in the crowd, dressed as Habirum. They used clubs they had hidden under their cloaks to beat and murder many people that day."

I remembered my father talking about that day, the cruelty and excess of the Roman response. Many died from the beatings and more from the stampede away from the slaughter.

Yeshua asked how the Romans went from town to town getting the coins the tax collectors accumulated, the times of the month the coins were taken to the treasuries, how the Romans guarded those coins during the transport to the treasuries, where the treasuries were located, and of the forces that guarded those treasuries.

Eighteen million drachmas! I could see that Yeshua's plan and his quest included far more than just fighting the Romans. It was to also be a war at the very heart of their greed.

Levi Matthew expressed his shame at being a tool of the Romans and their heavy taxing of his fellow Habirum. "What can I do? What can one man do? The Romans control the very lifeblood of the Galilee. I wish there was a way to be released from their hold on our throats."

Yeshua then told Levi Matthew of his vision and the quest ADONAI had commanded of him. Yeshua told Levi Matthew, "Take heed and beware of the leaven of Caesar and of the Sadducees and of the leaven of the Herod tribe. There shall be weeping and gnashing of teeth when our army strikes. We shall come from the east, from the west, from the north, and from the south. You, Levi Matthew, think on what I have told you and think on what you have told me. Think on the Romans and the treasure they have stolen from our people and our land."

Yeshua said to me, "Judas, I am going to the hill to think and pray." To all of us Yeshua said, "At the dawn I will return. In the meantime the people are filled. Of the food left, gather up the fragments that remain so nothing be lost and the people will have a bite to break their fast at the dawn." Yeshua stood and beckoned me to follow. "Levi Matthew must prove himself. Until then watch him closely so he does not stray." Then he left us for his solitude and the time alone that I knew he required.

I set the watches, to each captain was assigned an appointed time. I took the last hour before the dawn. The next morning I was awakened by Andrew for him to rest and me to keep watch. For a long while all was quiet and still. In the very early hour, before the dawn when the darkness transforms to a grayness that plays tricks on the eye, I saw a moving shadow among the trees on the hillside. I had my bow in hand, an arrow at the string. Then I heard the whistle of the first morning bird and I knew it was Yeshua. I answered with a morning bird call of my own.

Yeshua stepped softly to my side and said quietly, "Your eyes and ears are keen my friend."

I replied, "I am accustomed to how you arrive silently. Our enemies will not be so vigilant or so fortunate in their awakening."

When the sky lightened and the people awakened, Yeshua stepped to his perch on the hillside and told them, "I journey to Gennesaret. Any who wish to join this army and join this quest to free our land from the Romans are welcome. Remember the words from Isaiah. – *Fear not, for I have redeemed you. When you pass through rivers they will not wash you away. When you walk through fire no flame will burn you –*. And the words of Mattathias. – *Follow me, every one of you who is zealous for the law and strives to maintain the covenant –*. Prepare for war! Rouse the warriors! The time for freedom from the Romans is at hand!"

All the captains, Yeshua, Levi Matthew and myself, boarded Philip's boat. We rowed away from the bank and then raised the sails to catch the morning breeze. I looked back to the shore and saw a multitude walking the shoreline, south to Gennesaret, to join the army and join Yeshua's quest.

Pointing, I said to Yeshua, "Look, my friend. Your words call the warriors to gather. They join your quest."

Yeshua clapped me on the shoulder and told us, "Our quest. This is our quest. One man may speak, but all who join and all who fight are counted as liberators. No one man can be counted as the savior. All must save themselves."

Yeshua asked Philip how far away the town of Gennesaret was. Philip told him if the wind was blowing it was about one movement of the sun dial. Philp pointed at the limp sail, "Those walking may get there faster than us. We will have to row."

We took up the oars and soon the water passing the bow was churned white with our progress. From where I sat I could see the land on both sides of the sea of Chinnereth. "This sea is but a small body of water. I wonder if the Great Sea is like this, where one can see land in both directions."

Philip told me, "No. The Great Sea is truly great. This is just a puddle compared to the Great Sea where the waters are vast. I once sailed from Joppa to Athens in the land of the Greeks. That journey was a sail of a half moon. The mariner I sailed with told me it was a journey of four or five moons to get to the far west of the Great Sea. At the western edge of the Great Sea are the Pillars of Heracles. Beyond that is the Sea of No End. The Romans call the Sea of No End the Sinus Occidentalis. In the Sea of No End great serpents lurk, pulling boats and sailors into the Sea and to their deaths. Those waters have great storms, the waves are taller than a temple. They say the Sinus Occidentalis has no end going to the setting sun. The Romans go through the Pillars then follow the coast northward to Hispania, and to western Gaul, and even farther west, to the island of the Roman Provincia Britanniae."

Philip stopped talking for a moment to adjust the sail, to try and catch the breeze. Then he continued, "They say the island of Roman Britanniae is a violent brutal place of cold rain and fog and dark forests. Their warriors fight naked, painting themselves with mud and clay to hide like smoke in the forest. It is said these savages come silently from the darkness, striking like daemons. In battle they cut off the heads of their vanquished. They place the heads on sticks and stand the sticks upright with the faces of the heads pointing out and surrounding their camp. They do this to strike terror and render evil unto any who may approach."

Philip turned to me and pushed his face close to mine, looking at me in a crazed manner. He opened his eyes wide and stretched his lips back to show all his teeth, "It is said if you are caught alive, the islanders of Britanniae will eat your human flesh raw. They keep you alive for weeks while they peel your skin off and cut you up into morsels to be eaten and devoured slowly."

ADONAI, protect us! I asked Philip, "Are these naked savage flesh eaters also in the land of the Gauls?"

"I have heard it said by Romans who have been there and fought the Gauls, that the Gauls are indeed fearless fighters. But I have not heard anyone say they are flesh eaters. It is said the weather in Gaul is sunny and pleasant, not cold, rainy and foggy like on the island of Roman Britanniae. Perhaps it is the foul weather that makes the primitives on the island of Roman Britanniae suffer madness of their minds, and makes them flesh eaters like wild dogs. Perhaps they are daemons. Only ADONAI knows."

We landed on the shore to find that runners had spread the word of our quest to free the Habirum from the Romans. The town of Gennesaret was full to bursting with people who wanted to hear Yeshua speak. We beached the boat then set off walking. We were making our way to the inn Philip recommended but the walking was slow due to the crush of people along the way.

The word of Yeshua's healing had spread before him and people in the street were asking his help. Yeshua told them, "Follow me to the inn and I will see you one by one." We arrived at the inn and Yeshua settled in the forecourt to minister and treat those in need. A boy on a stretcher was brought to Yeshua by his mother and father. The boy had burns on his face and chest. His mother told Yeshua their son had fits of madness that came on suddenly without any warning. When he was in a fit of madness he would foam at the mouth and gnash his teeth and he had no control over his body. Usually the father would hold the son down to the ground until the fit passed. But when he was in the grip of his last fit he had fallen into the fire.

The boy was conscious but moaning in great pain. Yeshua took from his pharmacopoeia some small black kidney shaped seeds and ground them with a mortar and pestle. He had the boy open his mouth and he placed the powder on his tongue and told him, "Let the powder dissolve in your mouth."

In a short time the boy was lying peacefully. Then Yeshua took the green leaves of a plant, he squeezed the leaf from the top down and a clear thick mush came out of the base. Yeshua gently spread the substance on the boy's burns. While he did this Yeshua spoke in that strange language, the words were musical and soothing. In just minutes the ugly red burns on the boy's skin seemed to transform to a pink healing color. Yeshua told the parents, "This is the plant aloe barbadensis. The juice of the plant heals skin damage." The leaves were thick as a finger with serrated edges and wide at the base tapering to a point at the top.

He told the mother and father, "Take these leaves and spread the juice of the plant on his burns each morning for five suns. If your son is gripped by another fit of madness place this powder on his tongue and he will become calm. Some say daemons cause madness and council exorcism. Do not listen to any magician who tells you this. The madness is caused by a defect in the brain. Do not feed your son honey, or dates, or drink the juice of fruits for the sweetness may trigger a fit to come on him. If he seems confused or stares without speaking, that is a sign of a fit to come. Give him a pinch of the powder on his tongue. Over time, as he becomes a man, he may grow out of these fits so you must be patient with him until then."

The boy's mother and father were full of joy for their son. The father asked how he could repay Yeshua. Yeshua told him, "Freely ye received, freely give to others. Show mercy to others in need and your debt is paid."

All the rest of the day people came to Yeshua and he counseled and treated all. Yeshua took no payment for his services from anyone, which all thought extraordinary. Most healers, and the magicians, and those who claimed to have the power of exorcism, and fortune tellers, sorcerers, and speakers to the dead, all charged and required payment even before they rendered their services. But not Yeshua. He greeted all warmly and at the end repeated, "Freely ye received, freely give to others. Show mercy to others in need and your debt is paid."

Toward the end of the day the crowd was gone. The sundown was approaching. A woman in a cloak with the hood over her head and a veil covering her face showing only her eyes in the dim evening light came to Yeshua. I heard her ask him, "Do you have a treatment for what torments the heart?"

Yeshua had been sitting and counting up his diminished supply of pharmacopoeia. Her words caused him to look up sharply. He bid the woman to sit and join him. When she was seated, he asked her, "Tell me fair lady, what torments the heart?"

"My heart is tormented because I have lost my friend."

Yeshua told her, "I too have a tormented heart for I too have lost a dear friend."

The women said, "Perhaps we can search together for our friend?"

Yeshua replied, "Yes, Mariam, I would like for us to search together. But I see I have found my friend, right here in front of me."

The woman pulled the veil and hood away exposing her face. The woman replied, "Yeshua, my friend, also is right in front of me."

Yeshua introduced us, saying, "Mariam, this is my good friend and strong right arm, Judas. Judas, this is Mariam, the angel that saved me in the wilderness."

I saw that Yeshua's angel was a beautiful woman with long red hair. Her hair was redder than mine. My hair is a dusty copper color but Mariam's was a brilliant lustrous red like a polished apple. I greeted her with enthusiasm, "Welcome and thank you for saving my friend's life."

I could see their reunion made them very happy. I left, so they could talk alone.

GENNESARET. MY NAME MARIAM OF MAGDALA

Yeshua was surprised to see me. In fact he was speechless for a moment while his face lit with a radiant smile. His happiness I shared for to find him fit and healthy had been my wish. I wanted to take him in my arms to feel his warmth but there were people about and that would not have been seemly. He did take both my hands in his hands and in his grasp I felt the strength of his welcome.

He was looking at me in astonishment.

"It is you. The keeper of my heart. What are you doing here?"

We took our supper in the forecourt by candlelight instead of at a table in the inn so we could talk privately. Yeshua asked me what I was doing in Gennesaret. I told him the word of his quest and healings had spread to the eastern shore of the sea and thus to the Temple. I thought that his healings may have depleted the supplies in his pharmacopoeia so I thought to bring more.

Yeshua asked, "How did you get here? Did you travel alone?"

I told him, "We sailed across the sea from Gergesa to here, leaving this morning. I brought with me three donkey loads of pharmacopoeia"

"We?"

"Yes. My uncle and aunt have come with me. To join me on my quest.

"What is your quest?"

I told him, "There is talk of your quest through the land. Many are joining your quest. I see some of your other followers are women. I too have come to join your quest. And my uncle and aunt willingly share your dream to rid the land of the Romans. Your quest is my quest."

Yeshua's smile turned to a grim look. He took me by the arm, leaning in to talk quietly. He said, "I told you before there is danger. I cannot let you be placed in danger. You must go back." Yeshua squeezed my arm. "Seeing you again is a dream come true, but you must go." He released my arm and said in a firm voice, "Go. Now."

I sat looking at Yeshua. Under his cloak I saw the sword and a dagger at his belt. I asked him, "Are you of sound mind and good judgment right now?"

He looked puzzled, "Of course."

"Then do you remember you once promised to honor anything I asked?"

He shook his head, "Please don't ask this thing of me. You cannot stay. It is too dangerous, I would die if anything were to happen to you. I could not live if something happened to you."

"Oh, that is not what I ask of you. What I ask is something else."

Yeshua looked relieved. "Then I will honor it, whatever else you ask."

"Then I ask that you protect me. If I am under your protection then there is no danger."

Yeshua looked stunned. Then slowly he grinned. "You are a wily woman, to trick me."

"I told you it was dangerous to promise anything to a woman that she asks. You tricked yourself, not I."

"I confess. I left you the tyet because it brought us together once before. I thought the magic of Isis might grant me good fortune to bring me back to you and be with you again someday. I never thought to see you now under these circumstances. What of the Temple and your duties? How can you leave?"

"My second sister's daughter is more than ready to take over. She knows more of the Belief than I. The Temple is in good hands."

Yeshua looked at me long and hard, "Is this truly what you ask?"

"Yes truly, this is what I ask."

"Then I will honor my promise to you. You have my protection. In return you must make me a promise, yes?"

"Yes. Anything but go back. I will not promise that. What is it you ask?"

"I will think on it. When I have decided what I desire to ask of you, then I will tell you."

I had to laugh at myself. "Yeshua, you are the wily one. You have tricked me!"

Yeshua smiled. When he smiled his whole face lit up. He told me, "Yes, you see. I had a good teacher!"

Yeshua stood and pulled me to my feet. He folded me into his grasp and placed his arms protectively around me. His body heat radiated through to my heart. I felt that my new life was to begin here and now together with my friend.

"Very well, then. I will honor my promise to you. I will protect you with all my heart and strength. And this has taught me a great lesson. In future I must be more careful of what I promise!"

"I should too!"

Happiness. For the first time in my life I understood what the Song meant. – *I sought him whom my soul loveth. When I found him whom my soul loveth, I held him, and would not let him go* –.

We stayed in the inn at Gennesaret for five more days. Many people came to Yeshua to be treated for their ailments. Word of his healing had spread throughout the Galilee. Of course many people exaggerated the tales, saying Yeshua could raise the dead and other miracles. These stories made Yeshua shake his head in disbelief, amazed at how gullible some people could be. Really, though, this was not unusual for there were some magicians who roamed the Galilee and would use their assistants to stage such theatre. Then they would charge coins to trick the desperate to pay for the healing and miracles they sought.

Yeshua was very busy talking to and organizing the men of his army but he made time to be with me when he could while I treated any and all who came. Yeshua observed the treatments in order to learn more of the healing arts. Also, the people wanted Yeshua to heal them as word had spread far and wide of his abilities. He assured the people that under my care they would get the best treatment for what ailed them. Eventually I took over all the duties required for the healing so that Yeshua could concentrate on the task that had been commanded of him in his vision.

Yeshua did not sleep at the inn in comfort. Each of his captains had their camp outside of the town. At the end of the day Yeshua would go among the men of the camps, meeting and talking to all. For sleeping, Yeshua would go off to a private place and make his camp with the moon and stars for his companions.

Yeshua would take his morning meal with me at the inn and tell me the progress of organizing the army. He would seek my counsel, listen and respect my words, I felt I was a part of his army and his quest. One morning Yeshua and I took food together, breaking our night fast. His captains joined us to discuss their progress.

Yeshua said to them, "There are many who have come to our quest. As we agreed, you have gone among them and chosen the men to be your right and left hands. We need three more captains to make the twelve new tribes. Of the men you have spoken to, are there any who you recommend for that task?"

Simon Peter replied, "Yes. Just last night a man came to me to join. He has a great fervor and zeal. I have known him for many years. He lost his land to the tax collector during the drought and has been living in the wild as a bandit, preying on the Roman caravans. He brought with him five of his warriors. He is called Simon the Zealot."

Yeshua said, "Send for this man and bring him to me here." Shortly Simon Peter returned with the man called Simon the Zealot. I was seated with Yeshua in the forecourt of the inn when the men arrived. As they took their seats, I rose to go. Yeshua said to me, "Mariam stay with us, please. Your counsel is of great value." I listened as Yeshua talked with this man, Simon the Zealot. Simon the Zealot told Yeshua his experiences raiding the Romans and dodging their patrols. He said he and his men lived in the wild lands of Idumea to the south of Jerusalem and west of the Salt Sea. "The caravans we attacked traveled north on the Roman road, Via Maris, and east on the King's Highway, bringing trade goods from Aegyptus."

Yeshua asked, "Did these caravans you attacked have Roman military as guards?"

"Not at first. At first the guards were hired men. Some were skilled fighters but most were not. As our attacks became more frequent and successful the tetrarch, Herod Antipas, began to assign military patrols to the roads and sometimes they would accompany the caravans."

"How did you fare against the protected caravans?"

"We became like night creatures, using the darkness to overcome their sentries. Then when the sentries lay dead, we would fall on the sleeping men. All was going well but then the Romans began to bring dogs with them on their patrols. That made it harder to sneak up on them."

I asked Simon the Zealot, "Did the Romans keep their dogs at their sides or did they tie them to one place and leave them?"

"They would tie the dogs at the outer edges of their camps and the sentries would rely on the barking to alert them."

"So there were times when the dogs were alone?"

"Yes, the creatures were mostly alone. Sometimes the Roman guards would be comfortable enough to sleep, knowing the dogs were keeping watch. A good dog on watch can scent a stranger for a great distance if the winds are blowing to it."

Yeshua asked me, "Do you have an idea for dealing with the dogs on watch?"

I told them, "Yes. I have just the thing. I will mix a potion for you to use."

Simon the Zealot asked me, "What will this potion do?"

"The potion will make their watch dogs sleep. The potion will be a powder. You will place a spoonful on a piece of meat. Then use a sling to throw the meat to the dog from a distance. Count one hundred heart beats, then the dogs will not bark. This potion will make a dog sleep for several hours."

Yeshua asked, "Can this potion be used on men, to make them sleep?"

"Yes. You can use it on men if you can sneak it into their drink or food. I can make another potion of a deadly pharmacopeia from which they will never awake, if that would suit your purpose."

GENNESARET. MY NAME IS JUDAS ISCARIOT

I could see that Mariam was a warrior herself. A bold, decisive woman warrior like Jael. Jael tricked Sisera, the Canaanite commander of King Jabin's army. Jael gave Sisera a sleeping potion and then used a mallet to drive a tent peg into his eye, splitting his brain. Jael then used a sharp knife to saw off the head of Sisera. Jael put his head in a bag. She snuck out of the enemy camp and put Sisera's head on a stick and paraded it among the warriors commanded by Deborah, inspiring them to victory over the Canaanites. Another great woman warrior was Judith, the widow, who used the sword of the Assyrian army general Holfernes against him. One night in the enemy chieftain's tent, while Holofernes lay in a drunken stupor, Judith raised his sword and cleaved him through his forehead between his eyes. Like these women warriors who acted bravely to save the Habirum, Mariam would fight alongside us.

Yeshua told Simon the Zealot, "We welcome your strong arm and your experience. I would like to make you the tenth captain. Would you join our quest?"

Simon the Zealot told Yeshua, and us all, "I am happy to find you. I will fight with you on this quest. The warriors I bring with me to join your quest are hungry for freedom from the Romans. We will all fight."

Yeshua stood and reached out his right arm. Simon the Zealot and Yeshua grasped each other by the forearm. Yeshua said, "It is our quest together. You are welcome to join and fight with us for freedom from the Romans and make our land free."

Yeshua turned to look at everyone. "Listen to my words. There are now ten of what will be twelve military captains of the twelve new tribes of the land of Israel and Judah. Our work does not end after we have defeated the Romans and drove them from our land. After that you will have authority within your area. But you must use that authority wisely. – *In all the settlements that ADONAI is giving you, you shall govern the people with due justice. You shall not judge unfairly, you shall show no partiality, you shall not take bribes. Justice, justice shall you pursue, that you may thrive and occupy the land that ADONAI is giving you –."*

Yeshua studied each man carefully. "The Word of ADONAI should guide the word of man, but the just man, the good man, the honorable man, knows that to be righteous means to do right by all citizens. Justice. Justice for all, shall you pursue. Let us now go to the others."

As we left the inn there was a commotion down the road and the sound of horses running. We stopped and looked to see what might be happening. Now I could see three men on horseback riding hard towards us. In a moment their faces became clear. I told Yeshua, "It is our cousin, Thaddaeus Barabbas."

Thaddaeus Barabbas and the two others pulled up, Thaddaeus Barabbas leaped off his horse and embraced Yeshua and myself with rib crushing greetings. Thaddaeus Barabbas told us, "I bring good news, my friends. Let us talk."

Yeshua told Thaddaeus Barabbas, "We are going to meet the army who have gathered. Walk with us and tell us your good news. But first let us get you and your men water to wash the dust from your mouth and a bite of food."

At this time there were a number of women who came to the quest, mostly as wives and companions to the men who gathered. There were also some girls and women who were with their fathers and brothers. One of the young women was named Rachel. I thought she was very pretty and had spoken to her several times. Rachel had a sister named Jehosheba and the two of them were always together. Now they happened to be standing by and they volunteered to get water and food for Thaddaeus Barabbas and his men.

They rushed into the inn and soon came back with food and water. Rachel had a pitcher of water in one hand and a jug of wine in the other. Jehosheba had a plate of chicken and drinking mugs. Jehosheba smiled at Thaddaeus Barabbas telling him, "A strong man such as you needs nourishment so I brought you three chicken legs."

She was a very pretty girl. She stood blushing while Thaddaeus Barabbas took a bite of a chicken leg and told her, "You are a fine cook. This is the best chicken I have ever tasted."

Jehosheba smiled and told Thaddaeus Barabbas, "I did not cook it. But I am pleased it eases your hunger."

I introduced Thaddaeus Barabbas to Jehosheba and Rachel. I smiled at Rachel as we watched Thaddaeus Barabbas and Jehosheba talking. It had been a number of years since Thaddaeus Barabbas had lost his wife. Perhaps it was time for him to stop mourning and start living again. I thought perhaps this was a sign. The morning prayers start with blessing the rooster for waking us up to a new day. The taste of the leg of the hen seemed to wake Thaddaeus Barabbas to the possibility that he could awake and live again.

We walked to the ruin by the shore where the others waited. On the way there Thaddaeus Barabbas told us his good news.

"A shipment of arms will be transported from the port of Caesarea Maritama to the garrison at Zippori. They will travel the Via Maris road across the Plain of Esdraelon and through the pass between the Mount Tabor and Mount Carmel into the Valley Jezreel. They must cross the River Kishon. It is a perfect ambush site."

Yeshua asked, "How many men will we need?"

Thaddaeus Barabbas told him, "We should have at least forty men, half of them skilled with the arrow and the same with sword and spears."

Yeshua said, "We will have them."

Yeshua and I, with Mariam and Simon Peter and Simon the Zealot and Thaddaeus Barabbas and his men arrived at the ruin. This was the site of an old Roman fort from the days of Pompey from about eighty years before. This had been another in the long history of Roman attacks on the Habirum. Pompey had invaded and destroyed the temple in Jerusalem and wrought havoc throughout the land.

The warriors were organized by divisions with their captains. Simon Peter went to his men as did Simon the Zealot. So now there were ten captains. The two Simons, Andrew, James, John, Philip, Nathanael, Levi Matthew, Thaddaeus Barabbas and myself.

Each of those had different numbers of warriors gathered about them according to their recruiting of the men who had come to the quest. Yeshua told Levi Matthew that his men would need to be knowledgeable about the Romans means of taxing and the whereabouts of those taxed coins. Levi Matthew would be gathering about him fewer men but those men would be specialists in their work. The other captains recruited men for their skills in archery and with sword. All seemed eager and willing to launch a bloody attack on the enemy. I stood on a low rise with Yeshua and looked about me. Already the army counted fifty men. The men quieted when Yeshua began to speak.

"The words of ADONAI tell us what we must do. There is a time to love, and a time to hate. A time for war, and a time for peace. There is no love for the Romans, only hate. There can be no peace with the Romans. We will have no peace until the land is free of the Romans."

"ADONAI goeth with you, to fight for you against your enemies, to save you. ADONAI sends you forth like a mighty warrior. You will arouse vengeance like a man of war. You will shout triumphantly. You will overpower your enemies."

"Your hands are trained for war. You are the weapons of war for ADONAI. You will shatter the horse and his rider. You will shatter the chariot and the rider. ADONAI sends you out not as sheep in the midst of wolves but wise as serpents and hungry as the lion."

"If thine enemy be hungry, give him iron to eat. And if he be thirsty, give him his own blood to drink. Thou will heap coals of fire upon his head. And ADONAI will reward thee. And when ye go to war in your land against the adversary that oppresses you, then you shall be remembered before ADONAI and ye shall be saved from your enemies. He that hath ears to hear, let him hear. Ye draw nigh this day unto battle against your enemies and ADONAI goeth with you, to save you. Soon all of the Habirum will join our quest. Soon Israel and Judah will be free of the Romans."

I saw Yeshua's words were smoother than butter but his blood was hot like a fiery sword. His words were inspiring to the men. Yeshua finished by pulling his sword from its scabbard and raising his arm in the air shouting, "Freedom!"

The men cheered Yeshua's words. I saw that they were all of a fervor to fight and be free of Roman rule. Yeshua told them, "Soon there will be swords to fill the hands of all of you. You will have swords to strike at the Romans."

Yeshua went to their midst and drew the captains to him. He gave the marching orders and the captains sent their men to make ready. Yeshua gathered in a group the captains and Mariam and me, to discuss strategy. Yeshua asked Thaddaeus Barabbas to tell the others of the caravan and ambush site. When Thaddaeus Barabbas had done that, Yeshua questioned him of what he had learned spying out the land.

Thaddaeus Barabbas told us, "The information I have gathered show that the actual number of soldiers in the army of Herod Antipas are only a few hundred. The Romans are trusted to be officers. The troops under those officers are mercenaries from the lands the Romans rule. Many are from Germania and Galatia. Some are Greeks, some are Cuthites, and the cavalrymen are mostly from the land north of Roman Italia called Thrace. The mercenaries fight for coin and after twenty five years of service to the emperor become Roman citizens. Their homelands were conquered by the Romans and these mercenaries have become dogs to their masters. Herod keeps ten Roman officers and one hundred troops and a turmae of thirty cavalry at his palace in Caesarea Maritama. There is half that number guarding the armory at Zippori. Herod's second capital, at Tiberias, has an officer and twenty troops. There are five officers and fifty soldiers plus a turmae of thirty cavalry at the Fortress Antonia in Jerusalem, mostly to guard the Temple treasury. At Herod's other fortress, Machaerus, there are two officers and only ten soldiers."

Yeshua said, "The Romans rule mostly by threat of force. When Herod travels between his palaces, he has a heavy bodyguard that makes him seem more powerful than he really is. The land, our land, is spread out so the Romans with their few are vulnerable."

James said, "The Romans are only a large force if they invade from Roman Italia."

Yeshua replied, "Yes, but it takes weeks for a message to get to the emperor in Rome and then more time for an invading force to land. By then we will have our defenses set. We will have traps in the harbor to stop their ships. Then we will set fire to their ships with burning arrows soaked in pitch. If they are within range we will use the Roman catapults and fireballs against them. The ones who do get to the beach we will slaughter and paint the sand red with their blood. We will have scouts at the far borders to warn us if they attack by land. That will give us time to set traps for them."

Levi Matthew told us, "If the Romans do come from Italia they must also provide provisions for their army. When Pompey invaded Syria, his army numbered over 30,000 infantry, 7,000 cavalry and 4,000 archers. His army included the thousands of horses for the cavalry, plus a herd of several thousand cattle from Aegyptus to feed all the troops. A Roman army of this size also requires hundreds of wagon loads of grain. Each day a Roman soldier is given three libra of grain to cook his bread. That is enough grain to fill both his cupped hands twice over. Forty thousand soldiers is thus a mountain of grain, given each day. They also require oil of olives, vinegar and wine. His army included those with special skills such as carpenters, cooks, and slaves for the officers. There were men to operate the catapult and other war machines. Also engineers, surgeons and clerks. An army is not just those who fight but those who support the fighters. Make no mistake, the might of the Roman army may be slow to arrive but their endurance for the triumph is legendary."

Simon the Zealot remarked, "You sound as if you admire them."

"Admire? No. Respect? No. See their strengths and abilities? Yes. If we are to be victorious over them we must see who they are. Know this, the Romans rule with the fist of iron all the lands that border the Great Sea. Will they turn the wheel of their army toward us? Yes. Can they be beaten? Yes. But we must make them pay in rivers of blood for their trying. It will take a greater army to beat their army."

Yeshua said, "Levi Matthew speaks the truth. We can free the

Habirum from the Romans. To do so will require the might of the entire land. All Habirum must be warriors. That is why we go about the country recruiting warriors. We must also pick the time and place of our battles. We will lure the enemy into the canyon and we will fight from the high ground. The swiftness of their cavalry will be stopped by the tribulus when we cripple their horses. Their archers will be trapped in burning pitch, and we will flank their infantry and push them into the path of our own archers. And we need weapons. Which brings us to this ambush."

Thaddaeus Barabbas drew a picture in the sand of the ambush site. He described the terrain and the hidden places we would use to lie in wait. We discussed strategy and tactics. Yeshua set the captains their tasks and then we were on the move.

Our war was to begin.

THE RIVER KISHON. MY NAME IS JUDAS ISCARIOT

Yeshua, Barrabas with his three men, and I traveled with Simon the
Zealot and his five men. Yeshua had sent the other captains and their
men out from Gennesaret in separate groups and separate directions
so as to not draw attention to the movement of so many men. Each
captain had handpicked a number of men to join us at the ambush
site, all skilled as archers and as charging fighters.

We traveled through the night. We crossed the Valley Jezreel
to the foothills of Mount Tabor and Mount Carmel where we set
the ambush. In the early morning light Yeshua I were lying in the
shadow of a rocky cleft overlooking the Via Maris Road where it
crossed the River Kishon. Our vantage point on the hillside was
that of the hawk eyeing his prey. The heavy winter rains this year
had washed torrents through the trough, making the road deeper
and rockier than normal. The caravan would have to slow for the
crossing. The Roman road ran northeast from Caesarea Maritama
across the foothills of Carmel Mount, through this pass at Mount
Tabor then north to Zippori. The caravan would not make it to the
garrison at Zippori.

Most Habirum men have a proficiency with the bow and arrow
and the best had been situated around the ambush site. I had an arrow
at the string with brush soaked in pitch lashed to the tip. Yeshua had
the flint and iron in his hand and would strike the spark setting the
brush afire. I would shoot the arrow high which was the signal for
all the archers to unleash their arrows at the Romans and the attack
would begin.

Thaddaeus Barabbas, Simon the Zealot, Yeshua and I had spied
out the caravan the day before. We counted twenty camels loaded
with burdens. There were twenty camel tenders along with their
leader and ten Roman cavalry riding as guards. Simon the Zealot
was hidden in a rocky outcrop overlooking the hill leading down
to the trough. I was checking the men to be sure they were hidden

well when Yeshua nudged me and nodded his head. I saw Simon the Zealot backing away from his hiding spot and signaling to us the caravans approach.

We lay in wait. The caravan appeared at the top of the hill and came down to the ravine. When the caravan was in the ravine, the animals picking their steps carefully through the rocks and the riders and handlers occupied with their tasks, Yeshua struck the flint to my arrow. It flamed. I had the bow already drawn and released the fiery arrow high up into the air. At that instant the archers shot their arrows. Not all the enemy were downed in the first attack as the Romans had their armor of metal breastplates and some arrows missed their targets.

A handful of our men rose from their hiding among the rocks and showed themselves from the top of the ravine. The Romans were seasoned fighters and those not immediately downed from the arrows galloped toward the fighters. Our men turned to run from the charging Romans. When the Romans saw them retreating they spurred their horses to greater effort.

On the ground we had spread dozens of the Roman tribulus. These were the four sided metal spikes that were sized to fit in the palm of the hand. They were made to lay on the ground in such a fashion that the tribulus rested on three of its legs with the fourth pointing up. The Romans called these weapons the iron jagged killing things. The Romans used them over the years to great effect on their foes.

When the charging horses ran to the ground where the tribulus were set some of the horses feet were instantly crippled. Those horses fell, spilling their riders hard to the ground disorienting and slowing them. That was what we were waiting for.

Our warriors came out of hiding and attacked the Romans. Yeshua and I joined them. Our swords were soon wet with Roman blood. The Romans were outnumbered and also now did not have the advantage of being horseback. Other warriors fell on the Roman collaborators. The bloody end came swiftly. We had a few with slight wounds but no casualties. It was a fine start to our quest. Our army now had twenty camel loads of the emperor's weapons to use against Herod, Pontius Pilate, the Roman army, and the emperor's bloody rule over the land of the Habirum.

Yeshua had the arms divided amongst the captains. There were the short and long swords, the javelin, daggers, iron tipped arrows, bows, and shields. There were weapons enough for many warriors. The uninjured horses we took for ourselves. The camels we loosed to run in the wilderness as we did not need the creatures. Before the attack Yeshua had given his orders for our next movement. Now the captains and their men dispersed in the directions according to their orders. We would all meet at the Tir'an Mount where there was a fresh water spring. This was a day's ride from Zippori. The next attack would be on the armory at Zippori. This would be done to deny the Romans their own weapons, and to arm the more of our warriors to free our land from the Romans.

The captains and their men left for Tir'an Mount. Yeshua, Thaddaeus Barabbas, Simon the Zealot, their men and I went another route. We would go east to Nazareth then north to Cana. Mariam, Rachel and her sister, Jehosheba, and the other women had left Gennesaret to go to Cana where we would meet them. It was a half day's journey to the outskirts of Nazareth. I looked forward to seeing my mother and father. I had news for them. I was to be married. I had asked Rachel to be my wife and she had agreed. We would wed in Cana. Our union would be sanctified at the synagogue there before the attack on the armory at Zippori.

NAZARETH. MY NAME IS JUDAS ISCARIOT

We traveled hard, arriving at Nazareth just before sundown. As we came up the hill we could hear voices raised in lamentation, indicating a funeral procession was in progress. Yeshua and I spurred our mules into a run, worried as to who the funeral was for. The women were keening and the men blowing their pipes behind the men carrying the shrouded bundle. They were followed by a crowd of people. Yeshua wailed when he saw his mother at the front of the procession. He jumped from his mule and hurried to her, renting his garments as he ran.

Mary Salome, Yeshua's mother, saw him and fell into his arms. Yosef, she told him, had woken with an ache in his head that morning, complaining of weakness. At midday he had fallen to his knees, clasping his hands to his head. Mary had grabbed ahold of him and helped him to lie down. Mary Salome told Yeshua Yosef's last words were, "My wife. You have done me good and no harm. You are more precious than jewels."

My parents and most of the villagers were in the procession. Yosef had been a respected elder in the village, always willing to help others with their building needs. I joined with them as did Thaddaeus Barabbas, Simon the Zealot and their men. Paying respect and assisting with the burial was a community responsibility. I saw that Yosef's corpse had been wrapped in a clean shroud scented with spices. I regretted not being here to assist with the preparations. I could see that Yeshua was beside himself with grief.

The procession continued to the cliffs at the eastern edge of the village where families had carved tombs into the soft reddish colored rock. Yosef had been a wise man. A sage and believer of the word of ADONAI. He was an honorable man. A fair man. A friend to his neighbors. A good husband. And Yosef had been a good stepfather and teacher to Yeshua. His presence would be missed sorely by all.

Yosef was carried into the tomb. Yosef was laid on the carved stone shelf. There he would rest for a generation and then his bones would be placed in a stone carved ossuary marked with his name to be preserved until ADONAI called him to His home. The funeral was finished and I assisted Yeshua to roll the rocks to block the tomb. Everyone escorted Mary Salome to her home after the service. Yeshua would stay in his home for the seven days of mourning.

I went with my father and mother to our home. I was thankful to find them in good health. We brought food with us and added them to the table for supper. I introduced Simon the Zealot and the other men and they were made welcome at the table. Thaddaeus Barabbas was quiet, saddened by the memory of his wife and stillborn child. My father said the prayers, thanking ADONAI for His blessings and asking for our safety in the quest. The next morning I sent the men to Cana to meet the others and tell them of the delay due to Yosef's death. I waited respectfully for the period of mourning to end and for Yeshua to rejoin us.

The morning after the seven days, I met with Yeshua who told me his mother and stepsister Salome would travel with us on the quest. The other women of the household would stay in Nazareth and be looked after by Yeshua's stepbrothers Simon and Jude. I agreed that his mother and stepsister were now his responsibility and told Yeshua I would be especially vigilant for their safety and see their needs were cared for.

Yeshua and I went about the village, Yeshua approached and talked to the men, seeking warriors to fight the Romans. But the men of Nazareth would shake their heads and not listen to Yeshua. My original impression of the men of Nazareth seeming to disregard Yeshua for some reason, was brought back to my memory. I did not know the reason for their disrespect, except perhaps some of them had fallen to his fists during fights when they were younger.

I was standing to the side of a gathering of village men and heard one saying, "Is not this the tekton, the son of Mary? By what right does he say he will proclaim liberty to the captives and to set at liberty those who are oppressed?"

The fellow standing next to him, a fat man who I didn't recall seeing at Yosef's funeral, replied, "This son of stada, I will listen to no more of his talk. His birth should not have been. The unclean babe should have been left out for the dogs to eat."

I watched the men walk away. The fat man went around a corner and I decided to follow him. I saw him enter a hutment in bad repair. I went to the door and knocked. The man opened the door and looked at me in surprise. "What do you want?"

"I heard what you said. Is there something about this Yeshua that may change my mind about following him?"

"You do not know the truth of this Yeshua?"

"I only know what he has said."

The man beckoned me to enter. The inside of the home was foul with trash and stink. The fat man lived like a swine. The fat man picked up a bowl of beer and drank thirstily, then he belched, loudly and rudely. "You don't know the truth about the mother of this Yeshua, the one whose name is Mary but who is called stada?"

"No. What of her?"

"Mary the stada, fornicated with a Roman soldier. This Yeshua, the one who talks so boldly, is the bastard son of this Roman."

"Do you know the name of this Roman?"

"It is said the Roman's name is Panthera. That is the Roman curse word for the javelin. Panthera." The fat man grabbed his crotch. "So you see, this Panthera stuck the stada with his javelin!" The fat man laughed at his own joke.

I asked, "Mary must have been very young when it happened, just a child. Was it rape or did she go willingly?"

The fat man shrugged, "Yes, it was rape, but who cares? Fornication is fornication, what does it matter how it started. This Yeshua who speaks so boldly is unclean. When the mother's pregnancy showed the truth became known. She was to be stoned and driven from the village to die a whore's death. But that tekton, Yosef, took pity on her and took her for his wife. She screamed birthing the Roman's little bastard. The mother, stada, and the son, are both unclean."

The fat man threw back his head and barked a loud laugh, his mouth open wide, showing me his black rotting teeth. He lifted the beer to his mouth and slurped a mouthful. I took a quick step forward and drove my fist into his fat belly with all my might. He spat out his mouthful of beer, dropped the beer bowl, bent over and careened backwards into the centerpole that held up the roof. The whole shack shook from the collision and brush fell from the roofing. I kicked hard between his legs, crushing the rotten core of him. I smashed his face with my fists. I jerked him to the ground and fell on him, pinning him down. I put the point of my dagger to his eye. He started to yell. I told him, "Shut your fat mouth or I will blind you. Then I will castrate you and you shall be a blind eunuch. They will put you in the Roman brothel. You will be a whore for the Roman soldiers."

The fat man was terrified. I sliced a thin bloody line on his cheek with my dagger, and told him, "Hear this you fat loathsome slug. You will never say these lies about Yeshua again. You will never even utter his name again. Do you hear me? If you ever speak of him again I will know. Then I will come back for you. I will take you out into the wilderness. I will stake you to the ground. I will slit a hole in your fat belly and pull your guts out. You will lie there and watch the wild dogs eat your guts. The dogs will eat your guts and you will die. Then they will eat your stinking carcass and scatter your bones. I will set off a distance and listen to your misery until you are dead." I pushed the point of my dagger under his eyebrow. "Do you understand me?"

The man whimpered, "You are a daemon!"

"Yes, I am your daemon. You will do well to remember me. Do you understand what I have said?"

"Yes. Yes. I will say no more."

I stood and kicked the fat man about his foul body. Then I left the fat man lying there, crying and moaning, in the wreckage of his miserable life.

I saw that Yeshua and the others were preparing to leave the village. I joined them. Now I understood why Yeshua had gone mad that day in Zippori when he saw the Roman soldiers were going to rape that girl. Now I understood why Yosef was Yeshua's stepfather. Now

I understood why the people of Nazareth had always shunned him. Now I understood who his real father was. And now I understood why Yeshua wanted to catch and kill the Roman soldier, Panthera. Lastly, I understood that my friend, Yeshua, must be protected from the foul talk of stupid people. I would protect my friend, Yeshua, with all my strength.

CANA. MY NAME IS JUDAS ISCARIOT

We left Nazareth for Cana. It was about two movements of the sundial to Cana. Yeshua's mother, Mary Salome, rode a donkey as did his stepsister Salome. Yeshua and I each rode mules. Each of us had lead ropes for another mule. One mule carried the possessions the ladies would require. Our weapons were hidden in bundles of straw and hay on the other mule.

We had taken the surviving horses from the Roman soldiers at the ambush. Yeshua sent them with the men to the spring at Tir'an Mount to be hidden until the attack on Zippori. We did not ride the horses on our journey from the ambush to Nazareth and now on to Cana as it would be a provocation to any wandering Roman patrol. The typical villager did not own horses because of the expense of acquiring them and the cost of care including feed. Only the Romans and wealthy Sadducees kept horses. The riding of horses would be questioned by the Romans. The Romans might see it as a call to arms or an indication of collaboration with the Romans. Either one would draw attention to our small group. We did not want any attention, especially since the women were with us. So we used the mules and donkeys. The smart little donkey with the long ears is a steady, patient beast, able to carry its load without complaint, walk all the day, climb the hills and ford the streams, asking no more than a handful of barley in the morning and evening. Of course the horse was faster and more useful for combat than the mule or donkey, and we would soon need the horses we had taken and more.

One day, the words of Ecclesiastes. – *I have seen servants upon horses, and princes walking as servants upon the earth* – would be revealed as surely as the sun rising in the east. The Habirum would be free to travel as they pleased. For far too long the Romans had sat upon their elevated equine roosts as lords, but their time was coming to an end.

Horses from Aegyptus had been forbidden by the Law as given to Moses. – *He shall not multiply horses to himself, nor cause the people to return to Egypt* – because of the temptation to trade with the pharaoh. But King David saw the necessity of warhorses and horse drawn chariots that bowmen could shoot arrows from. King David's son by Bathsheba, Solomon, continued his father's use of the horse. – *Solomon had four thousand stalls for horses and chariots, and twelve thousand horsemen. They brought horses for Solomon out of Egypt, and out of all lands. And he ruled over all the kings –*. Yeshua and I knew we would need war horses to triumph over the Romans. Yeshua was determined to fight the Romans with whatever weapons we would need. We would have horses and chariots, just as King David and Solomon.

Our journey took us north. We arrived at Cana in the morning of the sixth day. We entered the village where we found the women with the men who had accompanied them for protection. They were at lodgings in the town that Mariam had found and organized. Our reunion was joyous, tempered only by the passing of Yosef. The family was now in the mourning period of thirty moons, which was a reentering of the world where prayers are said each day.

All joined for a meeting to discuss the planned weddings of Rachel and myself and the joining together of Thaddaeus Barabbas and Jehosheba. It would be a double wedding with twice the festivities. Mary Salome, the widow of Yosef, insisted that the weddings take place as planned as the joy of our unions would be a balm to her aching heart.

It was now high sun on the sixth day, at sundown the Shabbat would begin and end at the morrow's sundown. At the end of Shabbat the nighttime wedding ceremony would commence. We had a handful of hours left today to make arrangements for the weddings on the morrow's eve, as no such work could be done on Shabbat. The women pitched in to organize the foods. The men gathered the tables and seating for the supper and festivities after the weddings.

In Gennesaret I had gone to Rachel's father to ask his permission to marry his daughter. Her father and mother had joined Yeshua's quest to free the Habirum from the Roman's rule. I had offered the traditional fifty shekels of silver as the marriage price but Rachel's father had refused. He told me, "Love and protect my daughter. Defeat the Romans. And the price is paid. As is written in the Book of Joshua. – *Whoever attacks and captures Kirjath Sepher, to him will I give Achsah my daughter to wife* –. Give my daughter a good life. Give her a life of freedom." Rachel's father was referring to the land in Caanan the tribe of Judah conquered. Yeshua and Thaddaeus Barabbas witnessed my signing the ketubah, the marriage contract, and I and Yeshua witnessed Thaddaeus Barabbas signing his.

After the wedding ceremony there was a week of festivities where each evening the guests would take supper and dance. With two weddings there would be two weeks of festivities pushed together into one week. Thaddaeus Barabbas and I were standing together talking, worrying about the quantities of food and wine and barley beer this would require. Yeshua came to us, smiling "My friends, you look worried. Are you having second thoughts about your upcoming nuptials?"

We explained our concerns, Barabbas saying, "There are only a few jugs of inferior wine to be found in the whole town." Yeshua told us, "Do not concern yourselves with minor details. Both of you have more important things to consider. I have the answer to your dilemma. I shall return."

With that Yeshua turned to leave. Thaddaeus Barabbas said to him, "Shabbat is soon upon us. There can be no work done to gather wine."

Yeshua waved his hand in the air, "Fear not my friends. I shall perform no work. All that I do I am sure ADONAI would approve." The sun touched the horizon as Yeshua mounted a mule and disappeared into the gathering darkness.

Yeshua did not reappear for the rest of that night and had not returned by morning services. Thaddaeus Barabbas and I were talking when Mariam approached. "I have not seen Yeshua since late yesterday. Do you know where he is?"

"He told us he would be back before sunset today," I replied.

"Is there trouble"

This put me in a perplexity. I did not want to cause Mariam undue worry. Thaddaeus Barabbas and I were very concerned as to Yeshua's disappearance and his mission. I had no ready answer to Mariam's question but Thaddaeus Barabbas replied, "Yeshua will return shortly. I am certain of it. He is most capable."

Mariam raised her eyebrows, "I trust you will let me know if I can be of assistance." Then she returned to the brides to assist them in their preparations, of which certain of the activities were limited by Shabbat.

Thaddaeus Barabbas and I fretted the rest of the afternoon. We agreed that we should have accompanied Yeshua to assist in whatever he was up to. When the sun began leaning to the west we discussed organizing a search party. Then there was a yell from someone in the gathering and we turned to see Yeshua riding his mule leading an oxen pulling a wagon. We ran to him and saw the wagon was loaded with a stack of crates and barrels and six carved stone water pots that were sealed at the top with wax.

These stone water pots were used to maintain the purity of the water and were more costly than amphora made of fired clay. The stone water pots were heavy when empty but filled would require a strong man to handle. Each stone pot was cut different, depending on the boulder it was fashioned from, and each could hold more than twenty or more jugs of water, each jug being about the size of a grown man's head. The stone pots were lashed together with rope and had dried moss packed between them for cushion during traveling.

I saw that Yeshua was covered in road dust, and he had dried blood streaked on his tunic. Thaddaeus Barabbas asked if that was his blood. "Are you injured?" I know the difference of wine stain and blood stain but Yeshua shrugged, "That is of no concern. Just call it spilled wine. I am well but thirsty." Yeshua gave Mariam his quick smile, "Hello, Mariam. Would you please pour me a drink of water?"

CANA. MY NAME IS MARIAM OF MAGDALA

I went to the spring to get fresh cool water for Yeshua to drink. I returned to the wagon to hear the men talking. It was still Shabbat so Yeshua insisted that we wait for the sun to set before we unloaded the wagon as there could be no lading of asses. I heard one man say to Yeshua, "But for you to fetch this wagon on the Shabbat is a violation of the law."

Yeshua shook his head and told the man, "If anyone does not provide for his friends and relatives, and especially for members of his household, he has denied the faith and is worse than an unbeliever. It is written. – *Whatever your hand finds to do, do it with all your might. Whether you eat or drink, or whatever you do, do all to the glory of ADONAI –*. So whatever I have done, I have done to provide for my relatives and friends and the glory of ADONAI who, I believe, will not judge me harshly."

The same man said, "Then if there is no violation of the law let us unload while there is still light to see."

Yeshua told him, "We will wait. I will not have you violate the law on my account." Then Mary Salome, Yeshua's mother, touched the man's arm and said kindly to him, "Do whatever he tells you."

Yeshua reached for the pitcher in my hand. "Many thanks for the water, Mariam. I am very dusty and thirsty. First I will wash off the dust." He held the pitcher over himself and poured water over his head, soaking his shoulder length unruly hair, his beard and face. He put the pitcher to his mouth and drank the last swallow, tipping it over to show it was empty.

Looking into the pitcher he remarked, "It is all gone. I need more water. Wait. I will get water from this stone pot." Yeshua reached into the wagon, broke the wax seal, tilted the pot and poured liquid into the jug. He raised the jug to his lips and drank. Lowering the jug he looked closely at it, and then looked at us in wonder. He said, "Now that is very odd. This stone pot was supposed to be filled with water, but it tastes like wine."

I took the jug from his hand and tasted. "Yes, it is wine. The best quality of wine. The best wine will be served first. – *A feast is made for laughter, and wine maketh glad the life* –. Now that we have wine for the festivities, the weddings can commence!"

Yeshua pointed at the sky. "Look. The sun has fallen and there are the three stars." He smiled and turned to the impatient man, "It is a time of joy, my friend. Would you be the first to carry the load?" The man leaped up to the wagon and began wrestling the stone jugs. Yeshua told him, "The wood barrels contain the finest barley beer and the crates have grain for bread, olive oil and fruits and nuts. Oh, yes. My friend, when the load is off, we should get rid of the beast and wagon. Let us make of them a burnt offering sacrifice. The meat will make a tasty stew and the wagon will make fire to light the festivities."

What would happen now was not work but celebration. The two grooms, Judas and Thaddaeus Barabbas, dressed in their finest clothes, were escorted by their parents to the place where their brides resided. There, the parents of the brides, being the same for both brides as they are sisters, presented Rachel and Jehosheba to the grooms. The brides were dressed in fine colorful robes, their faces pretty and radiant.

Judas and Thaddaeus Barabbas each in turn said to the parents of Rachel and Jehosheba, "I came to thy house for thee to give me thy daughter to wife. She is my wife and I am her husband from this day and forever."

Rachel and Jehosheba were asked by their fathers, "Wilt thou go with this man?" and each in turn said to Judas and Thaddaeus Barabbas, "I am for my beloved, and my beloved is for me."

According to custom, Judas and Thaddaeus Barabbas then lowered the veil over the bride's faces. The grooms had seen the face of their brides, and now the veil covered her face, giving her privacy, and this also showed the groom respected his bride's dignity. The bride would hide her face until the ceremony was complete thus showing her man that she was giving herself to him alone.

There was now a throng of people carrying candles, singing and dancing and joyously accompanying the grooms and brides as they moved to the wedding canopy where the nuptials would take place. The wedding canopy symbolized the new home the couples were establishing in the sanctity of marriage.

A wise man, an elder of the community, conducted the ceremonies. "Therefore shall a man leave his father and his mother, and shall cleave unto his wife, and they shall be one flesh. Let thy fountain be blessed. Drink waters out of thine own cistern, and running waters out of thine own well. And have joy of the wife of thy youth. With her love be thou ravished always. And have joy of the husband of thy youth. With his love be thou ravished always."

The men in turn said to their brides, "One who has found a wife has found goodness, and has brought forth favor from ADONAI. I will do my wife good, not harm, all the days of her life. My bread also which I give thee, fine flour, and oil, and honey, wherewith I fed thee. I hold her, and will not let her go. Let her kiss me with the kisses of her mouth, for your love is better than wine. I am for my beloved, and my beloved is for me. She is my wife and I am her husband from this day forevermore."

Rachel and Jehosheba said to their men, "One who has found a husband has found goodness, and has brought forth favor from ADONAI. I will do my husband good, not harm, all the days of his life. With the fine flour you provide I will make bread to dip in the oil and honey. I hold him, and will not let him go. Let him kiss me with the kisses of his mouth, for your love is better than wine. I am for my beloved, and my beloved is for me. He is my husband and I am his wife from this day forevermore."

Then Judas and Thaddaeus Barabbas placed a ring on their brides right index finger, saying "Behold, you are consecrated to me with this ring." Rachel and Jehosheba placed a ring on their husband's right index finger, showing wife and husbands are equal, saying, "Behold, you are consecrated to me with this ring."

Yeshua and I were witnesses for the weddings. I saw Yeshua's smiling face. I was pleased for his happiness. We watched as the brides and grooms were escorted away by the candle holding and singing crowd to their chambers to consummate their vows. The

144

eating and dancing would commence, waiting upon their return after the consummation.

Yeshua and I stood sharing in the warmth and joy of the ceremony and occasion, and in the candlelit darkness of the night, our hands found each other. We turned to each other. Yeshua put his arms over my back and I circled his waist with my arms. We stood looking at each other, smiling and, perhaps, anticipating.

Yeshua said to me, "Sweet is thy voice. Thy countenance is comely. Thy lips are like a thread of scarlet."

ZIPPORI. MY NAME IS JUDAS ISCARIOT

After the week of celebration, we got back on the move to organize the warriors to free the Habirum from the Romans. We needed two more captains to make the twelve tribes. Yeshua was determined to find those two from the land of Judah. As he said to us, "The entire land must be rid of Romans for all of the land to be free. – *Moses said, If ye will arm yourselves to go before ADONAI to the war, and every armed man of you will pass over the Jordan until he hath driven out his enemies from before him, then this land shall be unto you for a possession before ADONAI –*. We must unite the northern and southern tribes as in the days of King David and Solomon."

We left Cana at the ending of the next Shabbat after observing the week of festivities of the wedding ceremonies. Simon Zealot, his warriors, and the other men who had been with us in Cana, went directly to the spring at Tir'an Mount. Yeshua and I, with the women, struck due east to the town of Magdala to deliver them to a safe place. The town is on the west shore of the sea of Chinnereth. Mariam's family was there and she could rely on them for any assistance she and the other women might require. She would arrange quarters for the women to await our return.

We went to the spring at Tir'an Mount after leaving Magdala where we would meet the others. There we would prepare for the raid on the armory at Zippori. From the armory we would get weapons for our warriors. Yeshua and I had not been back to Zippori since the day he appeared at the fountain after his exile in the wilderness. Thaddaeus Barabbas had left Cana to go directly to Zippori to spy out the land. Upon our arrival at the spring at Tir'an Mount, we met with Thaddaeus Barabbas who had returned from Zippori. Thaddaeus Barabbas gave us the information he had acquired on his scouting mission

The tetrarch, Herod Philip, the half-brother of Herod Antipas, had arrived at the Zippori palace of Herod Antipas for a visit. Herod

Philip ruled for Rome the area east of the sea of Chinnereth and the River Jordan south to Bethabara and north to Caesarea Philippi. This is the lands of Iturea, Gaulanitis, Auranitis, Trachonitis and Batanea. Most of this country was rocky arid hills and ravines. Only at the western edge of this land where the River Jordan flowed south from Lake Merom and along the east coast of the sea of Chinnereth was the land fit to live in. Herod Philip had a modest palace at the town of Caesarea Philippi. Herod Philip's lands were not rich with resources and trade as was the Galilee that Herod Antipas ruled. Most of his land was forlorn and – *Utterly empty and utterly plundered* – as my father had used the words of Isaiah to describe it from his travels as a young man.

One particular tribe of this region, the Itureans, relied on hunting to survive and were excellent archers. They were also dishonorable thieves and mercenaries, warriors for hire, loyal only to the buyer with the most coin to pay. Those with the most coin were the Romans. Herod Philip ruled the land for the Romans using his mercenaries, the Itureans.

Yeshua asked Thaddaeus Barabbas what was the number of Romans and Itureans with Herod Philip in Zippori. "There are five Romans on horseback with lance and twenty of the Itureans on foot. They lead five mules laden with taxes for the Romans and gifts for the brother, Herod Antipas."

"How long do they stay in Zippori?"

"I was told by a man who works for the Sadducee merchant who supplies the garrison with food that they are to increase the amount delivered by a half for another moon."

"And before these arrivals, how many Romans in the garrison?"

"Thirty Roman cavalry and twenty foot soldiers."

"So now there are seventy five of the sons of dogs at the garrison. We must rethink our plan."

Around the fire that night we discussed the untimely arrival of Herod Philip and his men. Our group were all seasoned warriors who had killed Romans and who were ready to kill more, but the doubling of the Roman forces made the attack less likely to succeed. Yeshua said the delays caused by the mourning for Yosef and the marriages of myself and Barabbas plus the time required to travel to Magdala and return were not to trouble us. Yeshua told us the opportunity to strike will come again. "Our eventual success means that – *So shall thy barns be filled with plenty, and thy vats shall overflow with new wine –*. We must be patient and attack on our terms, not giving the Romans any advantage."

Yeshua said we needed a place where the entire group could comfortably and safely camp. Barrabas suggested we move everyone east, to the land beyond the River Jordan, in the area called Decapolis. This land was a confederation of ten cities that were awarded some autonomy by Rome. Yeshua said this would put us far from the reach of Herod Antipas while we made the final arrangements for the strike against the Romans.

I told them I knew that area well. I had been to Kerioth in the Wilderness of Kedemoth many times to visit my father's people. I sketched a map in the dirt, showing a hilly region with a natural spring that flowed down to feed the River Arnon. "The hill has good views of any approaching forces. It is heavily forested with steep sides, being easily defended, and grows good grasses for the animals. It is about a three day horse ride east of Jerusalem."

Yeshua told us this would be a good central location. "The time is drawing near. The might of righteousness is with us, as ADONAI said unto Joshua – *Tomorrow will I deliver them up. Thou shalt have their horses, and burn their chariots with fire –*. We need supplies. We will attack a convoy, then move to the camp right away."

ON THE VIA MARIS ROAD TO ZIPPORI.
MY NAME IS JUDAS ISCARIOT

In the middle of the darkest hour, the moon and stars were obscured by the thick roiling clouds which promised a much needed rainfall in this desperately arid region. Tonight there would be more revolt against Roman rule and more Roman dead.

"A rain would be good," said Yeshua to me in a whisper. Yeshua and I stood together in the dark shadows of a cliff. Yeshua was covered by a dark cloak of rough material, his face hidden by the hood of the cloak. He turned to look behind him and to the sides as he marked the locations of our men, myself next to him, and another two dozen spread out and cleverly hidden in the shadows.

The enemy, the Romans and the Roman collaborators, had pitched camp for the night beside the road. Yeshua and I both turned our attention to a sudden movement on the outskirts of the camp as two wild dogs fought over a piece of rubbish in a pile of trash. The dominant beast sent the other scurrying, licking its wounds. The winner of the fight took the rancid meat in its jaws and ran in the other direction.

Yeshua and I looked at our quarry. A Roman soldier was on guard, watching over the camel train. The guard stopped walking. He watched the dog fight, then resumed his patrol. The camels were lying down and one, a mare, had a calf resting against her side. The market goods were stacked on the ground in crates and baskets. There was a large quantity of foods, wine, and other items. At sunrise the camels would be reloaded and the convoy continue on to Zippori. A few yards away from the camels the men were sleeping on the ground. These were Roman soldiers who were not on watch and the camel tenders and the caravan's leader. These men were all enemy, Roman soldiers and the despised Roman collaborators. We had the enemy marked, all of their numbers and positions carefully targeted, and now it was time to begin.

We watched as the Roman guard reached the end of his patrol near the sleeping men and then turned to walk back the other direction, right to us. Now the guard was in range at the end furthest from the sleeping men. I had my bow in hand, an arrow fitted to the string. Drawing the bow to full stretch I took careful aim. The Roman guard walked into the killing field. I released the arrow and it found its target. The arrow went in the guard's chest, the velocity pushing the arrow all the way through. The arrow came out the guard's back between his shoulder blades, a mortal wound. The guard gasped. He fell to his knees and placed his hands over the arrow's end, as if he were caressing the feathers that gave the arrow its true flight. He stared at the end of the arrow for a moment then lifted his head, looking into the darkness as if attempting to divine its origin. Even at a distance and in the darkness I could see the look of shock on his face.

Yeshua blended into the night in his dark cloak. He ran out silently and with a strong swing of his razor sharp sword removed the guards head from his shoulders. Now the others came out of the shadows and fell on the sleeping men with swords and spears. In just moments, with hardly any noise, the Romans and collaborators were all dead. Yeshua walked over and raised his hand in the air. Everyone stopped and listened to the night. There was no alarm, all was quiet. Yeshua lowered his arm. All clear. The horses and mules were brought up and the booty loaded. We moved away into the night, leaving the dead men on the bloody ground. Then the rain began, washing the blood into the sandy soil.

RAKKATH. MY NAME IS MARIAM OF MAGDALA

Yeshua, Judas, and Barrabas, with their trusted men, arrived at the dawn. Our reunion was sweet. They came to Magdala to get me and the rest of our people. Yeshua said we were all going to the place of our new encampment. We straightaway left Magdala. We traveled in the dress and manner of fishermen and laborers with their women. The weapons were hidden under fishing nets and sheaves of straw strapped to mules.

We journeyed south along the west coast of the sea of Chinnereth. Herod Antipas, in his arrogance and ignorance, renamed this body of water Lake Tiberias, to honor the Roman emperor Tiberius. Only the Romans and the Sadducees called it that. The true Habirum, the Pharisees and Essenes, call it Chinnereth. The Greeks call it the sea of Galilaías. In this land of conflicting peoples, even the name of a large lake was a point of contention.

We arrived at the town of Rakkath, or Tiberias as the Romans called it, in the morning before the high sun. Rakkath was once a fortified town of the Naphtali tribe, as told in the Book of Joshua. The town was captured, razed to rubble, and burnt to ash by Nebuchadnezzar II. It lay desolate for many generations, unused because of the multitude slaughtered there by Nebuchadnezzar, their bodies weathering into the soils. This made it unclean and no Habirum would walk the ground. The father of Herod Antipas, Herod the Imudean, decided the mineral hot springs could be used for soaking and healing, so he had his Sadducee priests call upon ADONAI to bless it. Herod the Imudean built a palace and fort atop the ruins, making the town another of his strongholds. The Romans used the springs of Tiberius as a spa. Herod Antipas dedicated the town to the Roman emperor, further showing his abject subservience to his Roman masters.

We passed outside the town walls to avoid the cursed land. The town had outgrown its walls, being heavily populated with Romans and Sadducee. The market was now so large it continued outside the walls and we had to go through it to get past the town. The merchants in the market sold the usual items and there were also stalls that specialized in the types of meats the Romans ate as delicacies. One could see this was a Roman town from the displayed meat of the unclean swine. I saw pig's feet soaking in pickled brine, blood sausages, strips of sliced bellies and thick haunches. There were jars full of live whiskered dormice. This filthy creature would be drug, alive, through a batter of wet flour, then dropped in boiling grease and fried. It would be eaten whole, held by the tail and biting the crispy revolting thing off at the end of the stiff fried tail. I saw clay pots filled with salted water, swirling with swimming eels and the floating gonads of sea urchins. There were dead birds of all types hanging from strings and one merchant sold the long maggot looking tongues of the flamingo bird. I saw the brains of lambs, the testicles of rams, the vulva of the ewe, the teats of heifers, and the wombs of sows. The Romans used all parts of a beast in their banquets. The Sadducee, even though claiming to be Habirum, were lined up with the Romans to trade coin for these hideous foods.

There were men and women from the desert lands of Arabah at the market. The men with their chest length beards were dressed in long tunics and colorful robes with turbans on their heads. The women were completely covered from head to foot in plain dark colored robes. How the women could see to walk was a mystery. They were haggling with merchants over the price of the camel's foot. This revolting meat, which they considered a delicacy, was sickening just to look at. The Arabah's worshipped the god they called Ahura Mazda who was the overlord of lesser gods they also held in thrall. They deified the daemons called gallu who were the devils of their underworld, and they used sorcerers to ward off or call the invisible djinn. Their gods and their worship was a baffling mystery, as I suppose ours is to them. If I had one wish, it would be for all the people to embrace the compassion, common sense, rational thought and humanism taught by the Goddess Isis. But as the philosopher says, wishes, like miracles, are few and far between.

Passing through the market place, seeing and smelling this repulsive collection of unclean foods, made me break in a sweat and become faint. It was with relief when we finally made our way past the crowded aisles to the fresh air beyond the town.

Habirum of the Pharisees and Essenes ate a simple diet of breads from wheat and barley. We used the oil of olives and ate honey and nuts, the fruit of figs, grapes, olives, pomegranates, and dates. We prepared dishes of fish but only those with fins and scales. – *Whatsoever hath no fins nor scales in the waters that is a detestable thing unto you* –. Meat, usually goat, lamb and mutton, was cooked for special occasions. We ate lentils, fava beans and chickpeas for endurance and strength of muscle, we grew various vegetables and herbs and gleaned wild plants from the fields. Since clean water was difficult to find unless one was near a flowing spring, we used yayin, the fermented juice of grapes to drink and satisfy thirst.

We had gone a few paces past the town's southern gate when I heard someone calling my name. I turned to see a woman, a veil covering her face. As she came nearer she pulled aside her veil and I saw it was my friend, Joanna. I had known Joanna since we were both young girls, having grown up on the same street in Magdala. Joanna was Pharisee of the tribe of Zebulun. Joanna had been a stunningly beautiful girl and was still beautiful, though I saw some grey strands in her hair. It struck me suddenly that Joanna and I were both in our thirty five years of age. The time had passed so quickly! Joanna had been courted by the son of an influential man, a knowledgeable and respected scribe. The son's name was Chuza. He had been trained to also be a scribe, like his father.

I was surprised and happy to see my dear friend. Our greeting was joyous. Joanna told me she was the mother of two children, which was another mark of the passage of time. I asked her, "Does your husband still serve as house steward to Herod Antipas?"

Yeshua raised his eyebrows at the mention of the tetrarch's name.

Joanna replied, "Yes. He is at Zippori, due to return here after the next Shabbat. We will winter here then we go to Jerusalem for the Passover festival. What are you doing in Tiberias?"

I had not seen Joanna for many years. Her mother had raised Joanna in the belief of Isis and she and I shared many good memories. But she had been near to the court of Herod Antipas for most of her married life. I wasn't sure of her thoughts on the usurper. Before I told her of our journey I first sought to rest my mind concerning her loyalties. "How has life in the royal court treated you?"

A sour look came across Joanna's face. She looked at the ground and shook her head. "I would give my life to bring my family away from the Imudean and his Roman masters. My husband is kind to me and patient with our children but we rarely see him. Herod Antipas is greedy with my husband Chuza's time. Herod is like a covetous, insecure wife. Herod is jealous of even his loyal steward's wife. Chuza is at Herod's beck and call the whole day and even during the night hours."

"Is it true what I hear, that Herod Antipas is petitioning the Roman Caesar Tiberius for the lands that had been given to his brother, Herod Archelaus?"

Joanna told me, "Yes. Since the Romans exiled Herod Archelaus and made Judah a Roman province, Herod Antipas has coveted that territory. Herod Antipas is a greedy swine. May his death be as painful as his fathers was."

It was known throughout the land that the father, Herod I, had been eaten from the inside by worms, suffering for years. He was a cruel man to begin with and then the pain had rendered him completely insane. He had his wife, his wife's mother, and three of his sons executed. None of the Roman medicine men had been able to cure him of the worms and the treatments of the heathen magicians fared no better. It was said that Herod I feared no one would mourn his death, so before his end he had ordered that a group of distinguished men be brought to his palace and executed at the time of his passing. He thought this would cause the sounds of mourning he craved.

I was comfortable with Joanna now, hearing and seeing her disdain for the employer of her husband. I felt she could be trusted. I introduced her to Yeshua. We were standing under the shade of a grove of olive trees. Yeshua and the others gathered around us. I placed my hand on Yeshua's shoulder. "Joanna, this is my friend, Yeshua."

"Yeshua! I have heard tales of your healing. I am pleased to meet you."

Yeshua smiled, "Joanna, it is my pleasure to meet you. Mariam is the healer. All I know I have learned from her. It is Mariam's knowledge and skills that make the healing miracles you have heard of. Not I."

I told Joanna, "If you want to free your husband of the demands of Herod Antipas, perhaps Yeshua may be able to help you."

BEIT SHE'AN. MY NAME IS JUDAS ISCARIOT

We journeyed south on the Roman road Via Maris with a fine view of the sea of Chinnereth on our left. This far south, where the sea of Chinnereth once more joins the River Jordan, both shores became high cliffs looking out over the water. We came to the ruins of the abandoned town of Tarichæa.

For generations Tarichæa had been a thriving port city. But over half a hundred years before, the Roman governor of Syria, named Gaius Cassius Longinus, had attacked it. He destroyed it and took thirty thousand Habirum into slavery. Now, a natural gully led down to the shore and this was where the few residents lived, making their living by fishing from the boats we could see spread over the waters.

This Roman, Gaius Cassius Longinus, was the leader of the assassins who had murdered their emperor, the one called Caesar Julius. The Roman sons of dogs were those who – *Eat the flesh of their sons and the flesh of their daughters, and they shall eat every one the flesh of his friend* – and they will be punished by Yeshua's army of the Habirum for their greed and sins. I will be at Yeshua's side to witness their destruction.

Our next stop would be the town of Beit She'an, called Scythopolis by the Greeks, where we would take shelter for the night. We traveled from the high sun hour to the hour for supper. We took rooms where we would rest. While eating we discussed whether this town may have anyone we could recruit but decided against it. This town had a large Roman population as it was on the important trade route from the Great Sea to Damascus. It was the only town of the Decapolis on the west side of the River Jordan.

The town, in generations past, had been an Aegyptus fortress ruled by the pharaoh who allowed the Canaanites some freedom. Then it passed through several hands being conquered by the Assyrians, then the Persians, then the Greeks, then freed for the Habirum by the great fighters of the Maccabees. It was now in Roman control.

Yeshua told us, "We will have to secretly bring a large number of fighters into the city gates before they close at dusk and take this town from within. They have strong walls, able to withstand an attack. Judas, after we eat we will walk about and take the measure of the defenses. We will hold the information for the day of our future attack. In the meantime we will sojourn and make our camp in the land of the Decapolis."

This town, Beit She'an, where we rested for the night, was the place where King Saul's decapitated body had been hung from the walls after he was defeated by the Philistines at the battle of Mount Gilboa. When Saul and three of his sons were defeated, it was a dark time for the Habirum. It was the valiant men of the tribe of Benjamin who in the dark night hours had braved the sentinels and archers on the walls and retrieved Saul's body.

In previous times the other eleven tribes had decimated the tribe of Benjamin slaying the men, women, and children down to the last six hundred warriors. This was done as a revenge for the gang rape of a woman of the tribe of Levi. Six hundred of the last warriors of the tribe of Benjamin hid in a cave at the rock of Rimmon for four months to escape the vengeance and certain death in the war. For their dedication to Saul, even in his death, by rescuing his body, the other eleven tribes agreed to assist those six hundred warriors to rebuild their tribe. As a reward, these last warriors of the tribe of Benjamin had been spared. Then the other eleven tribes attacked the city of Jabesh-Gilead. The attackers killed all the men in the city of Jabesh-Gilead, as told in Judges. – *Go and smite the inhabitants of Jabesh-gilead with the edge of the sword. And this is the thing that ye shall do, ye shall utterly destroy every male, and every woman that hath lain by man. And they found among the inhabitants of Jabesh-gilead four hundred young virgins, that had not known man by lying with him, and they brought them out* – as a gift to the six hundred warriors of Benjamin.

There were still two hundred of the warriors without a woman, so, as they were told in Judges. – *Behold, there is the feast of ADONAI from year to year in Shiloh. Go and lie in wait in the vineyards. Behold, if the daughters of Shiloh come out to dance in the dances, then come ye out of the vineyards, and catch you every man his wife of the daughters of Shiloh and go to the land of Benjamin –*. Thus was every warrior of the tribe, the last six hundred, allowed a wife to take into their home.

The next morning we left Beit She'an going east into the land beyond the Jordan. We did not use the bridge on the Roman road leading to Pella so we could avoid the tax collector at the toll. At a spot north of the bridge we crossed the River Jordan at an unused ravine called Cherith. This was the place where Elijah sojourned during the drought he prophesied, that would be the punishment of Ahab for the worship of ADONAI's wife, the queen of heaven, Asherah. – *And the word of ADONAI came unto him, saying, Get thee hence, and turn thee eastward, and hide thyself by the brook Cherith, that is before the Jordan –*.

RABBAH. MY NAME IS JUDAS ISCARIOT

After crossing the River Jorden we went through the back country until we came to the Old Caravan Road leading south and east. We journeyed all the day, making camp as the sun leaned to the west in a high spot off the roadway for privacy and security. The next morning we were up early and continued the journey until we came to the town of Gadarenes at the junction of the River Jabbok and the King's Highway. To the far south on the King's Highway was the land of the annihilated Nabateans and their city of Petra carved from the sheer face of the mountain cliff. If one traveled north on the King's Highway, it would lead to Damascus in the land of the Syrians.

Our destination would be the town of Rabbah, two days ride south of the river. Rabbah was known as the City of Waters. It sits on a high bluff overlooking the River Jabbok. This was in the land formerly of the Ammonites. The mother of Ben-Ammi was Lot's youngest daughter, the father being Lot himself, and so Ben-Ammi was conceived in incest. Ben-Ammi was the first of the Ammonites tribe.

This town had many fresh water springs that fed the river below. We were about a three days ride east of the River Jordan. In the days of King David, Rabbah had been besieged and overthrown. As it is told by Ezra, in the Book of Chronicles. – *And David took the crown of Malcam from off his head, and found it to weigh a talent of gold, and there were precious stones in it, and it was set upon David's head, and he brought forth the spoil of the city, exceeding much. And he brought forth the people that were therein, and cut them with saws, and with harrows of iron, and with axes. And thus did David unto all the cities of the children of Ammon –.*

Rabbah had been taken from the Habirum by the Assyrians, who were then defeated by the Greeks under the rule of the one called Ptolemy Philadelphus. Ptolemy married his older sister, Arsinoe II. These two were known as the Philadelphoi, which means lover of a sibling. He had renamed the town of Rabbah to Philadelphia to honor his sister.

We traveled for two days before we arrived at the inn where we would take shelter for the night. The clean rooms were a welcome sight. Yeshua, Barrabas and I with Mariam, Rachel and Jehosheba were sitting by the fire taking our leisure after supper. Yeshua asked Mariam and me, "Remember when I spoke to each of you concerning the Nephilim of the Book of Genesis?"

I shook my head and mumbled to myself, "Oh, no. Here we go." Yeshua will tell one of his wild stories that will frighten the women and probably give them the troubling dreams. I attempted to interrupt his chain of thought, "Yeshua, pass over that flask of wine and be of good cheer." He took the flask in hand and while passing it to me Mariam said, "Yes. I have thought over what you said then. Why do you speak of it now?"

"ADONAI spoke unto Moses. – *When thou comest nigh over against the children of Ammon, harass them not, nor contend with them, for I will not give thee of the land of the children of Ammon for a possession, because I have given it unto the children of Lot, the Rephaim and Zamzummim, a peoples great, and many, and tall as the Anakim* –. So, I ask you. Who was ADONAI speaking of when he says the Rephaim, Zamzummim, and the Anakim? Could ADONAI be speaking to Moses of those who came first, who came before the time we know? Could they be the ones who came from the place beyond the stars?"

Barrabas said, "What is this you speak of?"

I said, "The Ammonites were enemy of the Habirum having denied them passage through the land during the Exodus and then joined forces with the Assyrians and the Moabites against the Habirum. As it is told in Joshua and Amos. – *Now these are the kings of the land, whom the children of Israel smote, and possessed their land. So will I kindle a fire in the wall of Rabbah, and it shall devour the palaces thereof, with shouting in the day of battle, with a tempest in the day of the whirlwind, And their king shall go into captivity, he and his princes together* –. Any tales of times before that are just that, strange tales, to conjure up unknown spirits of the imagination."

Yeshua looked at me with a grin of mischief on his face. "Judas is a practical man. He will not entertain any thoughts not grounded in the dirt of the earth. Perhaps Judas is right. Perhaps tales of those from beyond the nighttime stars have no place here in this cozy room made for relaxing and talk among friends."

Barrabas laughed, "Horse apples! Tell us a story!"

And with that encouragement, Yeshua was off. "I will tell you of the wonders of the Aegyptus gods, but first," he told us, "We will prepare ourselves for the awakened dreams. This will enable your mind to see further and to know the unknown." He took from his pouch of pharmacopeia a clay vial with a carved wood stopper. From the vial he shook out a portion of the dried green herb Kannabaeus into his pipe. Yesterday, at the river's edge, I had seen Yeshua walking through and inspecting a patch of reeds. He had taken several of the reeds, now he selected one from the bundle. He told us, "Breathe this and hold it in your lungs as long as you can." He lit his pipe with a coal from the fire and turned the pipe around so the stem was inside the reed. He put the bowl in his fist, then his fist against his lips. He blew into the bowl making the smoke pass through the reed. The smoke had cooled by the time it reached the end of the reed, making it easy to breathe in. Taking turns we all inhaled the smoke into our lungs. My skeptical hesitation soon turned into a feeling of relaxed peacefulness, a clarity of vision, and a new awareness.

Until the late hour we listened to Yeshua telling tales of the Watchers in Enoch, and the Nephilim in the Book of Genesis. Yeshua told how the Watchers saw that the daughters of men were comely and how the Watchers lay with the daughters of men and made babies called Nephilim. The women were shocked by the thought of the Watchers taking and laying with the daughters of men. Shocked to their core! – *The Nephilim were in the earth in those days, and also after that, when the sons of God came in unto the daughters of men, and they bore children to them, the same were the mighty men that were of old, the men of renown* –.

Yeshua said in Aegyptus he had seen carved onto the stones of the monuments unexplainable pictures. The pictures were of strange beings that were not people but not creatures of the natural wild either. They were something else. The Aegyptus people said the strange beings came from the sky, riding chariots of fire. These beings had miraculous powers they used to build the monuments. They used a sword that shot a streak of lightning bright as the sun to cut through rock like a hot knife cuts through butter. Their powers enabled them to lift the huge blocks of stone on a cushion of air. Yeshua told us, "I have climbed on the stones to the top of the monuments. The monuments are higher than the Temple! Some of the stones are bigger than this building! Enoch tells us the Aegyptus people acquired knowledge and learned skills from the Nephilim. Some knowledge was good and some was bad. ADONAI punished the Nephilim for teaching people the bad things."

Yeshua asked us, "Who were the babes of the Watchers and daughters of men? Could some of the Nephilim be called Rephaim and Zamzummim? Could they be the giants, the Anakim? When the archangels destroyed the Nephilim in the war between the sons of light and the sons of darkness, was all of their knowledge and skills lost? What about the angels in the Book of Enoch? Are they still among us? If we know the right words, can we summon the angels? – *Behold, I send an angel before thee. If thou shalt indeed hearken unto his voice then I will be an enemy unto thine enemies, and an adversary unto thine adversaries* –. Will the angels go before us as in a storm and cut down the Romans with their swords of lightning?"

The fire had burned down to red coals, emphasizing the darkness beyond its light. The air had the night chill. Yeshua, with his eyes wide open and looking like a seer divining the mysterious, asked us, "We are in the old kingdom of Og. We are told that Moses destroyed Og of the Rephaim. Og was a giant. – *Behold, his bedstead was a bedstead of iron. Nine cubits was the length thereof, and four cubits the breadth of it* –. Were all of the Watchers and Nephilim and Anakim destroyed? Did Og lay with the daughters of men and have babes, children who were uncounted by the sons of light? Babies who survived the war? Do some of them, perhaps still walk among us?"

Rachel was sitting close to me, gripping my arm. I felt a shiver run through her. Everyone set quietly for a moment, spellbound by the wonder of Yeshua's story.

Suddenly Barrabas laughed, "Horse apples!" And he added wood to the fire, lighting the room and chasing the chill away.

Yeshua, I had to admit, could spin a story. A story that could make one wonder, what was the reality? What was the real truth of the world we think we know?

Mariam said, "I have been thinking on this since we first discussed it. I wonder why ADONAI allowed Asherah to be denied by the Habirum? Was she not the queen of heaven? Was she not the wife of ADONAI?"

Jehosheba said, "Yes. ADONAI and Asherah were brought back from the exile in Babylon by Ezra. Why has she been forgotten by our people?"

Mariam told us, "It is said in Jerimiah. – *Offer unto Asherah, the queen of heaven, and pour out drink offerings unto her, for then had we plenty of food, and were well, and saw no evil. But since we let off to offer to the queen of heaven, and to pour out drink offerings unto her, we have wanted all things, and have been consumed by the sword and by the famine* –. And I wonder, could it be that Isis and Asherah are one and the same? In the beginning, if all was made by ADONAI, of which men are the image, did not ADONAI need an Asherah of which women are the image? Has the name of Asherah changed through time, becoming Isis?"

Rachel reached out and took a stick from the fire. She lifted the burning end up like a signal flame. "The messenger of ADONAI, the angel, spoke to Daniel. – *His face as the appearance of lightning, and his eyes as torches of fire* –. Why are the messengers described as lightning and fire and their chariots blazing? Is the magic of fire the breath of ADONAI?"

We talked through the night, seeking answers to mysteries that are truly unknowable.

THE DECAPOLIS. MY NAME IS
MARIAM OF MAGDALA

The stories of the miracle healer, the one called Yeshua, had spread amongst the people all the way to the land of the Decapolis. That Greek word, Decapolis, means ten cities and those cities were allowed a measure of independence by Rome. Of these ten cities the town of Rabbah was the largest and most prosperous. The town was situated on the King's Highway and north of the Joppa Road that ran west to the shore of the Great Sea and east to the ruins of Bozrah in the land of the Edomites. As told by Jeremiah. *−Bozrah shall become an astonishment, a reproach, a waste, and a curse for their worship of Qaus, the Imudean god of the Edomites −*.

The morning after the night of our arrival there was a group of people waiting outside for Yeshua, seeking the healer. A man was holding a child in his arms and the mother was standing next to him holding the child's hand. The parents of this child told Yeshua the child was deaf and could not speak words. They begged Yeshua to place his hand on him. Yeshua beckoned them to follow him into the courtyard of the inn.

Yeshua sat down and the father handed the child to him. With the child in his lap he asked, "How old is the child and how long has he suffered from this ailment?"

The boy's father said the child had recently turned two years. He never had seemed to hear sounds and had never been able to form words. The mother sat quietly with tears on her face. Yeshua waved his hand in front of the child's eyes to get his attention. The child was looking at Yeshua and Yeshua snapped his fingers next to the child's ears. The child did not respond. Yeshua spoke to the child, and again, he just sat looking up at Yeshua. Yeshua then lifted the child, putting the child's face directly in front of his own. Yeshua said loudly, "BOO!" and made a comical face, smiling and laughing. The child blinked his eyes as if startled then smiled and laughed his own self.

Yeshua said to me, "The child may not hear or speak but he does not seem to be deficient in his mind. He knows humor and can laugh."

I leaned in and inspected the child closely. "Turn his ears to the light of the sun so that I may see inside." It was then I saw the child had wax clogging his ears. "The child cannot make words for he has never heard anyone speak words. His ears are blocked with wax."

I told Yeshua, "Place your throat against his ears and sing. I will watch his face for his reaction. If he has no reaction then he may suffer from an injury of the brain. If he does react, then the tissue in the ear that creates sounds most likely works. The problem then is that sounds cannot get past the blockage to the inner ear."

Yeshua lifted and turned the child so his ear was directly against Yeshua's throat. Then Yeshua began to sing a melody to a lively tune, "ADONAI is a man of war, ADONAI is His name. Pharaoh's chariots He cast into the sea and dasheth the enemy," ending the last word on a high note, stretching the sound EEEEEE out for long moments.

As I watched the child's eyes opened wide, he seemed to be listening or sensing the vibrations. His mouth opened and the noise EEEEEE came from his throat. "He hears. It is the wax blocking the sounds. Let us treat him with the tincture of garlic boiled in the fermented juice of the wheat grains."

Yeshua said to me, "Yes. I remember we have spoken of this. Let us heal this child."

I got a pan of heated water from the cook at the inn. I soaked a clean rag in the hot water. I placed two drops of the tincture in each of the child's ears. I wrung the water from the rags and covered his ears with the warm rags. I massaged the child's ears in a circular motion while Yeshua pointed at himself and opened and closed his jaws as if he were chewing. Yeshua took the child's chin and got the child to mimic his face movements. The cook brought more warm water. I reheated the rags and continued the massaging. Yeshua continued the jaw movements while making comical faces, getting the child to join in the game. Then I held the child while Yeshua took a mouthful of warm water and blew it through his lips forcefully into the child's ears. Taking a clean rag I dried and cleaned his ears of the dissolved wax and splattered water.

Then Yeshua snapped his fingers by his ears and the child jumped and looked to both sides. Yeshua turned the child's face so the child was looking directly at him. Yeshua said loudly, "Ephphatha!" At this, the boy's ears were opened, his tongue was loosened, and he began to speak sounds, not whole words but at least speaking.

Yeshua told the boy's parents, "Since he will be really hearing for the first time, he does not know how to speak words correctly. You must be patient and talk with him and teach him the words. He seems to have a bright mind and will learn quickly with your help."

I told them, "Watch his ears carefully. If the wax begins to build then heat a rock in the fire, wrap it in leather and cloth, and hold it near his ears to warm and melt the wax. Wipe the melted wax away from the ear passage. But be careful to not stick anything in his ears. Do not puncture the ears nor introduce any unclean water, dirt, or foreign matter."

The mother was hugging the boy to her breast, crying tears of joy. The father was telling Yeshua he would bring him all the produce of his garden for payment. Yeshua told the man he owed no payment, but he commanded them not to talk to anyone of this healing. I knew Yeshua was trying to keep our presence in this land quiet, so we could make an encampment without worrying about the Romans. The man, his wife and child left, blessing Yeshua and me for our kindness.

During the day more came for the healer. Everyone was talking about the healer. His fame went throughout all the land. The people were saying that those brought to him, sick people with diseases and torments, those that were lunatik and possessed with devils, and those that had the palsy, he healed. People were overwhelmed with amazement. "He has done everything well," they said. "He even makes the deaf hear and the mute speak." Yeshua was kind to all but worried this would draw attention to our group. He instructed those he healed to not say any word concerning him. But the more he healed the more they kept talking.

All the captains came to Rabbah to meet before we moved to the place of our new encampment. At the end of the day, Yeshua called us all together to give instructions for the next steps in our fight against the Romans. We gathered in our room for privacy. Yeshua told them, "We are near the time to make war against the Romans. As it says in Joshua. – *And they smote all the souls that were therein with the edge of the sword, utterly destroying them. There was none left that breathed –.* And then we shall see our victory. But our victory does not begin and end with ridding the land of the Romans. For our victory to be complete we must bring to the land the words of Isaiah. – *And of peace there be no end. Through justice and through righteousness, from henceforth forever –* and that is our covenant with ADONAI."

Levi Matthew stood and said to all, "As ADONAI said to Abraham. – *And I will establish My covenant between Me and thee and thy seed after thee throughout their generations –.* Our leader, Yeshua, is as King David, bringing strength and unity to the land. I say we should make Yeshua king of Israel and Judah and leader of all the Habirum."

Yeshua shook his head. "I will not wear the crown. It is only freedom for our people I seek. You shall each be head of a tribe, the new twelve tribes of the land of the Habirum of Israel and Judah. But neither shall you be kings. There will be no king. All will be equal."

Levi Matthew insisted, "We must have a king!"

"No. It is written. Samuel forewarned the elders. – *This will be the manner of the king that shall reign over you, he will take your sons, and appoint them to plow his ground, and to reap his harvest, and to make his instruments of war, and the instruments of his chariots. And he will take your daughters to be perfumers, and to be cooks, and to be bakers. And he will take your fields, and your vineyards, and your olive yards, and the tenth of your seed, and give to his officers. And he will take your men-servants, and your maid-servants, and your goodliest young men, and your asses, and put them to his work. He will take the tenth of your flocks. Ye shall be his servants –.*"

Yeshua pointed his finger at each man in turn. "Psalms tells us. – *Put not your trust in princes –.* Each of you are good men. Each of you have it within yourselves to govern. You can be fair and just with those of your tribe, as captain of your tribe. But if someone abuses the trust of their tribe then the tribe will have the right to replace that captain. No one man can be king. It is too much power to entrust to one man. Even King David proved himself unworthy by the murder of Uriah and seduction of Uriah's wife, Bathsheba. The death of the child of David and Bathsheba was ADONAI's punishment of David. Proverbs tell us. - *As a roaring lion, and a ravenous bear, so is a wicked ruler over a poor people. The prince that lacketh understanding is also a great oppressor -*."

John insisted, "We have seen and do testify that ADONAI sent you, the son of man, to be the savior of the world."

Yeshua shook his head, mumbling to himself. I could see he was becoming aggravated. Then he asked in a challenging tone of voice, "Whom say the people that I am?"

They answered, "Yokhanan HaMatbi the Baptizer, but some say, Elijah, and others say that one of the old prophets is risen again."

Yeshua asked, "But whom say ye that I am?"

Simon Peter said, "The son of man. The malka meshiḥa, the king messiah, the anointed one, sent by ADONAI."

And Yeshua straitly charged them and commanded them, "Tell no man that thing! For this son of a man is not come to be a king. No man can be king. All must rule themselves with wise thoughts, judicious actions, and peace to their fellow man. They must also be willing to raise arms against those who would suppress and dominate for their own glory. But the violence must be measured out carefully so the action is for justice and not for revenge, and not for taking of wealth or personal gain. It is those who would call themselves king who are the ones that are most willing to shed the blood of others. Some who would be king, once they taste the power and once they feel the gold, only want more. Those who would be king, those who lust to be king, are those who are the least worthy to be king. And, verily, what is the son of man but a child of the Habirum. Is he not? The son of man should be a good man, a fair man, but indeed, he is only a man. We are all sons of man on earth. Perhaps we all are sons of ADONAI but ADONAI charges us to be responsible for ourselves in the here and now. We must all earn salvation. The price is that one must first save themselves. Even the pagans, the heathens, the uncircumcised, the Romans, are all a son of some man, are they not? Those words, son of a man, mean nothing more than that. A man is born of a woman who lay with a man. Put no other significance to those words."

Yeshua looked hard at us all. "Tell no one I am their messiah, or the anointed, or that the prophecy of David has come, or that there will be a new king. If the people believe they have a king or messiah to save them, then they become lazy and let others fight their fight for them. All must be responsible for their freedom. Having freedom is not a gift. It is a job that must be worked at steadily. I tell you I will not be king. In the twelve new tribes, all will be equal. All will share in the rights and responsibilities needed to govern the land. Note I say, govern the land, not govern the people. The people must be free. And hold onto this. We do not want the Romans to hear words like king or messiah and send their centurions against us. We must prepare and then attack in secret. I will not be as Judah of Gamala to be hung from the cross as a false messiah. Bear in mind that the Romans also crucified thousands of his fighters along with him. We must tread carefully and firmly to win this fight."

Yeshua looked at each of us in turn. "Heed my words. We strike when we are ready. We must not waste blood in useless battles. And we must not cause the people to think ADONAI or a messiah will save them. The people must save themselves. It is their task. It is their fate. And it is their treasure. A treasure they must find for themselves. No one else can find freedom for them. Freedom is a treasure and that treasure must be guarded carefully. Freedom means one must choose. Only slaves cannot and do not choose. They do not have the freedom of choice. Men must choose to be free as they choose what sacrifices they are willing to make for that freedom. ADONAI does not give men freedom, only the chance to pursue that freedom. ADONAI expects the sons of men themselves to make the choice to be free."

I saw that Yeshua's words gave direction to the men for they moved with purpose and conviction as they left. Yeshua truly was a wise man, a teacher, and a leader of men.

THE PLACE OF ENCAMPMENT. MY
NAME IS JUDAS ISCARIOT

We left Rabbah and ventured south into the desolate landscape north of the River Arnon. Atop an unnamed mount there was a fresh water spring that bubbled from the rocky depths making a flowing stream. We made camp alongside the stream. There was good grass for the animals which the men had brought from the spring at Mount Tir'an. As Ahab said unto Obadiah. – *Go through the land, unto all the springs of water, and unto all the brooks, so that we may find grass and save the horses and mules alive* –.

For food we had lambs, a flock of chickens for eggs, goats for milk and cheese, and the trade goods we had plundered from Zippori. Everyone in the camp was ready to march in our mission to free the Habirum and the land of Israel and Judah. The camp was a place of communal harmony that was pleasant to see. As Psalms tells us, in a melody of David. – *How good and pleasant it is when ADONAI's people live together in unity* –. Soon all the Habirum would be united in harmony.

Yeshua, Mariam, the other captains, and I discussed the need for two more captains to make the twelve. Yeshua said they should be Essenes. "To fairly represent the Habirum people of the true faith, the twelve should be both Pharisee and Essene. Yokhanan HaMatbi the Baptizer was Essene. A third of all Habirum are Essenes, the rest are Pharisees. The Sadducees are few in number and they only keep control because they are Herod's dogs. All of the Essenes want to avenge the murder of Yokhanan HaMatbi. My step brother, James, is Essene. I will talk to him about joining us." Levi Matthew told us his brother James barAlphaeus was Essene. "Let us speak to him also," said Yeshua.

We left the camp at dawn. Yeshua, Levi Matthew, Philip, and Simon Zealot and I, plus two of Simon's men, would make our way downstream by boat on the River Jordan to its mouth at the Salt Sea.

170

Our destination was En Gedi, on the west shore of the Salt Sea. We arrived before the high sun at the town of Heshbon. This was the junction of the King's Highway and the road leading west to Jericho. As it is told in Numbers. – *Sihon would not allow Israel to pass through his territory. So Sihon gathered all his people together and went out against Israel in the wilderness. Then Israel defeated him with the edge of the sword –*. Moses gave the land of the defeated king of Heshbon to the Tribe of Gad. The Romans would suffer the same defeat as the other enemies of the Habirum.

We rode hard, switching from tired horses to the fresh horses on lead ropes. At sundown we came to the hillcrest overlooking the River Jordan. We were on the east side of the river in the Plains of Moad. Across the river was the Plain of Jericho. Barrabas, Bartholomew Nathaneal and a group of men had gone ahead three days earlier and we met them at the river's eastern edge. They had a boat ready for us. We made camp for the night and at dawn we loaded into the boat for the journey downstream to where the River Jordan flowed into the Salt Sea.

The boat was sturdily constructed of thick fir wood planks, joined together by clever notches as nails of iron would rust. The entire hull and seams were painted with pitch to make it watertight. We took up our oars and Barabbas gave us a push into the river. The current was running fast. The rainy season had passed and the river was full but not at its crest. Barabbas and the other men would take the slower overland route. They would meet us at En Gedi.

We floated downstream at a fast pace using the oars only to guide us past the many rocks that threatened to wreck us. South of the landing that led to Jericho, the River Jordan narrowed and ran faster. Between the high cliffs the river twisted upon itself like a snake, east to west, then back again. At several places where the river narrowed even tighter, we encountered racing rapids. The sudden surge of the rapids was thrilling, like the racing of a horse, as we dropped to the next levels below. After a rapid the river might suddenly turn calm for a short distance giving us a chance to catch our breath and laugh over the near escape. In some places the river fell over a rocky ledge so steeply we had to disembark and lower the boat down by sturdy hempen ropes. We did this by either clambering along the cliff face or by wading chest deep in the river. Here a slip of foot could throw you into the tossing river amongst the rocks. The river claimed many lives each year. The level of the river seemed to be falling at a measured pace, like it was rushing to a lower region. The river pulled us steadily downstream. What would we find at the place where the river finally stopped?

During a period of calm I had a chance to observe the surroundings. At this point on the river, at the bottom of the cliffs, there was a strip of green vegetation, canes, bushes, flowers and trees growing in a multitudinous bounty. Branches of willow trees hung over the water creating a welcome shade. If the water by the bank was deep we took advantage of the shade, if not deep then we were in the middle of the river under the fierce sun. The green plants and trees were in stark contrast to the brown dry hills on both sides of the river. Sometimes the cliffs were so high and close it seemed we were passing through a tunnel. Caught in the rocks of the hillsides were thick tangled branches and even trunks of trees that Philip told us were testimony to the power of the river during the height of the rainy season. Philip said it would be very dangerous to navigate the river during the annual flood.

We saw a wild boar swimming across the river. The swine made it to the shore then turned to look at us. It was as tall at the shoulder as my waist. It lifted its fleshy, grotesque snout and squinted its near sighted eyes, turning its head to catch our scent. Its tusks were longer than a man's hand and the bristles along its back stood erect. The beast snorted loudly then turned and crashed into the thick brush. We could see its progress by the wildly bending brush and sound of breaking branches as it made its clumsy way to its lair.

A chorus of birds sang to us and we watched an eagle plunge into the river, then flying off with a large fish in its talons. For a distance the cliffs dropped shear to the water, giving no opportunity to land the boat. The rocky cliffs towered above us where the river narrowed and the water ran swift. We were constantly using our oars to push off from the rocks jutting up from the water that threatened our safe descent down the river. Rounding a turn the river widened with a small sandy island jutting from the middle of the river. The west side narrowed to a fast running current and rocks but the east side seemed suddenly placid. There was a wide bank with green willow trees and plants on that side and we could see a waterfall running merrily down the face of the brown rocky cliff. We rowed that direction and pulled the boat ashore. The splashing waterfall cut down the rocks and created a small gurgling stream that fed the river. The water was clear, cool, and fresh tasting. We filled our water containers, praising ADONAI for this timely gift as the water of the River Jordan was mostly muddy and undrinkable. While we drank and rested we pulled food from our bags and ate ravenously as the exercise had sharpened our appetites.

I walked off a ways to relieve myself and explore a little. The soil by the stream where it entered the river was soft and I found the tracks of a full grown lion. ADONAI! All my senses suddenly sharpened. The tracks were new, the muddy edges crumbling to the touch, and the nearby scat was still fresh with flies buzzing around it.

I crouched and the hair on my neck literally rose in respect of the danger. I fitted an arrow to the string of my bow as I turned in a slow circle. I examined closely the area around me. The brush was thick here, a dim little forest, with trees, bushes, canes, and weeds in a plentiful variety. If the beast were lurking, watching me, thinking to make a meal of me, his tawny coat was well hidden. He would only make his presence known by a sudden rush. The lion had rubbed against a tree and stuck in the bark was long black fur from his mane. This showed the lion was a male and it was known that male lions with black fur on their manes were the most aggressive. My bow and arrow, in my hands, seemed like a trifling defense against such a threat. I crept from that spot with great caution. There were tracks of other animals here and there, showing that the strip of green along the river's banks were alive with the splendor of nature.

I spotted Yeshua walking through a patch of flowering greenery, bending to pluck and then put in his bag some small yellow leaves.

I asked him what the plant was and he told me it was Senna. Yeshua said the leaves were used for treating burns, wounds, and ailments to the skin. He said the boiled roots cured colic and constipation, and a hot drink from the boiled leaves would act as a purgative and induce labor.

Yeshua chuckled and said, "The words of the pharmacopeia of Isis also lists the pulp of ground Senna leaves as a cure for the back passage boils, what the Romans call the haemorrhoidaes. But as my healing skills do not include treating that ailment, I will collect the plant and its flowers for its other fine uses."

In the deep river canyon, between the high hills on both sides, the sun set quickly. During the middle of the day with the sun directly overhead the light and heat had funneled and concentrated directly on the water. The glare off the water had been blinding and the heat oppressive. Now in the shade of evening the air cooled rapidly. We gathered wood and built a blazing fire. We determined to make camp at this spot for the night rather than risk being caught in the darkness at a tricky spot of the river. The rapids and the unseen rocks were like daggers beneath the surface that could dash our boat to splinters. This was a constant hazard we wished to avoid in the dark of night. We did not want any damage to the boat as it would be a long rough walk out of this wild place.

The contrast between the heat of day and chill of night was extreme in this desert land. As we took turns during the night standing guard, the watchman fed the fire to keep at bay any wild beasts. Yesterday, back in camp, I had told the others to arm themselves with sword and spear and follow me. I wanted them to see something. I led them to the stream. When I pointed to the tracks of the lion, its paw prints as big as a man's fist, everyone's eyes popped wide open. I pulled the long black fur threads from the tree bark. They too understood the meaning. I poked at the scat with my spear point. It squashed easily. In a low voice I told them, "The high sun. No later." All heads swiveled to peer about and there was gained a newfound appreciation for our camping site. That night all had kept their weapons close at hand while resting. When it was my turn for watch, I kept my back to the fire and my eyes trained to the surrounding darkness, searching for the glitter of golden eyes. I thought the presence of a lion was a good omen, for as told by Zechariah and Jeremiah. – *Hark! The roaring of young lions. Behold, he shall come up like a lion from the thickets of the Jordan –.* While I trusted in ADONAI, as Isaiah says. – *Fear thou not, for I am with thee. I strengthen thee, yea, I help thee –* reliance on one's own vigilance and strength was expected by ADONAI.

At the dawn the breeze and temperature was so cool as to make me shiver. We climbed into the boat and set off once again downstream. Past the end of the island we rounded a turn and were immediately thrust into a white foaming fast current. The river narrowed once again, the cliffs on each side lifting high above us. While the water ran fast here it was deep. Our oars could not find the bottom and we saw no rocks blocking the surface so we only steered to keep in the middle and let the water carry us south. The rocky cliffs were of a brown color with cream colored streaks showing the change in levels of the earth. There were many birds. I saw a large hawk, herons, and others soaring through the air. Halfway up the cliff on the west side was a dark opening, an entry to some sort of cavern. An underground stream emerged there and a brilliant stream of water shot out of the cavern falling into the river far below. The spout of water made a great splashing spectacle creating a rainbow to delight the eyes. We steered toward the edge of the waterfall's furious entry into the river. The rain of water drops and mist cooled us and made us laugh like joyful children.

On we traveled the rest of the day through this land that was a tribute to the bounty of ADONAI. The River Jordan was a vein of liquid life that nourished this strip of land through what was mostly barren country past each side of the high cliffs. Toward the end of the day we noticed the temperature becoming even warmer. The breeze carried a smell of salt that was bitter tasting where it landed on my lips. This indicated we were approaching the end of the river and the beginning of the Salt Sea. The river widened and slowed. We were obliged to take to the oars to make progress. The sun was so bright and the glare off the water so blinding as to make the head ache. The heat from the sun was like standing too close to a fire.

Around another bend the twisting river brought us to a place where suddenly the height of the cliffs was lowered, the mouth of the river opened, and spread out before us was the shimmering Salt Sea. We rowed to the west bank and prepared to make camp for the days end. We were at the far southern edge of the Valley of Achor and there we took shelter. The sun and the heat was so intense we dug holes and stuck the blades of our oars into the ground. Then we leaned and lashed the tops of the oars together and draped a canvas over it to make a spot of welcome shade. The shore here was wet and marshy, the source of water coming from the northwest out of the Valley of Achor. There was driftwood aplenty attesting to the high water mark. At the very edge of the Salt Sea, the ground was a slimy mud. When my sandals sank into the slushy mess, the mud was so hot from being broiled by the sun it felt like my toes and feet were cooking.

We rested there until the dark before dawn. We began early to take advantage of the cooler morning air and make progress before the sun blasted us once again. We rowed further south down the western shore of the Sea. We passed the narrow ravine where the River Kidron fed water to the Sea in the rainy season. Now it was just a trickle. The low sweep of the Valley of Achor had ended and the ground had lifted so that a high cliff towered over us on our right western side. The cliff appeared too shear to climb though I saw dark areas that could be the entrance of caves. Did people inhabit those caves? I could see no way to get to them from the top or bottom. Perhaps there were ledges or footpaths, but they could not be seen from our low spot on the water.

One towering mount showed evidence of a fierce conflagration. There was nothing growing, no plants or even a speck of weeds. It was as if the soil was poisoned. The top looked as if it had been rent asunder by thunderbolts and charred by lightning blasts. Could this be evidence of another burning mountain, like the Mount at Sinai? This whole land looked desolate and uninhabitable. I was very curious to see how these Essenes adapted to this strange place. At the hottest part of the day we rowed for shore and pitched camp, meaning to start before sunrise in the early morning cooler air the following day. The driftwood was so caked with dried salt it would not catch fire, so that night we had a dark camp and cold supper.

We rested until the middle of the night hour and pushed off. We would make progress down the Salt Sea before the sun cooked us again like a piece of meat on the coals. Hours later, at the high sun, we came upon a particular mount that revealed itself to have been split in two, as if by a giant wielding a large ax. We saw the fissure was used as a walking path, for there were people standing looking and pointing at us. We rowed to shore to greet them. They were the first people we had seen since the day we boarded the boat on the river.

Getting closer we saw it was a group of three men, dressed in white waist cloths who yelled at us to continue south as there was no place to land the boat where the cliff met the water. We rowed another two hours and came upon the path leading to the settlement of En Gedi.

QUMRAN. MY NAME IS JUDAS ISCARIOT

I was watching Yeshua walking with his brother, James, alongside the water channel. I was in a small cave I found and explored. The cave was above the level of the ground higher than the height of a tall man. I climbed the side of the cliff up to it. There was nothing in the cave of interest, but it was out of the bright sun so I lingered there for a spell sneaking a nap. The intensity of the sun's rays in this desert place was like a heavy thing, a burden one could only put down by finding the shelter of shade. Even then the heat wrapped one in its embrace like a serpent made of wool. I was awoken by the sound of voices. The heat and sleep made me so lethargic I could not move my limbs. I leaned back against the wall of the cave, blinking my eyes, looking groggily past the dark shadow into the bright light of midday. Yeshua and James approached my spot, still talking. It was my intention to call out to them and let them know my presence. I did not want to eavesdrop on their conversation, but my mind and body was so heat drugged, my vocal cords were slow to respond to the thought.

From our starting place on the River Jordan it took us five days to arrive at the place of the Essenes. We left our boat on the shore when we had landed at En Gedi. After a half day walk across the searing barren landscape of the wilderness of Judah we came to Qumran. The rocky bluffs, the caves, and caverns of this place had been carved and shaped into an unreal landscape by the countless years of the forces of nature. Some of the caves had been enlarged. They were dug out by hand, and were used as storage and living spaces for the people who settled in this place.

Atop a small, flat topped mount was the habitation of certain of the Essenes. They occupied several buildings. The buildings were surrounded by a rock stacked protective wall with a high tower at the northwest corner. The wall and the tower gave it the appearance of a small fortress. This particular group of Essenes had passed through a three year probation, and were then admitted into their secret society. These were the most pious and dedicated, and Yeshua's stepbrother, James, was their leader. He was their Teacher of Righteousness, the latest from a long line who had come before him. The other priests called Yeshua's stepbrother, James the Just. I suppose he had earned the title and position because he demonstrated wisdom amongst his fellow Essenes. What I had seen of him showed him to be haughty and arrogant, at least in his manner to Yeshua.

They had stopped walking just steps from where I lay hidden in the shaded cleft above them. Yeshua was talking. "Consider for a moment. What if ADONAI and the angels are only symbols?"

And I heard James reply, in a disrespectful, scornful manner, "Symbols? What do you mean? Symbols!"

"There is a common waking dream among all men. Call it a trickery of the mind, of a lost paradise and a longing for a return to that lost paradise. There is a common hope that an eventual return to that lost paradise will give meaning to this harsh mortal struggle, in the end. So if ADONAI and angels are symbols of that final perfection, that is what we strive to, even if our rational minds tell us such striving is in vain."

"That is blasphemy. – *And he that blasphemeth the name of ADONAI, he shall surely be put to death. All the congregation shall certainly stone him. He shall be put to death –.*"

Yeshua said, "I only suggest that we let the ending, whatever it may be, take care of itself and we take care of ourselves in the here and now. Ask yourself, how far can we see? Does that not depend on what we are looking for? You look for salvation at some end time but I look for salvation now. Freedom from the Romans is the salvation our people need right now. Then we will have the leisure to wonder about end times."

"The studying of the Aegyptus legends damaged your mind."

There was a sudden stir of gravel underfoot. Yeshua walked away from the cliff and I could now see him. He turned to look at his brother, "James, you were a sickly child. You could not leave the house and had to stay with the women all day. You did not get the advantage of studying with the wise men like I did. If you had done so, you would see the world more clearly. You cannot, or will not, see reality because of your superstitious fear of the unknown."

James also stepped into view. "I see clearly your ambition. If you are able to defeat the Romans with your puny army, then what? Then will the people call you messiah? Call you the King David of our time? Will you take on David's crown and rule the Habirum of Israel and Judah?"

"I have told you I do not seek the crown. The people and the land will live under the twelve new tribes, each tribe led by a wise captain of those twelve who have the courage to follow me. This end of time war you speak of is nonsense. Good angels fighting bad angels? Nonsense! If you wait for these sons of light to bring you salvation, you will still be waiting when the Romans knock down your puny fortress. The war is now. The Romans are the enemy. They are the army of darkness that you speak of. We must defeat the Romans now for the Habirum to be free. My brother, you can bring your bibliotheca and scrolls and librarium to the Temple in Jerusalem. You can share your wisdom of the Essenes with our entire people. There are Essenes in every town and village throughout the land. They may not be priests like you, but they are people who also desire freedom from the Romans. They will listen to you. Help them to be free. And why would you hide your knowledge? Share it. You have read the writings of Hillel the Elder, he tells us, 'Whosoever destroys one soul it is as though he had destroyed the entire world. And whosoever saves a life, it is as though he had saved the entire world.' Help to save the Habirum. Share your knowledge with our people. It is your destiny my brother."

"Yeshua. Do not call me brother. We are not brothers. My mother died of fever when I was two years. It was then my father took your mother for wife when she carried you as an unborn babe. There is no blood between us. There is not even the bond of friendship between us. I despise you. When you were born it brought shame into our

180

home. – *A bastard shall not enter into the assembly of ADONAI* –. The son of the pagan Panthera cannot rule the land of ADONAI. You will not rule the Habirum of Israel and Judah."

From my spot in the deep shadow I saw Yeshua move as fast as an attacking lion. Yeshua slammed his fist into James chest. Yeshua jerked James around, pinning James arm behind his back. Then Yeshua had his knife at James throat. It all happened in an instant.

"Shut your mouth or I will kill you. You will not speak of that."

"Fight. Yes. Violence. Go ahead. Kill me now and ADONAI will take me up as he did Enoch, and ADONAI will cast you out to burn in Sheol forevermore."

My muscles tensed to rise. My heart thumped in my chest. Should I interfere? If I made my presence known now at this late minute, then it would be embarrassing for all. They would know I overheard their entire conversation. James I cared not about, but Yeshua, he was my friend. If he knew I knew his secret, it could change our friendship. I hesitated a moment. Then Yeshua pushed James away from him. James tripped clumsily and fell to the ground.

"I hoped you had become more mature in your reasoning, and that the training you received in this place might have given you wisdom. But I see I was wrong. You are not mature nor are you wise. You are a coward. The reason you hide here in this forsaken place is you lack the strength of heart to fight. You would rather hide here like a mouse and dream your dreams of salvation by angels. You will be hiding when the Romans attack. Like a mouse in the corner, the Romans will catch you and they will crush you."

James stood and brushed the sand from his robe, "Do you know why you fight so well? Since we were children you were a good fighter. The reason you are a good fighter is because my father taught you how to fight. My father knew you would be plagued all your days by the curse of your father's rape of your mother. He knew if you could not fight someone more skilled would kill you in your anger. And someone will kill you, the Romans most likely, and soon if you persist in your foolish fight. And know this. If the Romans attack us here, attack all the Habirum, it will be because you have aroused their wrath. You will bring your house down upon your head and all Habirum will be made to suffer for it. You are possessed by a madness. Your great friend, your mother's cousin, Yokhanan HaMatbi, the one they call the Baptizer, he was deranged just like you. For many years he was Essene and then he left. He took our ritual of bathing for spiritual purity with him. He thought he would convert the whole world and save the whole world. He proposed to convert and save not just Sadducee but also Romans, heathens, pagans and the uncircumcised. He was barking mad. If he had not left when he did, I would have run him off, sooner than later. You too should go. Go now. You are not welcome in this place. Thou hast a devil who goeth about to kill thee. Take your devil from our midst."

Yeshua stood with the knife still in his hand, breathing hard, his muscles tensed, on the edge of his toes. I thought he would again go for James. But then he took a step back and lowered the knife.

In a calm voice he said, "James, Yosef was my father too, as I was his son. He was with me more than you because you were weak and sickly. Yosef talked to me more. He taught me more. That is why you hate me. You hate me because you think he loved me more than you. But that is not true. Yosef was a good man. He loved us all. He loved and cared for all his wives and all his children. I tried to be a brother to you, and a friend, but you would not have it. Your hatred drives you like a harnessed beast. That is why you left when we came back from Aegyptus. You left at thirteen years to come to this place. You have done well to become their leader. If being the leader of men who hide from the world and dream starry eyed nonsense is considered worthy. The Romans will come for you. Their actions are driven only by a lust for power. The Roman's power comes from their god Jupiter who hurls the lightning bolt and Jupiter's son, Mars, who kills Rome's enemies with the spear. Your existence is a threat to their power. The Romans barely tolerate the worship of ADONAI and they keep control of the Temple by occupation and threat of force. They will not tolerate your angels when they realize the true meaning of the Essenes beliefs. And make no mistake, the Romans know of you.

The Romans will come for you. They will slaughter you like the fox slaughters the chickens in the hen house. The Romans will wipe you from the earth. It will be as if you never existed. If me and my men don't stop them and stop them now, then your days are numbered. Even ADONAI and your beloved angels will not be able to help you. Before I go I will give you one piece of advice my …step… brother … and that is to guard your precious writings well. The Romans will use your writings to fuel their campfires."

Yeshua sheathed his knife. "You say we are not even friends, and with that I agree. I leave now. Not because you say so, but because I see there is no further purpose to my staying."

Yeshua turned and walked away. I stood slowly and watched both until they were out of sight. James walked fast toward the Essenes buildings. He bent over and went through a low doorway. Yeshua walked toward the wilderness past the water channel. I watched as Yeshua, in the distance, seemed to be swallowed up by the heat waves rising from the ground. I realized I had been holding my breath. I exhaled. I shook my head. I tried to erase what I had witnessed from my mind. Yeshua and James had lived under the same family roof for ten years. Brothers? Step brothers? Not even friends. Worse than strangers. Cain and Abel? Worse than that. The only difference being that one had not killed the other. Yet.

I waited in my shadowed place, catching my breath, trying to relax my thoughts. Then I took a roundabout way to the cave where I and the others had camped while here at the Essenes place of habitation. I was thinking perhaps it was a mistake to come to Qumran. Perhaps we should look elsewhere for the final two captains. Thinking that it was time to leave this place. If nothing else it was too hot here. I did not care for the climate. I thought that only madmen would make a home in such insufferable heat. I knew without a doubt that I could not tolerate another day here.

I arrived at the cave and to my surprise Yeshua was there. He was sitting with Philip and the rest of our group. There were two others also, both of the Essenes. They turned at my entry. Yeshua saying, "Good. Judas is here. We can now make our plan."

I saw one of the two Essenes was James barAlphaeus, Levi Matthew's brother, and the other was a man I had earlier met named

Thomas. The other Essenes called Thomas, in jest, the Doubter, as he was constantly questioning what they said. Indeed, his favorite expressions were, "Why do you say that?" and "Prove what you say is true."

I sat and listened while Yeshua talked to these two men. Yeshua looked as if his earlier confrontation with James had had no effect on him. He was his usual calm self, composed and in charge. I suppose the walk in the wilderness had allowed him to cast any worrying thoughts from his mind. After a short discussion we all agreed to go back to En Gedi to meet Barabbas with the horses. We gathered our belongings and left straightaway. James barAlphaeus and Thomas had nothing but the clothes they wore as the Essenes possessed no private property. We would outfit them with everything they would need, including the arms for war.

The sun had reached its westerly limit and we used the cooling night air to make the journey back to En Gedi. While walking, I thought upon what I had learned about the Essenes these past days. One would think it would be impossible to exist in this desert for lack of water. The reason the River Kidron had been only a trickle, as we had seen from the boat, was the Essenes had built a rock dam and diverted the water course to their area of abode. Using lined up piles of rocks and channels cut into the landscape, the water from the river was brought to reservoirs chiseled from the bare rocks. It was an ingenious means of survival in this otherwise unlivable dry place. Some of the water reservoirs were for storing drinking and cooking water. Other reservoirs were for the daily ritual bathing that each Essene practiced for physical cleanliness and spiritual purity. The reservoirs were replenished by the channels from the river and the rains, but during the occasional season when drought would hit rationing would be strict. The diversion of the river had been generations of work. The Essenes did the work themselves, laboring in the heat for years and years as they did not have slaves. The Essenes believed, as we Pharisees did, that the practice of slavery was an abomination before ADONAI.

Alongside the water channel the Essenes grew vegetable patches and flax plant. They used the nutritious flax seeds in their simple meals. They cultivated the long green stalks of the flax plant, with its pretty purple flowering buds, for its fiber. The Essenes used the fiber from the flax to make linen for their white robes and waist cloths. All the Essenes, including the priests, only wore these simple flax linen unadorned articles of clothing for everyday use and during their rituals and ceremonies. Also grown in great quantities was the papyrus plant for their writing materials. The Essenes had a bibliotheca of amazing proportions, an uncountable number of scrolls, in which certain of them busied themselves studying and copying.

The plain white robes were the complete opposite of what the Herodian Sadducee priests at the Temple in Jerusalem wore for their rituals. The high priest, Caliphas, wore a white linen undershirt under a fine, costly purple robe and over that a vestment of many colors to signify his rank. The sacred vestments were dyed and woven of the finest materials. The brilliant purple color was made in the town of Tyre, using a dye from blue mollusks harvested from the Great Sea. From the mollusks was taken the fluid of glands located near the creature's rectum. This purple dye was in miniscule quantities, difficult to render, rare, and thus more valuable than gold. The purple dyed robe was worn only by the Sadducee high priest. The lesser Sadducee priests wore a white knee length robe that included a colorful woven belt around the waist. The sacred vestments of the Sadducee high priest in Jerusalem were kept behind a locked door in the Roman Antonia Fortress. The Romans only allowed the vestments to be taken from the Fortress and used by the high priest during celebrations on holy days. The symbolic power of the sacred vestments was such that the high priest could not officiate on holy days without wearing the vestments. The Roman's strict control of the sacred vestments was one of the methods the Romans used to maintain order. Without the vestments, no worship could be done. Without the worship, no link to ADONAI could be made. Without the blessing of ADONAI, the Habirum were doomed. Such was the teaching of the Sadducee priests. The sacred vestments in the wrong hands would be a potent force to be reckoned with. The question is, whose are the wrong hands, and whose are the right hands?

In the caves of this area lived those who practiced the Essene's beliefs but were not of the priestly order themselves. This included men and their wives and children. Only the priests had taken the vow of celibacy. While the people added new Essenes through procreation, the priests only took volunteers to their order and sometimes they adopted orphan male children and raised them in their faith.

I talked with James barAlphaeus, the brother of Levi Matthew, who told me of the Essenes and their history. Really he only told me what he could divulge without violating his pledges of the brotherhood. Much of the Essenes beliefs and practices were secret amongst themselves only. James barAlphaeus counted the beginning of the Essenes from the time of the Enoch. From Adam the first man, it was seven to Enoch, so their beliefs were old as time itself. Enoch was a righteous man who ADONAI summoned to His side. Then Enoch – *Walked with ADONAI, and he was no more, for ADONAI took him* – and ADONAI set Enoch to rule over the angels of ADONAI in the House of ADONAI.

James barAlphaeus told me the history of their order. The first of the Essenes was the high priest Aaron, the Levite. Aaron, the prophet, was the brother of Moses. ADONIA made Aaron the first High Priest of the Habirum, with his male descendants to follow him for all time going forward. James barAlphaeus looked around to be sure no one would overhear him and whispered to me, "The magic Aaron displayed to the pharaoh was gifted to him by a Messenger, an angel. This Messenger was Moses guide who brought them out of Aegyptus. That Messenger accompanied them for forty years, teaching Aaron the secrets we practice today."

James barAlphaeus told me, "Generations later, Zadoq, who was a descendant of Aaron, was the first of the line of the Teacher of Righteousness. Zadoq was high priest during the time of David and Solomon. The lineage of Aaron continued until the Seleucid Empire controlled the Temple. After the death of Alexander the Macedonian, Menelaus of the Tribe of Benjamin became high priest of the Temple by bribing the Greek king, Seleucus IV Philopator. Once Menelaus was in charge of the Temple, he looted the treasury to pay the bribe to the Greek king. It is written in the Book of the Maccabees. – *The treasury in Jerusalem was full of untold sums of money, so that the amount of the funds could not be reckoned* –. Onias III, an official at the Temple, came into conflict with Menelaus after the treasury was plundered."

Onias III was a pious man. He accused Menelaus publicly of the thievery, causing Menelaus and his Greek allies to threaten the life of Onias III. Onias III was forced to flee from Jerusalem. Menelaus, aided by his Greek allies, hunted down and assassinated Onias III. Menelaus usurped the position of High Priest and continued to plunder the Temple. Thus Menelaus earned the title of Wicked Priest, a position passed on to the unworthy of each generation who defiled the Temple. The Wicked Priest now was Caliphas, leader of the court of Sanhedrin at the Temple in Jerusalem. Caiaphas was the Sadducee High Priest and subservient to the Romans.

After Onias III was assassinated, many of those who followed his teachings were also killed by Menelaus. The rest fled from Jerusalem.

Some went to the Habirum community in Alexandria, Aegyptus. The rest ventured south into the wilderness of Judah on the west shore of the Salt Sea. Those were the Essenes whose brothers now, many generations later, formed this community of Qumran.

After a couple of days talking with James barAlphaeus, I gained his confidence and he told me some of the Essenes beliefs. He described the Malakh, the Messengers. These are the angels, the Sons of ADONAI. The Messengers, according to Enoch, were sent by ADONAI to advice men, to reward men, and to punish men for their transgressions. Angels appeared to Hagar, to Abraham, to Moses, to the prophet Balaam, to Gideon, to Manoah and his wife, to Daniel, to Zechariah, and an angel of ADONAI removed the sins of Joshua. But two hundred of these angels chose to go the wicked path and they were those who have fallen. These are the Watchers. The Watchers rendered defilement amongst the daughters of men, birthing the Nephilim. The fallen angels brought the curse of ADONAI upon all the peoples of the earth. ADONAI sent the archangels to destroy the Watchers and Nephilim, to destroy the fallen angels. Then ADONAI cleansed the earth in a great deluge. ADONAI washed evil and sin away in a great flood that was so devastating that people still tell the story of The Great Flood to this very day.

Some of this I knew already. The Flood and Noah was common knowledge. But I listened closely to James barAlphaeus hoping he would divulge some new information. He only smiled and told me, "I can tell you there are more Messengers, but of them I cannot speak. Of them, only the initiated in our order have the knowledge. I will tell you this. To know their names and to know the words of the rituals, is to have the power to summon them. If one summons the Messengers without forethought, purpose, or knowledge, one brings great peril upon one's self. That knowledge is sacred and secret among the initiated of the Essenes only."

I asked, "But for what purpose are these secrets? I ask not the details of the secrets themselves, but what is the end? If the Essenes know of beneficial information to assist our people, why keep it hidden?"

"Those secrets we hold until the day of the final battle."

"The final battle?" I asked him.

"Yes. There will be a war between the Sons of Light and the Sons of Darkness."

"When will this war happen?"

"At the end of time. The war will last forty nine years and one day. Then the messiah will rule in justice and peace. As it says in the Book of the Maccabees. – *And the dominion of the Kittim shall come to an end, so that wickedness shall be laid low without any remnant, and there shall be no survivor of the sons of darkness –*. The Kittim were the Seleucids during the time of Judah Maccabee. The Kittim now are the Romans, but the real final enemy will be the Sons of Darkness, the sons of the fallen Messengers."

I scratched my head, wondering, where have I heard such thoughts before? Then I remembered Yeshua telling one of his stories about the Aegyptus gods. Some tale of a final war where AmunRa, the sun god, brings victory against Apophis, the god of evil and darkness. This all seemed strangely interconnected somehow. But I did not debate the issue with James barAlphaeus. It was too hot for debating. The temperature was oppressive. I felt like I was bread dough being baked inside a hot stone oven. I only nodded at him as if what he said made perfectly good sense, even though I privately questioned the clarity of his thinking.

The Essenes had festivals the Sadducee priests at the Temple in Jerusalem did not observe. The Essenes had the New Barley Festival, the New Wine Festival, and the New Oil Festival. It seemed all the Habirum, Pharisees, Essenes, and the Sadducees, had more differences than similarities. I scratched my head again. How did Yeshua intend to unite these people, these children of the patriarch Abraham, who had been at war with each other since the earliest days? Although we all recognize the same ADONAI, it seemed that His intent to us, and our response to Him, was composed of points of disagreement that could warrant the most extreme responses.

James barAlphaeus took me into their librarium. There they kept thousands of scrolls. Some were written on papyrus sheets and others on the processed skins of ritually slaughtered sheep and goats. The Essenes used skins of young lambs to make a finer quality writing material. This was reserved for especial works, such as the one James the Just was busy making. James barAlphaeus told me this was the Temple Scroll. It described how the new Temple was to be constructed, among other items of interest, after the Sons of Light defeated the Sons of Darkness. This scroll was longer than three horses with many columns of writings on it. James barAlphaeus said it was not yet complete.

James barAlphaeus introduced me to the priest in charge of this scholarly work. His name was Nahman barIsaac. He was a very old man with a ready smile and bright shining eyes. He seemed to get boundless pleasure from his work. He had started in the librarium as a talented boy, an orphan raised by the Essenes. His work in the librarium had kept his mind sharp. He quoted Proverbs at me. – *Happy is the man that findeth wisdom, and the man that obtaineth understanding. For the merchandise of it is more precious than rubies –.* Nahman was one of those blessed people who had found his calling and was happy in his life's work.

There were a large number of the priests who were knowledgeable scribes working in the librarium making copies of scrolls of ancient writings. I was shown scrolls that dated to the time of the Temple of Solomon, nine and a half hundreds of years before. The writings on the scrolls from different times were in the Habirum language of our ancestors, some in Aramaic and some written in Greek by the philosophers.

Some of the olden writings were copied true to the original words and meaning by the Essene scribes but others were reinterpreted according to their beliefs. They might change a single word, which could give a sentence, a paragraph, even the entire message of that writing a different meaning. Observing this work I saw that the Essenes were making new prophecies and new stories not found in the Books of ADONAI. I thought that this was indeed the way of the sons of men, to interpret the world through their own focus of vision.

I noticed one of the craftsman scribes, a skinny old man bald as an egg with a long white beard, working on a metal sheet of thin copper. The sheet of copper was a cubit wide, the distance of a man's forearm from elbow to fingertips, and the scroll was longer than fingertip to fingertip of a man stretching both of his arms. He was hammering small chisel strokes onto the metal, making precise marks. James barAlphaeus told me this was a treasure map. It showed the locations where the Temple priests hid wealth from the Temple treasury before the invasion of the Babylonians. He was copying words from brittle papyrus scrolls onto the more durable copper. I was told the papyrus scrolls themselves were six hundred years old. They looked it as they were cracked and faded and ready to fall apart at the slightest untutored touch.

A treasure map! I was intrigued. Sneaking a peek over the craftsman's shoulder I saw the letters and words were in a language I did not recognize. They were not Aramaic, nor Habirum, nor Greek, and not the Latīna of the Romans. James barAlphaeus said this Essene craftsman was from Aegyptus, on the Isle of Elephantine, where his family had fled at the time of Jeremiah's prophecy. – *Be ye horribly afraid. Destruction followeth upon destruction. The whole land shall be desolate, thus saith ADONAI* –. James barAlphaeus told me only this Essene knew the secret to this Aegyptus writing and he was teaching it to the Teacher of Righteousness, James the Just. James barAlphaeus looked around to be sure no one could hear him. He whispered, "Apparently James the Just is a slow learner. This craftsman tells me James cannot catch the sounds of the words. But he will not admit it and let someone else be taught."

James barAlphaeus said there were sixty three locations of treasure being marked on the copper scroll. He said these treasures were of gold and silver bullion and coins, precious jewels, and sacred Temple objects. The man looked up from his work. He smiled at me, pointed to some of the markings and said, "Young man, can you read these words?"

I looked closely, shook my head and replied, "No. I can make no sense of the marks."

The old man seemed to delight in a private joke, "I will tell you what this says. 'In the ruin that is in the valley of Achor, under the steps, with the entrance at the East, a distance of forty cubits, a strongbox of silver and its vessels with a weight of seventeen talents.'" The old man shrugged, "That is only a small amount." He waved a hand over the scroll and copper sheet, "There are many larger, greater, treasures told of here." Then he smiled and returned to his work.

Seventeen talents of silver? One talent is more than the weight of a healthy lamb ready for market. To lift that lamb is a both arms full load. Seventeen lambs! Of silver bullion! Imagine that! Yeshua should see this. If the writings were in the Aegyptus language, maybe Yeshua could read it. Treasure!

JERICHO. MY NAME IS JUDAS ISCARIOT

We left Qumran late in the day so we would not travel in the hottest hours. We arrived at En Gedi before the sunrise. Barabbas and a group of our warriors were there with a string of horses. After a brief rest and a meal we were horseback and headed for Jericho. Our route was due north across the Valley of Achor. This land was called the Valley of Trouble, as this was where – *Achan and his sons, and his daughters, and his oxen, and his asses, and his sheep, and his tent, and all that he had, brought them up unto the valley of Achor. And all Israel stoned him with stones, and they burned them with fire. And they raised over him a great heap of stones, unto this day* – because Achan had taken gold and silver from the wreckage of Jericho, against the Word of ADONAI.

The Valley of Achor was an area of rocky ridges divided by deep chasms. The low areas were swampy, treacherous wetlands. The going was slow as we had to pick our way through the changing landscape, fetid morass one way and dizzying mountain passes the other way. It was late in the day when we arrived at Jericho. The town was set on a plateau above the Valley of Achor. We had experienced a coming down from high to low on our river journey to the Salt Sea. Now the land climbed back up out of that low spot to Jericho.

Jericho was another warm climate. The land near the Salt Sea had been dry desert heat, but all the water springs in and around Jericho made the hot temperature humid and sticky. The springs at Jericho drained south and east to the Valley of Achor. The springs made the ground swampy in the Valley and was the source of the mudflats where the River Jordan met the Salt Sea. That was the muddy ground we first camped on when we came out of the River Jordan and arrived at the Salt Sea. The town of Jericho was an oasis, known as the city of palm trees. There were also banana trees, figs, balsams and sycamores.

Sixty four harvests in the past Jericho was hit by an earthquake when the earth shook and the rocks were split, and a great rendering tore the land. The earthquake was felt all the way to Bethany and Jerusalem. The town of Jericho was completely destroyed with three thousand people being killed in the calamity. Twice before this had happened, once as told by Amos, in the days of Uzziah king of Judah, and again in the days when Joshua was appointed leader by Moses upon his death. The Habirum under the leadership of Joshua crossed the River Jordan going westward and Jericho was the first city to fall to them, the first victory in the defeat of the Canaanites. – *The wall fell down flat, so that the people went up into the city, and they took the city* –. Joshua had pillaged what remained in the town of Jericho. – *And they burnt the city with fire, and all that was therein, only the silver, and the gold, and the vessels of brass and of iron, they put into the treasury of the house of ADONAI. All the surviving inhabitants being killed without mercy, both man and woman, both young and old, and ox, and sheep, and ass, with the edge of the sword* –. All were killed except for Rahab, and all her brethren, who were spared. Joshua cursed the town. – *Cursed be the man before ADONAI that riseth up and buildeth this city* –.

Jericho had been rebuilt by the Roman's pawn, Herod I. Jericho was now an oasis of springs, baths, palm trees, and gardens for the relaxation of Herod Antipas and those in his favor. Perhaps Joshua's curse was the cause of the worms that ate Herod I from the inside, killing him painfully. Soon Joshua's curse would fall upon the Herodians by the edge of the sword we would wield to cut them down. We would go through Jericho on this trip as we had business there and it was on our way to Jerusalem for the next Passover festival. Yeshua's plan was for the next Passover festival to be the time of the ax falling on the Romans' heads. We were nearing the end of our journey.

As it was late in the day and the city gates would be closing soon, we made camp on the far outskirts of town. We would enter the following morning with the crowd milling about, rather than draw attention to ourselves from the Roman guards. Our reason for going to Jericho was to find a man named Zacchaeus. This man was the chief tax collector at Jericho. Levi Matthew told us Zacchaeus had information we would need. We all gathered together, Yeshua gave the instructions for the morrow, then he went off into the wilds for his rest and solitude. I appointed the watchmen to stand guard, each to wake his relief, with myself taking the last hour before the dawn.

The next morning Yeshua, Levi Matthew, Simon Zealot with two of his men, and Barabbas with two of his men, and myself, entered the city singly or in groups of two. The others waited at the camp for our return. The city was surrounded by two walls made of stacked stones with the outer wall being the height of four men and the inner the height of five men. The city defenders could bombard an attacker from atop the inner wall if they breached the outer wall. Both walls were thick and stout, they were formidable barriers. I could see this city would need to be taken by deception from within rather than from frontal assault. The reason for the massive fortifications was Herod Antipas usually spent the winter months here as the weather was warmer than anywhere else in Judah or Israel. Herod Antipas had constructed an arena to entertain his guests with horse and chariot racing. He also had new aqueducts built to bring irrigation from the springs to his winter palace, all at the expense of taxing the Habirum.

Levi Matthew led us through the streets of the town to the home of Zacchaeus. After knocking at the door and being invited in, Levi Matthew introduced Yeshua and myself to this man while the others waited on guard in the street. Zacchaeus took us from the entry hall into his home. I saw this man had benefitted from his tax collecting duties as his home was luxurious with carpets and many valuable objects. Jericho was famous for its balsam plants and the production of the balsam spice that was used for its medicinal and aromatic qualities. Zacchaeus' income was from the taxes on the sale of this product. The greater part of the money went to Rome, further enriching the emperor. Levi Matthew had been friends with Zacchaeus all their lives, and our conversation proved that Zacchaeus was a Pharisee in whom a mighty zeal for justice for our people burned brightly.

Yeshua told him, "The curse of Joshua on Jericho continues. The town is cursed now by the presence of the Romans. We need for you to act as Elisha and cleanse the waters of this place. Cleanse the stench of the Romans from the waters. Levi Matthew is captain. He will return with many warriors. In the meantime you will survey the defenses and make a plan of attack. Can you take Jericho from within for the glory of Israel, and Judah, and the Habirum?"

Zacchaeus answered, "Yes. It will be done. I will pledge half of all I own for the purchase of arms and bribes to make it so."

Yeshua told Zacchaeus "Very well. We take Jericho right after the Passover. You will survey the defenses, count the Roman soldiers, count the night guards, and make a plan of attack. Hark the words of Ezekiel. – *A sword, a sword, it is sharpened. It is sharpened that it may make a sore slaughter* –. We will drain the blood from the meat of the Romans in Jerusalem, in Jericho, and throughout the land of the Habirum."

Zacchaeus stood and offered his hand to Yeshua. They gripped at the forearm, "It shall be done. You may count on it." We took our leave from Zacchaeus. We returned to the camp for the other men and horses. Our journey would now take us to Jerusalem.

MOUNT OLIVET. MY NAME IS
MARIAM OF MAGDALA

Yeshua arrived in Bethany at midday on the Shabbat. The next Shabbat would a High Shabbat because it occurred during Passover week. Our reunion was sweet, as I had missed him sorely. He and Judas and Barabbas and the other men were darkened and weathered by their days in the sun. Yeshua's brown hair and beard was streaked with gold from the sun's rays, like fresh cut straw. His blue eyes sparkled like sapphires, the stone of truth and sincerity. We sat and took food straightaway as they were famished from their hard travels. While we ate, Judas and Barabbas lavished attention on their wives, Rachel and Jehosheba, and the women glowed in their happiness.

I and the other women, and the men Yeshua had assigned to be our guards, had been in Bethany for ten days. I arranged lodgings for us, not all in the same quarters, but in various locations about the town. Bethany was nigh unto Jerusalem, about fifteen furlongs off, on the eastern slope of the Mount Olivet. This distance was less than a one hour walk. Bethany was a pleasant town with many trees of olives, figs and almonds growing about it. Mount Olivet had numerous oil presses and was famous for the quality of its oil from their centuries old olive trees.

Our lodging was in the house of Lazarus who was born and lived the life of a good Pharisee. He had taken the vows of an Essene. The home of Lazarus was built of four solid surrounding walls, with all the rooms opening to a garden in the center. One wall had a strong gate that opened from the street into a greeting room with another gate leading to the garden and household. I had chosen this dwelling so Yeshua could meet with his men in the garden in private.

Included in these meetings would be Joanna, my dear friend and the wife of Chuza, the steward of Herod Antipas. I had sent word to her when I had arrived in Bethany. We met the first time on the market street in Jerusalem and there we made other arrangements for the times and places of meeting. Joanna was desperate to take her family away from the court of Herod Antipas. Over the years she had seen many sickening things in Herod's court and she was worried for her children to be raised in the vicinity of Herod's perversions. Joanna had been horrified when the drunken Herod had Yokhanan HaMatbi beheaded at the whim of his new wife, Herodias. Chuza had also become disillusioned with his duties. He feared his insane master and was willing to assist Yeshua's quest for freedom.

This night, the day of Yeshua's arrival, Joanna came to the home of Lazarus. With her was Chuza and two other men. One was Joseph of Arimathea. Joseph was a prosperous man and on the Sanhedrin council. He was also secretly the leader of the Essenes in Jerusalem, secretly so that he could function within the Sadducee controlled Sanhedrin council for the benefit of the Essenes and Pharisees. The other man was Nicodemus of the land of Damascus. Nicodemus was also Essene, and he and Joseph and Chuza were bound to ridding the land of the Romans. They knew that for the Habirum to be free the Romans, Herod Antipas and all his family, and the Sadducees must go.

Nicodemus was one of the merchants whose business was supplying the Romans at the Antonia Fortress with food and drink. He had firsthand knowledge of the number of soldiers and what was happening in the Fortress. Joseph of Arimathea was the person who communicated between the Sanhedrin council, the priests in the Temple, and the governor, Pontius Pilate. Chuza, being the right hand of Herod Antipas, was informed of all that occurred in the royal court. Joanna would be the one who communicated to us any news and information they had to share as the week progressed. I would meet her each day at the high sun in Jerusalem at the market. When necessary she would come to the home of Lazarus in the evening. Yeshua would meet or exchange messages with his captains each day at the Garden of Gethsemane which was halfway between Bethany and Jerusalem on the western slope of Mount Olivet.

When Nicodemus of Damascus was first introduced to Yeshua, Nicodemus told him, "Yeshua, we know that you are a teacher who has come from ADONAI. No one could perform the signs you are doing if ADONAI were not with him. And this is the condemnation, that the Romans have come into our world, and Sadducees love the darkness of the Romans rather than the light of ADONAI. The Sadducees are evil and these evil men conspire with the Romans to enslave us. But he who does the truth comes to the light that his deeds may be clearly seen."

Yeshua bid them to be seated and asked, "What is the strength of the Roman guard in Herod's palace? How many soldiers are in the Antonia Fortress? How many are in the night patrol of Jerusalem and at the gates?"

Nicodemus had a drawing that he referred to while he gave his detailed accounting of the Romans. This was valuable information and I could see Yeshua was listening intently. The captains, Judas, Barabbas, Simon Zealot, the brothers James and John, the brothers Andrew and Simon Peter, the brothers Levi and James barAlphaeus, Philip, Bartholomew Nathaneal, and Thomas were all paying close attention.

"There are usually sixty soldiers at the fortress. Most of these men are mercenaries. The fighters on horseback are from Thracia. The soldiers are Macedonian, with some from Lycia and Galatia. They are commanded by two Roman officers. The mercenaries are trained in the Roman method. They work for coins and eventual citizenship. When Herod Antipas comes to Jerusalem for the Passover festival, he travels with another sixty soldiers to provide additional security for the Temple and for his own protection. So now there are one hundred and twenty soldiers at the Fortress Antonia. The soldiers of the Fortress are responsible for security on the outside around the Temple and in the city, but not within the Temple itself."

Yeshua asked, "Will these mercenaries fight to the death, for the glory of Rome?"

"Make no mistake, these men fight like Romans when they take up the sword. Whether they stand to the last man if outnumbered and see the cause is lost, only ADONAI knows. I suggest you be prepared to show no quarter."

Simon the Zealot said, "The fact is, none may leave. We cannot risk their reporting back to the Romans our numbers and strength."

Yeshua looked at each of us in turn. "It is agreed then. – *And thou shalt consume all the peoples that ADONAI shall deliver unto thee, thine eye shall not pity them* –. No mercy."

Nicodemus pointed at his map, "The Antonia Fortress has four towers, enclosed by walls between each tower. The south tower walls are next to the north wall of the Temple. The towers are also tied together by four bridges. The bridges at the two north towers span from roof to roof. The two towers on the southern corners are higher, so the bridges from the roofs of the north towers lead to doorways on the walls of the south towers and from there to inside stairs leading to the roofs. The two south towers are built higher so that from their roofs the Romans can overlook, see, and dominate the entire Temple. From that height they can rain arrows down onto anyone they see as a threat. The southeast tower is connected to the Temple courtyard by a set of stairs from inside the tower, and this is the Guard's Gate. The southwest tower has a bridge that leads onto the roof of the porticoes surrounding the Temple. From there they have complete access to all parts of the Temple." Nicodemus told more details of the Romans forces and when he finished Joseph of Arimathea told us about the Temple.

Joseph of Arimathea gave details of who the important priests are and what their functions were. He described the daily schedules of the Temple, in particular the preparations for the Passover week leading to the observance of High Shabbat, which was six sundown's from the next day. "The high priest, Caiaphas, is in a private room located at the rear of the Temple, behind the holy altar. According to the Sadducee's the high priest must stay at the Temple the week preceding his officiating the rituals. If he stays at his home he risks becoming defiled by the touch of a woman, whether it be his wife or a consort." Joseph also told us how the Romans of the Antonio Fortress controlled the high priest's use of the sacred vestments. "The Romans hand the sacred vestments over to the Temple treasurer before the high priest needs them for the rituals. Then the vestments are taken back by the Romans. This is done at the Guard's Gate, from the southeast tower directly into the Temple portico. The Romans normally do not come into the Temple as it would then be defiled. They are also not welcome into the Upper City because their spittle makes the area unclean. The Romans will, in the event of troubles, ignore these rules and go wherever they choose."

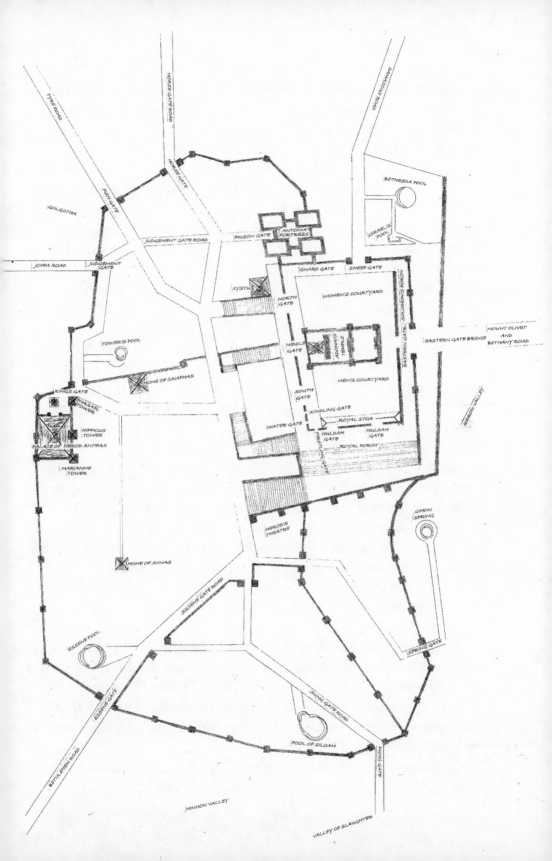

Joseph told us about the Sanhedrin council. He said this was the assembly of seventy one elders and leading men who exercise authority at the Temple and in Jerusalem. Their word is the law in all religious and legal matters, but they have no authority over military decisions. The Sanhedrin was sanctioned and allowed by the Romans who agreed to this independent authority, as long as it suited the Romans purposes. This Sanhedrin nobility consisted primarily of Sadducees. Leading the council was the high priest, Caiaphas, who was the son-in-law of Annas, the former high priest. The Sanhedrin meet each day in the Chamber of Hewn Stones except Shabbat and during festivals. Sometimes they would meet at the home of Caiaphas, as the need and hour of day dictated. The Chamber of Hewn Stones is a room located at the northwest corner of the Temple portico. Joseph gave Yeshua the parchment on which was drawn the gates and doors of the Temple.

Then Joseph described the Temple priests in order of authority. The captain of the Temple, a man named Joezer, was in charge of security in the Temple area with the power to arrest wrongdoers. Under the captain were priests stationed at the doors as gatekeepers, providing security in the sanctuary, and also patrolling the Temple area by day and night. The chief doorkeeper was Gudgeda. He was the keeper of the keys and responsible for opening, closing and locking the gates each day. The treasurer, Nahum, was the superintendent of the priestly vestments which the high priests wore. The vestments were the tunic, robe, headpiece, and other symbols of the high priests office. The Romans kept all these things under lock and key in the Fortress, only allowing the treasurer to take them out for the services.

Yeshua asked Joseph, "Where exactly do the Romans keep these vestments?"

Joseph pointed to a particular place on the map, "At the Guard's Gate, into the Fortress, in the passageway beyond the door leading to the Chamber of Hewn Stones is the locked room where they are kept. The Roman military commander at the Antonia Fortress gives the key to the Fortress captain of the guard on duty for that day when the vestments are required for services."

Yeshua said, "So. There are only two doors between us and the vestments."

FIVE DAYS BEFORE PASSOVER. MY
NAME IS JUDAS ISCARIOT

This was the day when Yeshua would enter Jerusalem for the first time as a warrior, with zeal and purpose. Yeshua gathered us, and he said, "We must bestir the passions of the people to make them see freedom is at hand. This week, beginning today, will become known as the week of passion. This will be the week of passionate bloodletting, when the Habirum take up the sword. This will be a week of violence and sacrifice, and that sacrifice will be our redemption."

We left Bethany and crossed over Mount Olivet. We came to the road running east and west that led to the Eastern Bridge over the gorge of the Kidron Valley. On the west side of the Kidron Valley was Mount Moriah, where Abraham built the altar to sacrifice his son, Isaac. We bypassed the bridge road and took the rough path down and through the gorge. We came to the old wall built by King David after he had taken the town from the Jebusites. At the hill of stacked stones, covering over the Spring of Gihon, we entered the Lower City through the Spring Gate. The Romans and Sadducees call this part of Jerusalem the Lower City. The true believers, the Pharisee and Essenes, know it as the City of David, as it was King David's first settlement at the southeast end of Mount Moriah. David founded a new city which he called Jerusalem, meaning, City of Peace. The Temple was constructed by David's son, Solomon, over one thousand years before for the glory of ADONAI. The Romans and the Herods had no rightful claim to their presence here. This week, this fight, would be the end of them.

Mount Moriah was divided by the Tyropoeon Valley that ran north to south. Herod I, the one called Herod Great by the Romans, had conspired with the Roman general Pompey Magnus and seized Jerusalem, Herod I then embarked on ambitious building projects. Herod I brought in designers and planners from Rome and Aegyptus who had completely rebuilt the Temple. Herod I filled the Tyropoeon

Valley with stones and rubble, doubling the size of the crest of the Mount. On this new plateau Herod I rebuilt the Temple and added a new part to the city on the western side, called the Upper City. At the Upper City Herod I built his new palace and the Antonia Fortress. Herod I started his Temple rebuilding project forty six harvests ago. The Habirum had been heavily taxed to finance this work, all done for the glory of Herod I himself, not for the glory of ADONAI. His son, Herod Antipas, had inherited all of his father's work as he was the Roman appointed tetrarch of Galilee with rights and privileges in Roman administered Judah.

It was our intention today to survey the city and entry gates to verify that our attack plan was as solid as the foundation of the Temple itself. After entering the city through the Spring Gate, we followed the walkway south along the inside of the wall to the next gate, the Dung Gate that led to the Hinnon Valley. Outside the Dung Gate was the city dump. After a careful look at the area near this gate, we continued west to the Essene Gate. From there we retraced our steps to the Spring Gate road and made our way into the City of David. The thousands of people who lived and worked in this part of Jerusalem were the majority of the residents of Jerusalem. They were mostly Pharisees and Essenes. In the Upper City, the newer section, was where the wealthy Sadducees and Herodian's made their homes.

Looking at the residents of the City of David, Yeshua said, "These people bringeth forth that which is good out of their hearts. The others, who live above them, bringeth forth that which is evil. These good people here shall be like roaring lions. – *They shall roar like young lions, yea, they shall roar. And lay hold of the prey, and carry it away* –."

An older woman approached Yeshua. She was bent with age and a lifetime of struggle. With her was a boy carrying a load of palm fronds upon his back. I took another look and saw that this was not a boy, it was a man with a wrinkled face and beard. Apparently he had been born or acquired some deficiency making him small and twisted. He must be her son. They collected the palm fronds from where they fell on the ground and were carrying them about, making their livelihood from selling them. These fronds were useful for thatching roofs and for fencing yard gardens to keep chickens from pecking. The price they could charge was next to nothing as the fronds lay on the ground to be gathered for free. Their customers were those who did not have the time or inclination to gather them, or who purchased out of a sense of charity. I did not see how anyone could make enough coins to survive from this type of work.

The woman clutched the sleeve of Yeshua's robe and spoke to him, so softly I could not hear what she said. Yeshua leaned over to speak in her ear. I suddenly recognized the woman. She was the woman who had donated the mites to the Temple years before and who Yeshua had assisted. They talked privately for a few moments, then Yeshua introduced her to Mariam. They talked in low voices, then the woman raised her head and spoke in a surprisingly loud voice to all the passersby, "I know this man and his kindness and strength. I know that he is a mighty man of ADONAI. Word of his deeds go before him, like Elijah before him, I know that he is a man of ADONAI and that the word of ADONAI from his mouth is the truth. ADONAI has put His spirit upon him, He shall set a covenant of the people." Then she took several fronds from the man's load and spread them on the ground before Yeshua, proclaiming to all, "Hark! Hear, ye deaf, and look, ye blind, that ye may see. The king enters!"

When Yeshua and I were both children about eight years old, me living in Bethany and him living in Aegyptus, the Roman Imperator Caesar Augustus directed Publius Sulpicius Quirinius, the Roman governor of Judah, to make a census of the land of the Habirum for taxation purposes. It was this imposition of Roman rule that brought countless multitudes of angry Habirum from Galilee to gather in Jerusalem. Judah of Gamala organized these Habirum into a fierce fighting force to resist the Romans. Jerusalem, as the holy place, was then and now the focus of revolt against Roman rule. It was prophesied that Jerusalem was where the messiah would appear. Everyone knew this prophecy. The Pharisees expected it and the Sadducees feared it. This is what the old woman was telling the crowd of people gathered around. – *Behold, the days come, saith ADONAI, that I will make a new covenant with the house of Israel, and with the house of Judah* –. After the death of Solomon the land of the Habirum was divided, and all awaited the day when a messiah would bring the Habirum together again.

As much as Yeshua tried to keep such talk tampered down, word of his medicinal curative powers and especially of his resistance against the Romans seemed to be much talked about amongst the Habirum. He smiled and patted the old woman on the back. He nodded his head at us to continue walking.

We followed the Spring Gate road. At the old City of David wall was the Greek style theater Herod I had constructed. The north and west sides had been carved from the Mount. The east side was adjacent to and defiled the wall of the City of David. The south end was built up in a half circle style for seating on raised tiers. Here the Romans and Sadducees would watch the shows of Romans playing Greek stories the Romans had translated into their harsh sounding Latīna. The intersection of the Spring Gate and Essene Gate roads inclined upwards, leading to the Temple and Upper City. The Temple was perched high above us, at the very top of Mount Moriah. At this corner of the Temple, on the roof of the portico, is where the trumpeter would stand before sundown and blow his horn. This was a signal to everyone in the city to – *Remember the Shabbat day, to keep it holy. Six days shalt thou labour, and do all thy work, but the seventh day is a Shabbat unto ADONAI, in it thou shalt not do any manner of work, thou, nor thy son, nor thy daughter, nor thy man-servant, nor thy maid-servant, nor thy cattle, nor thy stranger that is within thy gates* –. This had always been a major point of disagreement between the Habirum and the Romans. The Romans, greedy swine that they are, did not want anyone, freeman or slave, to lose a day of laboring. The trumpeter would blow his horn from this raised position to signal the start and end of Shabbat.

The thousands of Habirum who came to the Temple for the festival entered it from four directions. At the southwest corner was a wide set of stairs leading up the southern entrance and the two Huldah

Gates at the Royal Porch. Also from the Royal Porch were the smaller Kindling Gate, Water Gate, and the Firstling Gate that allowed entry for supplies to be delivered for the rituals. On the west side were three stairs leading to the North, Middle, and South Gates. Entering from the east, from the Mount Olivet and Bethany direction, they would cross the Eastern Bridge onto Solomon's Porch then go through the Eastern Gate. The Eastern Gate was where the morning sun shined directly into the Temple. At the north was the Sheep's Gate through which the sacrificial victims were led to slaughter. Also on the north was the Guards Gate from the Antonia Fortress, leading directly to the portico inside the Women's Courtyard.

We walked the entire city, ending up in the northwest at the market stall of a food vendor. The market stalls ran alongside each of the main roads through the city. One could find all manner of foods and products in Jerusalem. From the food vendor we bought a dish for a high sun meal. The cook spread olive oil on a piece of thick bread and while the bread crisped golden over hot coals, the cook quickfired onions in a smoking hot iron pot. The onions were stirred in a drizzle of olive oil with spices. The quick frying kept the onions still crispy. A spread of cooked fava beans was slathered on the bread, then the onions were added, then the bread was folded over so the piping hot mixture could be held in the hand. We ate hungrily as the hot olive oil dripped from the onions and ran down our fingers.

While we ate we studied the palace of Herod Antipas just south of where we stood. Herod's palace was substantial, solidly built, and surrounded by four tall walls. The western and north walls were built on the edge of the Mount, at the sheer face of the cliffs. The view from there looked out over the Wilderness of Judah. The other two walls separated the palace from the Upper City. These walls had the Tower Phasael, Tower Hippicus and Tower Mariamne. The Tower Mariamne was named for the wife Herod I had suspected of treachery and who he murdered. Each of these towers gave the palace a defensive fighting position with good fields of fire into the Upper City. A direct assault on Herod's palace would be pointless. The palace would have to be taken by siege. We had a plan for that.

South of Herod's palace was the home of Caiaphas, the high priest. We had a plan for him also.

We were at the intersection of four roads. One led south to the western Temple staircases, one north to the Fish Gate, the third west to the Judgment Gate, and the fourth east to the Prison Gate of the Antonia Fortress. Roads came to the city from all points of the outside world. The Fish Gate road led northwest to Tyre. The Sheep's Gate road ran northeast to Damascus. The Horse Gate led to Mount Gerizim in the land of the Cushites. The Eastern Gate led east to Mount Olivet and beyond to Jericho and the River Jordan. The Essene Gate at the southwest of the city led to Bethlehem. The Dung Gate went into the Valley of Hinnon, the Valley of Slaughter. On the west side of the city, The Judgment Gate went just outside the city to the place of the skulls, called Golgatha, and then further west to Joppa and Lydda. That town, Lydda, was once the center of an affluent agricultural area. The people of Lydda grew all manner of crops and raised cattle from the time of Solomon and after Judah Maccabee freed the Habirum from the Seleucid tyrants. Lydda was captured by the Roman general Gaius Cassius Longinus when he was the governor of Syria. The town was razed and the inhabitants of Lydda were sold into slavery. This Roman, Cassius, was one of the conspirators who assassinated the Caesar Julius. The Roman greed for power, conquest, and blood knew no bounds.

Directly east of us was another structure built by Herod I. This was the Xystus. It was a raised platform with columns supporting a roof for shade. It was open on two sides, one facing west, the other north. The south side was the wall of the staircase leading to the North Gate of the Temple, and the east side of the Xystus, was the Temple wall itself. This structure being tied to the Temple in its construction and sharing a wall was a constant point of disagreement between the Herodian Sadducee priests and the Pharisees and Essenes. The Romans and Sadducees used it for exercising and wrestling in the Greek and Roman style, meaning they cavorted in the nude. The Pharisees and Essenes saw this display as an abomination before ADONAI at his very Temple.

We discussed our plan and refined the details. Yeshua looked at us, he said, "Yes. It will work. It will work just as we thought." We left the city through the Horse Gate. At the northern end of Mount Moriah we studied the outside of the Antonia Fortress as we made our way to Solomon's Porch. We crossed the Eastern Bridge over the Kidron Valley to return to Bethany. Our plan was set.

FOUR DAYS BEFORE PASSOVER. MY NAME IS MARIAM OF MAGDALA

The Passover festival did not start before spring and not before the barley was ripe. The Passover festival is a command for all Habirum to appear before ADONAI. The only persons who were not obligated to attend were a deaf-mute, those who were not in their right minds, children too young to be without the assistance of a parent, one of double sex who carries the organs of both man and woman, those who had been made eunuch, slaves not of Habirum descent, and those who were blind or lame.

We left Bethany, going down the west slope of the Mount Olivet where the burial grounds lay. Some of the Habirum of Jerusalem were entombed in burial caves on the west slope of the Mount. The stone of the Mount was made of soft chalk and flint and was easy to dig for caves. Judas told me the stones were not good for building as it had no strength and would easily collapse on itself. Every Habiru wanted to be buried here as from this height they could look upon Jerusalem in their final rest. From here I could see down and across the Valley of Kidron to the Temple. It shined splendidly under the sunlight. The Temple was located at the northeastern edge of the Mount. On the northern wall of the Temple was the Antonia Fortress, where the Roman soldiers lived and from where they exercised control of Jerusalem.

At the bottom of Mount Olivet we would cross the Eastern Bridge over the dry rocky Valley of Kidron to the Eastern Gate of the Temple. Before the bridge we stopped under the shade of some trees where Yeshua nodded to two of his men, Yeshua told them, "Just past the end of the bridge you will find a man waiting with a donkey and her colt. Untie them and bring them here to me."

The men walked onto the bridge and crossed to the city. While we waited for them to return, Yeshua began speaking in a loud voice and many stopped to listen. Soon there was a multitude gathered about him. Yeshua spoke of a rich man and a beggar.

"Now there was a rich man dressed in purple and fine linen, who lived each day in joyous splendor. A beggar named Lazarus lay at his gate, covered with sores and longing to be fed with the crumbs that fell from the rich man's table. The dogs came and licked his sores. One day the beggar died and was carried by the angels to Abraham's side. The rich man also died and was buried. The rich man was cast into Hades, where he was in torment. He looked up and saw Abraham from afar, with Lazarus by his side. So he cried out, 'Father Abraham, have mercy on me and send Lazarus to dip the tip of his finger in water and cool my tongue. I am in agony in this fire.' But Abraham answered, 'Child, remember that during your lifetime you received your good things, while Lazarus received bad things. But now he is comforted here, while you are in agony.' 'Then I beg you, father,' he said, 'send Lazarus to my father's house, for I have five brothers. Let him warn them so that they will not also end up in this place of torment.' But Abraham replied, 'They have Moses and the prophets, let your brothers listen to them.' 'No, father Abraham,' he said, 'but if someone is sent to them from the dead, they will repent.' Then Abraham said to him, 'If they do not listen to Moses and the prophets, they will not be persuaded even if someone rises from the dead.'"

I watched the people while Yeshua spoke. I could see they were shocked at his words. Many gathered in groups to discuss what they had just heard. "What is this new teaching?" I heard a man say to the others about him. Just then the two men arrived with the donkey and Yeshua climbed aboard the beast. Yeshua's legs were long enough for his feet to rest easy on the ground. While this may have looked sort of comical, I knew that Yeshua was fulfilling the prophecy of Zechariah, telling us. – *Rejoice greatly, O daughter of Zion. Shout, O daughter of Jerusalem. Behold, thy king cometh unto thee. He is triumphant, and victorious, lowly, and riding upon an ass –*.

I knew that Yeshua did not aspire to the crown of a king, but he knew the power of the Words. It was this vision of freedom he wanted the Habirum to carry in the eye of their mind. All of the people showed enthusiasm for Yeshua's words. They were speaking in an excited manner. It was this very vision I could see was scandalous to a Sadducee who had stopped to listen. He was a wealthy merchant or landowner, dressed in a colorful costly robe. This Sadducee spoke angry words to a man standing with him. The Sadducee pointed at Yeshua. The Sadducee slashed his hand across his throat in an unmistakable gesture. This Sadducee's reaction would be typical of all the Sadducees. They feared any threat to their rule, and apparently this Sadducee perceived Yeshua had spoken this parable against Herod Antipas. I could see Yeshua had begun his visit to the Temple in a striking manner. Barabbas had also noticed the Sadducee and the man he was talking to. He leaned in to whisper in the ear of Judas, then Barabbas slipped away into the crowd. I wondered what he was up to.

Judas was walking directly behind Yeshua who was riding on the ass. With him were Simon the Zealot, and the two brothers, Andrew and Simon Peter. I walked with Rachel and Jehosheba. Behind us were Barabbas and Simon the Zealot's men as guards. I was listening to the men talking about the bridge over the Valley of Kidron that made an entrance to the main Eastern Gate of the Temple. While they admired the structure and the hard work of building it, they had only harsh words for Herod I, the son of the Imudean slave and the grandfather of Herod Antipas.

Judas was describing how the two ends of the bridge were cleverly stacked stones that squared the two opposing ends of the ravine. The stones were carved so fine they needed no mortar. The stones supported the cedar timbers spanning the open middle. Judas was explaining to Simon Zealot that the bridge and the entire Temple were built of finely carved stones set without mortar, as the wood required to burn the limestone rock and make the lime for mortar would have used more trees than grew in all of Judah.

Herod I, during his siege of Jerusalem, had cut down almost all of the trees around the city. He used the timbers to erect an encircling wall with guard towers. The Roman army that supported Herod I was fifteen thousand soldiers who stood guard at the wall. No one inside the city could escape and the wall denied them supplies. The residents of the city suffered starvation. Those who dared to attempt an escape, and were captured, were crucified on timbers from the cut down trees within sight of the city walls. Thousands of Habirum met their death from cruci fixus during the three year war. The trees, some hundreds of years in age, had never grown back, leaving the area around Jerusalem a barren landscape to this very day. Only the trees on the slopes of Mount Olivet had been spared as this was the main camp of Herod I.

Suddenly from behind us was the panicked neighing of a horse and people yelling. We turned to see a horse rearing and people scattering out of the way of the beast's hooves. Then there was a scream, a man howling hopelessly that ended with a loud thump noise. I looked over the bridge railing to see the body of a man lying twisted, broken, and bleeding on the hard stones of the valley below. I saw it was the Sadducee who had spoken harshly about Yeshua's parable. Straightening I saw Barabbas pulling on the horse's reins trying to control the animal. Then everyone started moving again and we were pushed from behind to continue the crossing. I was not sure what had just happened but I was sure Barabbas had played a hand in the Sadducee's seeming accident. That Sadducee would not be witness against Yeshua. I did not see the other man, the one the Sadducee had spoken to. If this Sadducee was a landowner, growing foods for sale, he most likely had so many slaves the slaves did not know the name of the man who owned them. Most likely, also, he accumulated his land by seizing the farms of Habirum who could not repay their loans he had given during the drought. His demise was no great loss.

At the end of the bridge we came to Solomon's Porch, a wide paved area that spanned the entire eastern side of the Temple that then turned and continued around the southern end of the Temple for the Royal Porch. On Solomon's Porch were tables of those who exchanged foreign coins for the Jerusalem silver shekel, which was the only coin the Temple accepted. Also in this area were those selling the sacrificial victims, sheep and doves. All Habirum were expected to offer a sacrifice, a sin offering or blood offering, in order to remain true with ADONAI. In reality, the sacrifices were directly advantageous to the Sadducee priestly hierarchy. The priests bled and butchered the sacrificial victims, then kept a portion of the meat. The Sadducee priests also kept the hides of wool and sold them. From my perspective as a healer, I knew the meat rich diet from the daily eating of the sacrificial animals kept the priests in constant bowel sickness. It was common knowledge the temple physician was kept busy treating the priests for their bowel sickness. I did not envy the Temple physician or his duties which were, no doubt, very unpleasant.

According to the last mandatory census by the Romans, the population of Jerusalem equaled fifteen thousand inside the city walls and another five thousand in the surrounding area. The pilgrims who came to a festival from all over, would at least triple the population, equaling a massive gathering of people during the week of the festival. If one table consisted of ten people eating one sacrificial sheep that means there are thousands of sheep sacrificed during the Passover festival. The temple priests were very well off financially as they drew their income from the treasury and all the money from the sold hides went directly to the Temple treasury. The high priest had control of the treasury so the high priest and his family were very wealthy. The income from the sale of the hides, the sacrificed unblemished sheep, was supposed to be shared among all the priests. However, the Sadducee high priest used the Temple treasury as his own private bank. The shamelessness of the high priest was unbounded. The high priest would often plunder the hoard of the lower priest's hides and not share the coins from their sale.

Ordinary priests who lived outside of Jerusalem and who were not of the Temple class lived in great poverty, some of them actually dying of hunger during a famine or when an entire harvest was destroyed by warfare or weather. During normal times the prices of all commodities inside the city was higher than in the surrounding countryside. The price of fruits and vegetables cost several times more than in the countryside. During the last famine, the price of wheat was increased twenty times. Only the wealthy could eat their daily bread.

We crossed the bridge onto Solomon's Porch. Directly in front of us was the Eastern Gate. The double doors of this main gate facing the sunrise were sheathed in solid hammered bronze, with gold and silver trim. The doors were the height of two men. The doors were set into the walls that were three men high and surrounded the Temple. Beyond the double doors was the Temple courtyards. Inside the courtyards was the Women's Courtyard on the right and the Men's Courtyard on the left. The Women's Court was limited in size due to the addition of the Chamber of Wood, the Chamber of Lepers, the Chamber of Oils, and the Chamber of Nazarites.

The Nazarites had taken a vow abstaining from fermented drink. They ate only fruits and vegetables, they never cut their hair or beards, and never touched a dead body. Indeed they could not touch a corpse even of their own family to prepare for the funerary rites. They vowed to dedicate all their thoughts and actions to the service of ADONAI. They had their own space in the Court of Women to ensure they did not come into contact with unclean persons. There was debate as to whether women could be Nazarites. The Sadducee's said it was impossible for a woman to be Nazarite and to be of a clean spirit when once a month a woman would menstruate, becoming defiled. The Pharisee's and Essenes allowed anyone to take the Nazarite vow. It was said that Yokhanan HaMatbi, the one called the Baptizer, had renounced his Essene vows and taken the more strict Nazarite vows. No one knew the truth of this matter. Yokhanan HaMatbi was as unknowable as the place of landing in the desert of a starfire that streaks across the night sky. The shooting stars were known only by ADONAI. When Joshua was in battle with all the kings of the Amorites. – *ADONAI cast down great stones from heaven upon them and they died, they were more who died with the shooting stars of fire from the night sky than they whom the children of the Habirum slew with the sword* –.

At the Eastern Gate were Temple priests who acted as guards to stop anyone not Habirum from entering and to forestall any unruly behavior. We walked past them through the gates into the Temple grounds itself. The area was packed with Habirum engaged in the functions of worship, bringing to the priests their sheep to be sacrificed on the ritual tables. The ground was paved stones, sloped in particular directions, so that the blood from sacrifices would drain into open culverts. The blood was diverted by the culverts into stone carved tanks and used as fertilizer for the planting of gardens. Gardeners had to buy the blood from the Temple. To use the blood without paying was to incur sacrilege.

All these people gathered at the Temple making sacrifices, made me recall the words of Psalms. – *We have done iniquitously, we have dealt wickedly* –. According to the Sadducee priests, the words of that verse required the different offerings. There was the sin offering, the burnt offering, the guilt offering, the trespass offering, the incense offering, the wood offering, the meal offering, and many more. According to the Sadducee priests some of those offerings were specifically related to women and the cleansing of their defilements.

This also made me remember the words of Hosea. – *For I desire mercy, and not sacrifice, and the knowledge of ADONAI rather than burnt offerings* –. These words from Hosea, which showed the grace and wisdom of ADONAI, made this practice of bloody animal sacrifices all the more unnecessary and repugnant.

The practice of the ritual sacrifice of animals had been brought back from Babylon. When the Habirum had been taken slave and exiled in that foreign land, they learned to worship the Babylonian god, Anu, who was the Babylonian Great Creator and Sky God. Their God of Darkness was Nergal, who brought war and famine, sickness and plagues, and the accompanying devastation and destruction. Both of these Babylonian gods required the slaughter of animals for confession, for atonement of sins, and blessings.

The panicked bleating of the pitiful terrified beasts was heartbreaking. Hundreds of sheep were lined up to be offered as sacrifice. The barnyard stink and the stench of burnt blood and raw flesh made me feel nauseated and woozy. My stomach had been tender for several days. I had just this morning complained to Yeshua that the drink or perhaps the food did not agree with me. Yeshua had kindly expressed sympathy and asked what he could do for me.

When I told him he could do nothing, it would pass, he had playfully suggested, "Physician, heal thyself."

I determined to ignore the smelly slaughter. I put my back to the sorry spectacle and turned to the task at hand. I looked at the Temple in a new way, with the eye of a warrior, as Yeshua and Judas and Barabbas were seeing it. But while they counted guards and doors and access, I cast an eye toward the Temple in a more brooding manner. I wondered how this unholy Herodian state of affairs had come into being. When Moses came down from the burning mountain with the stone tablet, and when Joshua had brought the Habirum tribes together at Shechem to make their covenant with ADONAI, could they have foreseen the stranglehold of Herod's Sadducee priestly aristocracy? Could they have foreseen the Temple being used as the Roman's tool to subjugate the Habirum people in their innocence and desire to worship ADONAI?

I turned to the south and looked at the structure atop the colonnaded aisle, the Royal Stoa. Columns supported the roof of the shaded area where Herod Antipas and his court could sit in comfort and observe the mass of people below in the Temple courtyards. The Royal Stoa overlooked the Men's Court of the Temple where the Habirum worshiped under the blazing, unforgiving sun. The shade of the Stoa was so dark, and the sun's light so bright where I stood, that I could not make out whether Herod Antipas was there or not. I knew in which direction his royal chair was located. With a grim smile I mentally sent an arrow flying straight for his cruel heart. If my arrow did not find him then I hoped the drink he took for pleasure would be – *Grapes of gall, bitter clusters, and his wine is the venom of serpents, the cruel poison of asps –*.

When his father, Herod I, had murdered the last of the Hasmonean line, Aristobulus III, and the freedom won by Judah Maccabeus had been lost, the Temple had in essence ceased to exist as ADONAI's home. It became the pinnacle of Herod's power, being then called Herod's Temple. The Sadducee Herodian priests continued their line ruthlessly. A Sadducee priest was compelled to marry a daughter of a Sadducee priest and her purity had to be confirmed for five generations. If she or a woman in her line had ever lived in a town occupied by an enemy she was considered impure, because she may have gone aside in secret with a man and been defiled. A priest's daughter who was accused and found guilty of adultery, judged by the Herodian Sadducee priests, could be burned at the stake publicly in Jerusalem.

Looking at the Temple with a calculating eye, I remembered a conversation the men had when they discussed getting into the Temple. They talked of the twelve gates for access, and the number twelve had stuck in my mind. I thought it odd that this number had such significance. Ishmael, the son of Abraham, had twelve sons. – *Twelve princes shall he beget, and I will make him a great nation –.* Jacob, the grandson of Abraham, had twelve sons who became the twelve tribes of the Habirum. There were twelve Judges who led the children of the Habirum through dark days and to victories over their enemies. A Habirum girl on the day she reaches her twelfth year, becomes a woman. We study the twelve prophets, Hosea, Joel, Amos, Obadiah, Jonah, Micah, Nahum, Habakkuk, Zephaniah, Haggai, Zechariah, and Malachi, whose writings are brief, concise and convey the wisdom of ADONAI.

The Greeks have the twelve Titans, who were overthrown by the twelve Olympians. The Greek hero, Heracles, the son of the Greek god Zeus and the mortal woman Alcmene, performed his twelve great labours. The Romans, untutored dogs they are, have no gods of their own and worship the twelve Olympian Greek gods, giving the Greek gods new Roman names. The Romans call the gathering together of their twelve gods the Dei Consentes, the Council of Twelve.

Twelve hours mark day and twelve hours mark night. Twelve full moons mark one harvest to the next harvest. Twelve harvests, twelve years, mark the return of the bright wandering nighttime star, the star the Greeks call Zeus and the Romans call Jupiter. The Greeks gave names to the twelve zodiakos, the circle of animals, the concentrations of stars that shine and frolic in the night sky.

The people in the land of Aegyptus use a twelve based numbering system, counting the knuckles of the fingers on one hand. The goddess Isis' birthday is celebrated on the twelfth day of the twelfth month. The Essenes believe the end times will bring a great wonder from ADONAI, when a woman will appear in the sky. She will be bright as the sun and she will stand on the moon. Upon her head will be a golden circlet of twelve shining stars. She will be the mother of the new messiah, according to the Essenes. Yeshua recruited twelve captains for his army, honoring the twelve tribes of the Habirum. Yeshua says he will rename the gates into the Temple after the names of the tribes. All the tribes will have equal rights and equal responsibilities and this will fulfill the prophecy of Ezekiel. It is said that even before the Babylonians there was a people, long since dead, who worshipped a forgotten god. Their god divided the sky into twelve gates, leading into a place of eternal rest. Twelve. What an interesting number. I shook my head. My mind was wondering. Perhaps whatever ailment was causing my stomach to be weak was also affecting my brain.

While I was standing to one side of the colonnaded aisle in the Women's Courtyard, lost in thought, I suddenly heard the noise of yelling and fighting. The sounds of violence were coming from outside the Temple, on Solomon's Porch. I ran with the other women to see what was happening. The women were frightened and running and to avoid being trampled in their midst I had no choice but to be carried along in the rush. At the gate I saw Rachel and Jehosheba and grabbed at their robes so we could stay together. The occurrence of the packed crowd panicking, and death by stampede, was not uncommon. With so many people packed into such a small restrictive area, there were numerous occasions over the years of mass hysteria, a mad dash for the gates to exit, and many deaths by being crushed underfoot.

Outside on the Porch, Barabbas was being wrestled to the ground by a handful of Roman soldiers. Even though he was outnumbered, it took all the Roman's might to subdue him. He was eventually subdued when a soldier bashed Barabbas on the head with a stout cudgel. Another ten or so Roman soldiers were joined in a circle, their swords and spears leveled outwards holding all the gathered

Habirum at bay. In just moments Barabbas was being dragged away to the Antonia Fortress.

Yeshua and Judas ran up. They had to wrestle their way through the crowd to get to us from the far south end at the Royal Porch. I told them Barabbas had been arrested but I did not know why. Yeshua looked fierce in his anger. He consoled Jehosheba, telling her, "Do not worry. Have no fear. We will rescue Barabbas from the clutches of the Romans." Looking about we could see the mass of people were fearful and crowding toward the bridge. The situation had become very dangerous. Yeshua told us we should leave now. He told Judas to lead us across the bridge. I asked Yeshua if he was coming with us. He said, "I am right behind you. Go! Now!"

As Judas shouldered us through the packed crowd, I looked over my shoulder to see Yeshua walk up to the tables of the money changers. He went down the row overturning the tables, scattering their stacks of coins all over the paved stones. The people were in a state of extreme anxiety from the actions of the Roman soldiers. They were ready to panic and stampede, but they turned back from mobbing the bridge to gather the fallen fortune of silver coins. The people were yelling in excitement, the soldiers forgotten for the moment. Yeshua was creating a diversion so we could safely exit the Temple grounds and cross the bridge. But he was placing himself in extreme danger. I saw a man, a money changer, pull a leather whip from inside his robe and slash at Yeshua. The man got one stroke then Yeshua slammed his fist in the man's face, took his whip from him and began whipping the money changers who rushed to attack him. He whipped the money changers out of his way as he made his way to the bridge. On the other side of the bridge Yeshua caught up with us and we hurried for the safety of Bethany.

That evening Joanna, Joseph and Nicodemus came to the home of Lazarus. They brought news from the Sanhedrin council and the court of Herod Antipas. Joanna said that Herod Antipas was enraged about the events at the Temple. Herod Antipas frothed at the mouth like a rabid dog in his anger. Herod Antipas had been told about the words a man said on the Mount Olivet side of the bridge. Herod

Antipas understood he was the rich man in the parable, and that this was a direct challenge to Herod. Herod Antipas had called a full meeting of the Sanhedrin council. The high priest, Caiaphas and his father-in-law, the former high priest, Annas, had been shouted at by Herod. Herod told Caiaphas and the Sanhedrin council they must get their Habirum under control or Herod would do it for them. Joanna described how Herod Antipas stormed about the palatial room in his palace. He kicked over a table laden with wine and plates of food. He screamed "Bring me this man. I will make a eunuch of him. I will make him eat his own testicles!"

Herod Antipas, like his father before him, had the power of life or death to those he perceived as enemy. I shuddered to think of the countless thousands of men, and women and children over the last seventy years who had been killed tortured to death being hung from the cross by these wild dogs. While Herod's boiling anger was very upsetting to me, Joseph had more bad news. He told us he had a spy in the city, a man who brought him information to trade for coins. This man was a Greek Habirum from the province of Cyrenaica, the port city of Cyrene. This man had recently come to Jerusalem and was unknown by most. This man, said Joseph, was Sadducee and believed Joseph was Sadducee also. The man reported to Joseph any actions by a Pharisee or Essene that could be a threat to the Sanhedrin or the court of Herod. Joseph told us he cultivated this man as his spy so Joseph would have advance notice of any actions against Pharisee or Essene. Joseph could warn them of impending arrest or danger.

Joseph told us the Sadducee merchant at the bridge who had been thrown into the gorge had been talking to this man from Cyrenaica. The man went to a Roman guard at the Temple and told the guard he had seen Barabbas create the trouble with the horse in order to throw the Sadducee off the bridge. This was why Barabbas was arrested. The man from Cyrenaica was to be a witness against Barabbas. Barabbas was charged with murder. Thankfully Jehosheba and Rachel were in another room and did not hear this. I would explain the situation to them in private.

"What is this man's name?" asked Yeshua.

Joseph replied, "He is called Simon the Cyrene."

"Do you know where this Simon the Cyrene can be found?"

"Yes. I know his place of lodging."

Judas said, "Describe this man, so he can be taken without mistake."

THREE DAYS BEFORE PASSOVER.
MY NAME IS JUDAS ISCARIOT

Early this morning the captains came to the home of Lazarus. We met in the garden. It was then we realized there was a setback in our plans. Yeshua had assigned seventy warriors to return to their homes to recruit more fighters. Yeshua had sent them out in pairs and we had expected each pair of men to bring at least five men, hopefully ten, back with them. That would have increased our forces by several hundred fighters. The last of the seventy with their recruits had arrived during the night, reporting to their captains at their camps on the outskirts of Jerusalem. The captains now told us they had only managed to bring a total of sixty nine warriors. This would require a change to our plan. Also the arrest and absence of Barabbas was a problem.

We gathered over a drawing of the city. Yeshua assigned the captains their points of attack. By the middle morning hour everyone knew their assignments. The captains left to return to their camps to prepare and to brief their men, and to hone the edges of their weapons sharp for the kill.

Yeshua and I went over our plan once more. During the evening hour Joseph of Arimathea and Nicodemus of Damascus came to the home of Lazarus with news. The Sadducee priests were all on the alert. They had been instructed to look for a man in the city who spoke treasonous words. If they came upon such a man they were to engage him in conversation, to provoke him to speak of many things. They were to be lying in wait for him, and seeking to catch him in something he might say that they might accuse him.

Nicodemus of Damascus told Yeshua, "If you were any other man I would advise you to get out and depart for Herod Antipas will kill thee. But you are not any other man. You are sent from ADONAI."

Joseph of Arimathea said, "Caiaphas the chief priest and the Sadducees of the Sanhedrin council seek to destroy thee. But even

Caiaphas worries that if this man they seek be executed during the feast week, there would be an uproar among the people. Caiaphas and the Sadducees would have you taken unawares and kill thee in private. But Herod Antipas has decreed that you be hung from the cross as an example. Herod Antipas has sent word to the governor, Pontius Pilate, that to be hung from the cross is to be your fate."

I watched Yeshua. His face showed no emotion. He told Joseph of Arimathea and Nicodemus of Damascus, "The Sadducee priests of Herod Antipas and his Roman overlords defile the Temple with their practice of selling and profiting from the offerings right at the doorstep of the Temple. For where their treasure is, there will be their hearts also. Our fight is twofold. For the freedom of the Habirum people and to free the home of ADONAI from the vipers within. The man who sells his cloak to buy a sword is the man who knows the true value of freedom. We will fight. We will prevail."

Joseph of Arimathea and Nicodemus of Damascus left. Then we rested for the dawn would bring us to the day of the positioning of our forces and the sunset on the morrow would begin the attack.

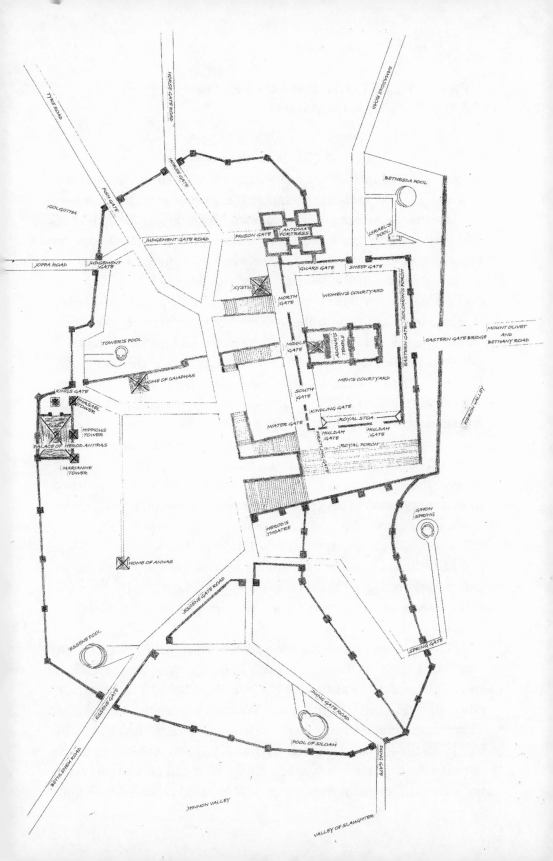

TWO DAYS BEFORE PASSOVER. MY
NAME IS JUDAS ISCARIOT

At the dawn we met all the captains at the Garden of Gethsemane. Yeshua told them to take to their men these words from the prophets. "Tell them – *Draw near, every man with his destroying weapon in his hand. And fear not, nor be dismayed, be strong and of good courage, for thus shall ADONAI smite all your enemies against whom ye fight –.*"

Every captain knew their assigned positions, what they were to do, and how to direct their men to accomplish their tasks. All during the day, from morning until the late hours before the gates were closed, the men of our forces infiltrated the city and took up their positions. Yeshua and I walked the entire city during the hours after the high sun and before sunset, double checking our arrangements. We left to return to Bethany satisfied that all was ready. We would return before the gates were closed for the night.

We were at the home of Lazarus sitting with the women taking supper. Yeshua raised his drinking cup in a toast, "This is our last supper under Roman domination. By sunrise we will be freed of Roman perversion. This time on the morrow we will take supper in the city as free men and free women." Yeshua said to Jehosheba, "Barabbas will also be freed. He will take supper with us." Yeshua and I finished our meals. The women were brave. They smiled at us as if we were going out for a walk and would return shortly. We went to the Garden of Gethsemane, collected our men, and then went into the city.

The sun would set shortly. We entered through the Spring Gate just before the two Roman guards closed the gate. As the guards turned their backs to us to close the gate, we attacked and took them efficiently and silently from behind. We left four men to hold the gate. Then Yeshua and I and six other men who had been waiting inside the city, proceeded to our next target. Around the city, at the other gates, our men overpowered the guards. Going west and north these were the actions of the men. Bartholomew Nathaneal captured the Dung

Gate. Simon Peter took the Essene Gate. Andrew took the Judgment Gate. Simon Zealot and his warriors took the Fish and Horse Gates. John took the Sheep's Gate. John left his men controlling the Sheep's Gate, then he and other warriors proceeded onto the north end of Solomon's Porch. From the south end of the Temple, up the stairs onto the Royal Porch, James barAlphaeus came around the corner onto the south end of Solomon's Porch and met John coming from the north end where they rushed the guards at the Bridge Gate. While this was occurring the remaining captains James, Levi Matthew, Philip, and Thomas took the roving guards whose movements we had carefully tracked each night for the last several days.

The city gates were now in our control and the patrols eliminated. It was time for the next steps. Certain of the captains with their warriors united at their stations on the main road to the west of the Temple where the three staircases were located.

All this took a set period of time. It was now approaching the hour when the Roman guard would be changed. The Roman army divided the day and night into watches of three hours, so there were four day watches and four night watches. Since the days and nights were shorter or longer depending on the season, and since clouds could obscure the sun and moon, their officer of the guard used water clocks to track the hours. The accuracy of these water clocks are constantly confirmed by the sundial when the sun would cast a shadow.

Inside the Temple, a man loyal to Joseph of Arimathea and Nicodemus of Damascus was standing at the Kindling Gate that he opened for me and my men. Quietly we entered the Temple grounds. We captured the four priests on guard duty who were huddled around a fire in the Women's Courtyard. We did these priests no harm, merely tying them securely and gagging them. I and a handful of my best archers climbed the stairs onto the roof of the porticoes. From there we quietly crossed the southwest tower bridge. On the roofs of the Antonia Fortress towers were two guards that needed to be eliminated. From the darkness we sent arrows flying to the guards then followed the arrows wielding sword and spear. Those guards were taken. I left some men on the roof of the southwest tower. Then we went back down the stairs to the north end of the Temple at the Guard's Gate that led from the Temple stairs into the Antonia Fortress.

In my mind's eye, knowing the plan, I envisioned Yeshua and his men standing in the darkness of the Xystus, awaiting the Prison Gate's opening and the change of guard coming out. I could see Yeshua, when he heard the creaking of the gate, tap the man holding the flint who struck the flint to iron igniting the arrow the archer had ready to fly. Just then I saw the fire signal arrow arcing into the air and heard yells breaking out from the direction of the Antonia Fortress. The battle was started.

All the men who were not at the gates, came running from their hiding places among the yards of the residents homes and from the market stalls and attacked the Roman soldiers at the Prison Gate. At the Guard's Gate leading into the Antonia Fortress, I used the key Joseph of Arimathea had provided to open the lock. My men and I rushed into the passageway. I knew the first door led into the Chamber of Hewn Stones and passed it. It was the second door, where the vestments were kept, that was my target. There were two locks on this door. I had the key to one. Joseph had not been able to get a copy of the other one, the Roman lock. That lock would have to be forced. In the original plan I was to be with Yeshua on the direct attack at the Prison Gate and Barabbas was to get into the vestments room.

I used my iron tools, hammer and chisel, on the lock to force it. I could hear my men at the end of the passageway. They were blocking the door against the Romans who were now on the alert. The Romans were yelling and banging against the heavy door made of thick timbers. The door swung inward to the passageway and my men used the building materials we had brought with us, wood and nails, to construct a stout frame to keep it from opening. They were giving me time to open this door. The air in the passageway was hot. I sweated like a running horse while I hammered at the stubborn lock.

I knew I had only a few minutes left. If the lock could not be forced, then I would have to use the alternate plan. Suddenly a man ran up to me from the Guard Gate. He told me the Romans were coming out of the tower roof doorways and our men were having trouble holding them at bay. Apparently Yeshua was holding the Romans at the Prison Gate and the Romans were coming out of the Fortress from the top of their structures, the tower roofs.

I knew they would be counter attacking, coming across the Temple porticoes. It was time for the alternate plan. Coming into the Temple we had brought buckets of pitch with us. The pitch came from the black oily pockets of Lake Asphaltites at the southern area of the Salt Sea.

We poured the buckets out onto the floor and onto the wood of the doorways, leaving a thick coating on everything. I ordered the men at the Fortress door back, and as we went out the Guard Gate, a man struck a spark to the torch I had in hand. The torch ignited. The heat in the closed passageway was intense against my sweating face. I lit three other torches that men were holding, and we threw them into the passageway. The great quantity of pitch exploded with a flaming whoosh. We shut the Guard Gate door and quickly used wood planks and nails to block the door from opening. Then we ran out of the Temple and down the North Stairs. We ran to where Yeshua was engaged in fighting the Romans trying to come through the Prison Gate.

The timber Prison Gate doors were on fire from pitch that had been thrown on them, lighting the scene of bloody fighting. Some Romans were outside the Fortress. These Romans had apparently come down a ladder from an upper opening. Our men were engaged in deadly battle. I saw Yeshua. He had two Romans dead at his feet and was swinging his sword against a tall, heavily built Roman. The Roman was wielding his long sword like a man possessed and was forcing Yeshua back. On the run I pulled an arrow from my quiver, put notch to string, pulled to full draw, and let the arrow fly. The arrow caught the tall Roman between his shoulder blades. The impact caused the Roman to raise both his arms into the air, giving Yeshua an opening to thrust his sword into the Romans chest.

By then I had reached Yeshua. He shouted, "Now! We draw them away."

Yeshua yelled in his loudest voice, "Horns! Blow!" Several of our men had shofars, the ram's horn, and now they put the horns to their lips and blasted the signal all of our men in the city had been waiting for. Our men turned and ran south, past the Xystus, past the west staircases, all the way to the Dung Gate road. Yeshua and I waited until we saw the last of our men past us, then we followed them. The plan was to draw the Romans south, straight down the Dung Gate road to the ambush. Our efforts had been designed to draw the Romans outside the city walls into the Valley of Hinnon, the town dump.

Running through the Dung Gate, I saw lying on the ground the brute who was the overseer of the town dump. He lived in a hovel inside the city wall, just a few steps from his beloved stench pit. I suppose he heard the noise of our men and had come out to investigate. For his curiosity he had been rewarded with a handful of arrows that punctured his stinking skin. Someone had silenced him and finished him off by cutting his throat. He would be a meal for his rats. His wretched workers picked the trash for food and the necessities to survive. They lived in rude huts that backed up to the wall at the very edge inside the dump. Our men had freed them then put them to work building the barricades. The barricades were finished, and the dump workers had scattered to the winds for none of them were to be seen.

Bartholomew Nathaneal and his men had the workers stack piles of trash to form a barricade of three sides, the open side being the wall and Dung Gate. Our men with swords and spears were on the outside of the barricade. The Romans would have to reach and fight over the mounds of trash to get to us. Yeshua and I quickly climbed over the barricades to join our other men. We waited for the Romans who were pursuing to come through the Dung Gate, into the trap. I looked up and saw our archers. They were on the top of the wall, the ramparts, overlooking the killing ground below. The ramparts were designed to allow defenders to repel an attack from outside. We would use their device against them.

We wanted as many Romans as possible through the Dung Gate and inside the barricaded enclosure, into the Valley of Slaughter. Here they came. The Romans ran through the Dung Gate and into the killing field. The space was packed with Romans trying to breach the barricade of piled trash. We were holding them, the iron of swords ringing. Our men on the inside of the city wall slammed the Dung Gate closed. Yeshua told the man beside him to blow the horn. At that signal lit torches were thrown over the barricades and the ground and trash inside the barricaded enclosure exploded into flames from the pitch that was spread. The Romans were trapped like rats in a box. The archer's unleashed arrow after arrow into the Romans below. We slew with the edge of sword any who made it over the barricades who tried to escape the fiery inferno. The dark night was lit by the flames like a vision of Hades. The screams of the burning Romans were like the mournful cries of the damned.

This was only part of our plan. It was our intention to kill as many Romans as possible during the taking of the Gates and the ambush in the Valley of Slaughter. Then we would have control of the City and control of the Temple. Any Romans who were left in the Antonia Fortress and inside Herod's palace, would be isolated. We would cut their flow of water from the aqueduct, causing them to eventually perish of thirst. No foods or supplies would enter the Fortress or palace. No reinforcements would be able to get into the city to help them. To further force their desperate position, we would use the Roman catapult against them. We would use the catapults to throw the dead bodies of their soldiers over the walls, into the Fortress and Herod's palace. Any Sadducee priests and merchants who were taken and judged guilty of collaborating with the Herodian Roman dynasty would be immediately executed and also flung over the walls. The rotting, stinking, flyblown corpses of the dead, inside their walls, would be an encouragement to them to negotiate terms of surrender. We would tell them they could leave the city through the Sheep's Gate, on the road to Damascus. But the men would be taken through the Judgment Gate to the Place of the Skulls and wiped from the earth. The women and children would be allowed to leave unharmed. Executing the men is exactly what the Romans would do to their vanquished foes, except the women and children would be sold into slavery. We would show the women and children mercy.

My inability to get the holy vestments was a discouragement but not a complete failure. The vestments might be burned and unusable or they might not be, but possession of the vestments wasn't a necessity. The vestments were merely a symbol of the Sadducees stranglehold on the Temple. With control of the Temple, we would bring back the rightful worship of ADONAI in the true manner of the Pharisees, according to the Word of ADONAI. The priests would henceforth appear before ADONAI as humble servants wearing unadorned robes of simple cloth. The Sadducees of the Herodian Roman dynasty in their colorful costumes, would be no more. They profited by corrupting the worship of ADONAI. The Sadducees worshipped the coin of Caesar. Render unto Caesar the things that are Caesar's, and unto ADONAI the things that are ADONAI's. The requirement to purchase the blood offerings with the coin of Caesar was an abomination. Hosea tells us – *Any seducer who says unto thee, Let us go and serve other gods. Thou shalt not consent unto him, neither shall thine eye pity him, neither shalt thou conceal him, but thou shalt surely kill him, thy hand shall be first upon him to put him to death. The hand of all the people shalt stone him with stones that he die. –*

The Romans inside the barricaded enclosure were being slowly but surely wiped out. Yeshua and I would leave a force here to finish them off. We would go back inside the city through the Spring Gate. We would check our forces, as there was more to do before this battle was finished. We must secure the Temple. The Romans left inside the Antonia Fortress must be held at bay. We would maintain an armed presence on the Fortress tower roofs. And we would meet our men who had gone into the homes of the high priest Caiaphas, and Annas, and the members of the Sanhedrin, to isolate them.

The plan seemed to be working. Yeshua and I were about to turn for the Spring Gate when a large group of our warriors came careening around the wall at the corner of the Essene Gate. The men were panicked and in full retreat from some attacking force. Just then, over the other sounds of battle, I heard the galloping of many horse hoofs. A man rushed to Yeshua, telling him the Romans had broken through the Prison Gate and had come out on horseback with spears and swords. Just then the Romans came galloping around the corner and charged full speed at us.

Some men of our warriors panicked at the sight and turned to run. Yeshua yelled to the men, "Follow me. Stand and fight." Most of our fighters were farmers and fishermen who were not ready to fight a man on horseback wielding a spear and long sword. Yeshua waved his sword in the air to attempt to rally our men. Some of our men followed Yeshua and I to make a stand, but many of them turned and ran.

Yeshua dodged an attack and thrust his sword into the belly of a horse. The horse reared and the Roman fell off backwards to be slain by the edge of Yeshua's sword. Yeshua yelled, "Men, fall back to the Spring Gate. We will go to the Temple and make a stand." We fought our way to the Spring Gate only to find more Roman soldiers coming out through that gate. We were caught between the horsemen coming from the west and the soldiers from the city. It was obvious that our forces had not been able to hold the Prison Gate. The number of soldiers we had killed were not enough to make the difference we needed to win the battle.

I looked around to see that almost all of our forces had fled. Yeshua and I stood back to back, swinging our swords and slaying. I told Yeshua, "We must cross the Kidron Valley. The horses cannot follow through the rocks and we will have a better chance fighting the soldiers on foot."

Yeshua's face showed his fierce frustration. "Fight. Stand and fight," he screamed at the backs of our men as they ran. I grabbed Yeshua's arm, "We must go or we will be taken. We do not have the men to fight from both sides."

A Roman foot soldier charged Yeshua with his spear. Yeshua stepped to the side. The spear missed him by inches. Then Yeshua swung his sword down onto the Roman's neck at the shoulder cutting the man's head half off. Yeshua yelled to the remaining men of our forces, "To the valley. Into the rocks. Save yourselves."

We retreated into the Kidron Valley, fighting as we went. At some point in the next blur of time, the Romans fell back to the city. The desperate fight had ended. Yeshua told the men with us, "Go. Go away from the city. Back to your homes. Do not speak of this as some Sadducee viper may hear your words and report you to the Romans. Do not let yourselves be taken."

The men dispersed in all directions. Yeshua and I stood on the slope of Mount Olivet looking down into the city. Yeshua stood there shaking his head. "Ah, Jerusalem, Jerusalem. The city where David encamped! There shall be mourning and moaning. Rome will encamp against thee round about. And will lay siege against thee. And they shall not leave in thee one stone upon another."

I looked at Yeshua. In the moonlight I could see tears streaming down his cheeks. "It will be dawn soon. We must go." I turned toward Bethany. Yeshua, in his desolation, followed.

ONE DAY BEFORE PASSOVER. MY
NAME IS MARIAM OF MAGDALA

"You should have seen them run! Cowards! One turned and the panic spread like a fire. If they will not save themselves, then no one can save them."

I asked Yeshua, "What will you do?"

"I am sorely tempted to leave them to their fate. If they have not the strength within themselves to fight for and save themselves, then what am I to do for them? I cannot perform this miracle for them."

"But what of your vision?"

"I think now the vision was merely a dream of my own mind. One sleeps at night and dreams of things with no explanation. The dreams are not real. The dreams are not reality." Yeshua jerked his arm in the air. "This is the true reality. The dreamer awakens and sees that the world has not changed. Only the dream changed it and the dream fades with the rising of the sun. I see now that the words of ADONAI in my dream vision was my own mind conjuring up those words." Yeshua sat, shaking his head. "I was only dreaming of freedom. It was only a vision in my mind. This. The Romans and their power. This is the cold hard reality."

Yeshua sat moodily, staring at the candle flame. I ached for him. His dilemma was truly vexing. He and Judas arrived in the dark just before sunrise. They were bloodied and battered but most of the blood was on their clothing, attesting to their strength of arm against the enemy. Rachel tended to the wounds of Judas as I attended Yeshua. Jehosheba cried silently that Barabbas was not with them. There was food in front of Yeshua but he had no appetite. He was gripped by a burning sorrow that their efforts had been in vain.

Yeshua opened his hands and looked at them, closely, as if he had never seen them before. "The teacher, Qohelet, tells us – *I looked on all the works that my hands had wrought, and on the labour that I had laboured to do, and, behold, all was vanity and a striving after wind, and there was no profit under the sun. The wise man, his eyes are in his head, but the fool walketh in darkness. As it happeneth to the fool, so it happened even unto me –.* Why did I think I was wiser than the fool? Men believed me. Men followed me. Now they are bandits and outlaws. They are on the run from the Romans. Where is the profit in that?"

I had no answer. I knew Yeshua did not want to hear that he had tried his best, for then he would think his best was lacking. I knew all I could do was to sit with him, listen to him, and hope that eventually he would come to a reckoning in his own mind. He had tried, not for his own vanity or his own reward, but tried because he believed the Habirum deserved to be free. He had tried. And no matter the outcome, his strength of purpose was moving. My heart swelled with love for him.

Yeshua and Judas, exhausted after a full day and night of strenuous activity, slept for several hours. I awakened Yeshua to tell him Joanna, Chuza, Joseph of Arimathea and Nicodemus of Damascus had arrived with news. Joseph of Arimathea told us the Sadducees of the Sanhedrin council were in an uproar that the Temple had been breached. The council ordered the captain of the Temple guard to double the men on watch for the rest of the festival week.

Chuza told us news from the court of Herod Antipas. Herod had decreed that all talk of the activities of the night were to be suppressed. Herod was torn between rage and embarrassment. His rage was directed at the perpetrators of the insurrection and he wanted their heads. At the same time he was humiliated that the attack had even occurred. His soldiers and spies were to sniff out any information that might lead to the capture of the ringleaders, but his men were hampered by the order to pretend the attack never took place. The official story was to be that drunken buffoons had made noise but done no damage and that they had been quickly dealt with by the Roman guards. All the dead Roman soldiers were to be quietly removed from the city and buried in the wilderness.

Herod had demanded of the high priest, Caiaphas, what he knew of the insurrectionists. "Who is their leader?"

Caiaphas told Herod Antipas the name he has heard is "Yeshua."

Herod Antipas complained that Yeshua is a common Habirum name. "Yeshua, who?" he demanded.

When Caiaphas confessed he did not have any other information about the leader, this Yeshua, Herod Antipas commanded, "This Yeshua must be known to the Pharisees. Find this man!"

Simon the Zealot arrived just then with news of the men. Joanna and Chuza left to return to the city while Joseph of Arimathea and Nicodemus of Damascus stayed behind to listen to Simon the Zealot's report. Simon the Zealot told us that some of their men had suffered injuries but miraculously there had been no deaths. Most of the men scattered to distant points, to return home. Simon the Zealot told Yeshua that he and his men would stay with us in case the Romans came hunting in Bethany.

Simon the Zealot said, "I recommend we go soon. We should go north into the Galilee, get supplies, and then cross over the River Jordan into the land of Rabbah to our old camp."

Nicodemus of Damascus shook his head. "I suggest you go further. Go north of the Galilee into the land of the Phoenicians. Or from here just go south, to the land of Aegyptus." He looked at Yeshua, "You know that land? Could you lay low there?"

Yeshua shook his head, "The Romans are in both Phoenicia and Aegyptus. They are like wild dogs with the scent of blood in their nostrils. They never stop the hunt."

Joseph of Arimathea said, "Listen. Caiaphas and the Sadducees of the Sanhedrin council just want this to end. They will be satisfied with a bone if they cannot have the meat. Caiaphas and the Sanhedrin council worry that the influence of Yeshua is spreading. They worry that if they let him go on like this, everyone will believe in him and the Romans will come and destroy both our holy place and our nation. Herod Antipas wants this to end as he considers it a threat to his rule. If the Romans will not stop the hunt until they have the leader of the insurrection, perhaps the best course is to deliver to them their man."

THE DAY BEFORE PASSOVER. MY
NAME IS JUDAS ISCARIOT

It was near to the end of the day. Sundown would herald the sound of the shofar blowing to begin the new day and Shabbat. The priests in the Temple were busy making the final preparations for the Shabbat and Passover. Residents were going to and fro among the vendors in the market stalls making the purchases they would need to last them until Shabbat ended. I was standing near the Essene Pool waiting for Joseph of Arimathea to return. We had met here just minutes earlier. We discussed the plan then he walked away down the footpath. He went to a block of houses that were located near the Essene Gate. Now I saw him walking toward me and there was a man with him.

They approached, stopped, and stood before me. Joseph of Arimathea said, "Simon, this is the man who will take you to Yeshua, the bandit. Herod will pay thirty silver coins for the bandit's capture."

I looked at this man called Simon the Cyrene, and I blinked in astonishment. At the home of Lazarus, Joseph of Arimathea had told us his thinking on how to divert the Romans attention from the hunt. At first Yeshua and I had been skeptical. Could such trickery be possible? Now that I actually saw Simon the Cyrene, I was amazed. Perhaps Joseph's plan would work? It was the only plan we had so it must work.

I took a step closer and extended my arm for the clasp of peaceful greeting, which Simon readily returned. Joseph's secret informer was a man with startling blue eyes, brown hair, and of medium build. Of the tens of thousands of men in Judah, Galilee, and the surrounding area, this man, this Simon the Cyrene, looked remarkably similar to Yeshua. It was uncanny. Of course if you really knew who was who, the differences were obvious. But not everyone knew who was really who in this dangerous game we were playing.

Joseph said, "Herod will pay thirty silver coins. Judas, all you have to do is bring this bandit Yeshua to the place where he will be captured. His capture must be done on the sly in the absence of the multitude. The Roman guards will do the capturing. All you must do is identify the man."

Simon squinted his eyes, rubbed his thumb and fingers together, and said, "Thirty silver coins is the wages for a moon's work, even the price of a plot of land. How do you reckon we split it?"

I told him, "The coins are for you. I want no payment."

Simon looked dubious. He was obviously wondering how a man could not want payment. "Then why do you do this, if not for the coins?"

I told him, "This man, this bandit Yeshua, has cast a spell over the daughter of a friend. I have already paid the marriage contract. She was to be my second wife, but now he has ruined her. I only want revenge for her defilement."

A knowing smile crossed Simon's face. "Ah, I see. Yes, to desire a woman and then not have her. That is worth killing over. But why do you need me? Why not just hand the bandit over to the Romans yourself?"

"I know the man's family. I must still do business with them. They cannot know I am involved."

Simon looked pleased, "Very well, I will take the coins."

We made our plan. I would trick Yeshua with a story of women and wine and get him to come to the Garden of Gethsemane when the moon is high. Simon would meet me before Yeshua arrived and we would set the trap. Simon and I spit in our palms and shook hands on the deal.

Simon told me, "After the bandit is taken we will celebrate. I will introduce you to a woman. She is a lovely dark skinned delight from the land of Kush. She will take your mind off the woman you have lost."

I smiled, and told Simon, "I look forward to our next meeting in the Garden of Gethsemane at high moon. I especially look forward to seeing this woman you speak of."

We left in different directions. Joseph went into the city. Simon retraced the path to his place of lodging, and I left through the Essene

Gate. I walked south in the direction of Bethlehem to be sure I was not spied upon or followed by Simon. Then I cut across country, across the lower Kidron Valley, and made my way back to Bethany. Back at the home of Lazarus, I sat with Yeshua and told him what had happened. We made our preparations.

The moon was high and full, so bright it cast dark shadows in the darker night. In the Garden of Gethsemane I was leaning against an oil press, waiting, when I heard the sound of someone approaching on the footpath. I whistled, then heard a man's voice, "Judas? Is that you?"

"Yes. Over here." Simon the Cyrene walked out of the darkness. I saw he had a flask of wine in his hand. He offered me the flask, "Drink?"

Smiling, I told him, "With gladness." Not trusting the man, and not knowing if the wine might be drugged I raised it to my lips but kept my mouth closed. "Ah, that's good wine."

Simon nodded his head, "Yes, and plenty more where that came from." He took a drink, then licked his lips. "Where is this Yeshua you speak of?"

"He will be here any minute." Actually, Yeshua was already here, hidden in the darkness like a hunting lion. With him was Simon the Zealot and his men. If the plan went awry they would pounce, ambushing the Romans and wiping them from the earth. "Let us light a torch so that he can find us." I pulled a flint from my pouch and my iron knife from the sheath.

"Is the ambush all set? Are the soldiers waiting in hiding? Does Joseph have the thirty silver coins?"

I struck the flint to iron. The spark hit the torch that flared to a brilliant light. "Yes, I just spoke to Joseph. He is with the soldiers in the darkness. They will come out after I give the signal."

"What is the signal?"

I set the wooden handle of the torch in a notch by the oil press. I was sure the light showed us clearly. I turned to Simon. I crooked my finger at him and spoke quietly, "Listen. I will tell you the signal." He turned his head to point his ear at me, to hear the confidential information. I stepped close to him and raised my knee solidly, slamming him between his legs. The breath went out of him in a loud grunt. I slammed my knee into him again, forestalling any resistance. He was bent over and I slammed my knee in his face. I heard the bone of his nose crack. I jerked him to the ground, falling my full weight on his chest knocking out any breath he had left. I pulled my mason's mallet from where it hung on my belt and used my mallet to smash his already broken nose flat against his face. I flipped him over and kneeled on his back. I pulled his arms behind him. I hammered both of his hands, breaking his fingers to stop him from any writing he may try to do. I grabbed him by the hair and twisted his head around. I pressed my thumbs and fingers into his cheeks, forcing his mouth open. I bent over him and gave him the kiss of peace. My lips covered his open mouth. I sucked his tongue into my mouth, and with my teeth I grabbed his tongue and worried it like a dog chews a bone. I chewed at his tongue until a large piece of his tongue was severed. I felt the piece of his tongue in my mouth like it was a bloody gristle from a disgusting bite of rotten meat. I spat the chunk of flesh in his face. Simon was flailing and screaming incoherently.

The kiss of peace was the signal to identify the bandit Yeshua. Now the Garden of Gethsemane was lit by the soldier's torches as they fired them and ran to the capture. The Roman guards used their clubs to beat Simon the Cyrene into submission. In just moments, Simon the Cyrene was bound and being dragged away. Joseph approached with the centurion of the Roman soldiers.

Joseph said to me, "Excellent work. The bandit, Yeshua, has been taken into custody. Come with us and I will get you the silver coins you are owed."

The centurion of the Roman soldiers stood staring at me. His mouth was agape, his eyes were wide open. It was quite a feat to shock a Roman centurion who no doubt had witnessed many bloodthirsty things in his career. I must have looked a terrible sight, like a daemon. Standing in the light of a torch I grinned at the centurion. I hoped the sight of blood staining my face, my lips, and teeth would give him disturbed dreams of the night hours.

Earlier I told Yeshua and the other men my idea, but had not shared it with the women. I feared they might find it too disturbing. But before I had left the home of Lazarus, I had asked Mariam about the tongue. She told me the tongue was part of the mouth organ and had a thick artery that was fed from the large carotid artery in the neck. I mentioned that I had once bitten my tongue and it was very sore for a long time until it healed. "Yes," she said, "The tongue is very sensitive. We use it to taste, to help chew, to clean our teeth, and to talk. Tell me, Judas, are you interested in becoming a physician?"

"No. I hate all that blood and stuff. You and Yeshua can be the physicians." I smiled at Mariam, "I was just curious."

PASSOVER. THE DARK OF NIGHT.
MY NAME IS JUDAS ISCARIOT

I accompanied Joseph of Arimathea and the Roman centurion back to the city after the capture of Yeshua, or who the centurion thought was Yeshua. I knew that Yeshua had been in the darkness of the trees, watching and wondering, like me, if this performance would play out as we hoped. While I walked, I used Simon the Cyrene's flask of wine to rinse, gargle, and spit to clean the filthy taste from my mouth. I poured wine into my hand and washed my face. I noticed the Roman centurion watching me. He was still looking stupefied over what I had done.

Simon the Cyrene stumbled forward, barely able to walk, as he was led in chains by the Roman guards. They had to mostly support him as he could hardly stand upright. I suppose the shock of the pain, the beating, and blood loss had weakened him. He was moaning and blubbering and left a trail of blood on the stones of the paved roads. Near to the Essene Pool was the home of Annas, the former high priest and father in law of the high priest Caiaphas. The centurion said we would go to Annas first as he was closest to where we entered the city from the Spring Gate.

I knew the dramatic theatre to come had two main players, Simon the Cyrene and myself. Simon's role was fairly simple, he would not be talking. I knew that my role demanded far more skill. I had to be convincing that I was delivering the man they sought. This was a tricky part to play. I would not be truthful if I did not admit to a certain apprehension.

We came to the gate to the courtyard of the home of Annas. His guards quickly opened up when they saw the centurion. The house steward of Annas was sent for. Told of our reason for coming, he went into the home and awakened his master. In a few minutes Annas came out and listened, while the centurion told him our reason for disturbing him.

Annas was an old man with long white hair and a beard to his waist. He was wrapped in a long robe covering his sleeping clothes. A cap was on his head with the long peaked end folded over and reaching the belt of his robe. He held his head back in an arrogant manner and looked down his long nose at us as if we were accompanied by a bad odor. Simon the Cyrene was moaning and dripping blood on his gardened pathway. Annas did not look happy that this problem had arrived on his doorstep. When the centurion finished explaining, Annas demanded, "What is it to me? Why fetch it to me?" in an angry shrill voice. "Go to the high priest." And with that he swirled around and rushed through the doorway of his home.

The home of Caiaphas was not far from Annas and when we arrived there I saw the residents were already awake. Men with torches stood outside the gate and we were immediately ushered inside. The house steward of Annas had sent a boy running ahead of us with a message for the high priest. We were led into a large hall that was used as a meeting room. The place was brightly lit by many candles and a fire was burning around a stone circular hearth in the midst of the hall.

The house steward spoke to the centurion, "The master has sent for members of the council. You will wait." Then he left the hall through a doorway. We stood there, waiting. All was quiet in the hall except for the noise of Simon the Cyrene's moaning. The Romans had let him collapse to the stone floor where he lay curled up, one hand to his face, the other between his legs. I wondered how long we would be kept waiting. I had not foreseen this delay and it made me nervous. I looked at Joseph of Arimathea. He stood silently, watching Simon the Cyrene. In a remarkably short period of time, a couple dozen members of the council came in looking sleep disheveled. Apparently the summons of the high priest was not to be ignored or delayed.

A door opened and the house steward appeared. He stepped to the side, holding the door open for the high priest. I was surprised because not all the council were present. Joseph leaned toward me and whispered, "These are the Sadducee members only. Loyal to Herod." Caiaphas was a tall man. He walked briskly to a raised platform. He sat on the only chair then turned his gaze upon each in the room, one at a time. The first thing I noticed was his stern face, he had prominent cheekbones and his eyes were set back in deep dark sockets under bushy white eyebrows. A thick white beard that came to a sharp point covered his face. He was dressed in a costly purple robe over another robe of fine white linen that covered his legs and arms. Atop all that was a purple cone shaped hat that made him look taller even while sitting. I saw this was a man who was used to those who served him being subservient, and who expected his every word and gesture to be obeyed like a royal command. I determined I must be very careful in my dealings with this person.

Yeshua, or I should say, his substitute, was lifted to his feet, marched forward and forced to his knees. Caiaphas looked long and hard at him while Simon the Cyrene moaned piteously. His face was a mask of blood and bruises. His broken nose was a dark scar in the middle of his face, and the skin around both his eyes was darkening purple and black. The Roman guards had contributed to his injuries with the cudgel and whip. Under other circumstances I might feel pity for the man, but now I just hoped he would be convincing in the part he had to play.

Caiaphas had a deep voice that rumbled, "Is this the bandit? The one called Yeshua?"

I answered, "Yes, my lord."

At this disturbing piece of news, Simon the Cyrene squealed and tried to rise. The Roman guard on both sides of him pushed him roughly down.

Caiaphas slowly swiveled his pointy beard in my direction. "Who are you?"

"My lord, I am Judas. I am a stone carver from the Galilee. I live and work in the town of Zippori."

"How do you know this man, this bandit, this Yeshua?"

"I have seen him and heard him speak to the crowds in Zippori many times. Once in Bethesda I listened to him speak of revolt against the Temple."

"Against the Temple?"

"Yes, my lord. This man, Yeshua, said he was the anointed one, sent by ADONAI to cleanse the Temple. Then a few days ago, I was going to cross the bridge to the Temple and I heard him speaking against the tetrarch, Herod Antipas."

Joseph of Arimathea spoke, "My lord, this man, Yeshua, speaks as if he is sent by ADONAI. If we let this man go on like this, everyone will believe in him and the Romans will come and destroy both our holy place and our nation."

Caiaphas looked at the bloodied man kneeling before him. "Why do you speak against the Temple?"

Simon the Cyrene, who was Yeshua in this theatre, blubbered and cried. He could make no coherent sounds. He fell to his face before the high priest and tried to crawl to him but the Roman guards restrained him. He lay prone, making sounds like a wounded beast, the beast knowing the time of sacrifice is near.

Caiaphas shook his head in disgust. "What is wrong with the man? Why can he not talk?"

I began to be worried. I had hoped Caiaphas would make short business of this affair and return to his bed. Just then I heard a voice. I turned to see Simon Peter, the brother of Andrew walking into the hall.

"My lord, may I speak?"

"Who are you?" asked Caiaphas, in what I perceived as a voice growing short in patience.

Simon Peter approached the raised platform, stopping near to Joseph. "My lord, I am Simon Peter of Capernaum, a fisherman. I attest that this man is the one called Yeshua. I met him before, two harvests ago, and even then he was speaking against the Temple. He said he would destroy the temple and in three days he would raise it up. He spoke against even you, saying when he took the Temple for the glory of ADONAI that he would make you into a burnt offering."

The man, Yeshua, jerked himself on the ground, rolling and screaming like a person caught in a fit. Caiaphas yelled at the top of his lungs, "SILENCE! MAKE HIM BE QUIET!" A Roman guard smashed the man, Yeshua, on the head with a cudgel, stunning him to stillness.

Caiaphas turned to Simon Peter and lowered his head. He looked out from under his bushy eyebrows like a bull getting ready to charge. "You say this man, this Yeshua, claims he is sent by ADONAI. Do you believe he is sent by ADONAI?"

Simon Peter answered in a clear voice, "No, my lord, he is not sent by ADONAI."

"Do you believe he is the anointed one?"

"No, my lord."

"And do you believe that he is able to tear down the Temple and rebuild it in three days?"

"No, my lord."

"But you give witness this Yeshua claims all these things?"

"Yes, my lord."

Caiaphas turned his attention to me. "Do you give witness this Yeshua claims all these things?"

I answered, "Yes, my lord."

Caiaphas turned to the assembled Sadducee members of the Council. I knew from what Joseph of Arimathea had previously said that these men wanted to end this affair, to end the troublesome Yeshua. "You have heard two witnesses give testimony that this man is guilty of blasphemy! Now you have heard the testimony! What is your judgment?"

One of the council members, a man wrapped in a fine costly robe, stood and said, "He stirs up the people all over Judah with his teaching. He violated the Temple. He speaks blasphemy. He must be dealt with sternly, and quickly, before the multitude cause troubles that will bring Roman retribution on us. He is worthy of death!"

The other council members echoed him, saying, "He is worthy of death!"

Caiaphas suddenly stood. He stared at everyone threateningly. I could see how he had managed to keep the high priest position for over a dozen years. Power radiated from him. This was a very dangerous man.

Then I realized. He was not powerful nor was he dangerous. Caiaphas was just a man. If he was a stone carver he would only be a tall stone carver with a white pointy beard and bushy eyebrows. He merely used the power and danger of his office to intimidate, threaten, and rule. He was only a symbol, a symbol of all that was wrong with the sons of men. Some sons of men lorded it over other sons of men because their position gave them a strength they abused. They lacked any personal strength or morals and they deserved no respect. These men use the power of their position to abuse other men. If all men are created equal, then no one man should possess such power of life and death. The sons of men would have to eliminate such evil, ego driven men, from positions of authority before the sons of men could finally be free. I could split his heart with my knife before anyone in the room realized I had moved. Whatever happened here in the next moments, if our plan was not to work, Caiaphas would be the first to die. My muscles tensed for the rush. Then Caiaphas spoke.

He said in a loud voice of proclamation, "The council has judged this criminal to be guilty. But the council cannot render penalty. Only the Romans can render penalty. Herod Antipas and Pontius Pilate are the Roman authorities. Take this person to them. Both are here in the city for the festival. Take this man away from my presence. Deliver him to the Romans with my compliments." He ordered the Sanhedrin council members, "Go with them and tell Herod and Pontius of our ruling." Then he pointed at the blood smeared all over the floor. "Clean that mess up!" And a pair of slaves rushed to obey.

Caiaphas stepped down from the platform. His attendants made haste to assist him but he waved them away irritatingly. The steward opened the door and Caiaphas left the hall.

He would never know how close he had come to death.

We left the home of Caiaphas. It was still dark night. In the distance I heard a cock crow, signaling the coming dawn. Looking at the eastern sky, I saw a strange red glow low on the horizon, a warning sign of bad weather. The air was breathless, hot, and sultry. Miserable weather. The stink and smoke from the fires in the Valley of Slaughter was thick and sickening. It would be a long scorching day.

The centurion said we would go to the governor, Pontius Pilate. He stepped out briskly, leading the way. It was the opposite end of the city to the Praetorium at the Antonia Fortress where we would continue our ruse. The Roman guards marched Simon the Cyrene between them, cursing him for his weakness, ordering him, "Walk!" And to encourage him, they lashed him with the whip like he was a beast.

Yeshua, his substitute, Simon the Cyrene, vomited a pile of blood, noisily splashing the paved stones of the roadway. The Sadducee members of the Sanhedrin council expressed disgust girlishly. The council members hurried around the prisoner and guards to get in front of them so they would not step in the mess and become defiled.

Joseph of Arimathea, Simon Peter, and I held back to the rear of the procession so we could speak quietly. I said to Simon Peter, "Tell me what is happening? Where did you come from?"

"I have been lying low in the wilderness with my brother. He suffered a sword wound, a slash across his chest. I have been tending to him."

"He is healing?"

"Yes. He will live. As soon as I could I went to Bethany. Mariam told me what you were doing. I came to assist you."

"Many thanks for that. Two witnesses are better than one."

"Yeshua is in the city. He and Simon the Zealot and a few men came over the wall. He is somewhere close watching us now. He is ready to attack if the plan does not work."

Simon Peter handed me a flask of wine. I took a long pull. "Let us deliver this informer rat to Pilate and get ourselves gone. May our trickery be successful and over with soon."

"Praise ADONAI."

The sky in the east was lighter by the time we reached the Prison Gate at the Antonia Fortress. Entering I took my first good look at the inside of the Roman stronghold. Though it was still early, the Fortress was awake and Romans were busy with their morning activities. Soldiers were hurrying about, the officers shouting orders at them. Slaves worked busily at their duties, a pack of them shoveling manure from the stables into a wagon. The Fortress was a formidable structure, built solidly to withstand attack. Only a siege or treachery from within would take it. I shook my head, remembering our attack. We must have been insane. Only an army could beat this army.

The Sadducee priests among the members of the Sanhedrin council would not enter the Praetorium, claiming it would defile them on the day of Passover. We waited for Pontius Pilate at the Pavement, a roofed structure open on three sides and backing to the sturdy stone wall of the Fortress. This is where Pilate listened to judicial matters and rendered verdicts. Pilate took orders from the Roman legate in Syria, but here in Jerusalem his word was the final law, as only he could order capital punishment. Everyone knew Pilate did not hesitate to send those judged guilty to the place of the skulls, where the Roman soldiers were specialists at the cruci fixus. While we waited for Pontius Pilate, a senior centurion on his staff conferred with the arresting centurion and the Sadducee members of the Sanhedrin council.

Pilate resided at his palace in Caesarea Maritima on the balmy coast of the Great Sea. He made the journey to Jerusalem for every festival to deter any troubles among the throngs of Habirum. Pilate ultimately answered to Rome, to the Emperor Tiberius, and it was Rome's decree that the Roman province of Judah suffer no troubles from the troublesome Habirum natives.

Pilate walked up. He was freshly bathed, shaved, and in a clean uniform. His appearance was the picture of Roman correctness. He stepped onto the Pavement, sat in his chair and without further ado, he demanded, "State the charges against the accused."

Pilate had a sharp featured face with a pointy nose and ears that stuck out. His hair was trimmed short in the Roman fashion. He was average height and in good physical condition. He conducted himself in an authoritative manner, as one who is accustomed to decision making and who tolerated no dissent. His staff centurion said in a loud official voice, "The accused is named Yeshua. He is charged with sedition and mutiny. He is charged with being the leader of the insurgents who raided the city two nights ago."

The council member who had spoken to Caiaphas rose from his seat, "The Sanhedrin council has tried him and found him guilty of blasphemy."

I saw Pilate's jaw harden and his eyes narrow. "I have no jurisdiction over religious matters. I am only interested in charges relating to security of the state."

The council member said, "My lord governor, this man, by claiming to be the anointed one sent by ADONAI, is sending a direct challenge to Caesar for if, as he claims, he has authority, then Caesar has not. Anyone who claims to be a king opposes Caesar."

All this time the one they knew as Yeshua was on his knees before Pilate, his head hung low in weary abject submission. He was covered in blood. His hair was tangled and filthy, hanging down blocking his face. Pilate had his head cocked to one side with a quizzical expression on his face. "You there. Yeshua. Look at me." Yeshua did not move, Pilate nodded to the Roman guards and one of them grabbed his hair and lifted his head.

Pilate asked the centurion who had captured Yeshua. "What happened to him?"

The centurion replied, "The man resisted arrest, my lord governor."

Pilate told the centurion on his staff, "Add resisting arrest to the charges." Then Pilate addressed Yeshua, "Are you the King of the Habirum?"

Yeshua had no reply. His eyes were black and swollen shut. His face was a bloody mask. He could not speak. His whole body was one big wound. His broken hands hung useless. He was trapped in a concentrated misery he could not escape.

Pilate ordered him, "Speak man!"

Yeshua's head dropped to his chest in surrender.

Pontius Pilate looked grim. He tapped his fingers on the arm of his chair. He looked at the members of the Sanhedrin council, "Shall I crucify your king?"

The spokesman of the council replied, "We have no king but Caesar. If you let this bandit go on teaching, it will only bring troubles."

Pilate's demeanor slowly changed from imperious to angry. I suppose he did not like being told how to conduct his business. He asked a practical question, "Where is this man from? Where is his home?"

The arresting centurion pointed at Simon Peter and myself, and said, "These witnesses at the Sanhedrin trial say the man is from Galilee." Pilate looked hard at Simon Peter and me for long moments. I did not like being the object of his scrutiny. I steeled myself for his questioning. I was suddenly unsure of our position. There were a dozen Roman soldiers fully armed within sword thrust and dozens more between the Pavement and the Gate. Would our trick now come home to roost, like the proverbial chicken?

Instead of speaking to us, he suddenly seemed to come to a decision. He stood and ordered, "Since this man is a Galilean, take him to Herod Antipas. Galilee is in Herod's jurisdiction. This man is a subject of Herod. That will be all." And Pontius Pilate strode briskly away leaving Simon Peter and myself looking at each other with raised eyebrows. Would this never end?

Herod's palace was halfway across the city. It would have been full sunrise if the sun was visible but there was a thick haze blanketing the entire sky. The air was hot causing me to sweat even more and soak my already drenched clothes. Back across the city we walked. At Herod's palace there was a full muster of Roman soldiers who were Herod's guard. Since our attack the Romans seemed to be on full alert.

Our party was lead through the gate at the Tower Phasael then into the beautifully manicured garden courtyard of the palace of Herod Antipas. In the middle of the courtyard was a large tiled pool. In the center of the pool, on raised posts, was a roofed structure open to the four sides. There were four short bridges spanning the water, a bridge at each side of the structure. The water in the pool came from gently gurgling fountains, fed by the aqueduct system. The water was continuously replenished, keeping it fresh. The structure, pool, and garden screamed luxury. I could only imagine the extravagance within the palace. All of this overindulgence was paid for by taxes on the Habirum. In the structure I could see Herod sitting in the seat of the host at a table laden with delicacies for his dozen or so guests. I had to grit my teeth to keep myself from charging Herod, and using my knife to saw off his head. Another day.

Herod spoke to a man who I recognized as his steward, Chuza, who approached the centurion. They spoke for a moment, then the centurion turned and flapped a hand at us to come with him. We walked a wide path toward the structure until Chuza signaled the centurion to stop. We stood in the daylight, being observed by Herod and his guests lounging in the shade. This was as close as I had ever been to the tetrarch of Galilee. From where I stood I saw that Herod Antipas, the grandson of the Imudean slave, was a thin dark skinned man. He was a hatchet faced ugly man with a cruel demeanor. He was dressed in costly attire with many jewels sewn onto his clothing. When Herod finally spoke, his voice surprised me. He had a high pitched grating voice that irritated the nerves.

"Have you brought us entertainment? Something fun to amuse my guests?"

The arresting centurion replied, "My lord, this prisoner is called Yeshua. He is charged with multiple crimes. The governor, Pontius Pilate, has questioned him, and with the governor's compliments sends him to you."

"Why?"

"My lord?"

"Are you deaf or dense? I ask why send the creature to me?"

"My lord. The prisoner is from the Galilee and the governor says you have jurisdiction over him, not the governor."

"Did he commit a crime in Galilee?"

"I have no knowledge of that, my lord. The crimes he is accused of were committed here in Jerusalem."

Herod turned triumphantly to his guests, "There! You see? Ask the right question and you get the right answer!" His guests laughed as if their host was the cleverest man on the earth. Herod turned his attention to the man called Yeshua, on his knees before him. "You! You look more like a filthy beggar than a bandit. Are you guilty?"

Simon the Cyrene had only the strength to shake his head. "No? You shake your head at me but do not speak?" continued Herod.

"Well if you will not speak then someone will have to speak in your defense." Herod looked at the Sadducee members of the Sanhedrin council. "Who among you will speak for this man? Come now, someone must defend him! Who will it be?"

And then the Sadducee members of the Sanhedrin council all broke out in excited speech at once, but no one defended the prisoner. Instead they spoke words of condemnation and damnation, exhorting Herod to "Crucify him! Crucify him!" They got louder and louder, all trying to speak over the other, until Herod yelled, "STOP!"

Everyone instantly froze. Herod's expression was the essence of cruelty. His eyes were narrowed to slits, his lips were drawn back showing his teeth, and his long thin face reminded me of a snake. He had his hand on the dagger at his belt. He spoke, "The unanimous verdict then, is guilty. But this is not my problem. His crimes were committed in Jerusalem. Therefore, the prisoner will be taken back to Pontius Pilate, with my compliments. But before he goes to sentencing he must be made to look presentable. His clothes are rags. We will give him a new robe!" Then Herod pointed at one of his guests, "Flavius, give the man your robe."

The man, Flavius, was standing at the edge of the structure, the water gently swirling just below his feet. I saw that he was a short fat man with his black hair greased and curled. He looked shocked. "My robe, my lord?"

Herod snapped his fingers, "Yes, yes, come on, we don't have all day!"

Flavius looked sick. "Yes, my lord." He lifted his knee length robe over his head. Now he stood there with only a white linen wrap around his waist and covering his genitals. Those parts of him were buried under his obscenely swelled gut. His teats hung like the udders of a sow. His fat face was blushed red with embarrassment.

Herod ordered him, "Take the man the robe, Flavius. What are you waiting for? Go on!" Flavius stepped from the shade into the full light. He crossed the bridge, his fat jiggling as he walked. The women guests were giggling and chattering like little birds while the men roared with laughter. Flavius handed his robe to the arresting centurion, then he turned and scurried for the shelter of the shade. The piece of linen he wore disappeared in the crack of his big butt, a loose piece of it was hanging down like a tail with a brown stain on it. The wobbling twin cheeks of his fat ass were each like hams from a well fed hog.

Herod ordered, "Strip the prisoner! Remove his rags and put the fine red robe over him."

The Roman soldiers obeyed the command. They jerked Simon the Cyrene to his feet. They stripped him. He stood there naked. Simon the Cyrene was pathetic looking. Dirtied, bloodied, shamed, and humiliated. His scrotum was swollen and purple and his penis was shrunken and hiding. Herod and his guests were hooting and snickering. The soldiers put the robe over Simon but it was too short, barely covering the middle of him. Herod screamed with laughter and beat on the table.

Now I did feel pity for the man. I had not foreseen anything such as this. I looked at Joseph of Arimathea. He was studying the ground at his feet. Simon Peter was looking away to the side. They both had grim expressions on their faces. I felt ashamed that I had placed the man in this position. The shrieking laughter was making my brain ache. I felt sick. I thought I might throw up.

Suddenly Herod yelled, "ENOUGH!" Herod waved his hand in careless dismissal, and said to his steward, who was standing silently by this whole time, "Get them out of here!"

The Roman soldiers pulled the red robe off Simon and dropped it on the ground. We made our way from Herod's palace as fast as possible. Even the Romans looked stunned at the perverse display of Herod's idea of entertainment. I felt like this day would never end, and it was only the second hour.

When we left Herod's palace I was looking at the ground, lost in my thoughts, shaking my head, sickened. Then I heard a loud noise. Raising my head and focusing my attention, I realized there was a large crowd gathered. Men and women were standing to the sides of the roadway. It was the man Yeshua, or who they thought was Yeshua, they had come to see. Among the Habirum, Yeshua's healing had become well known and the word of his raid on the city had quietly spread, despite Herod's command for it to be officially ignored.

The noise was the people talking animatedly among themselves. Some were crying and wailing, seeing Yeshua's condition. But others, mostly Sadducee, and heathens, who had come to market, were yelling in delight for the unexpected parade. The crowd grew bigger as we approached the Antonia Fortress. We were still some distance away from the Prison Gate. There were soldiers outside in front. Then I saw an officer on horseback send a soldier running through the gate into the Fortress. That officer galloped out the Prison Gate road, reined up, and raised a hand, stopping our procession. He asked the arresting centurion, "What is the meaning of bringing this mob to the Fortress?" The centurion explained that Herod Antipas had sent the prisoner back to Pontius Pilate and the people had followed.

While they talked, more in the city had joined the crowd until it was a huge gathering. The Fortress was now on alert. I saw archers on the tower roofs and several dozen soldiers came through the Gate and made a line with their spears and shields at the ready. A man bumped into me and stood closely. He was dressed in rough laborers clothing, a hood over his head despite the heat. I looked at his face. Yeshua smiled and winked at me, then he moved off to the side. The crowd got larger and louder. The Romans were on high alert after the troubles in the city, I knew it would not take much to set them off probably causing a massacre if they attacked the crowd.

Just then more soldiers came through the Prison Gate and with them were two buglers who blew their horns loudly. Everyone stopped and looked toward the Prison Gate to see Pontius Pilate riding out on a fine black stallion. There was a large group of horsemen behind him. Pontius Pilate galloped straight toward us. The other horsemen rode out to flank him on each side. They stopped, the dust swirled. Pontius Pilate's horse snorted and pawed the ground. The other horsemen had long sharp spears pointing directly at the people in the crowd. I have to admit, it was an impressive display of military might. Standing there with only my dagger and mason's mallet for a weapon, I felt very exposed. I nudged Simon Peter. He looked at me and I quietly told him, "Holy horse dung. Get ready!"

Pontius Pilate demanded, "Why have you brought this man back here?"

The arresting centurion snapped to attention and reported, "Herod Antipas has judged the prisoner guilty, but Herod Antipas said since the crimes were committed in Jerusalem he has no jurisdiction to render sentencing. He sends the prisoner back with his compliments."

I saw that Pontius Pilate was greatly irritated. He obviously thought he had washed his hands of the matter. He looked at the swarm of people, with more joining the crowd by the minute. He looked at the man called Yeshua who was kneeling in the dirt, his rags of clothing hanging on him where the Romans had hurriedly redressed him. Someone in the crowd yelled, "Crucify him!" Others took up the words, the noise becoming a chant. The crowd was restless and pushing against those in front of them. The last thing Pontius Pilate would want on the eve of Shabbat and the day of the Passover feast was a riot he would have to forcefully put down, and then have to explain to the emperor.

Pontius Pilate said something to an officer on horseback beside him who issued an order. The horns blew loudly again. This quieted the crowd. Pontius Pilate ordered, "Bring out the other prisoners." Looking past him I saw three men being led through the Prison Gate. One of them was Barabbas. The other two I did not know. Apparently the prisoners had been made ready and brought to the gate when Pontius was told the man called Yeshua was being returned to him.

Now Pontius Pilate rendered his judgment. "The prisoner Yeshua has been tried and found guilty by the Sanhedrin council. The prisoner Yeshua has been tried and found guilty by the tetrarch Herod Antipas. As governor I now render judgment. The punishment is to be hung from the cross until dead. The prisoner will join a murderer and thieves at the place of the cross."

I heard a familiar voice yell, "Give us one in the spirit of Passover! One will be passed over! One will be spared! It is the custom! Give us Barabbas!"

Scores of others repeated the words, "One will be spared! Give us Barabbas! Give us Barabbas!"

I was watching Pontius Pilate. He looked angry enough to kill everyone no matter Rome's displeasure. He called out, "Who shall I release? Should I release Yeshua who claims to be your king? Should I release the thief Gestas? Should I release the thief Dismas? Should I release the murderer Barabbas?"

And the Mount echoed with the thunderous exhortation, "GIVE US BARABBAS!"

Pontius Pilate issued a brisk order to the officer on horseback next to him. Then Pilate displayed excellent horsemanship skills. He pulled the reins making the horse rear on its hind legs, neighing and striking out with its forefeet. The crowd pushed backwards away from the horse's hooves. The horse came down with a thud. Then Pilate pulled the reins again making the horse walk backwards. The horse stopped and whirled in a circle. Pilate spurred the horse and galloped away, going through the Prison Gate. I hoped it would be the last time I saw Pontius Pilate. The last time I saw him until the day I could hang him from a cross, until he was dead.

The Roman capacity for efficiency was now seen as the officer left in charge issued a quick series of orders. The prisoner Barabbas was released from custody and he quickly merged into the crowd. Four slaves yoked to a small wagon like oxen pulled it forward. Then at an order from a burly Roman centurion, the slaves stopped pulling and dropped their harness. The centurion had four soldiers to assist him. This was the cruci fixus squad. Exhibiting much practice they proceeded to prepare the three remaining prisoners for execution. The prisoners were stripped naked and forced to their knees by the soldiers. From the wagon the slaves took three timbers, each as long as the height of a man, which they laid on the prisoners shoulders and tied to their outstretched arms. This was the crossbeam they would carry to the post. The centurion pulled from a bucket pieces of wood that hung from a length of leather at holes in the top corners. These were signs the condemned wore about their necks that proclaimed their crime. The signs had seen much use as they were stained with blood. Two signs had the word THIEF written in block letters and these were draped over the heads of two of the prisoners. The centurion took from the bucket a piece of charcoal and scrawled the words KING OF THE HABIRUM on the one he hung over Simon the Cyrene's neck. The soldiers stood behind the prisoners and using leather whips gave the prisoners a solid scourging. The business ends of the leather whips were weighted with points of lead. The prisoners screamed as the flesh and blood flew from their backs. Then without further delay, the prisoners were jerked to their feet and told to "March!" The order was emphasized by continued scourging. The prisoners began their weary last journey carrying the crossbeam weight of their final judgment on their backs.

The Sadducee spokesman for the council came to me, and smiling said, "For he shall be delivered unto the heathen and shall be mocked, and spitefully entreated, and spitted on." I was very tempted to stick my knife in him, but Simon Peter came between us, saying, "Let us follow. To see the judgment executed." I stepped away from the Sadducee, breathing hard.

Simon Peter said to me as we walked away, "You have been sorely tested these last days my friend. Let us see the ending of this through, so we may then rest." The Prison Gate road led directly west to the Judgment Gate. People were lined up on both sides of the road to witness the march to judgment of the prisoners. The crowd mostly consisted of heathens and the uncircumcised, who came to Jerusalem as merchant or shoppers at the markets. Seeing three prisoners hung from the cross was a treat they had not expected. Looking at the crowd I saw a few who stood out by their better dress and I knew they were Sadducee. I saw no Pharisee or Essene who were the majority of residents in Jerusalem. The Pharisees and Essenes were Yeshua's people, and they would be mourning for Yeshua. The Sadducee minority, loyal to Herod and Rome, would welcome Yeshua's fate. It was now the third hour, early morning, and yet the air had no early day feel to it. The temperature was very hot and the air thick with moisture. There was no breath of wind, just an oppressive unseasonable heat. The march continued.

People were jeering at the prisoners, spitting on them and throwing rotten food at them. It was a display of uncivilized behavior that made me question the sanity of the sons of men. What was it burrowed deep in men's souls that allowed the daemon within them to be so publicly celebrated? Did ADONAI not have any influence on these sons of men to show them the error of their ways? I could not perceive any answer to that question.

At the junction of the Fish Gate and Judgment Gate roads, the line was jolted to a sudden stop. Looking ahead for the reason, I saw an old woman had stepped forward blocking the road. She was holding a flask of water to the lips of Simon the Cyrene. It was the woman of the mites, of the palm fronds, and she was pitying the man she knew as Yeshua in his torment. I experienced a sudden moment of panic. Would she recognize this person as not being Yeshua? Would she, in her shock, say the wrong word? Would she, at this late minute, give away the game causing our deception to fail? I felt a sudden exhaustion. I thought, 'Well, here we go.' Then she stepped back into the crowd and the procession jerked forward. In a few steps I came abreast of where the old woman stood. I looked at her. She smiled and winked at me! I laughed aloud. It was a day of smiles and winks! A sudden burst of optimism gave me new energy. The trick was working!

Past the Judgment Gate we continued to the final stop for those judged guilty of crimes, the place of the skulls. Golgatha. The Romans were so efficient at the work of cruci fixus they had Golgatha set to be used at a moment's notice. Holes were dug in the ground then lined with opus caementicium, the hardening mixture used for building. That way the tall posts could be lifted, leaned forward and dropped into the holes with a minimum of effort. The slaves tripped and pulled the condemned prisoners so they fell backwards, the cross beam landing on the post. The slaves kicked at the posts and crossbeams until the crossbeam fell in a notch carved into the upper part of the post. The prisoner's heads were pulled forward out of the way, then lengths of stout rope were used to lash the crossbeam to the post so it now formed a sturdy cross. Under the watchful eyes of the centurion and soldiers the slaves set to work on the prisoners. Holding down the arms they drove a long iron nail through the wrists between the bones of the forearm, being careful to miss the main blood vessels. A piece of wood with a hole drilled through it was placed between the head of the nail and the wrist so the prisoner could not slide his arm back off the nail. The legs were spread to opposite sides of the post, and the process was repeated, driving the nails through the heel bones.

Someone rushed from the crowd and placed a woven crown of thorny branches on the head of Simon the Cyrene. The centurion swung his whip at the man's buttocks, yelling "Get back!" The crowd jeered and laughed at the irony of the king of the Habirum wearing his crown. The slaves held flasks of liquid to the mouths of the prisoners. This was a mixture of sour wine and myrrh meant to deaden their senses. The two thieves opened their mouths wide, taking the libation willingly. Simon the Cyrene tried to drink but his wounded mouth would not allow him to swallow. Instead he puked the last of what remained in his stomach. One would think the Romans offered this pain numbing drink out of a sense of humanity but in reality they did it so they would not have to listen to the victim's constant screaming until they finally, mercifully, died. Sometimes, if the victim was to be hung from the cross and punished as long as possible for a particularly heinous crime, the drink would not be offered. The punishment of cruci fixus was refined by the Romans to a masterful degree. The Romans used the cruci fixus for all manner of crimes. If a slave killed his master, all of the master's slaves would be hung from the cross. This included all the men and all the women, and any children not young and attractive enough to be sold into slavery at the brothels. This mass cruci fixus was a lesson all slaves had witnessed and understood. A slave killing their master did not happen very often. The mass cruci fixus was probably the only thing that kept the masters, the slave owners, alive.

The posts were placed at the tip of the holes. The slaves lifted until the end of the posts slid down into the hole. The post, with the condemned hanging from it, was now standing upright. While two slaves held the post steady, the other two slaves chocked the post in place with wedges of rocks. In a surprisingly short time, all three prisoners were in the air, hung by their crosses. They faced west so the light of the sun would shine in their eyes and blind them all the last day of their life. Simon the Cyrene was in the middle and a thief on each side of him. The slaves squatted and threw bones, casting lots for the clothing of the prisoners that had been tossed into the wagon at the Fortress. The centurion and soldiers settled in for the long wait, taking food and drink from the wagon to ease the time.

Suddenly I was totally exhausted, too tired to move, too tired to even think. Two full days and two hard nights of preparation and warfare followed by disappointment. Then the ambush of Simon the Cyrene. Then the deception and tension and constant alertness to make no mistake so our trickery would not be discovered. All of that had taken its toll. It felt like it was forever since I had last slept. Simon Peter bumped my arm. He told me, "Let's go" and I followed him.

We moved away from the place of the skulls, walking north across the rough ground to the Fish Gate road outside the city walls. We came to a small stand of trees and stopped in the shade. There were others there. "Judas" I heard and turned to see Yeshua standing there with Barabbas and Simon the Zealot. We enjoyed a moment of gladness and greeting. A flask of fresh sweet water and a handful of fruit was given to me. I devoured the fruit and poured the water down my throat. The refreshment invigorated me. We discussed our next steps. I told both Yeshua and Barabbas," You should leave. Go to Bethany. Get out of sight of the Romans."

Yeshua said, "Yes, Barabbas, you should go. I will stay until Simon the Cyrene has perished. I owe him at least that for taking the cross for me." Yeshua took me in his arms and gave me a bone crushing hug. Then still holding me by the shoulders he leaned away, looking into my eyes, "Judas, you are my true friend and I owe you my life. You have done more than anyone could ask or expect. All I have, is

264

yours. You have only to ask and it shall be given. You too should leave this place. Go. Rest."

Just then a group of men and women walked up. It was Rachel and Mariam and Jehosheba, and with them was Yeshua's mother, Mary Salome. The men were Simon the Zealot's fighters who were accompanying the women to provide them protection in these troubled times. Joyful tears and happiness were shared amongst all. They brought food, bread, meat, fruits and wine. We made a festive meal under the shade of the trees on this grisly occasion.

After the meal I insisted that Barabbas should take the women and go. Go to Bethany. Get themselves away from this place. Yeshua agreed, and they departed. We promised to join them as soon as this was over. I was determined to see this to the end. So it was myself, Yeshua, Simon Peter, and Simon Zealot, and one of his men who Barabbas replaced as guard for the women. We settled down to wait for the death of Simon the Cyrene. We waited, for the end, to be sure our trickery had been successful. And truth be told, we wanted to show respect for Simon the Cyrene who had gone to the cross with such a minimum of fuss. As Isaiah tells us. – *And opened not his mouth. As a lamb that is led to the slaughter, and as a sheep that before her shearers is dumb –*.

It was now the sixth hour. The sun would be directly overhead but the clouds covered the whole sky. From our spot in the small grove of trees I could see the three men hanging on the crosses like slabs of meat. The wind had picked up, coming now from the south, from the desert land of the Imudeans. This was not a refreshing wind. It just blew the hot air even more mercilessly. This wind from the desert was called an Evil Wind. It was a wind that pulled the sand up from the ground and scoured the skin. These Evil Winds killed travelers, making the air coarse and unbreathable, sometimes burying people under a sky full of sand.

The crowd of heathens had lessened but many remained, wanting to prolong the entertainment that had brightened their normally dull days. Yeshua stood looking at Simon the Cyrene on the cross and the mob of heathens celebrating the sacrifice. "For my death, which they think happened, to them in their error and blindness, since they nailed their man unto his death. They know not that it was another, who tried to drink the gall and the vinegar. It was not I. It was Simon who bore the crossbeam on his shoulder. It was another upon whom they placed the crown of thorns. And I should be standing here laughing at their ignorance, but I cannot."

"Why can you not laugh? It is a good joke on them, is it not?"

I looked at Yeshua. He seemed different, changed. He looked older, worn, his shoulders slumped in some sort of defeat he had brought upon himself. There were lines and wrinkles on his face I had not noticed before. His voice sounded tired and he said, sadly, "They never knew truth nor will they ever know it, for there is a great deception upon their souls. May ADONAI forgive them, they know not what they do."

I was not sure who Yeshua was speaking of. Who he thought needed forgiveness. I was not in the mood to forgive any of the heathen swine. So I kept my silence, pulled a drink of wine and handed him the flask. Just then the wind suddenly increased to a forceful roar that made me stagger. The air was full of tiny darts, bits of sand that struck the skin so hard it stung. I turned away from the onslaught and yelled over the thunder of the wind, "Sand storm. Evil wind. We must take shelter!" The sky that had before been a dull haze, suddenly became dark, like night had fallen.

Yeshua yelled, "To the rocks!" and we all ran a distance to where there were bluffs. These bluffs had holes carved into them for tombs. We found a cleft between two hills and clambered down into the depression. The wind continued to roar but we were out of the direct thrashing of the sand storm. Everyone wrapped a bit of cloth over their faces. To me this only made the day darker, hotter, and harder to breathe. Holy ADONAI. Would this ordeal never end?

The Evil Wind blew for two straight hours. The entire land was darkened for those two hours. It seemed that the light of day was gone forever, perhaps never to return, as if ADONAI had cast down a punishment on mankind. We huddled and waited it out in the rocks. Finally the wind subsided enough that we could talk without having to yell. I climbed and stretched to the top and poked my head up out of the hole, like an animal seeing the first dawn. As near as I could tell without seeing the angle of the sun, it was the ninth hour. The three men still hung from the three crosses. I was amazed that the wind had not carried them aloft like giant birds. I saw the centurion, his soldiers and the slaves, stirring out from under the wagon where they had taken shelter. The centurion walked up to the men on the crosses. I saw his mouth moving as if he were saying something to them. I could not see if any of them answered him. The centurion said something over his shoulder to the other men. The centurion raised his spear. He pierced the chest of each man, probing deeply to be sure of hitting their heart. The Roman cruci fixus detail could not leave until the condemned were dead. The centurion was just helping them along, in their final journey. The bodies would be left on the crosses for several days for all to see. This was a warning by the Romans to any who considered committing a crime. Look, they were saying, this could be you. When the bodies began to stink, the overseer of the town dump would take them down, being sure to save the iron nails for the next victims as iron was valuable and not wasted. The bodies would be hauled off to the fire pits in the town dump, the valley of slaughter. The slaves harnessed themselves to the wagon and began pulling, following the centurion on his horse and his soldiers walking. They moved off jauntily, as if they had done a good days work and were heading for the Roman baths, food, and wine.

Taking other possible outcomes in consideration, we had done a good day's work also. But I did not feel jaunty, only weary to the bone. I wanted to get to Bethany, to lay in a tub of hot water with Rachel, to eat and drink, and to relax and sleep. I was about to tell the others the deed was done, the coast was clear, and we could leave, when I saw the centurion's horse shy and rear suddenly like a snake had crossed its hooves. The centurion was unseated, thrown upwards and backwards into the air like an acrobat at the carnival. He landed hard on his stupid head in a comical neck breaking fall. A harsh laugh exploded out of me. The horse breezed away as fast as it could run. The soldiers and slaves were moving as if they were dancing, cavorting back and forth as if they had gone crazy. The rock I was leaning against heaved as if shoved by a giant. The rock cracked with a noise that stunned my ears. The whole earth seemed to split, to lift then drop, making my stomach lurch. – *And the foundations of the earth do shake. The earth quaked, and the rocks were split. The earth trembleth and tottereth* –. The ground of the whole earth was moving, shaking violently. The others were climbing up out of the rock cleft when I was unseated and thrown backwards landing on top of them. Hands grabbed me and shoved me up. I climbed to the top and they followed. I slipped and fell from the rock onto the violently shaking ground. The earth had lost its moorings and we were tossed about like leaves in a strong wind. We cut and ran like all the daemons of Hades were chasing us.

HIGH SHABBAT AND PASSOVER EVE. MY
NAME IS MARIAM OF MAGDALA

At the home of Lazarus, Barabbas and Jehosheba were in their room resting. Rachel and I were waiting for our men. Just moments ago the sandstorm had finally blown itself out, and the silence made the previous howling of the wind even more remarkable. According to the water clock it was the ninth hour. That meant in about five hours the sun would set and the Shabbat would begin. At this hour, at the Temple, the slaughtering of the lambs for Passover would commence. I had the uncanny notion that the passion of Simon the Cyrene had passed, and I thought it a very strange coincidence that his death may have occurred at the same time the priests were making their sacrifices. I wondered if anyone in future days would remember the sacrifice of Simon the Cyrene, at the timing of the Passover slaughter. I knew I would carry a certain responsibility, and guilt, for his death, even though he deserved his fate. He would have sold Yeshua and Barabbas for blood money. These were times, all this, that troubled the soul.

I was about to start the preparation of the Passover meal we would take at moonrise when the quaking of the earth began. The whole house seemed to lift straight up and fall back down with a great booming noise. Then the rolling of the ground started. The entire building was rocking, furniture and other items crashing about. The roof where it met the wall separated and I stood looking at the sky, dumbfounded. I had lived through quakes before. They had been quick, nervous shakings of the earth but I had never experienced anything like this. This whole region of Judah, from the Salt Sea to Jerusalem, to the coast of the Great Sea, was prone to violent quaking. About sixty harvests past, during the early years of the reign of Herod I, a great earthquake killed thirty thousand people from one end of Judah to the other.

The movement of the earth was like being in a rudderless boat in a stormy sea. My heart hammered fast in my chest the whole time. As suddenly as it began, it stopped. Jehosheba and Barrabas came from their room. Rachel rose from where she had fallen on the floor. Lazarus and his wife came into the room. We all stood, speechless, staring at each other for a long moment, then everyone started speaking at once. Suddenly there was another quaking, even more violent, but lasting only a few seconds. Lazarus said, "That was the shock that comes after. It is normal. We may feel more but they will eventually subside."

Rachel had her hands to her face, covering her mouth, her eyes wide, "Judas and Yeshua! Where are they?"

Barabbas said. "I am sure they are safe and on their way. I will go now to meet them." Barabbas rushed into his room and came back out with his sword and his leather shoes. While he was tying the laces around his calves, there was a beating on the door. I heard Yeshua's voice, "Lazarus. Open up."

The last week had been difficult and tiring. Yeshua and I were resting in our room. He told me, "We will leave tomorrow, in the evening, after Shabbat. We will leave Jerusalem. I do not know how you feel about it, but I do not care to ever see the city again, as long as I live."

"And your army? The fight?"

Yeshua laughed without humor, "Army? I had no army! I was only fooling myself. I spoke to Judas about that very thing just before the sand storm hit. He told me about his last meeting with Pontius Pilate. Judas told me how the Romans dominated the ground. Just those handful of horsemen and the archers and soldiers could have slaughtered everyone in that crowd. There will be no army of the Habirum until all the Habirum join together. The Pharisees, the Essenes, and even the cursed Sadducee if they would open their eyes. All must join together. All of the Habirum must train together as a military force. There must be good weapons for every warrior. Only when we realize we must band together and fight for the land like Joshua and King David, only then will we defeat the Romans."

"Do you believe that may happen one day?"

Yeshua lay still and quiet. I thought he was thinking on my question, then I realized he had gone to sleep. I must have fallen asleep too because suddenly I jerked awake to hear the voice of Lazarus at the door, "Yeshua. You must come at once." Yeshua was already awake and at the door before I could move. I heard them talking in low voices. He closed the door and began to dress. It was dark so I lit a candle, "What is it?"

"Joseph and Nicodemus have come with news, go back to sleep," and he was out the door. Of course I could not simply go back to sleep, so I soon followed him. In the outer room were Joseph of Arimathea, Nicodemus of Damascus, Lazarus, Judas, and Barabbas, Simon the Zealot, Simon Peter and Yeshua. I sensed an urgency in their demeanor.

Joseph of Arimathea was saying, "I told him the evil wind and the quaking of the earth at the death of the bandit, Yeshua, had the citizens fearful that a blasphemy had been done. I told him many simple minded persons believed the bandit, Yeshua, was the anointed one, sent by ADONAI. They believed it was the fury of ADONAI that blew in the storm and shook the ground."

Lazarus said, "Pontius Pilate is the worst kind of Roman heathen. He believes only in the god of the sword. He probably thought you were speaking some sort of magician's hocus pocus, talking about the messiah of the god of the Habirum."

Yeshua asked, "What did he say?"

Joseph said, "Lazarus is right. Pilate poured scorn on the notion, but I changed his mind when I pointed out that the longer the body of Yeshua hung from the cross the more it could attract attention. The body could very well become a symbol to arouse the wrath of the people. I described to him Roman soldiers having to spill Habirum blood. Hundreds, perhaps thousands of citizens dead, and that would be a disaster for Rome. Pilate grudgingly agreed and gave me permission to remove the body from the cross. Just before sunset, Nicodemus and I wrapped it in linens and put it in a tomb I happened to own just north of Golgatha. We closed the tomb with a stone."

"The hills past the Fish Gate Road? That is where we waited out the sand storm. So, all is well now?" asked Yeshua.

Nicodemus of Damascus said to Joseph of Arimathea, "Tell them the worst part." Nicodemus looked at Yeshua, "You will not believe this!"

"A message was brought to my home from Annas. The message was. 'What is this rumor I hear that the dead man is not the bandit Yeshua?'"

Judas shook his head, and muttered, "Well, here we go!" Yeshua nodded his head at Judas, and said, "Yes. This is very inconvenient news." Yeshua asked Joseph, "So, what happened then?"

Joseph said, "While I was reading that note from Annas, another message arrived from Caiaphas. He and Annas are both questioning the dead man's identity."

Nicodemus said, "That's not the worst part. Tell them the rest." Judas was groaning and shaking his head.

Joseph said, "Herod Antipas has many guests for Passover so Chuza could not leave, but I spoke to him. Herod received the same messages from Caiaphas and Annas. Herod, Chuza told me, is raging, screaming like a mad man 'Can no one do anything right? Must I do everything myself?' So then I went straight back to Pontius Pilate. I thought it best he heard of this from me."

"And what did Pilate say?"

"Pontius Pilate listened, then he told me it was a good thing I had taken the man from the cross and put him in the tomb."

Lazarus asked, "Why did Pilate think that was a good thing?"

Then Joseph told us the most alarming news. "Because one of his officers, had just minutes before my arrival, mentioned that he knew a man who knew this Yeshua! And Pilate ordered that this man be brought to him, immediately. Pilate told me that taking the man from the cross and entombing him would keep the birds from eating his face so he could be identified by this man."

Yeshua asked, "What do you mean?"

"Do you recall ever meeting a Roman centurion by the name of Cornelius?"

Judas threw his arms in the air, loudly exclaiming, "Well, happy horse dung! Here we go!" He pointed an accusing finger at Yeshua, "I tried to tell you!"

THE WILDERNESS OF JUDAH. MY
NAME IS JUDAS ISCARIOT

Mariam had given me some leaves to chew that tasted terrible. She said it would awaken me for the task ahead. She handed me only a few leaves. I told her, "Give me the sack. I am beat." She looked worried, but handed it over anyway, telling me, "Go easy with this."

The juice of the leaves had jerked my eyes wide open. I munched steadily on the leaves as we rode until the sack was empty. I was wide awake. After six hours I was still going strong. The leaves had increased my heart beat alarmingly and made me sweat and grind my teeth, but they worked wonders on my exhausted body. I threw the last shovelful of dirt into the hole, wondering if this ordeal would ever end. I had had just a few hours of sleep before Joseph and Nicodemus had shown up at the home of Lazarus with their news. Then we had left to finish this, I hoped, final piece of business.

Joseph had taken us to the rock carved tomb where he and Nicodemus had entombed the body of Simon the Cyrene. We had to work quietly, in the dark, as the guards at the Fish Gate were not far away. We rolled the stone back, then Yeshua crawled in, grabbed Simon's feet and drug him out. As a joke, Yeshua tossed back in the tomb the soiled linens Simon the Cyrene was wrapped in, "We will let the Romans hunt for a naked man."

We rolled and tied Simon the Cyrene in a piece of hempen boat sail. Yeshua lifted Simon's carcass over his shoulder. Then we walked a distance to where we had left the horses and the mule with Simon the Zealot. The mule didn't like the smell of Simon the Cyrene, and complained as we tied Simon on the mule with stout ropes.

We rode south for several hours, alternating between galloping and walking. We did not want the horses to become lame. We passed to the west of Hebron, stopping at a stream to water the horses, then continued south for two more hours. In the hour before dawn, we finally stopped in the northern Imudean desert, a place so wild and desolate I wondered if humans had ever been here before. We dug a deep hole and placed the stiff corpse of Simon the Cyrene at the bottom. We filled the hole then placed large stones over the dirt to keep animals from digging.

Groaning, I stood and rubbed my sore back. I noticed Yeshua was looking at me strangely. He asked me, "Are you well?"

"Yes. I am fine. Why do you ask?"

"Because you have been talking ever since we left hours ago. You have said more words in the last hours than I heard you speak in all the years I have known you." He stepped close and looked at me as if he was examining one of his patients. "Your pupils are dilated and you keep clenching your jaw, making funny faces." Yeshua took my arm and placed his fingers on my wrist. I could feel the echo of my own pulse banging strongly. "Hmmin. I think the pharmacopeia Mariam gave you was over dosed. I know what will make you feel better."

Yeshua took some of the green Kannabaeus herb from his pouch, loaded his pipe, took a coal from the small fire we had set to work by, put the coal to the pipe, and puffed a few times to get it going. Then he turned the pipe around, cupping the burning end in his fist. He told me, "Breathe this." He put his mouth to his fist and blew air into the wrong end of the pipe. This made the smoke come out backwards from the stem end. I breathed deeply. Inhale, exhale, inhale, exhale, until the herb was burnt. I stepped back and looked at Yeshua. "So?"

Yeshua said, "Relax. Wait a moment while we get the horses ready to travel." And I sat there on the stones on top of the grave of Simon the Cyrene, and rested. I looked to the east and to the lightening of the day. I watched the most glorious, beautiful sunrise I had ever seen in my life. I sat there for long minutes, minutes lost in time. I realized I had never really seen the sunrise before. This wondrous, life giving sunrise, reminded me of the words from Joshua. – *Sun, stand thou still upon Gibeon. And the sun stood still, until the nation had avenged themselves of their enemies –*. This sunrise was an epiphanea, a striking and sudden understanding. I knew what it all meant. Everything suddenly made perfectly good sense.

Yeshua walked up, "Are you ready to go?"

My whole body felt comfortably and wonderfully numb. All the soreness was miraculously gone. I stood slowly. "Did you see the sunrise?"

Yeshua smiled, "Yes."

I looked at Yeshua, and the other men, and the horses and the mule. I looked down at the stones covering Simon the Cyrene. I looked at the surrounding countryside. Everything was bathed in a sparkling, beautiful golden light. Everything looked just right.

I told Yeshua, "I am suddenly very hungry. Did we bring food?"

THE THIRD DAY. MY NAME IS
MARIAM OF MAGDALA

It was close to sundown and the end of Shabbat, when Yeshua and the others returned. They were dirty, exhausted and famished. They were too tired even to eat. Yeshua kept nodding while I bathed him, and it was all I could do to support him to the bed where he fell like a tree and was instantly asleep. From sundown to sunrise the men slept. Then they woke and after dousing their heads in water to wake up, they ate like starved, wild animals.

We broke our night fast, actually a night, a day, and another night fast for the men. All were of good cheer. I prayed this ordeal, as Judas called it, was finally over. During the meal, guests arrived. The first were Philip with Andrew, Simon Peter's brother, who had been wounded in the fight. Andrew was healing. His sword cut was a healthy, pink color that would leave a scar across his chest for the women to admire, but no long term damage. Then came Levi Matthew and his brother James, the sons of Alphaeus. They had all gone into hiding in the wilderness after the fight was lost, not knowing if the Romans were hunting them. They told us James and John, Bartholomew Nathaneal, and Thomas were in the wilderness waiting for Andrew to return and tell them what was happening in Jerusalem and Bethany.

The men were discussing the battle, and like all men, were glorying over the cuts inflicted and enemy slain. Of course they forgot the desperate danger and close calls of their own lives, and did not remember the dangers they had placed others in. There was the light of battle still in their eyes as they relived the damage they had done to the Roman swine enemy. I could see it would not take much for them to assemble and charge again. Men! Foolish men! – *And he smelleth the battle afar off, the thunder of the captains, and the shouting. He goeth out to meet the clash of arms. He mocketh at fear, and is not affrighted, neither turneth he back from the sword.*

The quiver rattleth upon him, the glittering spear and the javelin. He swalloweth the ground with storm and rage –.

I thought there must be something wrong with men, all men, all the sons of men. There must be a deficiency in their brain that makes them storm and rage and battle and seek to shed the blood of other sons of men, as if that was heroic. If I could only turn them to the quiet love and peace and harmony of the worship of Isis. Or, if that were not possible, then take from them all the positions of authority and put women in charge of the game of life. Then and only then would there be hope that the sons and daughters of men could live without war and conflict. I laughed at my own musings. I was dreaming, only dreaming an awakened dream. I was dreaming of a perfect world. But I had a reason, a good reason, to hope that such a perfect world could be made real.

It was still early, the second hour, when Joseph of Arimathea, Nicodemus of Damascus and Chuza arrived at the door breathless, Joseph said, "We bring bad news." Judas sat shaking his head, mumbling over and over, "Here we go! Here we go!"

Nicodemus, being the food supplier to the Antonia Fortress, was in there often and kept his eyes and ears open. He told us the centurion, Cornelius, Pontius Pilate sent for, had rode hard overnight and arrived to Pilate's summons. Nicodemus gossiped with certain of the officers, making sure they always received extra wine and special food. An officer had bragged to him that Pilate was determined to verify the identity of the bandit, Yeshua, or burn the countryside until he had the truth.

Chuza told us that Herod Antipas received the high priest Caiaphas at his palace. Caiaphas told Herod the Sadducees of the Sanhedrin council were in an uproar because of the rumor the man hung from the cross might not have been Yeshua, the blasphemer. Herod Antipas told Caiaphas he would take care of the problem. The way Herod Antipas took care of the problem was to complain to Pontius Pilate that he, Pilate, was the person responsible for the cruci fixus of the man. Pontius Pilate shot a message back to Herod Antipas saying that he, Herod, and the Sanhedrin council, had judged the man guilty, Pilate had only rendered the penalty.

The solution that all agreed on was to let the centurion Cornelius open the tomb, take out the dead man, and verify the identity. The centurion would bathe and have food while a fresh horse was prepared for him, then he would meet with Pilate, Herod and Caiaphas at Herod's palace. He was expected to leave for the tomb at the high sun. It seemed that removing the body of Simon the Cyrene had not solved the problem. If there was no body to even attempt to identify, then Pontius Pilate, Herod and the Sanhedrin council might never cease looking for the bandit, Yeshua. They were determined to identify the bandit Yeshua, whether he was dead or alive.

While the men argued amongst themselves, making pointless remarks and useless suggestions, I sat thinking on the situation. Thinking of several different options, I quickly concluded there was only one solution. "Listen," I told them. "I have a plan. It is about three hours to high sun. We have just enough time but we must move fast."

THE FIFTH HOUR OF THE THIRD DAY.
MY NAME IS MARIAM OF MAGDALA

"It is too dangerous. This only brings you to the attention of the Romans. Besides, it is a crazy story and no one will believe it anyway."

Yeshua had been arguing with me from the very instant we left the home of Lazarus. We swiftly rode horseback south across the spine of Mount Olivet then down into the valley far past the city. We swung west then north to approach from behind the hills where the tomb was located. We stopped in the same ravine the men had used, so the horses would be out of sight of the city walls and the guards at the Fish Gate. The two women with us, Yeshua's mother, Mary Salome and Mary the wife of Lazarus, were not experienced horse riders but they had gritted their teeth and hung on for the ride. I was carrying clean linens, spices, and myrrh, to prepare the body as the entombment two days before had been hurried.

I told Yeshua, "All the Pharisee and Essene in the city believe Yeshua was the anointed one. They believe the evil wind and the earth quaking at the death of Yeshua was a sign from ADONAI. I am only taking the story a little further. You will be near. I will call if there is a problem." I smiled at him, "You can slay the dragon if we are in distress." I told the ladies, "Come on girls. Let us show the menfolk how to complete a difficult task." We walked away leaving Yeshua looking frustrated. He had Judas, Barabbas, Simon Peter, Simon the Zealot and two of his men to keep him company. I called over my shoulder to Yeshua, "Stay out of sight."

My plan was to complete the circle and sew together the ends of an age old tale and to make a spiritual ending, if not one that was entirely logical. Besides, it seemed that logic and reason played no part in the belief and acceptance of age old tales. This tale was as old as remembered time itself. As is written in the book of Daniel. - *Thy people shall be delivered. And many of them that sleep in the dust of the earth shall awake, some to everlasting life* -. And the stories of Enoch and Elijah, all echoing across the ages. And there were more. The Aegyptus god Osiris was resurrected by the goddess Isis. And still told to this day are other tales of death and resurrection such as Ba'al, and Melqart, Adonis, Eshmun, Dumuzi, Asclepius, and Heracles.

All of them lived forever in the hearts and minds of the sons and daughters of men, for one reason. That reason is because at their deaths they did not become just the clay of the earth or the dust blown by winds. They died, were arisen, and then lived again. That made them strikingly memorable, not just their deeds while they lived, but the belief that they lived forever. These tales of an amazing continuance made all of mankind yearn for such a rebirth, so that they too may arise to live again.

Among the Habirum there is different thinking on the end of life, the completion of the natural cycle, and what may or may not happen afterwards. Those of us who are Pharisees believe our bodies will be resurrected in which our souls always dwell. The Essenes think the soul is immortal, a spark like a star in the sky but that needs no bodily form. The Sadducees lived each day in excess, without conscience, for they believed that nothing remained nor would return after the flesh failed. The Sadducees embraced the Roman's way of life. Vinum et festum. Wine and Carnivals! Pecunia non olet. Money Does Not Stink! Because, to them, there was nothing after this mortal existence, so satisfying one's desires was the purpose of life.

The lessons of tolerance, as imparted by Isis, made me judge not how or what anyone else believed, as long as their beliefs did not infringe on any other's beliefs or way of life. But today, it was my intention to impress upon and influence another's way of thinking. This Roman, this Cornelius, would adjust his mind in the direction I wanted, or he would get my dagger planted in his heart. I had not told Yeshua that last part of my plan because then he would not have allowed this trickery to proceed. But I was determined. The Roman would believe, or the Roman would die. If he must die, he would take Simon the Cyrene's place in the tomb.

I had not told Mary Salome and Mary the wife of Lazarus about the dagger hidden in my wrist sheath. They would play no part in that final scene, if it became necessary. As we walked to the tomb I rehearsed with Mary Salome and Mary Lazarus the parts and words they played in this.

I had not wanted the women to accompany me, but Mary Salome told me, "I have come this far with you, I will be with you at the ending." Mary, the wife of Lazarus said, "Three witnesses are better than two." I now welcomed their company because, I admit, I had some anxiety about how this drama would work. There is probably a moment, right before the player goes on stage, when they seem struck dumb and all the lines they had so vigorously prepared just fly away from their minds. I wondered if words would fail me. I feared they would.

I had been to the theater once, many years in the past. I watched clumsy Romans butcher a smart play written by a clever Greek. I saw the obvious ending even before the deus ex machina untied the knot. The mangled story and the inept exhibition of it left me unsatisfied. I had never returned. Now I found myself on the stage in a starring role and I wondered if I could, as they say, make it play. My already twitchy stomach growled at me.

We arrived at the tomb to see the stone rolled back, I looked at the sun and saw it was close to high sun. As I looked around at our stage, the stage of the theater for our hurried play, I saw to my surprise that we were standing in a cabbage patch. These were not wild plants, someone had tended the field carefully. The purple and green leafy vegetables were growing in an orderly abundance, the weeds that might stifle them plucked from the earth. I saw that many of the cabbages near the tomb had been trampled and were ruined. I suppose Yeshua and the men, working in the dark, had done that.

The sight of the waste of the food, the waste of someone's efforts, the stress and fear of the past week, the exhaustion of the past year, the fright of the part I had to perform, the hot temperature and searing blinding sun, my unruly stomach and its implications, fear for the future, and the knowledge that I may have to commit cold blooded murder and kill one man, a stranger, to save another man that I loved with all my heart, suddenly seemed overwhelming.

My stomach nearly revolted. My heart was heavy, and all my courage was suddenly gone. Fight it as I might, the swelling of emotions overcame me. I choked. I could not take air into my lungs. My eyes became flooded till I could not see, I thought I might fall.

Then I burst into tears. The brave front I put on for Yeshua had been for nothing and now I stood in the midst of smashed cabbages weeping. Like Yeshua had said about his vision, my wild plan was a trickery of my own mind. This was not going to work. The worst of it was my tears caused Mary Salome and Mary Lazarus to break down. We leaned our heads against one another and bawled like babies. My weakness infected them, now all of us were defenseless in the face of this threat. I had led them here and now failed them.

Then I heard a voice, "Woman, why weepest thou?"

I jerked my head up fearing it was the Roman centurion. Who I saw before me was not a dangerous centurion in his clean red uniform but a small man in a filthy robe. He had twisted, knotted hair and a grey beard that reached to his waist. Blubbering, I asked him, "Who are you?"

"I am Yuda. I am Yuda the gardener. Do you come to buy cabbages?" He pointed, "The men who took up the dead man, they did this to my cabbages but I have more. I will get you the best."

The poor man had some sort of speech impediment. He stuttered and stammered over his words. "The men who took up the dead man? What do you mean?"

Looking at and listening to the gardener, I realized he was a gentle soul who had a weakness in his brain making him a simple minded lunatik. But he was harmless as a child. He lived in a cave he had scratched from the side of the hill, and his livelihood was tending his cabbages. It was no wonder he was strange in the head, living his solitary life with only the dead resting in their tombs and his cabbages to keep him company.

He told me that late in the night he had awakened to see men armed with swords and spears in his cabbages. He was afraid and lay still, watching, saying nothing, as the men took the dead man out from the tomb and away. He told me he had not gone back to sleep. The dawn had revealed his cabbages destroyed. He had cried and now his head hurt and he felt sick from not sleeping.

I suddenly saw a way out of our predicament. For since by man came death, by woman will come the resurrection of the dead. What I proposed was a trickery, probably cruel, and maybe would not work anyhow, but it seemed it was our only chance. Then I thought, perhaps Isis or maybe ADONAI sent this man to us? Perhaps this is meant to be? To be safe I sent up a quick silent prayer to Isis. I promised this would be the last of the trickery. If she would help me with this one last effort, I promised that I would go and sin no more. I looked at the sun. We had just enough time.

I would use the knowledge and skills I had studied since my childhood, the knowledge and skills of Isis. This knowledge was older than remembered time. Yeshua had described to me pictures and writings he had seen on the monuments in Aegyptus. The writings were so old the knowledge of the language had been lost. The pictures Yeshua had sketched from his memory showed the Goddess Isis and the pharaoh, Imhotep. They were the first physicians. Isis and Imhotep had mysterious powers. They used secret rituals and medicinal herbs and incantations to make physical and mental healings. The Aegyptus knowledge had traveled across the Aegyptus desert, across the Great Sea, and arrived in Greece, brought back by Alexander the Macedonian. In Greece there had been temples where people were cured of their ailments by the priests who studied the special arts of Isis and Imhotep. The Greeks called their healing god, Asclepios.

The Romans learned, or stole, from the Greeks this knowledge, and continued the practice, dedicating their healing places to the god, Apollo. But over time the perfection of the Aegyptus knowledge had been diluted and lost. The Greeks lost some and the Romans lost even more. That Aegyptus knowledge was practiced now only in the Temple of the Goddess Isis.

One of the special skills I learned in my training was how to alter a person's perceptions and their memory of experiences through the use of mind control. I focused their eyes and their mind and all their attention on one single point until they were susceptible to the power of suggestion. Normally the person would be prepared by fasting and purification and ritual bathing, but we had no time for that. Instead I would use a certain concoction to speed the procedure. I told the man I was a healer and I could cure the pain in his head, "Will you allow me to treat you?" I asked him. He readily agreed with the innocence of a child. I spread the linen on the ground, seated myself, and bid him to sit.

I had Mary and Mary quickly gather some twigs and dry sticks and start a fire. I told them to move out of his line of sight and to sit quietly, "Do not move. Do not make a sound." I took a small pot from my bag of pharmacopeia in which I poured some wine and added some leaves and plants which had very extraordinary properties. When the wine heated to its first bubbling I took it off the fire and told him to drink it down quickly. I told him to close his eyes and relax. In just moments I could see the pharmacopeia was working as his whole body slumped to a very relaxed position. I told him, "Yuda, open your eyes."

When he opened his eyes the first thing he saw was an unusual rock I held in the fingers of my hand, right in front of his eyes. The rock was the size of a small bird's egg. It was perfectly round, a lustrous black in color, with a distinctive swirl of a white mineral embedded within it. By rotating the rock back and forth the swirl drew one's eyes to focus exactly on this one thing. I then said to Yuda those special words which induced a trance like state upon the patient. I spoke the special words of the ritual from the teachings of Isis. Yuda watched the swirling and listened to the words until I saw the change in the pupils of his eyes I was expecting. At that moment I told him to close his eyes, which he immediately did. Then I painted a picture, using words, a picture that planted itself upon his mind. I described a different reality. A reality not of what he had seen, but of what I wanted him to have seen in the dark hour of the night.

This procedure, this mind control, according to the teachings of Isis, was to be used only for healing of the body and the mind. It was only to be used for good, and that had always been my practice. This mind control, the doing of it, took all my focused concentration. Yet a part of my mind, a small voice, asked me if what I was doing was right. Was I using this man? Were my own needs so important that this could be justified?

I had no more time to consider this question of ethics. In the distance I heard the galloping of an approaching horse. Was it the centurion, Cornelius? I continued speaking the words to Yuda until the picture was painted. I said to Yuda, "I will say your name and you will awaken. The ache in your head will be gone. You will feel refreshed as if you had a good night's rest. You will remember only what I have told you to remember and nothing else. When you hear the words I speak that I have told you to remember, then you will say the words I have told you to say. You will now awaken. Yuda."

And hearing his name Yuda opened his eyes and looked at me. He smiled and his eyes twinkled. He told me, "The ache in my head is gone. Thank you!" I smiled, "Yuda, I am glad the ache in your head is no more."

I stood and grabbed up the linens. I put the pot in my pouch and kicked dirt over the small fire. I walked to the tomb and knelt in front of the opening. Mary Salome and Mary Lazarus knelt each side of me. Yuda asked me, "What are you doing?"

At that moment I heard the horse stop, heard a man dismount. I heard the man walking toward us. I told Yuda, "We are praying to the man who was taken up by ADONAI." And thankfully, Yuda heard these words I told him I would say and I told him to remember. Then, gloriously, I heard Yuda say the words of the picture I had painted in his mind. The man who had ridden the horse stopped walking just a pace away.

Yuda said, "The man was taken up by ADONAI. I saw everything. The man came out from the tomb. He was standing just there, where you are kneeling. A bright light surrounded him. I heard a voice from the clouds. The voice was saying words in a language I do not know. The man from the tomb looked to the sky and he too spoke in the strange language. The bright light lifted the man from the tomb up off the ground. I watched the man from the tomb who was surrounded by the bright light rising up to the sky. I saw it all. The man from the tomb was arisen by ADONAI."

A different voice, the centurion, said, "Man, what is this you say?"

We turned to see a blond haired clean shaven man in the red uniform of a Roman centurion. The centurion asked Yuda again, "Who are you and what are you saying?"

"I am Yuda. I am Yuda the gardener. In the dark of last night I saw it. I saw everything from there," pointing to his cave dwelling.

"What? What did you see?"

Then, playing his part, as I had told him, I watched as Yuda slowly raised his hands to the sky, pointing. "The man in the tomb was arisen into the sky. The light was a wonder to behold as he was raised up in it to the sky. ADONAI took the man from the tomb up into the sky."

The centurion looked at us, "You, women. What is this man talking about? Move aside so I can see into the tomb."

We stood and moved away from the tomb opening. As the centurion knelt to look inside, I told him, "There is no one there. We came to prepare his body but he is gone."

The centurion stood. He looked at the pots of myrrh and spices I had set on the ground at the tomb entrance. He looked at the clean linens in my hands. He grunted, squinted his eyes, and looked hard at each of us in turn. "What do you mean he is gone? Dead men do not walk."

I could not answer him. I had no words. As I feared, I became dumbstruck on the stage. And then Yuda did something that I did not understand then, nor do I understand it now, all these years later. Yuda underwent some sort of ecstatic invigoration. He howled joyfully. He whirled and twirled like a dervish. He danced among his cabbages like one possessed. He spoke like a magician making some sort of incantation. His speech impediment was miraculously gone. Yuda sang the words, his voice as clear as a ringing bell. These words from Yuda were nothing I had painted upon his mind. Where these words came from, to be spoken with such fervor by this simpleminded man, was a mystery then as it is now. Yuda told us of his apokalypsis, his revelation.

Yuda sang out in a loud voice, "I saw the red throne of ADONAI. His golden scepter was in his hand. His scepter was inlaid with shining red rubies. I heard ADONAI speak. The words of ADONAI are like the sound of thunder. Thus saith ADONAI. *Behold, I will open your grave, and cause you to come up out of your grave, and ye shall live.* ADONAI raised the man from the tomb. The man from the tomb was taken to the right hand of ADONAI. The man from the tomb was made whole by ADONAI. Then ADONAI showed me a coming war. I saw a great beast made of fire falling from the sky and landing in the sea. The beast boiled the water and moved the seas until all the land and the islands are gone and the mountains are covered with water and the tops of the mountains become the islands. Coming out of the boiling sea I saw four horses. I saw a white horse, a red horse, a black horse and a pale horse. I saw the four horses gallop in a river of blood. I saw the four horses breathing fire. The horsemen riding the four horses are on fire and they are swinging swords of fire that destroy everything in their path. There are peals of thunder and flashes of lighting and a great hailstorm and a great earthquake and I saw the sun go dark. I saw those of mankind who did not perish in the first cataclysms retreat to caves on the mountains that are now islands. I saw from the boiling sea locusts like scorpions flying to those left of mankind, bringing seven plagues that inflict foul and malignant sores upon them. I saw all the water that was left to nourish life turned to blood. I saw a beast, a great dragon beast emerge from the boiling sea. The dragon beast had seven heads and horns of fire. The dragon beast told the people to make an image of itself and worship it. I saw the dragon beast mark the people, burning the symbol 666 upon their skins. I saw the people fall down before the dragon beast and worship the dragon beast. I saw the people living in the darkness of an unholy spirit. And then I saw ADONAI lay his hand upon the man from the tomb.

I saw the man from the tomb call to his side four angels. I saw the four angels and they are a lion, and an ox, and a man, and an eagle. I could see through the eyes of the angels and I could see everything in all four directions at once. I could see north and south and east and west and all that was there. I saw the man from the tomb take his angels to the earth to do battle with the great beast dragon. I saw the battle last forty years and one day. I saw the last day. I saw the man from the tomb and his angels slay the great dragon beast. I saw the man from the tomb and his angels slay the four horsemen. I saw on the last day of the battle the man from the tomb bring forth from the clean air of ADONAI's temple a woman clothed in a white robe. I saw the woman standing on the moon and upon her head was a crown of twelve stars. I saw a new sunrise. I saw a new Jerusalem shining on the Mount. All this I have witnessed for the glory of ADONAI and for the glory of the man who was arisen from the tomb."

I stood dumbfounded during the revelation of Yuda. Mary and Mary also stood with their mouths open and eyes wide in amazement at this rapturous spectacle. I looked at the centurion. He too seemed struck by the wonder of it. Then Yuda whirled in one last spin of the dervish and ran off as fast as his feet would take him into the wilderness. We four stood silent until he was lost to sight over the hills, lost in the blaze of the sunshine. I wondered to myself, was Yuda real, or a figment of my own imagination? Of course he was real. But what had overcome him? Was it the drug I had given him? Had the drug expanded his consciousness and opened his mind and his eyes to give him a glorious vision? Was Yuda the gardener the vessel from which poured forth an answer to a divine mystery? I would never know because Yuda was never to be seen again. Had Yuda deserted his cabbages to make a new home in the wilderness? Or, had Yuda been taken aloft by the hand of ADONAI, to sit at the side of ADONAI, as had Ezekiel, who also was gifted a wonderful vision? To this day, many years later, I still ponder this mystery, and each day before I sleep, I pray for the welfare of Yuda and I thank him for his deliverance.

The centurion jerked himself, as if reviving from a trance of his own. He turned and asked me, in a tone of astonishment, "What was that?"

I raised my arms and face to the sky, "Yuda was witness to the rebirth of Yeshua! Yeshua has arisen!" And Mary and Mary joined in my cries of joy, "Yeshua has arisen!"

The centurion watched us celebrating the rebirth of Yeshua. "Wait," he ordered. "This man, this Yeshua, what did he look like?" And I described Yeshua's blue eyes and brown hair, the features of his face, the height and breadth of him, as if Yeshua was standing there with us.

The centurion nodded his head. "Yes, that is he." Then he asked me, briskly, "This man, this Yeshua, was it truly he who was hung from the cross?"

And I dropped to my knees with Mary and Mary kneeling beside me. "Yes, it was Yeshua who was arrested and hung and died on the cross. I witnessed his passion! I witnessed his body being placed in this tomb. But now he is arisen! It is the prophecy as foretold by Hosea. – *On the third day He will be raised up, that we may live in His presence.* – Yeshua is arisen!"

"He is arisen! He is arisen!" cried Mary and Mary.

A dawning realization seemed to come to the centurion. He said to me, "I know this man, this Yeshua. I know him to be a great healer." Then, quietly, as if to himself, "There was something about him. There was a calm, a strength, he seemed to be …"

It was like the centurion had no words to express his last thought. He looked at the open tomb, the stone rolled away, our unused spices and myrrh, the discarded linens, the clean linens still in my hands, and he said quietly, "Could it be? Could the gardener really have witnessed all that?" The centurion raised his eyes to the sky. He stood quietly for a long time. I waited, as still as I could be, to see what would happen next.

Cornelius suddenly turned to me. "Tell me, when did you get here?"

"In the dark of the night. We waited for the dawn."

"And tell me, truly, did you see anyone here besides the gardener?"

"Yes. At first light we saw the stone was rolled back. I looked inside and saw the tomb was empty. I was frightened. I stood and looked about, thinking someone was here doing a mischief. Over there on the road, I saw a man in a new white robe. He was walking. He was away a distance, too far to call to him. But he stopped walking, he turned, and looked right at me. He raised his hand to me, then he walked away until I saw him no more."

"This man, what did he look like?"

And then I finally found my rhythm and my voice and played my part for all it was worth. I put an amazed look on my face and told Cornelius, "The man looked like Yeshua!"

The centurion grabbed the sleeve of my robe. "Which way was the man going?"

I pointed, "South, towards Bethlehem."

The centurion let go of my sleeve, turned, and walked the few steps to his horse. In an agile movement he leaped atop the horse's back and then galloped away.

I looked at Mary and Mary. We all just stood staring at each other. No one had any words.

As we walked back to the ravine, we were silent. I was mentally, physically, and emotionally drained. I fought back the tears inside me that threatened to burst forth. I looked at Mary and Mary. They too seemed wearied and fragile. I told myself, for them you must be strong. You must be strong!

I saw Yeshua standing at the edge of the ravine waiting for us. I knew that he had been vigilant. His eyes and ears were open for my call if there was trouble. His concern for us caused another wave of emotion to break over me like a wave. Be strong, I told myself, we are not yet released from this ordeal. There is still a great distance to go. Only I really knew what was left in this journey. Only I knew what was really at stake. Only I knew the importance of our final release.

Finally we came to the ravine. Yeshua walked out to meet us. He said, "We saw the centurion riding south as if the hounds of Hades were on his heels. Where was he going? Who was that crazy man who was dancing and leaping? What happened?"

He took my shoulders in his hands. He looked closely at me. "Are you well?" He touched my forehead. "You are in a cold sweat. What happened to you?"

I stood looking at Yeshua. I shook my head, and told him, "You will never believe it."

THE FOURTH DAY. MY NAME IS JUDAS ISCARIOT

Joseph of Arimathea and Joanna and Nicodemus of Damascus came to the home of Lazarus. They were telling us what was happening in the city, at the Temple, at the Fortress of Antonia, and in Herod's court. We all gathered and listened.

Joseph told us, "Caiaphas has told the Sadducee priests to spread the word that the followers of Yeshua have stolen the body. Caiaphas says to tell everyone that whoever has done this thing has committed blasphemy. They must confess and show the hiding place of the body, or they will be forever turned from the face of ADONAI."

Joanna said, "The Pharisees and Essenes believe Yeshua has arisen and is at the throne of ADONAI."

"Pontius Pilate has sent the centurion, Cornelius, out to scour the countryside. Herod and Pilate are thick as thieves with their old enmity forgotten," said Nicodemus.

I said, "It sounds like a holy mess." I asked Nicodemus, "Do you know what the centurion Cornelius told Pilate?"

"The officer who gossips with me said Cornelius reported only that the tomb was empty."

Mariam said, "That is all? He did not mention the gardener or the three women?"

"Not that I was told."

"Perhaps Cornelius placed no importance on those details. From a military point of view the only thing that would matter is the empty tomb," said Yeshua.

"Or perhaps Cornelius thought those were indeed the most important details, to him personally, and he decided to not share them with Pilate," offered Mariam.

"Whatever. We are wasting time speculating. We must decide what to do next," I told them.

Nicodemus told us, "You must leave quickly and go far from Judah. The Romans will continue to hunt you. We discussed this once before. Galilee is the province of Herod Antipas. You would not be safe there. The port city of Alexandria in Aegyptus is no better. Since the former emperor, Augustus, defeated Antony and the pharaoh Cleopatra suicided herself, the emperor Tiberius has flooded the land of Aegyptus with Romans. The Romans must hold Aegyptus for its abundance of grain or the land of Italia would revolt from starvation."

Joseph of Arimathea said, "I suggest an alternative. It is a long journey but the Romans are not thick as ticks there. I suggest the port city of Massilia."

I asked, "Where is that?"

Joseph of Arimathea said, "Massilia is a town of Gallia Narbonensis in southern Gaul. There is a large community of Pharisees there. You would be welcomed. They have a synagogue that is a place of learning. I know the elder. I will give you a letter of introduction. But it is far. It would require a sailing trip across the Great Sea."

Yeshua and I looked at each other. I was remembering our conversation with the learned man years ago about sailing the Great Sea. Yeshua picked up his pouch he kept his treasures in. From it he pulled the piece of wood on which he had copied the learned man's map. I saw that he had taken a hot metal and carefully scored lines over the charcoal marks in case the charcoal rubbed off and the map be lost. It struck me that Yeshua had never forgotten his blood vendetta against the Roman, Panthera.

Philip was looking at the map in Yeshua's hand. "I would like to go to Massilia. I will captain the ship. But we need a good ship. That is not as easy to get as stealing a Roman's horse."

Then Levi Matthew said the words that made it possible. "For many years I have been holding back from the Romans some of the tax I collected. It was my intention to give it to the Temple of ADONAI after we had released the Temple from the Romans. I will use the coins to buy a ship. I would like to see this Massilia myself."

Shortly the plan was made. Those who would make the journey included Rachel and myself, Barabbas and Jehosheba, Philip and

Nathanael Bartholomew as captain and first mate, Levi Matthew and his brother James, and Simon the Zealot, and his woman. We all turned to look at Yeshua. He was staring at something or staring at nothing. He seemed lost in thought.

I asked, "Yeshua. You have not spoken. What do you say?"

THE FOURTH DAY. MY NAME IS
MARIAM OF MAGDALA

Yeshua turned to look at Judas. Instead of answering his question, Yeshua said, "I must speak with Mariam. Excuse us." And he took my hand and led me to a corner of the garden where we could talk privately. We sat on a bench, Yeshua still had my hand in his.

"I told you the vision I had must have been a trickery of my own mind, but I have thought more on it. I think the message I received in my vision, whether it was ADONAI speaking the words, or something my imagination conjured up, did have meaning. The Temple, the land of the Habirum, must be freed from the Romans. I thought I could do that or lead our people in doing that. I was wrong and I failed. I ask myself, should I stay and continue the fight, or should I go and forget it. I fear that if I leave you will hold it against me."

"Why would I hold it against you?"

"In my heart I know I should fight to my last breath. I fear you will think me a coward if I run from the fight."

"You did all that was possible. No one could have done more. There is no shame. Your friends are concerned for your safety. If they did not believe you had done all you could, they would not be prompting you to leave and save yourself. And know this, I love you all the more for considering how I may feel. And I love you for your bravery and for your sense of purpose."

Yeshua sat shaking his head. He was torn by indecision. I told him, "We must go. If the Romans catch you they will kill you and they will make slaves of me and our child."

Yeshua looked at me, his face blank. "Our child?"

I placed Yeshua's hand on my belly. "Yes, our child. It is the morning sickness that troubles my stomach. We must leave for our child's safety."

Yeshua looked shocked. "You are with child?" I told him, "Yes." And then I waited. I waited to see if he would be glad or sad. This was why the stakes were so high. We had danger from the Romans, but there was another danger. This sudden news of a shared new life and a mutual responsibility, was also a danger. How would Yeshua react? This was a moment that would set our destinies.

Yeshua's expression turned slowly from shock to wonder. Then he smiled and looked happy to the core of his being. My sore heart was filled with joy. Yeshua took my face tenderly in his hands and kissed me. He leaned back, still holding me, "Yes. We must save our baby."

I told him, "But I have a fear. I fear that you will hold it against me if you believe that you are abandoning your fight because of my safety and because of our child."

Yeshua looked at me. He studied me for a long moment. "Do you recall that you once promised to honor whatever I may ask of you?"

"Yes. I remember." I had to smile, "I remember you tricked me!"

"Then promise me this. Promise me that you will never worry with that thought again. I promise that I will love you and hold you and cherish you. Have no fear. Will you promise me that?"

My eyes were full of hot tears, "Yes. I promise."

THE FIFTH DAY. MY NAME IS JUDAS ISCARIOT

Yeshua, Barabbas, and I were walking on the beach. The shells and sand crunched under our feet. "Yeshua my friend, it is a great journey. All three of our women are with child. It will be difficult for them."

Barabbas said, "It will be harder for our women if we are caught by the Romans. We must go."

"Yeshua, perhaps we should go to the land of the pharaohs, where you went as a child."

"Romans rule the land of the pharaohs. There are more of them there than are rats in the butcher's stall. We must go far from the Romans."

"You remember what the centurion told you that day. There are Romans in Gaul, from the time of the Caesar, Julius."

"Yes, but you heard what the wise man said. There are not as many Romans further away from the coast. And he said it was a beautiful, fertile land where all manner of crops grow. We will go into the country of the Gauls, away from the cities. The Romans will never find us."

"Yes, you are right, my friend. Let us go to this new land."

We stopped and looked at the boat. The boat sat bobbing at anchor in deeper water a short stones toss from the beach. It looked seaworthy. Philip and Nathaneal Bartholomew and Simon Zealot were aboard, storing supplies and organizing. We had worked all day moving supplies from the beach to the boat, loading casks of water, cages of chickens, bundles of vegetables, and other provisions for the journey. Levi Matthew and James were loading, into a small rowboat, the last of the boxes and crates. Barabbas said, "I will help Levi and James," and he walked away.

Yeshua and I stood looking out at the Great Sea. The water was a dark blue that disappeared into the lighter blue of the sky, the water and sky merging way off to the west. There was something I had to say. "Yeshua. You once said you wanted to go to this Gaul, go there and find the Roman, Panthera. Are you changing this fight for another?"

Yeshua looked at me, then turned his eyes back to the water. "Judas, my friend. My need to kill Romans has been curbed. My concern now is to see our women and our children away from this land that is soaked in blood."

"Good. Let us leave this place." The women were aboard. The rest of us would now join them. Philip had told us we would leave with the evening wind.

We heard the galloping hooves of a fast horse. We turned to see it was Simon Peter. He rode up and dismounted from the blowing horse. I asked him, "What news do you bring?" Simon Peter told us Pontius Pilate had men on the roads seeking the bandit, Yeshua. "He has not given up the search." He looked over his shoulder, "There are four more coming to join you on the journey.

I asked him, "Four more? We have twelve already. Philip says it is a full load. Who are the four?"

"It is Chuza, his wife Joanna, and their two children."

Just then I saw three horses approaching. On one was Joseph of Arimathea. On the two others was Joanna and Chuza each with a child sitting in front of them. We waited and in a few minutes they rode to us and stopped. Chuza dismounted then helped his children and wife down from the horses. Chuza told us Herod Antipas was becoming more insane every day. Herod had begun looking at him in a strange way, as if he didn't trust his steward any longer.

Yeshua and I told Chuza, "You are welcome. We will make room." Then Yeshua looked at me sort of sadly I thought and said, "Besides. Twelve does not seem to be my lucky number anyway." Barabbas and James had taken the last load of supplies to the boat and were now pulling the rowboat on the beach. I told Barabbas to take Chuza and his family to the boat then return for us.

Joseph of Arimathea handed Yeshua a scroll telling him, "This is the letter for you to give the elder in Massilia. I have written it in our Habirum for security so Romans will not be able to read it." He gave Yeshua a clay bottle with a cork. "After you read it, place it inside here to keep it dry. I pray for you and Mariam and your child," Joseph placed his hand on my shoulder, "Judas, I pray that all of you find a safe harbor and peace in the new land. Farewell, my friends."

Yeshua looked thoughtful and told Simon Peter, "If the people believe the anointed one, the messiah they are calling him, has arisen, then perhaps they believe the words. – *Behold, a day of ADONAI cometh. And ADONAI shall come, it shall come to pass, that at evening time there shall be light. And there shall be a king over all the earth –.* Perhaps we have planted a seed and perhaps the people will grow their will to resist the Romans."

Simon Peter said, "Yeshua, one day the hunt for you will end. Then you can return and we will gather another army to fight the Romans and defeat them."

Yeshua smiled a grim smile. He grasped Simon Peter by the shoulders. "Perhaps I will return one day. Until then you will prepare and take the word to the people. I will call you Simon Peter, and upon you my rock shall be built."

We rowed to the boat and climbed aboard, then we pulled the rowboat on board with us for short trips to land when we were at anchor. We pulled up the large stone anchor that was tied to a stout hempen rope. The wind caught the sails. I felt the boat under me move as if it were a living thing. Simon Peter and Joseph stood on the beach. Simon Peter yelled to us, "Come back some day." And Yeshua raised his hand. In farewell or agreement, I did not know which. Philip turned the rudder and pointed us at the setting sun.

The wind from the south, the desert lands, pushed us and made the sails snap and tighten. Before the sunlight was gone, the sight of the land blurred into the distance until it was just a memory. The other time I had been on a boat under sail, was on the sea of Chinnereth early in our mission. That sunny day had been so pleasant I had fallen into a peaceful sleep. This first night on the Great Sea was not to be that.

The wind became stronger and the water became rougher. The boat rose on waves until it was pointed at the sky. At the top of the wave the boat fell down into a trough with a jarring slap and barrels of water washed over the bow. The sky was full of thunder and lightning and a driving rainstorm soaked everything. I could see no moon or land. I thought we were in the middle of a vast lost space. Everyone except Philip, who seemed to relish being captain of a good boat under sail, emptied their guts and became miserable. The wind got stronger until it was howling. The waves got bigger and the sickness worse until I wondered if we had made a terrible mistake taking to the water. A fast horse galloping across the steady land suddenly seemed like the best way to travel.

Philip yelled at us huddled together on the deck by the mast, "This is just a small storm. It will pass. Hang on!"

To catch the wind and keep the boat pointed in the right direction, all the men pulled on lines to adjust the sails as Philip directed. We passed a miserable night and I continued to puke until there was nothing left. Then I dry heaved my guts out. I wondered how the boat managed to stay in one piece in the face of this onslaught. The women suffered and I feared for them. Would they, or could they, take much more of this? In the darkest hour of the night, finally the storm blew itself out and the waves slowed their constant hammering of the ship. Where the storm came from and where it went next only ADONAI knew.

The sun rose on a changed world. The wind was blowing stiff but not violently. The sails were full and the boat cut through the water smoothly. The women recovered faster than I, and they laughed while they spread things on the deck to dry. Nathaneal Bartholomew hooked a fish as long as his arm, which would make food aplenty for all. Some wood wrapped in a sail was still dry and Yeshua soon had the brazier burning. We grilled the fish and after the meal I felt alive again.

We looked at Yeshua's map. Philip, who had previous experience sailing the Great Sea, added his knowledge to our discussion. "We sail west and north. The sun will rise behind us and set in the direction we will steer. The man you got this map from was right about the currents. We must not be pushed south or the current will swing us around back to where we started. We will keep land in sight to our right hand side. We must not land on the island of Kyprus. It is known for its copper mines and Roman savagery. The next islands are Rhodes then Krete. We go between them, passing many small islands where we can get driftwood for the fire. The current will take us north and west to the Strait of Messana. After the Strait we will be in the Tyrrhenian Sea and continue north and west to the Ligurian Sea. Then we will soon come to Massilia."

Rachel asked, "How long will the journey last?"

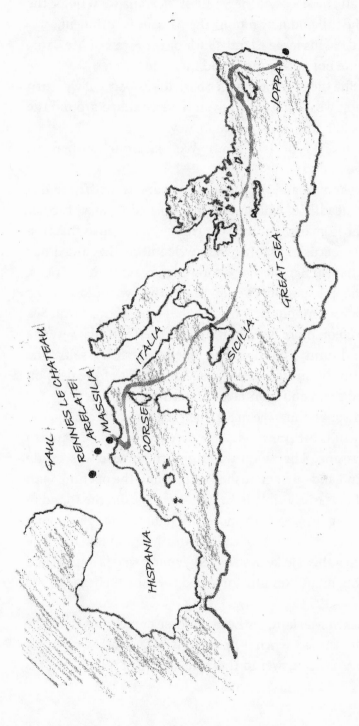

"A moon, if all goes well. At the Strait of Messana we wait for the half moon. At the full and new moons the passage is turbulent."

Yeshua asked, "This large island south of the Strait of Messana, Sicilia, why can we not go around it and miss the Strait?"

"South of Sicilia the current changes back to eastward. It will turn us to the direction we do not want. Even if we could go around the island it would add many days to the journey."

Yeshua told us, "Philip is captain. We place our trust in his knowledge and skills."

The sun rose and set and the moon waxed and waned. Each day was the same, a steadily blowing wind that pushed us west, further each day from the Romans. The weather was never as bad as that first night, though the occasional rains were welcome as they filled our water casks. Nathaneal Bartholomew showed me some fishing tricks, and I was soon happily pulling in enough fish that we could save the roosters and chickens for our new home. The water of this Great Sea was a deep blue color, more blue than the sky itself. The days were a delight, warm and sunny and the breeze smelled fresh and salty. The women soaked up the sunshine, the peace and quiet of the days on the water relaxed them and their faces lit with easy smiles.

We passed through the Aegean Sea then the Ionian Sea, stopping twice at small islands for firewood. After twenty moons we came to the Strait of Messana. The moon was right, the breeze was steady and fair. The wind and current pushed us through the opening with no difficulties. Land was visible in both directions. On the island of Sicilia was a large mountain with snow visible on its top. Philip told us this was the burning mountain called Etna. Mariam told us, "The Greeks have a story about a daemon called Typhon who is imprisoned below the burning mountain Etna, trapped there by their god of the sky, Zeus."

Jehosheba asked Mariam, "Is Zeus another name for ADONAI? Do we not look to the sky when we pray to ADONAI?"

"No one knows the answer to that question. Not I, anyway. It is a mystery."

Yeshua said, "Perhaps they are the same. Perhaps all the gods are the same, just one god called by different names. Or, perhaps there are no gods and they only exist in our imagination."

Jehosheba looked shocked by Yeshua's words. "Is that not blasphemy?"

"Perhaps blasphemy is just a word. A word with no meaning, if there are no gods."

I noticed that Yeshua seemed inclined to an even more skeptical frame of mind since our mission had failed. I did not know if that was good or bad. That was a question only he could answer in his own mind.

Jehosheba said, "Genesis tells us ADONAI created all. If ADONAI did not create all, then where does everything come from?"

Yeshua said, "On the seventh day ADONAI rested. Genesis does not tell us what he did on the eighth day."

Sensing one of Yeshua's jokes coming, I thought, here we go. But I asked him anyway, "What happened on the eighth day?"

"On the eighth day, god, whoever he or she may be, created Hades." Yeshua laughed, jumped to his feet and told us, "I am hungry. Let us catch fish for our supper!"

37 DAYS FROM PASSOVER. MY NAME
IS MARIAM OF MAGDALA

I was comfortably in Yeshua's arms, looking at his sleeping face. We were sitting on the deck, leaning back against some soft bundles. All these peaceful days had relaxed him and eased the stress marks from his face. I hoped our new home would be a place of rest for his mind and body. He wrestled with his thoughts. His constant struggle to understand what or who god is, and why god seemed to reward the wicked and punish the righteous, was a mental battle that could not be won.

I hoped he could come to realize that what happens next, the aftertime, is mysterious and unknowable. It was a mystery that would be revealed to all of us, someday. In the meantime it was not something to dwell so heavily on that it made one unbalanced in their own mind. I knew I could not force such thinking upon him. He would have to find that balance within himself. But I would help him in that journey any way I could.

The third Book, Leviticus, shows us ADONAI's words to Moses. I always thought the best of those words were. – *Thou shalt not oppress thy neighbour, nor rob him. Thou shalt not curse the deaf, nor put a stumbling-block before the blind. Ye shall do no unrighteousness in judgment. Thou shalt not disrespect the person of the poor, nor favour the person of the mighty. Neither shalt thou stand idly by while the blood of thy neighbour is spilled. Thou shalt love thy neighbour as thyself –.*

Those words and their simple message are also the teaching of Isis. If everyone would heed those words there would be less strife and conflict in this world and there would be no need to worry about what happens next. The garden ADONAI made was not some perfect world waiting for us in the next cycle of life. It was, or should be, and could be, the world we live in today. How could I communicate that to Yeshua? For all his good points, there was a hard knot of resistance inside of him that prevented him from recognizing that simple truth. Perhaps Yeshua would not allow himself to recognize that simple truth because he was angry at ADONAI. Perhaps Yeshua blamed ADONAI for ignoring the injustices heaped upon the sons and daughters of men. Why would ADONAI ignore those who prayed to Him? Why indeed. Only ADONAI knows.

Yeshua stirred, stretched, opened his eyes and yawned. He turned and smiled at me. He looked at my belly region, hidden under my robe. "How is our son today?"

"Our daughter is well."

"We will have a son, I know it, and he will be strong and brave and a good hunter."

"We will have a daughter. She will be beautiful and clever and will become a great healer."

Yeshua smiled at me, "Our child will be healthy and happy. That is what matters."

"Land ho!" yelled Simon the Zealot who was on watch. The day before, fishermen at a small village on the island of Corse told us to watch for a group of small islands at the head of a point leading into a bay. We turned and steered for a small cove east of the point. It was our intention to not sail directly into Massilia, but to land the boat and approach the town carefully from land so we could check for the presence of any Romans.

Yeshua, Levi Matthew, and Judas would venture into the town. The other men, the women and children, and I would wait on the boat. We insisted that we be taken ashore if only for a short time. I had to feel solid land under my feet for the first time in a moon plus seven days. The men went ashore first to make sure it was safe, then we were ferried from the boat to the beach in the rowboat with Barrabas pulling strongly at the oars. This peaceful little cove was quiet and still. The only sound was the splashing of the oars. To the right was a sheer cliff. The sun sparkled from a shining small waterfall, only the size of two hands, running down the cliff's face to splash into the sea.

The boat scratched onto the sandy beach. We stepped out onto this new land. The beach stretched in an oval shape. In front of us was a small hill with scrubby vegetation growing on it. Yeshua smiled and told me, "Let us walk to the top. I think you will like what you see." The little hill was not steep and in just minutes we reached the top. What I saw took my breath away. Before me, as far as I could see, was a wonderland. There was lush green grasses with green trees and green shrubbery. There were colorful wildflowers growing in abundance. I heard birds singing and watched them, singly and in flocks, as they flew from trees to bushes. A creek bubbled merrily, feeding the little waterfall. The sun was shining warm and comfortable on my face. The difference from the searing sun and bleak dry desert land we had left behind, to this seemingly magical green land of plenty, left me breathless in astonishment. The children were rolling in the grass, laughing in delight. Jehosheba and Barabbas were kneeling in a bed of clover amongst the flowering stems, praying. Rachel's arms were encircling Judas. She was crying in happiness and Judas was holding her tightly. Chuza and Joanna were kneeling and praying also.

Deliverance!

I fell to my knees, "Praise be to Isis. This is the heaven I saw in my vision!"

FIFTEEN HARVESTS FROM THE PASSOVER.
MY NAME IS JUDAS ISCARIOT

I have become more observant of the change in the seasons, of the times of planting and harvest. I am a farmer and a vigneron, and have been all these past years. Fifteen of them! Working the soil of the land has made me finally understand the words. – *ADONAI put man into the garden of Eden to dress it and to keep it. ADONAI said, Behold, I have given you every green herb, every herb yielding seed, which is upon the face of all the earth, and every tree, in which is the fruit of a tree yielding seed. To you it shall be for food* –. Surprising myself, I have found that I am a good farmer and happy at the work.

On that day of our arrival in the land of Gaul, Yeshua, Levi Matthew, and I ventured into the town of Massilia. The other men stayed with the boat to protect the women. We did not know how the men of the tribes in this new land would react to our presence. Would they be warlike or peaceful? The port town of Massilia was busy with commerce. There were ships being loaded and unloaded with all manner of items for transport.

We made our way to the synagogue Joseph of Arimathea spoke of. After introductions were made we were given a warm welcome. The wise man, the elder of the Habirum community, asked us as many questions about our old home as we asked about our new home. In our discussions of a place for us to settle, the wise man told us the region west and north was free of the Roman soldiers. He told us of a place called Rennes-le-Chateau that lie in a fertile region. He gave us the name of a trustworthy Habirum who had land for sale there at a fair price. To finance our future plans, I put into the pot the thirty silver coins that Simon the Cyrene thought he would receive. Barabbas had a bag of coins from his convoy raiding days that he added to the pot. And Yeshua sold his black rock from the stars to the wise man of Massilia. The rock fetched a substantial price, for a rock.

Rennes-le-Chateau was a six day walking journey from Massilia, but we cut the time in half by sailing across the bay. We sailed west along the coast to a landing, then walked north into the hills to our new home. We found the man who had the property, and made our deal with him. We traded our coins for land in a fertile valley, a land of promise. Arriving at the place where we would make our new home, I turned over a spade full of earth to find rich black soil. I crumbled handfuls and smelled the promise of good harvests. We are in a valley with mountains to the northeast and to the southwest. A perfect amount of rainfall and natural springs in the mountains feed the many streams that course through the valley. The streams and ponds are full of freshwater tasty fish that seem eager to be caught. The fishes fill the supper pot as often as you care to eat fish. The valley is a natural place for growing. The harvests are so plentiful there is plenty for our needs and to take to market for sale. I have found that farming suits me. Perhaps this is what I was always meant to do. I had no opportunity to farm in the desert land we left, so the possibility never occurred to me. Rachel bakes and sells bread and she teaches our children, a son and a daughter, to read and write. The son helps me with the farming and our daughter helps Rachel with her baking and selling the tasty, crunchy crusted bread loaves. Rachel and I and our children are happy.

Barabbas and Jehosheba did not stay long in Rennes-le-Chateau. Barabbas decided he would rather build than farm so he sold his share to us. About one hundred harvests ago the Caesar Julius defeated the Parisii tribe led by their chieftain, Vercingetorix. The Romans founded a new city on the arc of a river with two islands. The Gauls call the river, Sēquana. It is named for their goddess of the river. The Romans call the river the Seine, and they call their new city Lutetia Parisiorum. Barabbas told me the locals call the city, Paris. It is a fast growing area where he makes plenty of coins as a master builder. I see Barabbas every year or so. Barabbas tells me no Romans remember him from that Passover day in Jerusalem, and he never worries for his safety. Barabbas thinks it is a good joke that the Romans, who wanted to hang him from the cross, now make him rich with their coins and call him a leading citizen. Barabbas and Jehosheba and their two children are happy.

Chuza and Joanna and their two children also live in the city of Paris. Chuza works as a knowledgeable scribe and is an elder in the synagogue. Chuza and Joanna and their children are happy. Chuza tells me Joanna prays and says thanks each day to Isis for delivering them from the perverse insanity of Herod Antipas.

Philip, Nathaneal Bartholomew, Levi Matthew, and his brother James, used the boat that brought us to this new land, to start a shipping business. They haul goods from Massilia to Joppa, stopping at points to and from. Their business is so good they have added another boat to their business and have a trading house in Massilia for the items they import and export.

Simon the Zealot and his wife accompanied Philip on the boat and went back to Judah, then traveled to Aegyptus seeking adventure. That was a dozen harvests ago. No one has heard anything from him since. He was a strong warrior who championed our cause and I wish him well.

I see Philip and Levi Matthew each year in Massilia after harvest. It is to them I sell my barrels of wine. They bottle it and resell it. Their business is thriving. From their travels and from those they do business with, they get news from the land of the Habirum. The land of the Habirum has changed over the years.

Herod Antipas, the grandson of the Imudean slave, was arrested and charged with treason for plotting against the crazed emperor, Caligula. Herod was exiled to Hispania where Caligula eventually had him assassinated. Pontius Pilate was searching for treasure, supposedly buried by Moses, at the Samaritan village, Tirathana, near Mount Gerizim. Pilate's soldiers slaughtered the men of the village when they attempted to stop the digging and desecration of their holy place. The elders of Tirathana journeyed to Rome and complained to the emperor. Pilate was sent to Rome to be tried for multiple counts of murder. Pontius Pilate was disgraced and committed suicide.

The Pharisees and Essenes continue to focus their beliefs and practice on the words and true faith of ADONAI. The Sadducees continue to exploit the Temple for coins, but the true Habirum are increasingly moving away from the Sadducees strict interpretation of belief that the Temple is the only connection to ADONAI. The Pharisees and Essenes of the Habirum are finally seeing that the Sadducees are only using them for the financial benefit of the Sadducee priests. The true word of ADONAI is the home the Pharisees and Essenes dwell within.

Some of the things that changed in the land of the Habirum were totally unanticipated. The newest thing to happen is that the cruci fixus and resurrection of Yeshua, in the disguised form of Simon the Cyrene, has brought about a new philosophy. This new way of thinking, called Khristos by the Greeks and Mashiach by the Habirum, is inspired by the teachings and sacrifice of Yeshua. These people are called the Followers of the Way. This new thinking is spreading throughout Judah, Galilee, and the surrounding areas like it is blown by the wind. But, again, the sons of men compete for the minds, the hearts, and the souls of other sons of men.

Like the earlier beliefs that have come before, this new philosophy is interpreted differently by those who practice it. The Khristos, as a group, revere Yeshua and call him the Savior and son of ADONAI. They believe Yeshua, as their messiah, tells us, 'I am He who lives, and was dead, and behold, I am alive forevermore. Amen. And I have the keys of Hades and of Death. I am the way, the truth, and the life. No one comes to the Father except through Me.' A certain sect of the Khristos practice their belief in a calm, quiet manner, as befitting the way they think of Yeshua's teaching. Others are more clamorous in their belief. They beat their breasts and proclaim loudly they are the true believers and none others shall be saved.

James the Just, Yeshua's brother, in a bizarre move that would cause Yeshua to choke laughing, embraced Yeshua's ascension to the side of ADONAI and tries to convert the Essenes. The centurion, Cornelius, had a revelation like the gardener, Yuda. Cornelius says he was visited by an angel who commanded him to Follow the Way. Cornelius, along with some new fellow, a tax collector named Saul, who changed his name to Paul, busy themselves converting the pagans, the heathens, and all those who are uncircumcised. Their converts are being called by a new word, Gentiles.

Ironically, certain of the Sadducees have embraced this new Followers of the Way philosophy. These converted Sadducees speak of Yeshua as the savior sent by ADONAI. They say the words – *But he was wounded because of our transgressions, He was crushed because of our iniquities. The chastisement of our welfare was upon him, and with his stripes we were healed* – point to Yeshua as the messiah foretold by Isaiah. They too compete for the attention of the Gentiles.

These converted Sadducee priests wear beautiful, costly, tailored colorful vestments, robes, gowns and headpieces that apparently make them look more holy and believable to their flock of followers. The priests wear around their necks, hanging from a slender chain, a post and crossbeam made of wood or metal that signifies Yeshua's cruci fixus. The priests conduct elaborate ceremonies, holding and swinging a Greek thymiatírio that contains burning smoking incense. These exaggerated rituals are accompanied by the priests chanting in the Roman language of Latīna, apparently to make the rites more mysterious and appealing to their flock.

Philip has told me these costumed converted Sadducee priests are intent on organizing a large ekklisia, a gathering of their faithful that will span the whole world. The priests have their followers take a holy koinonía at each gathering. The Gentiles call this a communion, and it is a celebration that Yeshua is with them in spirit. During the communion the worshippers eat small breads and drink wine that symbolize the body and blood of Yeshua. Philip tells me this reminds him of the stories of the fierce warriors on the island of Roman Provincia Britanniae, who eat the raw flesh of their captured enemies.

These converted Sadducee priests end each service to the one they call Khristos or Mashiach, depending on their audience, with a plea for all to be immersed in the holy water. Just like Yehudah HaMakabi the Baptizer was doing on the River Jordan, the Sadducees use the water to make the converted believer feel pure and sanctified. They also have devised a scheme to enrich themselves, like the sacrifices at the Temple. During the service, the converted Sadducee priests go among the flock with a bowl in hand and collect coins. I suppose the Gentiles think this is a payment now, for their salvation in the future.

Philip tells me some of the Gentiles worshipping at the converted Sadducee Khristos meetings conduct themselves in strange and incomprehensible behaviors. In their worship of Yeshua they go into trances and talk in the tongues of peculiar languages. They roll on the floor, thrashing about. They leap to their feet and spin wildly around like dervishes. They sing and dance, in the grip of a passionate frenzy. They handle vipers with their hands and drink deadly poison, believing their faith in Yeshua will keep them from harm. They dive into the baptism water and delve deeply into their purses to fill the converted Sadducees collection bowls. They do all these things willingly and happily. They see the sacrifice of Yeshua as their eternal redemption and they express their love for him ecstatically. They believe this worship of Yeshua will cast out of their souls the daemons who persecute them and want to possess them. They believe the coins they donate will insure their seat at Yeshua's side in the afterlife,

It was Yeshua's dream to save the Habirum from the Romans. But what he accomplished, extraordinary sounding as it may be, was to give all manner of peoples a promise of salvation from their earthly misery. These people want to believe they too will arise to the House of ADONAI. They want to believe they will live forever in the love, the harmony, and the protection of ADONAI and His arisen Son.

The Sadducee converts and the newly baptized Gentiles argue even over the beginning of the new philosophy. The Gentiles say the words – *Bethlehem, Out of thee shall come forth the ruler in Israel. He shall be great unto the ends of the earth. And this shall be peace –.* While the Sadducee converts believe -- *Out of Aegyptus I called My son and raise Him up unto thee. He is the prince of peace –.*

Bethlehem? Aegyptus? I fail to comprehend the importance of the distinction. But neither will accept what the other believes. Indeed, Philip tells me the disagreement has led to war amongst the tribes. He says that whole villages have been slaughtered. The men, the women, and the children, all slain by the edge of the sword over this difference of interpretation.

I do not, and I know Yeshua would not, understand this. It is not what we set out to accomplish. I shake my head in puzzlement. I wish Yeshua was here to join me over a glass of wine and discuss this. We would laugh, and be grieved, over the absurdity of it all.

Yeshua and Mariam's question of whether their first child would be a boy or girl was answered just a few moons after our arrival in Rennes-le-Chateau. The answer to their question was one of each, as Mariam delivered of twins. The babies had the light brown hair of the father and the green eyes of the mother. Mariam has continued her work as a healer. When we first arrived, Yeshua, Barabbas and I built for Mariam a stone chapelle where she treats any who cross the threshold for their ailments. The chapelle is also a place of worship to the goddess Isis, and Mariam has opened the eyes and souls of many, spreading the words and gifts of Isis across the countryside. Their daughter is a sweet child who studies the art of healing and assists her mother to treat their patients. Already the daughter is becoming a renowned healer at her young age of fifteen harvests.

Yeshua and I taught our sons the art of hunting and both are masters with bow and arrows and trapping. Yeshua taught his son the skills of sword and knife and the boy is able to fight like a duelist. Yeshua's son showed his lessons to my son, of course, and they practice together like Yeshua and I used to do on Tabor Mount.

Two harvests ago Yeshua wrote Mariam a note, and left their home in the dark of the night. Along with his traveling gear he took his sword. He wrote that he was going on a trip. He did not say where or why or when he would return. The third harvest is approaching with no word from Yeshua. Everyone thinks he somehow returned to the land of the Habirum, to continue the fight against the Romans.

Each harvest I take to Massilia my barrels of wine and sell them to Philip and Levi Matthew. Mariam makes the journey with me. She goes seeking if anyone has heard news of Yeshua. She goes among the boats at the harbor, seeking information. Always she returns disappointed. Mariam wrote down her remembrances of Yeshua and their story. She gave it to me to read. I made a copy of it. It is here, her words, just as she wrote it.

I also wrote my recollection of those times. I added to the words some maps and drawings that show the people and the places of our adventures. I sealed the scrolls in a dry container and corked it, to await Yeshua's return. I would encourage him to write his remembrances of what happened and add his scrolls to the container. The scrolls in the container await its completion, waiting for the words of Yeshua.

Then, at the time of the last planting, I heard a disturbing story. A traveler told me that a stranger with blue eyes arrived at the town of Arelate, a place on the River Rhone founded by Caesar Julius, where he awarded plots of land to retired centurions. According to the story, this stranger with blue eyes dueled with a Roman centurion named Panthera. They fought with swords in brutal combat. After a desperate, clashing struggle, the Roman got inside the guard of the stranger with blue eyes and shoved his sword into the stranger's chest. It was a mortal wound. According to the tale, the stranger dropped his sword, pulled the Roman close with one hand and with the other hand pulled a dagger from a sheath at his belt, and shoved the dagger in the Roman's eye, through his head and into the Roman's brain. According to the tale, the stranger with blue eyes and the Roman, Panthera, fell to the ground in a dying embrace.

I do not know the truth of this tale. I do not know if the stranger with blue eyes was Yeshua. I do not tell this story to Mariam, as it would destroy all her hopes for Yeshua to return, eventually. The disappearance of Yeshua has cast a permanent shadow across Mariam's face. Mariam never smiles. Mariam never laughs. Mariam has forgotten how to be happy.

Yeshua's son is convinced the Romans have killed his father in the land of the Habirum. The son has grown tall and strong in his early manhood. The fate of his father, as he believes it to be so, has made him into a grim, stern, unyielding warrior, who talks only of revenge. He swears he will go to this land of the Habirum, and kill many Romans for what they have done to his father.

And so, the story of the sons of men continues.

Amen.

Printed in the United States
by Baker & Taylor Publisher Services